John Law

WASP-WAISTED

David Barrie was born in Scotland.
He has lived in Paris for 17 years, where he works as a
management consultant.

www.waspwaisted.com

David Barrie

WASP-WAISTED

John Law Media

Published by John Law Media Ltd.
P.O. Box 26515, Glasgow G74 9EF
www.johnlawmedia.com
contact@johnlawmedia.com
First published in Great Britain 2009.

ISBN 978 0 9562518 0 0

Printed in Scotland by Thomson Litho, East Kilbride.

Beauty is truth, truth beauty, – that is all
Ye know on earth, and all ye need to know.

John Keats, *Ode on a Grecian Urn*

A glossary of French terms can be found at the end of the book (the very last page inside the back cover).

It made the cover of *Exposé*. Newsstands the city over were plastered with a poster-sized version of it. Sales were high.

Normally *Exposé* – which, depending on whom you asked, was either a scandal sheet or a former pillar of photojournalism fallen with the times – dealt only in colour. This image, though, was in black and white. Somehow it made the photo all the more appealing, hearkening back to a mythical, more glamorous age when goddesses were captured in faultless white, shades of grey, and unfathomable black. An age when stockings and suspenders held an unassailable place in the canon of beauty and seduction. When white lace provided a virginal facade to slumbering sensuality. When generous breasts cradled in a scooped bra could hold a gaze hypnotised for hours. When a body curved on yielding sheets, its profile framed by a languorous arm, was an invitation that could stop the heart.

The other photos aligned on Franck Guerin's desk were in colour. Same pose, different angles – many different angles, as forensic photographers were trained to do. A few could even be said to be flattering, albeit colour was less forgiving with the subject's skin than black and white. Death's discoloration could be seen to be seeping in.

They were hastier too, shot in quick succession under overpowering light which banished shadow and flattened the corpse. Her curves were less in evidence, but the lingerie in which she had been left was caught in all its detail: an intricate pattern of lace surrounding an infinite number of tiny holes, each a window on the flesh beneath. Her nipples played fragmented hide-and-seek with the lens. Her pubic hair swelled slightly against the fabric stretched taught across her pelvis. Stockings, white as a bride's, hugged tight thighs that tapered down to form impressively long legs.

The wound, such as it was, figured on none of the photos. A pin-prick on the inside of the right forearm near the elbow, the flesh ever so slightly bruised, as if the hand that held the syringe had hesitated at the last moment. All this was detailed in the coroner's report, placed squarely in the top-right corner of his desk.

Franck looked back at the magazine's cover. "Laure Sarraute: a murderer's homage to a flawless beauty". No-one would contest the latter. She had earned her living from her anatomy. Its capacity to show clothes to their best, particularly those designed specifically to frame or slightly veil her considerable charms, had kept her on the right catwalks and in the right magazines for the past three years.

That said, she had never made *Exposé* before, which said something for her discernment and much for the discretion of her private life. In death, she could count on neither. The question of how, why and by whom a young model's life had been cut off at twenty-six would now be the object of frenzied and prurient interest from the media.

Not to mention a question of professional interest to Franck.

Had the circumstances been different, he might have smiled ruefully. So this was to be his new beat: celebrity crime. After thirteen promising years in national security, it seemed that he too had fallen with the times.

But he wasn't smiling. He was gazing at the black and white image of Laure Sarraute trying to understand what it exacted from him. Not desire – a half-naked young woman lying enticingly on a bed – nor outrage – a murder victim – but something else. Something akin to admiration, or reverence. As if he was looking at a canvas, a timeless masterpiece hung in unassailable majesty in the Louvre.

His profession had habituated him to a pretty ugly world: one of shadows and deception, of hatred and cupidity, of plots and traps, of violence and terror. When beauty turned up, it often proved venomous and always came with strings attached. Strings tugged upon by unsightly hands. Mistrust had become second nature, an instinct he had been taught to cherish for its power to clear the mind. Whether it hollowed the soul too remained an open question.

This time, though, things ought to be different. For once, he would be on beauty's side. A knight errant, albeit one who had arrived too late. That small detail aside, it was an attractive prospect – providing he was up to the job.

He pushed back from the desk – his desk, at least for the foreseeable future. The chair scraped across the parquet floor, whose once-varnished surface had endured such indignities from generations of uncaring *flics* cooped up in the maze of police buildings in the Ile de la Cité.

Unwittingly, Franck found himself in possession of what many pursued as the Holy Grail: an office within the quai des Orfèvres, the sombre heart of the capital's police force. A dingy cupboard with a single window looking out onto an inner courtyard, set at the end of a maze of neglected corridors and noisy stairwells, inhabited by fellow officers who – understandably, given the circumstances of his arrival – had not rushed forward to make his acquaintance. It was a far cry from the open plan workspaces and constant team meetings of the Direction de la Surveillance du Territoire.

But it was better than nothing. Better than being consigned to his apartment, as he had been for the eight weeks following his release from hospital, swallowing pills and taming the pain, taking increasingly long walks through Paris as he felt less fragile.

Franck retrieved a crumpled jacket from a coat stand jammed in a corner behind his chair, slid his arms in and tugged it down at the back to cover the holster carrying his service revolver. He reached out for the large manila envelope he had found in his mail slot two hours before and refilled it with the documents spread out across his desk. A neat inscription on the envelope identified who had sent it: Yves de Chaumont, *juge d'instruction*, office 513.

The copy of *Exposé* was the last item to go in. He slipped it in with care, so as not to wrinkle the cover. Laure Sarraute deserved at least that.

*

"I have a young man here who seems very keen to see you."

Madame Alba smiled as she listed to the reply, looking Franck straight in the eye as she held the phone to her ear.

"I'm sure waiting would do him a world of good. But not me. I don't want him pacing up and down in my office, making me nervous. The young man in question is a certain captain Guerin, and though he's not been with us for very long, I get the feeling he's rather skittish."

She put the phone down.

"He's all yours." She pointed over her shoulder, indicating a door that led into Yves de Chaumont's office from the antechamber she occupied. "You want to leave that envelope with me?"

"No thanks. It's why I'm here."

"Laure Sarraute?"

"The very same," confirmed Franck. "Is there anything that goes on in this office that you don't know about, madame?"

"I should hope not. It's my job to know everything."

"Including about me?"

Madame Alba laid a hand delicately against her cheek and contemplated Franck.

"I know you returned to active service yesterday. I know you came back from Corsica with a couple of bullets in you. I know there are people who are asking serious questions about what exactly happened while you were there."

She stopped. Franck waited. He had not faced a lot of questions since taking possession of his – hopefully – temporary office in the quai des Orfèvres the previous day. His intention was to stonewall any that came his way. He was not there to satisfy the curiosity of his new colleagues.

"Anything else?" he asked, his tone icy.

A smile crept across madame Alba's face.

"I know that monsieur *le juge* jumped at the chance when he heard that you were out on loan. That's good enough for me."

Suddenly feeling foolish, Franck apologised. "Sorry if I seemed curt. It's just ..."

She waved aside his explanation.

"I can well imagine what you have to put up with at the moment. If you didn't know before, you're about to find out – the DST is not the most popular service with the rest of the police force. When you work under the cover of darkness ..."

"... no-one can tell if your hands are clean," completed Franck. He had never before particularly cared about what was said or thought about the DST. That was when he was on the inside. Now he was no longer sure exactly where he stood – aside from being on secondment to Yves de Chaumont.

"I'd better not keep him waiting," said Franck and began to manoeuvre around her desk, heading towards the door she guarded day in, day out. Rumour had it that she had never been known to be ill. Aside from her annual absence every August, she was as constant a feature of the room as the piles of dossiers and folders in every corner, the available shelf space having been filled long ago.

Having grasped the round ceramic nub of the door handle he paused and shot a glance back at madame Alba, who had turned in her seat to keep her eyes on him.

"Any advice?" he requested.

"You look terrible," she offered. "Do something with your hair, get a proper shave, and ask a woman to have a look through your wardrobe. You're a waste of a handsome young man."

"Thirty-six," he pointed out. "Not so young."

"Believe me," she shot back, "from where I'm sitting, thirty-six looks very young indeed."

Franck threw her a smile, turned the handle and gently pushed the door open.

Yves de Chaumont was standing behind his desk – a wide and stocky table covered with worn but unstained green baize. A telephone, a laptop folded shut, a large leather-covered writing surface bearing a fountain pen, a small bottle of black ink and a stack of thick white sheets of paper were the only things to be seen on its surface. Clearly Yves had delegated his clutter to madame Alba.

The room was no larger than the one that preceded it. Two steps took Franck to the opposite side of the table from where he grasped Yves' outstretched hand.

"Monsieur *le juge.*"

"Captain, it's a pleasure to see you."

They released hands, each sinking into a chair.

"How are you settling in?" asked Yves.

"If I said I'm not planning on getting too settled, would you be surprised?"

Yves chuckled. "Not at all. But it'll grow on you – you'll see. Granted, there's not the frisson that I'm sure hovers over the DST every day, but there are compensations."

Franck said nothing.

"Polite scepticism," observed Yves. "Quite right too. I must say, you're looking remarkably good for someone not long off his deathbed."

"That doesn't seem to be madame Alba's opinion," Franck pointed out. "If I understood correctly, she's just told me I'm letting myself go."

"In which case, I bow to her opinion. I have rarely known Geneviève to be wrong," observed Yves solemnly, albeit with a smile tugging at his lips.

"I'll keep that in mind."

"Do," advised Yves. "Geneviève studies everyone who comes in and out of this office, and has been here even longer than me. If you ever want an honest appraisal of the state you're in, ask her. She's an excellent physiognomist, and a better psychologist than most."

"That wouldn't be hard, judging by the psychologists I've been dealing with recently."

Yves nodded sympathetically. "It's only to be expected. We can rarely afford the best. That said, I suspect you weren't the most receptive of patients."

"I'd have been happier talking with someone who's been in the line of fire himself. These past few weeks would have delighted Kafka – interviews, procedures, regulations, note-taking, ... Suddenly I'm confronted with a huge bureaucratic monster whose only purpose seems to be getting between me and my job."

"For what it's worth, my advice is to let it do its work and pay it no attention," suggested Yves. "Don't let it become an obsession. The best thing you can do right now is immerse yourself in something useful. And since the DST want to take a holiday from you for a while, why not set aside the cloak and dagger staff and try your hand at a little honest-to-god police work?"

"Like this?" Franck held up the manila envelope. "Laure Sarraute? I must admit, it surprised me. It's not exactly your usual line of work."

"That's true, but I had two good reasons to recover this dossier. One – I thought it would suit you. And two – based on the little I knew of her, I rather liked Laure Sarraute."

"You knew her?" asked Franck, surprised by this revelation.

Yves inclined his head slightly, a less definite reply than a simple nod.

"I met her once. At a reception at the Musée d'Orsay, organised by the Ministry of Culture as part of their obsession with transforming the nation's heritage into a money-making machine. The usual crowd – the boys and girls from the Ministry, eager as ever; curators and art historians, outraged as ever; assorted cultivated amateurs, myself included, perplexed as ever; minor diplomats from the friendly embassies, idle as ever. But there was also a bunch of fashion designers and entrepreneurs. I think the idea was to encourage the use of museums as backdrops for fashion shows. Something appallingly vulgar like that, anyway – one of those deceptively good ideas that brook no resistance and leave destruction in their wake."

Yves paused to mourn the ongoing decline of civilisation with a slight shake of his head and a short silence. He then leant forward and picked up his tale.

"There I was, forcing a description of the disgraceful state of some of the medieval churches in my bit of the country into the ear of one of the bureaucrats from Culture, when I noticed this young woman standing at the edge of the crowd holding an empty glass and looking, not quite lost, but disappointed and discomfited. As if she had expected more from the evening and hadn't known that it would just be a bunch of ageing civil servants rehashing gossip and complaints."

"What about the fashion crowd?" demanded Franck.

"All off in a corner. The corner where the drinks were being served, of course, and keeping very much to themselves. She wasn't standing with them, though. That struck me as strange, as she clearly came from that world."

"Too attractive to be in the service of the Republic?"

"False modesty Franck – you should listen to Geneviève. Get a decent haircut, a well-cut suit and walk in front of a mirror some time. You'd be surprised at the result – assuming you could afford the suit – which of course, you couldn't. That's what set her apart – she was too well dressed. Her dress looked as if it had been made for her. It was a simple thing – black, classic – but both distinguished and alluring."

"And yet no crowd of admirers?"

"No. It seemed to me at the time that no-one dared approach her. And likewise, she didn't know how to break into our closed ranks."

"So you walked over to her," Franck deduced.

"Of course. Her glass was empty. She was unaccompanied." Yves swept up his hands, emphasising how little choice he had had. "Someone had to do the gentlemanly thing."

Franck could detect not a hint of irony in this statement.

"Good for you. And?"

"And we had a most interesting conversation."

"About what?

"Rouen cathedral."

Franck' eyebrows shot up, instantly sceptical.

"This fashion model stood there and let you drone on and on about a cathedral?"

"No," Yves corrected. "This *juge d'instruction* stood there and let Laure Sarraute – for it was she – drone on about Rouen cathedral. Except she wasn't droning. She was making perfectly good sense, talking about Monet's series of paintings of the facade – a number of which are in Orsay, as you know –"

Yves paused, waiting to check that Franck nodded, which he did.

"– and how they had definitively influenced, if not polluted, the way she saw its exterior, even when she had her feet firmly planted on the cobbles of the square with the actual building right there in front of her."

"How on earth did you get onto such a subject?"

"I asked her from which region she had drawn her marvellous complexion. So fresh and unsullied – she couldn't be from Paris. And of course she wasn't – she told me she was born and raised in Normandy. From that point, it took a matter of minutes to arrive at Rouen and its cathedral."

"Naturally," Franck concurred. "Inevitable, really."

Yves glared at him. "For one with a modicum of decorum, yes it was. Dip into your eighteenth century authors and refresh your notions of civilised conversation. Faced with an extraordinarily handsome woman, you talk to her of things of the mind. Through force of habit she is deaf to praise of her beauty, and is sick to the teeth of fools who dance around her reminding her what a delight she is to their eyes. To win her esteem you must give her a chance to prove that she is more than a pretty face or a winning set of curves."

"And Laure Sarraute rose to the challenge?"

"Most impressively so. She had studied a little medieval history before coming to Paris. Enough, in any case, both to appreciate a cathedral and to know that no decent employment awaited her if she continued to concern herself with such things. So she chose to profit from her looks."

"By all accounts, she was doing quite well."

"I don't doubt she had secured financial independence. But I suspect there was a price to pay. Given the eagerness with which she talked to me – a tedious pedant with more than half a century weighing on his shoulders – I would say that the price was boredom."

"How long did you talk?"

"About an hour, while the drinks were served and the endless hand-shaking carried on around us. When the official speeches began, we left."

"We?"

"Yes. I suggested we go and have dinner somewhere quieter and more comfortable to continue the conversation."

"Does madame de Chaumont know about this?" asked Franck, incredulously.

"Of course." Yves frowned at Franck, letting him know just how foolish his question was. "I called her to let her know I was taking a delightful young woman to a restaurant and wouldn't be home for dinner."

"Does she often get calls like that?"

"Far less often than I get similar calls from her. My wife seems to draw delightful young men like flies to honey." Yves shook his head, smiling indulgently at the thought. "Never mind. I spent a most pleasant evening with mademoiselle Sarraute."

"And afterwards?"

Yves paused, looking askance at him. Franck raised both hands, palms up, and shrugged. Asking questions was his job, after all.

"Since then our paths had not crossed," Yves continued. "Until her corpse was found two days ago, and *Exposé* published their photo yesterday. That's when I requested that the dossier be handled by this office."

"What about the impartiality rule?"

"I scarcely knew her – just enough to care a little more than my colleagues, but not enough to put justice in peril. Anyhow, you'll be the one doing the investigating, not me. I'm prepared to bet she didn't even exist for you until you opened the envelope this afternoon."

Franck nodded. He had never heard the name Laure Sarraute until then. He did, however, wonder if he had unconsciously seen images of her before, which might explain how the photo on the cover of *Exposé* had snared him with its siren song.

"Good," continued Yves. "You're the man for the job."

"I hope you're right about that" observed Franck. "I haven't got much experience in handling what appears to be – excuse the term – a banal homicide."

"Banal?" echoed Yves, one eyebrow raised.

"OK, it's been given a lurid turn by *Exposé*. That means there'll be endless media interest until it's solved. The MO is unusual – I've not looked at the statistics, but I doubt we get many deaths by injection in Paris – and it looks as if it was done with a cool head, which has to make things trickier. That said, it's just another murder – and I don't know much about murder investigations."

"If you can handle a clandestine or politically sensitive operation – if you can defend the state and its institutions – then you ought to be able to do this. Don't forget that the Republic guarantees the lives and liberties of all its citizens, so this crime sullies it as much as many others, if not more so."

Franck conceded the point. "I'm not saying it doesn't matter. I'm saying that there are probably a host of competent detectives better qualified to clear this up. It doesn't have to be me."

"Actually," insisted Yves. "It does. Right now your former masters in national security feel you're due a rest and were delighted to farm you out to me. The Corsican incident has cast a long shadow, Franck. You're going to have to sit out what I predict will be a long period of doubt and mistrust, and you'll probably end up under the scrutiny of an official enquiry. Tackling something a little less controversial would be the best thing you could do, given the circumstances."

"This is scarcely a low profile case," Franck objected.

"True. But it is – as you pointed out – an eminently normal piece of police work. It wouldn't do any harm to demonstrate to a few people – whose names I won't mention – that you are more than capable of carrying out just such a job. Come in from the cold, Franck. It will help. It will help you, and it will help your friends and allies smooth things over."

Franck stirred irritably, "There is nothing to smooth ..."

Yves cut him off by extending a calming hand. "Yes, I know. The fact that I'm trying to help manage this situation and silence your critics doesn't mean I agree with them."

Franck subsided. He had worked with Yves on several occasions on the past when the DST found itself drawn into some of the delicate dossiers that the *juge* seemed to delight in handling. He believed him to be a man of forthright opinions and indisputable integrity. He ought to be glad to have Yves on his side. Not many people were, at the moment.

"Forget about the recent past. Concentrate on helping me placate the ghost of Laure Sarraute," suggested Yves.

"We're public servants. We don't believe in ghosts," Franck pointed out.

"Maybe we ought to. Now get out there and find out who did this."

Franck stood. "I'll do my best, monsieur *le juge*."

Yves too got to his feet. They shook hands.

"Keep me informed, Franck. I think you'll be surprised by this one."

"Surprised by what?"

"I suspect there was nothing banal whatsoever about the slaying of Laure Sarraute."

*

Once outside, Franck looked at his watch. Just after six. He was supposed to be at the Comédie Française at eight. He had more than enough time to head back to his office, but decided not to. Since he still had the manila envelope with him it scarcely mattered where he was, the important thing was to go through its contents once again. The first time he had skimmed. Now it was time to plod. Detail mattered.

He headed across the Ile de la Cité towards the Pont Neuf. Once there he gave his customary nod to Henri IV, proudly astride his bronze steed at the western point of the island. As kings went, old Henri had to be one of the least objectionable.

Paris vaut bien une messe, the height of cynicism for some, seemed to Franck a rare flash of lucidity in the midst of the religious fanaticism of the sixteenth century.

He left the island in the middle of the Seine and crossed to the Right Bank, dodging the clumps of idle Parisians or excited tourists who congregated on the bridge – the former with entangled lips, the latter with guidebooks and unfolded maps.

La Samaritaine rose before him, one of the city's more venerable temples of commerce, now supposedly facing financial ruin. If it were true, it was to be regretted. Franck had little interest in La Samaritaine's wares, but instinctively knew that if it disappeared something worse would take its place. Although not given to chronic nostalgia, he had yet to see a modern development in the city that could stand alongside what the nineteenth century, with Baron Haussmann at the helm, had done to it.

He turned to his left and walked alongside the river, passing the *bouquinistes* with their tattered wares of unwanted books and unexceptional engravings. He carried on, abandoning the riverside and crossing the road as the Louvre rose majestically alongside him. He entered the once-royal palace through the arch that gave access to the Cour Carré. This was the Louvre as Henri IV would have known it, when it was still a residence for kings and not just home to Napoleon's plunder. Franck crossed its cobbles, weaving around the odd tourist transfixed by the tiny eye-straining screen of a digital camera.

The noise and exhaust fumes of the rue de Rivoli awaited him on the other side. He spotted an opening in the traffic and dashed across to seek refuge under the arches that bordered the street, home at this point to a series of grotesquely overpriced antique shops. Still, worse awaited those who continued westwards, where vendors of perfume and poorly printed silk scarves battled with those proposing a thousand miniature variations of the Eiffel tower. Franck avoided this sorry spectacle by heading north-west, crossing a large open area taken over by roller skaters displaying their dexterity to a small crowd, passing before the seat of the Conseil d'Etat and arriving at square bordered by the Comédie Française, the entrance to the Palais Royal and the arrayed tables and polished windows of Le Nemours. This was where Sylvie had told him to meet her at eight.

Franck knew the place well and plunged inside, ignoring the coveted exterior tables. The counter stood just inside the entrance, the only seating options being a long and narrow space to the left or a boxed-in one to the right. As the furthest table to his left was empty, he headed for it. He figured it was best not to have anyone reading over his shoulder when perusing a crime scene report, replete with photos, in a public space. Doing so was a new experience for him: dossiers never left the four walls of the DST, except in encrypted form.

He sat down, shrugged his jacket from his shoulders over the back of his seat, and mouthed his order to a vigilant waiter, who nodded almost imperceptibly in reply. He then slid the contents of the manila envelope onto the table, arranged the documents in what seemed to him a logical order, and began rereading them.

By eight o'clock he had consumed three coffees, swallowed two painkillers, briefly glanced at the half a dozen customers who came and went at the tables around him, and begun the slow process of digestion that would soon make him a connoisseur of the victim's life and, more importantly, death.

Laure Sarraute's body had been found two days previously in a room on the seventh floor of the Lutetia hotel on the Left Bank. A housekeeper had found her body lying on the bed at eleven o'clock in the morning. The body was clad in a white bra, panties, suspender belt and stockings. A full set of clothes – underwear included – was found in a wardrobe. Hotel staff confirmed that Laure had arrived in these clothes around three o'clock the previous afternoon. Although she had frequented its bar and restaurants on a number of occasions, she was not a regular customer at the hotel. She had reserved the room by phone three days previously, having requested one that had a view of the adjacent public square and the decidedly upmarket Bon Marché department store, and which therefore was not overlooked by any of the neighbouring buildings. Her home address was in the Trocadero neighbourhood of the sixteenth arrondissement: she had sought out a hotel room in Paris by choice, not by necessity.

According to the forensic report death had occurred two to three hours after she took possession of her room. Potassium chloride, the executioner's friend, had been injected into an easily accessible vein running along her right arm. There was no sign of a struggle, which was scarcely surprising as flunitrazepam, a potent sedative, had been found in her system. Champagne in her stomach matched that of an open bottle in the room. The sedative had been concealed behind its sparkle: a nearly empty glass found in the room bore the victim's fingerprints, a centimetre of champagne, and traces of the chemical.

The bottle was half-empty, suggesting that three or four glasses had been drunk. When she checked in the victim had asked for champagne – a very expensive brand, Franck noted – to be delivered to her room. Room service had complied with her request around three twenty, depositing the bottle, an ice bucket and two tall glasses on a small table in a corner of the room. Only the victim had been visibly present at this moment. She had signed for the bottle, thanked the young man who delivered it, declined his offer to open it, and let him close the door when he left. The second glass that had been delivered along with the champagne had not been found.

The victim lay on her back, her shoulders flat but her waist twisted slightly, her right leg sliding up over her left. Her left arm was on the bed while her right one followed the curve of her body, her palm resting on the top of her thigh. Her head was cocked gently to the side, her hair gathered behind her and wreathed across her right shoulder. Not one hair was astray, suggesting that she had been posed, although whether this was done before or after the sedative robbed her of consciousness was not clear. In any case, her right arm must have been moved to perform the injection that killed her, and then draped back along her body.

The lingerie she was wearing was in pristine condition. No trace of detergent had been found upon it. It bore no labels, revealing nothing about its manufacturer or its size. The underwear found in the wardrobe with the rest of her clothes had been in contact with her body, presumably throughout her final day. While of quality and in good condition, it was clear that both the bra and panties from the wardrobe had been washed and worn before. It was thought the change had taken place before the victim was sedated as the lingerie sat upon her without a wrinkle and was smoothed perfectly against her flesh. Everything suggested that Laure Sarraute had clothed herself in lace and stockings before losing her life.

Fingerprinting the room had produced a vast quantity of prints. Although standards of cleanliness in the Lutetia were as high as could be expected of a luxury hotel, surfaces were at best lightly dusted between guests, allowing each one to leave a lingering trace behind, albeit invisible to the naked eye. Hair and fibre analysis was likely to run into the same problem. Once they had a suspect it would be worth checking to see if he had left behind a trace of himself in the room, but until then the crime scene report could only confirm that hotel rooms, being both private and anonymous, lent themselves well to homicide.

They were, no doubt, equally suited to a host of other crimes, but in this case it was only a question of homicide. There was no sign of rape, or of consensual sex for that matter. The virginal white of the lingerie seemed almost portentous in this context.

The Lutetia had security cameras in its entrance area, in the lifts, and a number of other locations. The hotel had been told to gather up and hand over its archives for the day of the murder. Franck would phone them tomorrow to hurry things along. Still, as there was no camera in the seventh floor corridor leading to the victim's room, nor in the stairwell that provided an alternative to the lift, he suspected that the tapes would be of little immediate use. The staff members interviewed the day the body was discovered recalled no-one having accompanied, asked for, or followed Laure Sarraute.

The Lutetia had been three-quarters full all week, with a constant turnover of guests. Foot traffic in and out of the hotel never ceased – all the more so on the ground floor, given the popularity of its restaurants and bar.

The victim's handbag had been left on a chair in a corner of the room. Alongside her ID card and the usual clutter of a young woman's bag, including three condoms, it contained two bank cards, nearly three hundred euros in cash, a slim-line mobile phone and the keys to her apartment. The code to the SIM card in her phone had been cracked by forensics so as to provide a printout of all the numbers in her directory and a list of recent calls made and received. The last flurry of communication had taken place between midday and two in the afternoon, before she arrived at the Lutetia. All the numbers called featured in her directory, all with first names appended – one male, four female. They would all be checked.

The victim's parents had been contacted the previous morning. They lived in Rouen, and had taken the train to Paris to identify the body in the late afternoon. They had given a short statement providing a framework to their daughter's brief life. Laure Sarraute was twenty-six when she was killed. Born and raised in Normandy, she had studied history and philosophy at Rouen University. She had come to Paris at the age of twenty-one upon completing her degree. For a year she did little of consequence – waitressing, working as a hostess at receptions and conferences, toying with various further study options – and then began picking up modelling work. For the past three years she had done little else, and had become a regular feature in the shows of a number of fashion designers. Financially independent by this stage, she maintained irregular but amicable contact with her parents. They knew nothing of her social or romantic life. Distraught at her death, they could not conceive of anyone wishing to hurt their little girl. Instinctively Franck felt certain that the roots of her death were to be found in Paris, not in Normandy.

That was it: the bare bones of the case; the fruit of twenty-four hours of interviews and forensic tests carried out before

Yves de Chaumont took charge of the dossier.

Franck slid everything back into the envelope with the exception of the copy of *Exposé*. Inside the front cover was a short text attributed to its photo editor:

> As a rule, we do not publish anonymous photos. As a rule, we do not receive anonymous photos – most photographers would do anything to feature in our pages, and we pay top money to get the best pictures for our readers. But whoever took the astonishing photo of the gorgeous Laure Sarraute that we publish today would not have revealed his identity for all the money in the world. The reason is simple – he murdered her. We received this photo before the police arrived at the luxurious Lutetia hotel to discover Laure Sarraute's dead body draped across a satin bedcover. This is the last picture ever taken of Laure: more beautiful and more sensual than ever.
>
> We hope that bringing this shocking murder into the public eye will help the police find the man who did it.

Franck twisted his lips at the patent cynicism of the final phrase. If *Exposé* was interested in the killer being captured, it was only in the hope of running his photo. He closed the magazine and looked down upon the cover. Empathy was not his strong point, but he could guess at the killer's delight on seeing his handiwork emblazoned across the city and beyond.

"*Exposé?*" came a voice. "Developed a taste for the frivolous, have we?"

Sylvie Thomas stood before his table in an open-necked blouse, a short-cut jacket, a skirt that stopped slightly short of the knee, dark stockings and modest heels. A single strand of pearls circled her neck, exactly level with the curved points of her ash blond hair. She rested a thin leather briefcase on the café table and smiled down on him.

"How's my favourite *flic*?" she asked.

"I would ask how's my favourite investment banker, but I don't know any others."

"Whereas I've had the privilege of meeting a fair number of

your colleagues," said Sylvie, pulling back a seat and sitting opposite Franck.

"That's the advantage of being arrested. Extends your social circle no end."

"Indeed it does," said Sylvie, leaning over the table to kiss Franck lightly on each cheek. "How are you feeling? You look good."

Sylvie had been a relatively frequent caller at the hospital, dropping in for brief visits and charting his progress – counting the tubes as they disappeared one by one. Having always been quite frank about how awful he looked, he was inclined to trust her current evaluation.

"Still a fair bit of pain if I move too fast or twist too far. Otherwise, no complaints."

"Glad to hear it. And you've reported in for duty at your new posting?"

Franck shrugged. He reached into the inside pocket of his jacket and pulled out one of his new business cards. A box of them had been awaiting him when he arrived at his office that morning. They bore his new address on the quai des Orfèvres, with his new fax, email and phone numbers. He handed it to her, without commentary.

"Still not happy about it, I see," she observed. "And yet you've always admired Yves de Chaumont. I seem to remember you siding with him against me first time we met. How is monsieur *le juge*?"

"Remarkably keen to make an honest detective out of me."

"I take it he's responsible for you reading this," she said, tapping the copy of *Exposé*.

Franck nodded.

"Your case?" she asked.

Franck nodded again. "As of this afternoon."

"Doesn't waste time, does he? So what's your take?" asked Sylvie. "A dead model in high-class lingerie – sounds like a sex game gone wrong, or at the very least a crime of passion."

Franck shook his head. "No sex, no violence, and nothing done on impulse. The killer came equipped to subdue and kill his victim, and we'll probably find that he took great care to slip in and out of the Lutetia unnoticed. If it was a crime of passion, it was passion long gone cold and sour."

"It happens."

"You speak from experience?"

Sylvie smiled. "We're sitting across from the Comédie Française. Years of watching Racine and Corneille have taught me a few things."

"I don't think this will turn out to be quite so decorous."

"Who's to say? If that photo really was taken by the murderer, you're dealing with an artist."

"The gentle art of murder?" mused Franck. "Not in the real world."

"Come on," said Sylvie, abruptly getting to her feet. "You haven't noticed, but I'm late. We have three minutes to take our seats."

Franck scooped up the copy of *Exposé* and slid it expertly into the envelope. He removed a crumpled ten euro note from a jacket pocket and laid it on the table. Sylvie was already at the café door. He hurried after, wincing as he did so. For him, speed and pain were now firm companions, although the doctors had assured him that time would prise them apart.

They headed towards the pillars that encircled the Comédie Française. Franck could hear the bell that rang just before curtain up, calling everyone to their seats. The hardened smokers, getting one last shot of nicotine before long hours of deprivation, were clustered around the main entrance. Scattered amongst them, eyes on their watches or scanning the streets that ran off from the theatre, were those who were slowly realising that they'd been stood up: an angry looking man in a suit, frantically thumbing the keys of his mobile phone; a young woman in a short skirt and leather jacket whose darkened eyes seemed unsurprised, used to disappointment.

Franck caught up with Sylvie inside the entrance while she was handing their tickets to the usher. He waved them through with little more than a frown, saving his ire for the smokers, who would endeavour to gain their seats seconds before the play's opening line.

Sylvie and Franck climbed a flight of stairs to reach the stalls. A soberly dressed young woman took their tickets and walked them briskly to a pair of seats eight rows from the stage. Good seats. That was one of Sylvie's many fields of expertise. Franck would compensate by paying for dinner later. The young woman slipped them a programme and stalked off.

The lights dimmed. Time for *Le Cid*: feuding nobles, love stymied by genealogy, crusading Catholics wiping Spain clean of Muslims; a tangled knot of honour, vengeance and passion that only royal sagacity could unravel. Standard fare for Corneille.

Chimène walked onto the stage in a golden gown of metallic fabric that flared aggressively under a spotlight. A prized daughter of the Castilian aristocracy, she was played by Marie Goubert, whose status within the Comédie Française could be described in much the same terms. Nearing her seventh year with the company, she had become its most celebrated heroine. On the verge of thirty, she had already run through most of the house's repertoire of young countesses, princesses, queens and scheming servants. She had brought to each role clear diction, intense concentration, and a willingness to risk whatever the director asked, not to mention her notorious beauty.

"She's incredible," Sylvie whispered as Goubert she took the stage. Throughout the theatre similar remarks were uttered, almost involuntarily, in most cases by women to their male companions.

Marie Goubert's arms were bare, her chestnut hair cascading down the back of her dress, her face radiant, made-up to echo the gold of her gown. She was the sun, warming hearts but threatening to blind insubmissive eyes. As she crossed to the front of the stage she seemed to sense the admiration that flowed through audience, already impatient to pay homage at the final curtain. She was at the height of her powers.

When the last verses had been spoken applause filled the theatre with resonant waves, beating back and forward every time the cast came to the front of the stage. The other players did their best to push Goubert forward on her own. She refused to do so. Never releasing the hand of the actor who played Rodrigue, the *Cid* of the title, she dragged him with her every time she stepped forward to acknowledge the audience.

Sylvie was a marathon hand clapper, never breaking her rhythm or lessening the force of her applause. She only stopped when the house lights came up and the cast finally stayed in the wings. Franck had watched her, rather than the stage, for the last few minutes. Her eyes were bright and her smile generous. To catch Sylvie with her guard down was a rare thing. So rare, in fact, that he could not be sure she was unaware of his gaze.

That was the problem with Sylvie: she seemed to do everything for a reason, and she took great care to ensure that those reasons were known only to her. Even now, three years after their paths had first crossed, he was not sure why she was sitting beside him. Aside from the fact that it was what she wanted.

The first time she had called him, a few days after being questioned in the course of an investigation into terrorist funding, Franck had politely but unambiguously turned down her invitation to lunch. She had not given up, eventually trapping him with the argument that refusing her offer was at best ungrateful, given the information she had provided, and at worst disturbing, implying that she might still be a suspect. Franck had given in, wondering as he did so if she had more to reveal. As it turned out, it was just a matter of eating lunch and answering – or avoiding – her questions. A few weeks later, a dinner invitation came along. About a month later, they found themselves at the cinema. After a longer pause, they spent an evening at the opera. Sylvie's determination – for, with very few exceptions, she was always the one who called him – had set a pattern that had lasted until this day. Given how little free time his missions left him, if it had not been for her, there would have been long periods in which he would have had no female company whatsoever outside the world of the DST.

And yet, he was not sure they were friends. Nor lovers, for that matter: neither had ever leant too close or caught a flash of desire in the other's eyes. They were infrequent companions, two busy professionals meeting up from time to time to profit from all the capital had to offer. It was not such an unusual configuration in Paris, yet such twosomes were normally formed by individuals who inhabited the same social sphere. Franck certainly shared some number of Sylvie's interests, but he was pretty sure no-one else she frequented resembled him at all.

In the end, he simply assumed that he amused and distracted her. She did much the same for him. Maybe there was no need to search for any deeper motivation. After all, she was not a suspect. Just an intelligent, attractive and wilful woman. And one who, as her energetic applause indicated, had a weakness for all things theatrical.

"You liked that," he observed. "A lot."

"Aren't you the detective," she declared. "Did you?"

"I think I prefer the film. Charlton Heston – now there's a *Cid*."

Sylvie elbowed him in the ribs. "Behave! Within these walls that's at least heresy, if not treason. It's the stake or the guillotine for you."

Franck breathed in sharply and winced, his hands curling into fists.

"Sorry," gasped Sylvie. "I forgot. Did that really hurt?"

Franck shook his head unconvincingly, and slowly released his fingers. "That's what I get for looking much better."

"Sorry," repeated Sylvie.

"Forget it," he insisted. "I'm supposed to be on the trail of a murderer. If I can't take a nudge in the side, I've not got much of chance against him."

He stood up and retrieved the envelope that had lain beneath his seat throughout the play.

"Goubert is impressive, though," he admitted.

"Impressive?" echoed Sylvie. "Goubert is a goddess."

She got up and they edged along the row, joining the slow moving stream that led to the doors. Very slow moving. When they reached the wide expanse of the lobby Franck saw bunching around the outer doors. Something was going on outside. Something punctuated by flashes of light. Those trapped inside interrogated each other, stopping what little progress there was by standing on tiptoes or craning their necks in an attempt to catch the spectacle outside.

"Stay here," said Franck, steering Sylvie to an abandoned ticket counter at the back of the lobby.

"They may have put you out on the beat, but I don't think they're expecting you to direct traffic too," she pointed out, but he was already gone.

Franck sliced briskly through the crowd, having first taken the precaution of holding his elbows tight against his sides and crossing his forearms across his stomach. He reached the exit and stepped out into the night.

Those leaving the theatre were hemmed in by a ring of seven or eight photographers who held their cameras at the ready, scanning those coming out. The flow of the audience stumbled against this breakwater of paparazzi, turning obliquely and shuffling laterally to escape around it.

Franck pulled his ID from his pocket, held it above his head, and walked to the middle of the line of photographers.

"Move back on both sides," he ordered. "Give these people a gap to move through."

The two photographers immediately before him simply sneered, shook their heads, and peered around him, anxious not to miss whoever might be coming up behind. Franck latched his left hand onto one's shoulder, and his right onto the other's. Instinctively they took a half-step back. He moved into the gap and extended his arms, pushing them to either side of him. He then released the one to his right and rammed his shoulder against the one to his left, propelling him back against his colleagues.

"Hey!" the man protested.

Franck stood back from him, his brow knotted in an effort

to ignore the complaints emanating from his torso. "Believe me, that hurt me more than it hurt you."

A couple of theatregoers took advantage of the gap Franck had created. More came up behind them, and soon a wedge was pouring through, forcing the broken wall of photographers further back on either side. Franck pushed his way to one of the pillars that ringed the theatre and took shelter behind it.

He waited till the crowd had thinned to a trickle before making his way back to find Sylvie. Whoever the paparazzi's prey had been, he seemed to have eluded them.

"Martin Freeman," said Sylvie.

They were at a corner table in the Le Colbert brasserie, right against the windows that looked out across rue Vivienne onto what was formerly the Bibliothèque Nationale. Both had ordered the moment a waiter brought them menus, not even bothering to open them. They had been here before.

"Vaguely rings a bell," said Franck.

"American film director. Big budget action movies. Did the last Bond."

"How do you know this?"

"While you were outside proving you can still throw your weight around, I asked one of the ushers what the fuss was all about. Freeman was in one of the boxes. He left by the cast entrance just as the play ended."

"Didn't bother staying to applaud? Probably doesn't understand French and was bored to death by then."

"How do you know he doesn't speak French?" demanded Sylvie.

"Fair point," conceded Franck. "Still, even if he does, I bet he doesn't speak Corneille. Can't see why he's worth half a dozen photographers. Must be a quiet night for celebrities."

"I bet he came to see Marie Goubert," said Sylvie. "She's the next Isabelle Adjani."

"Let's hope not. Hollywood had no idea what to do with Adjani. *Cat People* with Sharon Stone, and that's it, as far as I remember."

Sylvie thought for a moment, and was then forced to agree. Their food arrived: roasted suckling pig for her; steak tartare for him.

"*Bon appétit*," they chimed, simultaneously.

"You often publish pictures of the dead?"

Jacques Beaufort smiled slightly and nodded briefly over the top of Franck's head.

"Look behind you".

Franck turned in his chair. The wall behind him – like those on both sides of him, and the expanse behind Beaufort's desk – was covered with large photographic prints. None were framed, they were simply tacked or taped to the wall. All the easier to discard and replace, Franck imagined, as celebrities changed and new scandals leapt up, drowning their predecessors in the shallows of the collective memory.

When he had been ushered through the door of Beaufort's office Franck had been struck by its modest size and general disorder. Photo editor had to be one of the top jobs at *Exposé*, and Franck had interviewed enough executives to know that with rank usually went higher floors, bigger windows, and better furnishings. Beaufort's office recalled nothing more than a student bedsit, with posters, cards and photos claiming limited space and fast-fading attention. It sat on the ground floor of the *Exposé* building, just off a large open space area cluttered chaotically with desks, flat-screen terminals, and telephones. There was also a large quantity of photographic equipment carefully arranged on shelves in reinforced metal cases or hanging, bandolier-style, from rows of pegs clearly reserved for this purpose.

Beaufort sat surrounded by photos, and had even sacrificed most of his windows to them. Franck assumed he had either lost his battle for more wall space, or did not want anyone on the outside to know who came to see him in his office. *Exposé* was not above buying photos on the open market, of which unscrupulous freelance paparazzi were the principal, but not sole, suppliers. Even shadier sources had provided some of the prints that had fed readers' appetites in the past, ones with whom few would willingly associate.

"Which one?" asked Franck, unsure where he was supposed

to direct his gaze. He kept to himself the fact that his eyes had snagged on a photo of a middle-aged man in evening wear stumbling as he was hurried down a stone stairway, his hands hidden behind him, a dark-clad arm both pushing and steadying him from the right. He recognised the figure as François Salignon, being led away for peddling in enriched uranium. He also recognised the arm doing the pushing as his own.

"Try the coffin," suggested Beaufort. Diana's, drawn through London under the zooming lens of the same tribe of photographers she had tried to dodge when leaving the Ritz one night in Paris. "Or the Rwandan group shot." Further up, on the left, a pile of black corpses, most naked, none with all its limbs intact. "Or your colleagues." Across to the right, two Parisian policemen crumpled at the foot of a gunman who was himself thrown backwards as bullets slammed into his chest.

"We honour the dead almost every week," Beaufort concluded. "What's so different with the Sarraute cover?"

"How about the fact – as you pointed out yourself – that the murderer probably took it?" offered Franck.

"Strictly speaking, that's just a hypothesis," countered Beaufort. "We could be wrong. It could have been anyone who stumbled on the body before the police got there."

"A long time before the police got there. She didn't look quite as perky when hotel staff found her."

The remark did not perturb Beaufort. His job involved obtaining the most graphic photos of the world's catastrophes and atrocities. He was not one to be disturbed by the thought of a little rigor mortis or decay.

"Still doesn't prove beyond all doubt that it was the murderer, regardless of what I might've written. Have you looked closely at the print?"

Beaufort slipped his hand into an envelope and drew out an A4 sized print of the photo that had given such a boost to sales. His outstretched arm offered it to Franck.

"Is that the original?" Franck asked.

"Yes. It was pushed through the outside mail slot around midnight last Monday. I was in here, going through the final layout for the next issue's print run. I got a text message. Want to see it?"

Franck nodded. Beaufort let the print slide to the desk, picked up his mobile phone, flicked it opened, and stabbed at it a few times with his thumb.

"Here." He passed it to Franck.

The message filled the screen: "Killer photo. In the mail. Front page material."

Franck checked the date and time of reception: twelve minutes after midnight on the day Laure Sarraute was killed. The killer had wasted no time.

"Will you sign a paper authorising us to backtrack this call and search for any others from the same number in your phone records?"

Franck expected *Exposé* to cooperate, hoping for a place in the front line on the murder hunt. They would be looking for a follow-up: a culprit; a chase; a shoot-out, if at all possible.

"Sure," said Beaufort. "Just don't go copying my list of numbers. Can I count on your discretion?"

"That's funny, coming from *Exposé*," observed Franck. "But yes, you can."

He handed back the phone. Beaufort pushed the print of Sarraute to Franck's side of the desk.

"Was it in an envelope?" asked Franck.

"Yes. Along with a USB stick with the digital file for the picture. The file is time-stamped – nine twenty-two last Monday evening."

"The time-stamp indicates when the photo was taken?"

"No. It's when he stopped photoshopping the image. There's no metadata. He must have deleted the EXIF details when he created the JPEG file."

"Am I supposed to know what that means?"

Beaufort shrugged. "If you're handling this case, maybe you should. Normally a digital image file contains a lot of information about when and how it was taken – make and model number of the camera, lens size, date and time of image capture, aperture and shutter speed, that sort of thing. But you can wipe all that out, if you know what you're doing. That's what our man did. He didn't send us the raw image he caught when he clicked the shutter in the hotel room – he sent us a modified version. Actually, enhanced would be a better word."

"Enhanced how?"

"Changed to black and white for a start. Apart from that, I think he just cleaned it up a little. Nothing drastic – just the tiny touches that make all the difference, if you know what you're doing. Which he certainly did. Just look at it."

Franck turned his eyes to the sizeable print of Sarraute in the Lutetia. "What is it I'm supposed to see?"

"The fact that it's not a good photo – it's a great photo. One I'd be happy to call my own."

Franck looked at him with undisguised contempt.

"Professionally speaking, of course," continued Beaufort. "Look at the lighting, for a start. The body was found indoors, in a room in the Lutetia, right?"

Franck nodded.

"He didn't use a flash, which would have flattened everything. If the body was lit, it was by an indirect source. The light was reflected back down on it, falling like sunlight. Look at the shadows – all leaning the same way. Look at the way one breast steals the light from the other. Look at the depth of shade behind the suspender straps. If I didn't know better I'd say this was a studio shot. It certainly wasn't done by an amateur."

"Anything else?" Franck prompted.

"He had a camera that could take fourteen megapixels and had full manual controls. It was not some pocket snapshot machine."

"Anything else?"

"Look at the way she's lying. Sarraute was probably never better posed in her life. Who taught him to do that?"

"Anything else?" Franck repeated.

Beaufort threw up his hands. "Your turn now," he suggested, trying to dissemble the inquisitive hunger on this face. "Was the body exactly like the photo when you lot got to it?"

"I can't tell you," said Franck.

"Can't ? Won't ?"

"Won't."

"Maybe later, when you've got him?"

Franck was not in the habit of bargaining. He tried to nudge Beaufort back into his previous stream of thought. "You think he may have taken other photos, as well as this one?"

Beaufort held back for a second, but then relented, letting his own request drop. "He must have done. You don't take a photo this good with one shot. If he did, I want him on my team when you lot let him out of jail."

"You'll be long retired by then."

"Don't count on it captain. The criminal justice system has a short memory."

"I don't," insisted Franck.

*

On arriving back at his office, Franck headed straight to the evidence room to deposit the print, envelope and USB stick he had retrieved from *Exposé*. While down in the basement he signed out the box containing the items taken from the crime scene and carried it to his desk.

He extracted four ziplocked bags. Two for the underwear in which Sarraute was found. Two for the underwear left with the rest of her clothes. He held up the latter: a semi-transparent light blue bra and an identically coloured thong, both embroidered with a swirling, faintly oriental motif. The other clothes found were a short skirt and a v-necked top. All shared the same palette of colours.

Insofar as he could tell by looking at them in the bags, her blue underwear had a similar seductive potential to the white set with which it had been replaced. This very deliberate act – whether Sarraute did it herself, or with her killer's complicity, or at his command – had to be significant. For the moment all Franck could see was the change of colour, a preference for white, and presumably for its association with purity. Suspecting he was missing something he stretched out to the phone on his desk and dialled a number. It was answered almost instantly.

"Good afternoon, I'd like to speak with Sylvie Thomas. This is Franck Guerin. It's a business matter – she'll take it."

He was left on hold for a couple of minutes.

"A business call?" Sylvie's voice came on the line. "Don't tell me I'm about to be invited back into one of your nice interrogation rooms again?"

"Sorry to disturb you Sylvie," said Franck. "But I need some advice I don't think I'll be able to get in-house."

"Go ahead. I'll waive my usual fees. I know you can't afford them."

"You remember the photo of Laure Sarraute in *Exposé*?"

"Sure," said Sylvie, before correcting herself. "Well, the essentials – dead woman, white lingerie, no blood."

"Did anything about the lingerie strike you?"

"Other than the fact that it must have cost a fortune?"

"How do you know?" asked Franck.

"Because it didn't look cheap. How else?"

"Does yours?"

"Does mine what?"

"Does your lingerie look cheap? Whatever you're wearing right now?"

"Well, well, this is a new avenue for us. The time has come for a little phone sex, has it? Maybe I won't waive my fees after all."

"Seriously," insisted Franck. "You're a successful, attractive professional woman who earns far more than anyone should. You dress well and you like to look attractive to men."

"So you do notice these things?" interjected Sylvie, mimicking astonishment.

"Stop interrupting. What I want to know is whether you wear the kind of underwear that Sarraute was found wearing, and if not, what's the difference with what you do?"

"Look Franck, what I'm wearing – and I'll spare you a

description, as I don't want to raise too many eyebrows this end – is far from cheap. That said, based on what I remember, the Sarraute ensemble looked very high-end to me."

"Who could I show it to, to be sure?"

"Talk to those who sell such things. If you want easy access to all the exclusive brands in lingerie, try the Bon Marché."

"Thanks," said Franck. "I owe you."

"That you do," agreed Sylvie. "And if you want to redeem part of your debt, bring me back a little something from your shopping expedition. Just so you know – I prefer black."

"I'll keep it in mind," said Franck, and hung up.

He gathered together the four bags containing the two sets of underwear, found an empty cardboard box file and slipped them into it. Time to go shopping with the over-affluent.

Franck got out of the metro at Sèvres-Babylone. Looming to his left as he reached the surface was the Lutetia. Its proximity to the Bon Marché was quite deliberate, as the hotel had been built specifically for the department store's clientele in the early 1900s, at a time when shopping trips involved long train rides and could be multi-day affairs. It had traversed the subsequent two World Wars with little physical damage, and had largely succeeded in drawing a veil over its role as the requisitioned headquarters for German counter-espionage during the Occupation. Today it was simply one more luxury hotel in a Paris well-supplied with such establishments. Franck wondered whether Sarraute's death would prove a help or hindrance with its market positioning, aware that, for those who did not deal with it regularly, violent death could acquire a strange glamour.

He looked up at the facade, counting the floors and isolating what he guessed to be the window of the room which Sarraute had been given. She would certainly have looked out over the small square in which he stood – perhaps watching a man stride across it with one of the Bon Marché's signature stiff paper bags containing a freshly purchased present, which she would unhesitatingly agree to try on, with unexpected consequences.

He turned his back on the hotel, slightly troubled by this sudden flight of imaginative fancy. It was too early to start constructing possible scenarios. He had too little to hang them on. That was the problem with working alone: facts trickled in at a snail's pace. At the DST they worked in teams, amassing as much data as they could get their hands on until significant patterns floated to the surface almost by themselves. That was why it was called intelligence gathering – not a desperate quest staggering from one clue to the next.

The Bon Marché antedated the hotel by 50 years. It was the oldest department store in Paris, the only one on the Left Bank, and far more discreet than its brash and more youthful cousins across the Seine. Designed by Gustave Eiffel, its light iron infrastructure had allowed the construction of a vast multi-levelled temple of commerce organised like an open-air market whose booths were nowadays each dedicated to a single brand. Like the Lutetia, it catered to a very specific income group. Franck could not remember the last time he had set foot inside it, and was sure he had never purchased anything there.

With no intimate knowledge of the store's layout he wandered briefly between the boutique stands on the ground floor, balloted by the afternoon shoppers, before stumbling upon a directory indicating that lingerie was to be found on the first floor. He took the central staircase, open on all sides, that offered a panoramic view of the rows of booths. A well-heeled crowd flocked the passageways, the mere presence of each shopper furnishing proof of his or her individual purchasing power.

Once on the first floor it was not difficult to spot the area given over to lace, satin and all things sheer. At a loss before the sharply delineated territories of each brand, Franck chose one at random and presented himself to its reigning saleswoman.

"I hope you can help me," he started, wondering how strange his request would seem. He opened his box file and pulled out the white bra. "Do you recognise this make?"

The saleswoman, a veteran of many years, deployed an effortless smile, took the bag and unzipped the top. Before she could reach inside, Franck gently trapped her hand.

"I'd rather you didn't," he said. "This is evidence. It's a police matter."

In actual fact the crime lab had finished processing the lingerie, so there was no reason to stop her touching it – except the impression that his prohibition would make.

"I do apologise, sir," said the saleswoman.

She bent over the bag, peering inside, then held it up and turned it around.

"Du Bellay." she pronounced.

"Du Bellay?" Franck repeated. "The model? The fabric? The brand?"

"The brand, sir."

"Do you sell it?" he asked.

"Over there," he was told. "The young woman with the chopsticks in her hair and the rather long earrings."

Franck followed her gaze, for she was too well-mannered to point. What he saw first were a short, tight skirt and patterned stockings, but as his gaze rose he caught the identifying features he had just been given.

"Thank you."

"My pleasure, sir," replied the saleswoman.

"Can I show you another one?"

"Of course, sir."

He brought out the blue bra and watched the saleswoman study it in the same fashion – first through the plastic, then by looking closely at the item through the open top of the bag.

"I would hazard a guess at Aubade. It's a less distinctive item than the Du Bellay."

"Less expensive?"

"Far less expensive." The emphasis was firmly on the first word. "But still a quality product, sir, which we are proud to stock. Would you like me to show you to the boutique?"

"I think it's the Du Bellay that I'm interested in. Thank you very much for your help."

"My pleasure, sir. If required, you'll find the Ephémère stand on the floor below."

"Ephémère?" Franck recognised the name. One of the few fashion houses even he had heard of, Ephémère had been founded around the same time as Chanel and – proof that names were not always prophetic – had remained its great rival ever since.

"Eternal," said the saleswoman. "If my nose is not mistaken." She was referring to Ephémère's celebrated perfume, whose upmarket positioning was regularly reinforced by ruinously expensive but highly regarded ad campaigns. "Mademoiselle appreciates the classics."

Franck did not correct the tense. He offered his thanks one last time and headed towards the young woman with what looked like a pair of dark wooden skewers in her hair.

The Du Bellay boutique had little in common with those around it. Most had their daintiest wares, the lower-body garments, stacked in glass-fronted cabinets. Behind them upper-body ware hung in rows along easily accessible rails. Full scale or truncated dummies, each bearing a colour-coordinated ensemble, completed the panoply amidst which sales staff awaited their next customer.

Du Bellay displayed not one item of lingerie to the public gaze. Even the brand's name was nowhere on show. Its territory was marked on three sides by a waist-high wall of wooden drawer units, all facing inwards. The flat oak surface was home to a digital till, two credit card readers and a small pile of catalogues. All that was missing was a suite of private changing rooms, given which Du Bellay could have disdainfully denied any connection with the rest of the Bon Marché.

The salesgirl fixed her attention on Franck as he walked purposefully towards her. She did not, however, move from her vantage point right in the centre of her stockade. Franck noticed that the floor beneath her was covered with a parquet veneer. Thin, elevated heels supported what little weight she possessed.

As Franck stepped onto the parquet she greeted him.

"Good afternoon sir." She nodded slightly. Having dared to cross the threshold, he had to belong to the club, whatever his ill-tailored jacket suggested.

"Good afternoon," he replied. "This is the Du Bellay boutique?"

"Your first visit?"

"Yes, it is."

"I dare say it won't be your last." She offered him a smile of complicity. "I think you'll find that madame or mademoiselle will do anything to encourage you to come and see us again."

Despatched by a dead woman, Franck thought this unlikely.

"Are you looking for a particular item or model?" she asked.

Franck pulled out the two bags containing the white bra and panties. The girl showed not the slightest surprise and took them lightly from him.

"The Midnight Sun ensemble. A white that dazzles the eye and dizzies the head. The lightest possible gauze on the panties. The softest lace on the bra, almost melting on the breasts." She had to be quoting a rehearsed text, but she did so with a certain conviction.

"You stock this model?"

"We stock all current models. However ..."

"When you say current," interrupted Franck. "How long ago did this Midnight Sun come out?"

"Three or four months."

"Has it sold well?"

"It was selling at a respectable rate, until two days ago. Now I don't have a single sample left."

"Since *Exposé*?" asked Franck. Clearly there was no such thing as bad publicity.

"That's right. Midnight Sun was made for a figure like Laure Sarraute's. She couldn't have chosen better."

"You knew her? She shopped here?"

He received a stern look in return.

"We don't reveal our customers' identities. What if madame found out that monsieur has been shopping for a little something she has never seen, or vice versa? Our calling is passion and pleasure, not domestic strife."

"Laure Sarraute is dead. I don't think she'll mind," he pointed out.

"All the same." She raised both hands. "Policy is policy."

Franck offered a gesture of his own. His hand sneaked into an inside pocket and pulled out his official ID, holding it right before her eyes.

"Did Laure Sarraute shop here? This is a murder investigation."

Her eyes narrowed and a frown marred her carefully painted features. He was not a member of the club after all.

"No, she didn't. Or at least, not on my shifts."

"When are you on?"

"Mondays to Fridays, from two till closing."

"Were you here last Monday?"

"Yes."

"Did you sell one of these?" Franck brandished the ziplock bag.

"I couldn't say. Over the past two days it's like we've sold nothing but Midnight Sun. Before, I can't really remember."

Franck cared little about sales since *Exposé* came out. However, if Du Bellay was as expensive as they said, it could be that sales beforehand were few in number – and therefore manageable, from an investigative viewpoint.

"Do you know how many shops sell this model in Paris?"

"We only sell in our own boutiques. We have a shop in the rue du Faubourg Saint Honoré. We have another one in Nice."

"That's it?" asked Franck, encouraged by the news, and suddenly glad to be dealing with the rich and their jealously guarded toys.

"For France, yes. Then there's Geneva, Milan, London, New York, LA, Dubai, Moscow, Tokyo, ..."

For the moment Franck was prepared to ignore the rest of the world.

"I'll need your stock records for this model. I may need your credit card traces."

"I don't have the authority to provide such information."

Franck agitated his ID in the air. "I suspect that depends on who's asking."

She did not seem impressed, and stood her ground.

"I can't do it."

Franck backed off two steps and leant against one of the counters. He picked a catalogue from a pile to his right. The front cover was a stiff creamy white, embossed with the Du Bellay name. He flipped the slim volume over. On the back, at the bottom, was an address. He held it up.

"Is this the head office?"

The girl nodded.

"Can I take this?"

She took one step towards him, planting her heels firmly on the parquet.

"If you like. It's twenty euros," she informed him.

"Twenty euros for this?" He weighed the catalogue on his open palm. It could not contain more than thirty pages.

"If you were a customer you could have it for free. Otherwise it's twenty euros. I'll happily sell you some lingerie if you prefer."

Franck held up his two evidence bags. "I have a Midnight Sun ensemble. I think that makes me a customer."

He slipped them back into the box file and added the catalogue.

"Thank you for your time."

She offered no reply as he walked away.

Franck got out of the metro at Convention and headed northwest, looking for an address on rue Lecourbe. A few minutes later he stood before it, a tired and dingy café whose interior was dominated by a PMU counter taking bets on horse races. Large windows revealed an interior distinctly lacking in charm: broken tiles on the floor, scarred and neglected tables and chairs, and a similarly worn-down clientele. Unsurprisingly, given that it was a Saturday afternoon, there was a fair scattering of customers. Nonetheless, despair, rather than excited anticipation of future winnings, seemed to be the dominant mood.

Although the air inside was far from clear, Franck could make out Catherine Vautrin, who had commandeered a table not far from the entrance. She wore straight-legged trousers, flat shoes, and a formless cotton sweatshirt. All were black, as were the tangled hair that stopped short of her shoulders and the shapeless canvas bag that hung from the back of her seat. Although the only woman in the place, nothing about her attracted attention.

Her eyes moved lazily towards him and she raised a crooked finger to beckon him in. She had sent him a text message that morning, summoning him to this address at four o'clock. No explanation had been given. She was, after all, his boss.

Franck pushed the door and walked slowly towards her table, weaving around clumps of customers. She followed his progress, but did not stand up when he arrived before her.

"You look at lot better than the last time I saw you," she observed.

That had been in the hospital. Some three months ago. One visit, just to check he was still breathing, then nothing.

Not that Franck had felt slighted. She was a section head. As he had heard her say on many occasions: if she wasn't snowed under, she wasn't doing her job properly.

Which also meant she had certainly been keeping tabs on

him between times. She probably knew that he had spent the morning at the Val-de-Grâce military hospital, undergoing scans and examinations under the silent scrutiny of one of the doctors who had patched him together when he had been flown back from Corsica. His progress had been deemed satisfactory and his painkiller prescription renewed.

"I feel a lot better than the last time you saw me," he replied. "No catheter. Makes a world of difference."

She waved a hand dismissively.

"The fragility of men. A catheter is all it takes to turn you into martyrs."

Franck smiled and sat down opposite her, reassured that she was not pulling her punches. Any sign of sympathy from Catherine was always a very bad omen.

"I suppose I shouldn't ask how the section is doing?" he enquired.

"If you like – now that you're up and walking again, you presumably have the breath to waste. Just don't expect me to answer. You're not back on active duty. You know the rules."

He did. Then again, there were not many alternative topics of conversation that worked with Catherine. She lived in the corridors of the DST – five years' service under her had given him ample opportunity to confirm this fact. Many of his colleagues were convinced the only reason she ever stepped outside was to stock up on cigarettes.

She had one now, burning slowly between two outstretched fingers, impatiently awaiting her next breath. This could help explain her choice of café. Almost every customer in the place was smoking: those propping up the bar, those studying form in painstakingly folded newspapers, those lingering anxiously in front of the large television hung from the ceiling in one corner which provided live coverage of races, and the fortunate few draining the proceeds of a successful bet. No fresh air seemed to have penetrated the premises in living memory. It was just like being in Catherine's office in the DST, although she at least had the excuse that the windows were sealed.

"You a regular here?" Franck asked.

"The city has hundreds of places like this. They're the last refuge of impenitent smokers like myself. They're also one of the few places you can be sure no-one will pay any attention to you. Far more serious business is going on."

She nodded towards the television. A race was entering the final straight. Every pair of eyes in the room was riveted to the screen. Fingers were compulsively twisting betting slips.

"There's also the fact that anyone who wants to overhear you has to run the risk of lung cancer," she continued. "That ought to dissuade a few."

Not that such a prospect would worry Catherine in the pursuit of her professional duties. There was no theoretical limit to the risks she was prepared to run to obtain information. Or have her team run, for that matter.

"You have something secure to tell me?"

"Not really," she replied. "I just wanted to make sure you understood where you stand. First, though, you can get us something to drink. I'll have another of these."

There was an empty Pernod glass before her with a few drops of cloudy liquid at its base. Franck looked around for a waiter.

"Counter service only," Catherine informed him. "Another of the particular virtues of this kind of establishment."

Franck wandered over to the bar and came back with a circular tray bearing a new glass of Pernod, a small jug of water, and a bottle of Belgian beer for himself.

"Calories," Catherine remarked, motioning towards the bottle with her chin. "Do wonders for the constitution. Or so they say."

She herself seemed to get by on nicotine and strong spirits. Her face was hollow, her body without substance, her skin sallow, her eyes and mouth crowded by wrinkles. Although in the confines of the café she did not look much unhealthier than the average customer, within the DST, where a certain level of physical fitness was supposedly mandatory, she stood out like a recently reanimated corpse. Only her eyes belied the notion that she was teetering on the edge of collapse. Dark and small, they shifted continuously with a feverish energy.

She slowly poured water into her glass, letting a few ice cubes tumble with it, watching the liquor change colour until it reached what was presumably the right shade of translucent white. Franck sipped at his beer, waiting for her to start.

"A lot of questions are being asked about Corsica," she said. "Three bodies stretchered out and Gabriel Agostini still on the run. The minister is furious."

"Nobody ever explained to him that not all operations succeed?"

"Politicians don't have a problem with failure, as long as it's kept under wraps."

"Which is proving hard to do with Gerhart Lange, I imagine?"

"A dead agent is something we know how to handle. A seriously wounded German tourist ready to babble to the press back home is proving trickier."

"I haven't seen his statement," said Franck. "But I'd be surprised if he had anything to say against us."

"He certainly has nothing but praise for you. But he also provides clear proof that you didn't immobilise Agostini when you had the opportunity."

"Some opportunity!" protested Franck. "Had I tackled Agostini we would have had a dead German tourist on our hands."

"With a bullet from Agostini's gun inside him. Just another victim of a vicious terrorist operating under a spurious political flag. That is something we would have known how to deal with."

Frank shrugged. "I made the call. If I had to do it again, I'd do the same thing."

"That's what's worrying a lot of people."

"Including you?"

He fixed Catherine as he said this. She held his gaze for over a minute, offering nothing in return. She then reached for her glass and sampled it.

"I don't try to second-guess agents on the ground. It was

your call, not mine. All I'm interested in are the results. Frankly, they're not so good."

"You won't back me up?" demanded Franck. He had given twelve years to the service. He was owed something in return: the benefit of the doubt, for instance.

"What kind of a question is that?" she chastised him. "What's good for the service is good enough for me – and ought to be for you. The DST is a vocation, not a job."

Whatever Franck had sacrificed to the DST, he knew that Catherine had offered up much more. He was a neophyte in comparison to her. But he had never thought that her well-nigh mystical union with the service excluded all thought for the individual.

"You may have to be hung out to dry," she concluded. "If that's the decision, I can't help you. If you want my advice, here it is – try getting used to life on the outside. Yves de Chaumont can help you with that. That's why I called him."

"I didn't think you two got on," said Franck.

"We don't. De Chaumont thinks we're a shady organisation that's not to be trusted. And that's what's allowed him to work with us in the past. As a rule, we just ride roughshod over *juges d'instruction*. De Chaumont is an exception. He's come closer to forcing us to behave like normal policemen than anyone else. If you ask me, his unshakeable sense of right and wrong is proof that we didn't chop enough noble heads off when we had the chance."

She said this in a calm, matter-of-fact tone.

"Come on," objected Franck. "Yves is patently a good man and an excellent public servant."

"First of all, no-one is ever really patently anything. As for Yves, he may well be a good man, whatever that might be. But an exemplary public servant? Let's just say I have my doubts. In the end of the day, I suspect that his loyalty is to his aristocratic sense of honour rather than to the Republic."

"You're sure the two are incompatible?"

"Ask Robespierre. Or Saint Just."

It was not the first time Franck had heard her invoke the

tutelary spirits of the French Revolution, advocates of a deadly cocktail of terror and virtue. Being provocative had always been one of her favourite arms as a manager. As ever, the only way to handle it was not to rise to the bait.

"So why put me in the hands of such a reactionary?" he asked.

"Because he likes you."

"Despite the fact that I work for the devil?"

"By that, I suppose you mean me. Well, he probably likes you because you worked for the devil but never came to resemble him – or her in this instance." The change in tense did not escape Franck, but Catherine gave him no opening to bring it up. "That makes you stronger than Faust – which had to appeal to monsieur *le juge*. Whatever the reason, that's why I used you as liaison every time we had dealings with him. And that's why I knew he'd be interested in lending a helping hand in your hour of need."

"My hour of need, or yours?"

"You know I have your best interests in mind," she announced, a slightly wicked smile on her face. "So, what's he got you doing?"

"The Sarraute case."

"I'm supposed to know what that is?"

"Probably not," Franck conceded. Robespierre would not have read *Exposé* either. "A young model killed in mysterious circumstances."

"Makes a change from a government official blown to pieces. Should be easier to catch than Agostini."

"We'll see."

Catherine appeared surprised.

"Come on, Franck," she said. "How hard can it be – a murder investigation conducted in the bright light of day rather than a clandestine operation whose very name can't be pronounced in public?"

"That's what I'm about to find out."

He pushed back his chair, pulled out his wallet, and extracted two small plastic cards, both of which bore his photo and a microchip. One was his pass to the many electronic doors of the DST. The other gave him access to its secure network.

"I take it these are why you wanted to see me?"

Catherine held out her hand.

"I knew I wouldn't have to ask. You're a smart man, Franck."

"Sometimes I wonder," he said, depositing the cards on her upturned palm.

"It may just be temporary. We'll let you know."

Franck turned and walked away. Catherine returned her attention to her cigarette, not watching him go. As he stepped outside, the smoke and tobacco odour of the café came with him, stubbornly clinging to his jacket and his hair. This was the mark Catherine left on all those under her tutelage.

He felt stale, and wondered if this was a revelation.

Monday, 11th June

Three photos.

In the left foreground, a broad-leaved bush showing several shades of green. Behind it, a gnarled trunk, probably a chestnut. Slightly off-centre, a park bench with a cast iron frame and wooden slats, their green paint chipped and stained. A worn leather briefcase propped up at one end of the bench. Next to it, Franck Guerin in dark blue trousers, thick-soled black shoes, a light blue shirt worn without a tie, and a dark blue jacket with a noticeable bulge at his right hip. His hands cradle a mobile phone. His eyes are closed. A slight frown on his brow.

The baubled entrance to the metro in place Colette, its countless beads of Murano glass catching the sun and the attention of at least one tourist, visible in the upper right hand corner holding her pocket digital camera in front of her at eye level. A figure striding purposefully across the shot, dodging around a handful of people rising out of the metro entrance. Franck Guerin. A dog-eared briefcase in one hand. Jacket whipped out behind him by the speed of his progress. A holster half visible beneath it.

In the background, the arcade that runs around the inner garden of the Palais Royal. In the foreground, an unoccupied cast iron chair with a leather briefcase at its feet. To its left, a young woman in a short skirt and lightweight sweater with a widely scooped neck tumbling off one of her shoulders. She smiles, her head tipped slightly to one side. To the right of the chair, Franck Guerin gestures off to one side, his eyes on the girl's, a smile of his own echoing hers.

*

"My name is Franck Guerin. I've an appointment with Luc du Bellay."

It was nine thirty on Monday morning, the earliest appointment Franck had been able to secure when he called the

p.47

Du Bellay offices late in the afternoon on the previous Friday.

The receptionist was barely in her twenties. Perched on the edge of her seat behind a desk supported by thin rods of black steel, she leant forward intently as Franck spoke, offering a glimpse of her cleavage and the lace-trimmed cups that held it in place. He did not ask whether she was sporting one of the firm's products. His job was to pretend he had noticed nothing; hers was to make sure he did.

"Monsieur du Bellay is indeed expecting you captain Guerin, but unfortunately he is running a little late this morning. Can I invite you to take a seat?"

She waved towards an oval of polished translucent glass that hovered above the floor in a nearby corner surrounded by three chairs built of rods that echoed those of her desk. They did not look very comfortable, but there was nothing else on offer. Franck wandered across and sat down, wondering whether Luc du Bellay was simply late in arriving, or whether he had scheduled another meeting before his own appointment.

Fifteen minutes later he was still there. The receptionist had brought him coffee, kneeling alongside him as she deposited it on the low table. Franck did not notice how her short skirt inched backward across her thighs as she did so. He was too preoccupied leafing through the magazine that had been lying, all alone, on the tinted glass.

Its cover, printed on stiff and glossy paper, could not have failed to catch his attention. It bore a colour portrait of a woman seen from behind, her torso imprisoned in the unflinching grip of a corset. The lacing in the back of the corset was caught in loving detail, as was the grain of the woman's skin stretched across her shoulder blades. Albeit in colour, rather than black and white, it seemed a not-too-distant cousin of the photo taken of Laure Sarraute.

The pages inside confirmed this impression. Printed on paper so heavy it fought against his efforts to flick through the pages, the magazine consisted exclusively of photos of attractive young women clad only in lingerie. There were no articles and no adverts. The little text to be found was inside the front and back covers, which provided an address for subscription enquiries and the publisher's details. The only other words present were those of the title on the bottom right hand corner of the front page: *Wasp-Waisted.*

Franck was searching for the cover price when the receptionist called over to him.

"Monsieur du Bellay is free now. I'm sorry to have kept you waiting."

She indicated a pair of double doors and Franck stood up and headed towards them.

"Just go straight in," she instructed.

He gently pushed the two doors open and stepped through, letting them swing shut behind him.

Luc du Bellay stood waiting for him in the middle of a large room flooded with light from four large windows looking out onto the trees of the place des Etats-Unis. The floor was polished parquet, the walls stark white, the furnishings sparse and determinedly modern. Du Bellay was dressed in a tight-fitting charcoal suit framing a thin dark tie and starched white cuffs. He smiled at Franck from beneath copious, deliberately ruffled hair, a hint of the wolf in his handsome, elongated face.

He extended a hand for Franck to shake and guided him near the windows to a cluster of four angular seats poised around a coffee table surfaced with burnished zinc. Franck sat, laying his briefcase on the table. Du Bellay joined him.

"Captain Guerin, I do apologise for having kept you waiting. May I offer you some coffee, or something else?"

Franck waved a hand. "I'm fine. Your receptionist has been taking very good care of me."

"True to form. In which case, let us get down to business. You wanted to talk about Laure Sarraute?"

"More precisely, I want to talk about what she was wearing," Franck clarified. He released the lock on his briefcase and took out the copy of *Exposé*, laying it gently on the table. He then added the two evidence bags with the white lingerie taken from the corpse.

"I believe this is one of your products."

Du Bellay nodded, his regard switching between the bags and the magazine cover. "Midnight Sun. 85C, if I'm not mistaken."

Franck frowned. "The model number?"

Du Bellay smiled. "No, our models have names, not numbers. 85C is the size: 85 being the diameter of the body at the point of the breasts; C the size of the cup. But I'm guessing from the photo. May I?"

He pointed towards the evidence bags.

"Go ahead,' said Franck.

Du Bellay retrieved the bra from the bag, held it up by the straps, and turned it before his eyes.

"85C. Definitely."

"And you would say that's the right size for Laure Sarraute?"

"Oh yes," confirmed du Bellay. "Look at the photo. It's a perfect fit."

"So either she bought it, or somebody else did who knew her well."

"Not necessarily – it depends on what you mean by knew her well. Laure Sarraute was a model. Her measurements will have been public knowledge. Anyone who asked her agent could have known. Indeed, they're probably on the internet. She wasn't quite a top model – not just yet – but she was famous enough for someone somewhere to have put her on the web."

"You used her?"

"No, we didn't. Looking at this," du Bellay laid down the bra and tapped the cover of *Exposé*, "we should have."

"In a sense, you now have. According to your boutique in the Bon Marché, this model is selling out."

"It's true," confirmed du Bellay, with some slight discomfort. "When *Exposé* came out we sold every pair of Midnight Sun in stock in Paris. Milan, Geneva and London saw sales leap. No noticeable effect elsewhere as yet, but I think it's going to come. My phone hasn't stopped ringing. The fashion media is all over this. I've sunk a fortune – several fortunes even – into marketing over the past years and I've never seen half as much interest."

"You should just have had someone killed instead. Much more cost-efficient," suggested Franck.

Du Bellay glared at him.

"I don't find that particularly funny, captain."

"I'm glad to hear it," said Franck.

"Is that why you've come here? To cast such aspersions?" Du Bellay's voice remained indignant.

Franck raised his hands. He had said it on impulse, fishing for a reaction. He did not want the interview to stop there.

"No, I didn't. I came here to seek your help. I was just thinking aloud. Faced with a murder, we've got to ask who benefits from it."

"I would gladly sacrifice the sales income of the past few days if it would bring Laure Sarraute back. She was a lovely girl. Everyone thought so."

"I thought you hadn't used her?"

"I hadn't. But that doesn't mean I hadn't met her. I'm in the fashion business. I go to a lot of shows and events. So do models. Everyone knows everyone else, more or less."

"You were friends?"

"No. We may have talked on a couple of occasions. That's about it. But I knew her well enough to know that she was a lovely girl. Which, in this business, is rarer than you might think."

"Do you have any idea why she might have been killed?"

Du Bellay shrugged his shoulders. "A love affair gone wrong?"

Franck said nothing. A wronged or jealous lover sending a photo of his handiwork to *Exposé* seemed highly unlikely.

"A stalker? A pervert?" continued du Bellay. "I'm not an expert in these matters, captain."

"You're a fortunate man," said Franck. "Do you know anything of Sarraute's personal life? Who she was dating? Who she had dated?"

"No, I can't say I do. Have you asked her friends or

family?"

Franck changed tack. He had phoned her parents on Friday afternoon, but obtained nothing on this score.

"Let's talk about something you do know about." He nodded towards the bra on the table. "Why Midnight Sun?"

"Why not? She looked great in it."

"Yes, but could it possibly mean something? Does this model have any particular significance?"

Du Bellay shook his head. "No more than any other model we make. They all flatter the wearer and seduce the observer."

"What about the colour?"

"Midnight Sun is only available in white. Immaculate white. 'Innocence mixed with malicious intent'. One of our slogans."

"A rather prophetic one, at least as regards the malicious intent," observed Franck. "I need to know whether Laure Sarraute bought this or somebody bought it for her."

"I'd like to help, but we don't keep track of our customers. We have over twenty outlets around the world. We sell over four hundred thousand units a year."

"What about this model in particular?"

Du Bellay rose and walked over to a desk in the far corner of the room. Without sitting in the chair behind it, he reached out to a laptop that lay open on its surface and turned it around so that the screen faced him. After a few clicks on the mouse tethered to it he pulled up a series of three-dimensional charts.

"We released Midnight Sun in January this year. Up until the end of last week we had produced 1920 units – that's an individual piece, bra or panty – and sold 1284." He clicked again. "Sales were pretty even across all outlets, with New York in the lead."

"What about this size?" asked Franck.

"85C bra?" mused du Bellay, and clicked some more. "140 units produced; 98 sold."

"Sold in Paris?"

Another click. "24 units distributed to the Bon Marché and our boutique in Faubourg Saint Honoré; 17 sold."

Franck was encouraged by this. Seventeen was a

manageable number.

"You have credit card traces of those sales?"

"Of course," insisted du Bellay. "At least, for those bought by card. It if was a cash sale, we'll have nothing."

"How much did it cost?"

Another click. "2900 euros for the ensemble."

Franck whistled in astonishment.

Du Bellay looked across at him. "Given the quality of the product, it's not as expensive as you might think. Given my production, distribution and marketing costs, it's not as high margin as you might imagine either."

"Given the price tag," continued Franck, "you can't have that many cash sales."

"That varies from country to country. But, as far as Paris is concerned, you're right. Most sales go through a card."

"Can you give me those card numbers?"

"Not straight away. They're not on my laptop. But I can ask for them to be extracted from the system."

"My email and fax number are on this." Franck laid a card on the coffee table. "As soon as you can."

"Of course. However, I have to ask you to be discreet. If all my customers start getting calls from the police, they won't remain my customers much longer."

"I understand. But this is a murder enquiry. If that has to be done, it will be done."

"In which case, can I ask you to alert me before you do so, and provide the names and details of those you plan to contact? That way, I can send them a little something to make up for the inconvenience."

"After we call them – if we call them. Not before."

"Of course. I wouldn't want to seem to be interfering with your enquiries."

"You've been very helpful," announced Franck, standing up. "I'll do my best to make sure we don't harm your business. I'll keep you informed, and I may need to come back and ask you other questions."

"You know where to find me captain. Anything I can do to

help, I will. As I said, Laure Sarraute was a lovely girl."

Du Bellay waited for Franck to put away the evidence bags and the copy of *Exposé*. He then walked him to the door of his office.

As they moved, Franck asked, "You're restocking with this model?"

"Of course. It takes time though. We don't have the speed or the flexibility of the Chinese. We can't whip up tens of thousands of units from one day to the next."

"You're confident they'll still sell when they reach the shops?"

"I don't think this story is about to go away, captain. It's a terrible thing to say, but I think Laure Sarraute will sell every unit we put on the shelves."

"How many are you having made."

"2000 units."

"That's more than when you launched it."

Du Bellay nodded.

"She's about to make you a fortune," suggested Franck.

"She's about to save my fortune," corrected du Bellay, pulling open his office door and ushering Franck into the reception area.

"I've one last request," asked Franck. He pointed to the corner where he had waited for du Bellay to receive him. "That magazine over there on the table. Can I borrow it?"

"The copy of *Wasp-Waisted*? For personal or professional reasons?"

"Just in case it's relevant to the investigation," insisted Franck.

"By all means. However, can I ask you to return it to me afterward? I have the complete set."

"Of course," said Franck. "Where are the others?"

"Locked away. I never leave more than one out at a time. They're too difficult to replace."

Franck stepped outside the Du Bellay building. He paused to slip the magazine he had taken from the waiting area into his briefcase. He then walked past a statue of La Fayette and Washington and into the small park that sat at the heart of the place des Etats Unis. He pulled out his phone and tapped one of the many numbers in the DST directory he knew by heart. He was not optimistic, but he felt it was worth a try.

"Yes?" It was the curt, impatient voice he had been expecting: Pierre Halphen, connoisseur of money-launderers' dirty washing.

"This is Franck Guerin."

"Morning, Franck. How's life on the outside?"

"Not as chilly as you might think. If I ask you to help me, can you?"

"Officially or unofficially?" asked Pierre, always a stickler for precision.

"Either."

"No, and no. I'd say I'm sorry ..."

"But you're not."

"The service works in mysterious ways," offered Pierre, perhaps as solace, although that was unlikely.

"Indeed it does," observed Franck, as he ended the call. He then tried a different number, taking some satisfaction from the fact that this was someone who had once bested Halphen in his field of predilection.

"This is Franck Guerin. I'd like to speak with Sylvie Thomas. Business."

After a pause the assistant who had answered his call informed him that Sylvie was not available but could call him back shortly.

Franck moved towards a wooden bench and sat upon it, looking up through the trees at the windows of du Bellay's office. He could see no-one. He pulled out a notebook and wrote down the figures du Bellay had cited to him: 85C; 1920; 1284; 24; 17; 2900. His body might not be at its best, but his memory seemed to be working fine.

He then closed his eyes and sat still, ignoring the sounds around him, mulling over his next move.

Six minutes later the chirping of his phone broke through to him. He glanced at the screen before putting it to his ear.

"Thanks for getting back to me Sylvie. I've got a favour to ask."

"And here was me thinking it was an invitation to lunch," she replied.

"You want to have lunch?"

"Of course not. My next free lunch is probably in three weeks time. What do you need Franck?"

"I've sourced the Laure Sarraute lingerie. A brand called Du Bellay."

"Oooh, very upmarket. Even I would hesitate before splashing out on Du Bellay. In fact, I never have. I'm still waiting for someone to buy me some."

"At 2900 euros a set, I wouldn't hold my breath. Still, seems they're selling like hotcakes since *Exposé* came out."

"That's a very healthy revenue stream," observed Sylvie.

"That's what I'd like to know," said Franck. "How's Du Bellay doing, financially? Could you find out?"

"Of course. How fast depends on whether or not it's a listed company."

"There's no hurry. It's only a murder investigation after all."

"I love it when you're unreasonable," countered Sylvie, and hung up.

Franck looked at his watch. Time to move on. He had an appointment at eleven thirty at Laure Sarraute's modelling agency, which went by the name of Elegance, rue des Haudriettes in the third arrondissement.

He decided to walk to the Iéna metro station and to set off from there.

*

"Captain, good morning. My name is Frédéric Bonneau."

As they shook hands, Bonneau swivelled on his heels, stretched his free arm across Franck's back, and started walking him down a corridor away from the reception area. At no point did he stop talking.

"People call me Fred. I'm one of our talent managers. Laure was one of my girls. You can imagine what a shock it was to hear that she had – she was – oh, I still can't bear to say it! I can't even begin to imagine who could have done such a thing. Such a waste. All that beauty – gone. Gone forever, too. There will never be another Laure Sarraute. Whatever they say about identikit models, believe me, every one is unique. Every one has her own particular signature. That's what we look for here. That's what we cultivate…"

"What was Laure Sarrault's?" Franck cut in, stopping suddenly. As Bonneau's left hand was by this time nestling on Franck's far shoulder, he was forced to brake with him.

"Sorry?" Bonneau was momentarily thrown by the interruption. He loosened his grip so as to turn towards Franck.

"What was Sarrault's signature?"

Bonneau seemed stunned. The question, clearly, was too stupid to be asked. "Her décolleté. Those lovely breasts. Palm-sized and perfectly round."

"Palm sized?"

"Yes. You could cover them from bottom to top with an open hand. Cupped, of course."

Bonneau planted an open hand on Franck's chest – an inadequate demonstration, as there was nothing to cup.

"If the girl holds her own breasts – a classic shot – her hands are visibly full, in all senses of the term. But nothing spills over. No excess. It's sexy but not tacky."

"I see," said Franck.

"No you don't. You imagine you do, but you have no idea of the splendour of the thing. I'll show you some photos. I have all her work. From her juvenilia to her mature portfolio."

"Sarraute was twenty-six," Franck remarked.

"That's very mature, believe me. I'm twenty-nine and I'm an old man in this business."

Franck did not waste his time wondering what that made him.

"What do you think of her last photo?"

"The *Exposé* cover?"

They had reached Bonneau's office. Franck was ushered through the already open door. A dark mahogany desk brooded at one end of the room. An L-shaped leather canapé occupied the other, boxing in a square coffee table which had probably come from the same tree as the desk.

Bonneau motioned Franck towards the canapé and sat himself down on the facing section.

"I shouldn't say this," confided Bonneau. "It's quite scandalous."

"But?" Franck prompted.

"It was a super photo. I haven't seen the original, of course, and as for *Exposé*'s print quality, well, everyone knows they murder every image they publish. All the same, it was one of the best photos I've ever seen of Laure. Maybe even the best. The plumpness of her breasts! The shadows that fringed the lace cups! And the white! Who dares take white lingerie shots these days? Too virginal. At best, you get white undies on some posturing whore, just to play the extremes. But white was Laure's colour. Her skin was golden, even when it wasn't tanned, and white made it seem all the more so. Even though the shot was black and white you could still see it. Oh, I'd kill to have that print."

"Somebody did."

Bonneau fell silent and hung his head, chastised.

"You wouldn't happen to know who?" Franck continued.

Compunction turned to indignation.

"No, I do not. I do not frequent murderers, detective."

"Few do. At least, not knowingly. Yet statistics say we all have a decent chance of coming across at least one in our lifetime."

"That, surely, depends on your profession and the company you keep?" interjected Bonneau, archly.

"True. I don't know the statistics for the fashion world. That said, I'm not optimistic. But I'm not here to accuse you of killing Laure Sarraute, nor of aiding and abetting whoever did. I just want to know whether you have any idea of who might have done it, or why it might have been done."

Bonneau propped his chin theatrically on his left palm, fingers bunched, knuckles grazing his lower lip. Rodin would have been proud of him.

Franck studied the coffee table while waiting for the oracle's pronouncements. Fashion reviews were fanned out in a perfectly spaced circle, allowing a glimpse of about one third of each cover. Franck assumed that each cover figured one of the agency's girls.

"I didn't know Laure that well," began Bonneau. "I took great care of her, like all of my girls. We had lunch, we went to clubs, we went to *défilés*, but I can't tell you much about her life. She's been with the agency three years. Been with me for two. Got here before me. She must have had heaps of boyfriends, and even more admirers – breasts are one of the best weapons a girl can have. But more than that, I cannot say. You'd be better off talking to one of her girlfriends."

"As in friends who are girls?" asked Franck.

Bonneau threw a sly, reproving glance at Franck.

"As in friends who are girls," he confirmed. "I already said she'd had heaps of boyfriends. You're not listening."

Franck dismissed the comment with a wave of his hand. "She had girlfriends within the agency?"

"Yes. One in particular. Sonia. Sonia Delemazure. Fun girl. Great shoulders."

Bonneau bent over the coffee table and extracted one of magazines without disturbing its neighbours. Its name was *Ident*, a publication Franck had never heard of. The same was true of most of the half-hidden titles on the table.

On the cover a young woman turned to the camera, her head at forty-five degrees to her left shoulder. She wore a strapless dress, of which only the upper band was visible, just above the slight rise of her chest. The dress was dark green, as were her eyes. Her hair was cut short and spiky, exposing delicate ears and a long neck. She held her right hand against herself, one finger tracing her collarbone. She wore no jewellery or anything else that might distract from her taut bone structure.

Her shoulder was surprisingly round, although hard like marble rather than fleshy. It threw into deep shadow the fold between her collarbone and neck, a hint of darkness echoed by her witch's eyes, which looked up at the lens as she angled her head downwards.

"Off the shoulder, strapless, spaghetti straps – anything that leaves those shoulders exposed, she'll make it look great," Bonneau commented. "At least, until she gets her tattoo."

"Tattoo?" echoed Franck.

"Fashion, fashion, what fools it makes of them!" pronounced Bonneau theatrically. "In certain circles, if your flesh is not inked, you are no-one. In others, it has to be pierced if you are to count amongst the initiated."

"What circles is Delemazure moving in then?"

"Nothing sinister, captain. She's young, but not as young as she was. Twenty-eight. Her time is running out. She wants a tattoo as a mark of experience, to accompany her move from ingénue to mature beauty. She thinks it could become her calling card. After all, I can tell her shoulders apart from anybody else's, but not everyone can."

"And you agree?"

"No, I don't. I think it would be sacrilege. But I don't own my girls. I just try to guide them as best I can. But if you do talk to her, try to talk her out of it. You do share my opinion, I assume?"

Franck shrugged. Tattoos had spread like wildfire amongst the under-thirties over the past five years. That at least he was aware of. They were often useful in identifying suspects. Or corpses.

"Does she do lingerie?" Franck asked, tapping the photo of Sonia Delemazure.

"Cropped shots, yes. Not full bust shots. She doesn't fill well. The half-filled cup doesn't exist in our profession – there's full, there's feeble, and there's nothing in between." Bonneau clapped his hands together, clearly pleased with himself. "Can't remember who said that, but it's so true."

"So this Sonia was a good friend of Laure Sarraute?"

"Yes, I believe so. She was terribly upset when she found out about – you know – her disappearing. Had a whole weekend's shooting, and cancelled it all. Only started back today, and that's only because we've got really good make-up girls to hide her puffy eyes."

"She's here?" Franck demanded.

"No. There's no studio here. Anyhow, she's working with Antoine de Baune."

"Who's he?"

Bonneau slid out another magazine from his collection and tapped the cover. A long-legged beauty refusing to close her raincoat as she skipped across puddles in high heels.

"Took that. Does outdoor shoots. Refuses anything but natural light. A purist, in his way."

"Where's the shoot taking place?"

"The Palais Royal."

Bonneau glanced at his watch, an oblong face no wider than the narrow leather strap that held it in place.

"They'll still be there for hours. Antoine always believes there is better light to come. If the sun didn't set, he'd keep his crew waiting for ever."

"Thank you monsieur Bonneau. I'll be in touch."

"Anything I can do, captain. Anything at all."

*

With over an hour's observation under his belt, Franck felt qualified to say that a photo shoot was not unlike what veterans said of war: long periods of tedious inactivity punctuated by brief bursts of frantic action.

Antoine de Baune looked the part: a white silk scarf looped round his neck and draped over one shoulder; a leather jacket, hanging open but still tight on his frame; tailored jeans; ankle boots; unkempt hair; carefully cultivated stubble. Had a folding canvas chair marked with his name been to hand, his film director pose would have been complete.

As it was, he had three cameras, none of which remained in

his hands any great length of time, for he had two assistants to carry them, screw lenses on and off, take light readings and generally hover around him as he scanned sky, surroundings and model.

The latter, the object of his intermittent bursts of attention, was attended to by a make-up girl, a wardrobe mistress, a portable clothes rail on which hung six ensembles and one empty hanger, and a hair dresser. There were two more people whose role he had not yet worked out, unless it was simply to hang on the periphery of the others and smoke cigarettes.

Sonia Delemazure seemed a true professional. She did what she was told, changed costumes without hesitation – even though this meant stripping down to her underwear, her feet on a dainty mat provided by the wardrobe mistress, before the gaze of all those who happened to be wandering through the Palais Royal that afternoon – and waited patiently for de Baune to emerge from his periodical plunges into introspection or sky-gazing.

The costumes between which she switched all seemed to share the same characteristics: short skirts, wide-necked blouses, insubstantial shoes, and absurdly shaped handbags. Every time she tried on something new de Baune would swoop in to ask her to undo another button and tug the blouse off one or the other shoulder. She always complied, going through a series of poses that all looked equally exaggerated from where Franck was sitting.

At last, de Baune turned from his followers and stalked off to a nearby bench, instructing them all to take a break. One of his assistants amplified the instruction, adding that no-one should go very far, particularly not Sonia, and that they had thirty minutes at most.

Franck rose from the iron chair that he had placed alongside one of the row of trees that ran parallel to the arched perimeter of the Palais Royal. As he did so, Sonia tugged the blouse she was wearing over her head, exchanged it for a light sweater, and stalked towards him.

"I take it you're the *flic*," she announced as she drew up

before him. "Because if you're not, I'm going to have to have words with you about watching me undress so often."

"Franck Guerin. You knew I was coming?"

She nodded.

"Fred called me. You want to talk about Laure?"

"If it's convenient."

"Just don't get me crying. It ruins the make-up."

Franck looked around, trying to spot a free chair he could draw over to the one he had just left. Sonia had a better idea.

"I'm dying for a coffee. Let's go to the café down that way, by the Comédie Française."

"Le Nemours?"

"If that's what it's called. I never paid attention, but I suppose paying attention is your job."

"Part of it, yes."

"Let's go."

She walked off, not turning to see whether he followed. Within a few seconds Franck was by her side.

Sonia ordered two coffees. She drained one as soon as it arrived and toyed with the other, cupping its warmth in her hands, catching the steam it gave off with her chin. Franck limited himself to one coffee. He was impressed to find someone who could knock expresso back faster than he did and who understood it was a drink to be taken uncomfortably hot.

On the brief walk over Sonia had answered the basic questions about how she and Laure met – at the agency – and how close they had been – less so than Frédéric Bonneau had led him to believe. The tale of her grieving for days suddenly seemed a lot less likely.

Le Nemours was half full. Besides the idling tourists, self-absorbed couples, and businessmen hiding from whatever awaited them at the office, there was an eccentrically dressed group holding an animated conversation at the bar. He assumed they were from the Comédie Française. No-one had paid any attention to Sonia when she walked in. If she was famous, it was not in these circles.

"This was not a random killing," Franck insisted, Sonia having blithely declared that Laure had no enemies and no problems. "Laure Sarraute either knew or trusted her killer. I cannot tell you how she was murdered, but there was no struggle involved."

"Did she suffer?" Sonia was unable to resist the question.

"No. Not as far as we can tell. Indeed, she probably had no idea what was happening to her."

"That's good news."

Franck shrugged. "I'd rather go out fighting than unaware, blissfully or otherwise."

"Not if you knew you were going to lose," Sonia countered. "Not if you saw death coming."

"Even then," Franck insisted. "Nobody believes they're going to lose, not until the very last moment. That's how we're built. That's what's kept us alive all these millennia. We don't give up."

He knew what he was talking about, and the scars on his stomach could have provided illustrative detail, but he did not develop the point.

"Who did she know? Who should we be talking to?"

"People like me. Photographers, designers, stylists. Fashion people. A limp-wristed bunch at best. Scarcely murdering material. True, there're a lot of real bitches. Sharp nails and sharper tongues. But not that sharp."

"Did anyone have any reason to be jealous of Laure?"

"Only maybe ninety-nine out of a hundred women in Paris. Have you seen her photos? Have you seen her …"

"Breasts," Franck completed the phrase for her. "Yes I have. But on those grounds, you're next on the list of the same ninety-nine women because of your shoulders."

Sonia smiled but shook her head. She brought one hand up to the neckband of her sweater and pulled it even further down her left shoulder.

"It's nice of you to say so, but breasts are worth a thousand shoulders. Laure had the waist too. Not to mention her nose and cheek bones. And she was better looking at twenty-six than when she arrived in Paris."

"I thought you only met her two years ago?"

"I did. But I've seen her portfolio. When she got here from Rouen her features were too drawn. She looked scared all the time. She certainly didn't look like the future face of Eternal."

Franck thought back to his visit to the Bon Marché. The scent the elderly saleswoman had caught from Sarraute's lingerie.

"As in Ephémère?"

"As in Ephémère," Sonia confirmed. "She signed with them two months ago. She was due to start filming a new commercial with Luc Besson in three months' time. She'd already started offloading her future schedule. She'd have changed agencies by the end of the year."

"Why?"

"Elegance is a good agency, but it only covers Paris and London well. It does New York badly and Tokyo not at all. It's no place for an Ephémère girl."

"Would her leaving have been amicable?"

"If you mean, would Fred throttle her in a jealous rage, I doubt it. He even has trouble opening bottles of champagne."

"People are full of surprises."

"Not Fred. In his genre, he's about as predictable as you can get. In some ways, Laure's success was good news for him. She would have been the first supermodel groomed by Elegance. That's no mean feat. All he'd have to do in the future to recruit a promising girl would be to point to a billboard or walk her past a perfume store. Laure would be everywhere."

"She already is, if *Exposé*'s circulation figures are to be believed."

"Except that next week all those copies of *Exposé* will be in the bin, and some other celebrity will have taken her place on the cover. An Ephémère girl lasts two to three years, not seven days."

Franck felt sure that Laure Sarraute's last photo would be around a lot longer, albeit not on every wall or on every newsstand. It was too striking – too painfully beautiful, for those who knew its story – simply to be forgotten.

"So for you, professional jealousy is not a credible motive?"

Sonia shook her head firmly. "You may have a dim view of my profession, captain, but it's not a dangerous one."

"What else then? Who else did she frequent? What about her past? You mentioned Rouen."

"That's where she came from. That's where she went to university. Got a degree in history and philosophy. Didn't start modelling till she got out at twenty-one and came to Paris."

"She still had friends from her student days?"

"A few. Those who came to Paris at around the same time. They ended up in EDF, the SNCF, becoming teachers, that sort of thing. Mundane jobs. A safe and secure path to retirement. She saw them less and less. These last few years she was earning good money, moving in circles they couldn't afford. I met a few of her friends from Rouen. A bit too serious for me. Awed by what she had become. Especially the men."

"Any former boyfriends amongst them?"

"One. A harmless soul. Obsessed with art history, as I recall. Insurance agent with AXA. Hated his job but didn't seem to spend much time doing it. All he talked to me about was his blog on the web. He openly admitted Laure had always been way out of his league."

"What about since she became a model?"

Sonia laughed, shaking her head at Franck.

"She's had dozens of men since I've known her."

"Any of them stuck in your mind? Any painful break-ups?"

"No. On the whole, she was pretty lucky in her choice of men. Good-lookers, lots of cash, fun parties, expensive trips, classy hotels."

"She did better than you?" Franck was pushing, just to see her reaction, just in case a little jealousy had at some stage soured her friendship with Laure.

Sonia set down her second coffee cup, now empty, and drew herself up in her seat.

"I do OK, captain. How about you?"

Franck remained silent for ten seconds, watching her glare

defiantly at him.

"I apologise," he said. "Murder and manners don't always go together."

He got to say no more. One of Antoine de Baune's assistants burst into the café and bore down upon Sonia.

"Light's perfect. Quick! Quick!"

"Have to go," she said, getting to her feet.

"Thank you for your time," said Franck, rising in his turn.

They shook hands.

"One last thing," Franck interjected. "Forget the tattoo."

A cunning smile shot across her face. "See. I'm already the girl with the tattoo, and I don't even have it yet."

She moved towards the door, de Baune's assistant fussing in her wake like a deferential sheepdog.

"Could you provide a list?" asked Franck. "The boyfriends."

"Call me," suggested Sonia. "Just make sure you have a big sheet of paper to hand."

"How?" asked Franck.

"You have my number."

"I don't".

Only when she had disappeared through the door did he look down at the two empty cups of coffee she had abandoned. A card lay between them with her name and a mobile number. Where she had concealed it beforehand he could not say.

Franck pocketed it and then delved into his briefcase for the magazine he had borrowed from Luc du Bellay that morning. He turned to the inside back cover, where the publisher's details were spelled out in severe type.

He pulled out his mobile phone and tapped the number that was given. A young woman answered.

"This is captain Franck Guerin of the Brigade Criminelle," he said, attracting a few glances from those sitting nearby. Had he said he was from the DST there would have been less of a reaction. The Brigade Criminelle – his temporary home – had been made famous by a host of films and books.

"Good afternoon captain. My name is Claire. We were

expecting your call."

"You were? Why?"

"Mademoiselle Sehati believes you wish to see her. That is why you're calling?"

Franck's eyes flitted to the magazine. Sehati was the name given for its publisher.

"Yes, I need to see her on a police matter. It's quite urgent."

"Would eleven o'clock tomorrow morning suit you?"

"This afternoon isn't possible?"

"I'm afraid not. Eleven tomorrow is the earliest free slot I have."

"OK, I'll take it," said Franck.

"51 avenue Montaigne. If you have any problem finding us, just call me on this number."

"Thank you," said Franck.

"Don't mention it," said Claire. "We'll see you tomorrow." She hung up.

Franck closed the back cover, hiding the name of the clairvoyant mademoiselle Sehati. He slid the magazine back inside his briefcase, keeping it from prying eyes.

He had not eaten since he had got up that morning. Although it was past two in the afternoon, it was not too late to do something about it.

Tuesday, 12th June

Three photos.

Wide, heavy double doors in dark, varnished wood, studded with chunky brass handles. To either side of them the regular stone blocks of a classic Hausseman-era apartment building, overlaid with a column of brass plaques. In the middle of the shot, looking off to the right, Franck Guerin, in jeans, brown shoes, a plain blue shirt and a jacket. A leather briefcase hangs from one hand. The other holds a mobile phone before his face. He looks perplexed, or perhaps just preoccupied.

Two cars, parked nose to tail, one somewhat the worse for wear. In the background, a brick building with evenly spaced windows, each decorated with a flower box and folded iron shutters painted blue. Standing behind the bonnet of one of the cars, Franck Guerin, one hand reaching inside his jacket while the other holds it open.

Zoom shot. The bricks in the background are slightly out of focus. Franck Guerin's face fills the frame, telephone held against his right ear. His brow is furrowed. If not shouting, he is at least talking forcefully to someone.

*

Franck got out the metro at Franklin D. Roosevelt. He dodged the never-ceasing stream of people wandering up and down the Champs Elysées: the inevitable tourists, who ought to have been wondering how a stretch of cinemas, brand outlets and undistinguished restaurants succeeded in touting itself as the most famous street in the world; the packs of youth from the outer suburbs, who adored it because it was nothing more than a roofless mall; and the occasional besuited businessman sharing his thoughts with his cell phone.

A few paces down avenue Montaigne things were quieter. The tourists were better-heeled, predominately Asian, and all avid collectors of the over-sized carrier bags provided by the avenue's vertiginously upmarket designer shops to transport and advertise their wares. Franck paid little attention to the stores of the big names in prêt-à-porter and concentrated on dodging around those who stopped without warning before him, suddenly hypnotised by the goods on display in the windows. He was alone in walking fast – or what counted as fast for him these days – probably the only person in the street who had an appointment, or perhaps just the only one who cared whether he arrived late.

Number 51 was a stone-built apartment building, its entrance framed by sufficient plaques to prove that no-one lived there anymore. Three advocates, two doctors, one dentist, one psychoanalyst, and three firms, one of which was *Wasp-Waisted*. One half of the heavy wooden double door that faced the street was ajar. Franck slipped through into the entrance hall. A few paces further and he faced a glass partition that ran up to the hall's high ceiling. The chrome-outlined glass door in the centre resisted his touch. An intercom was set in the wall to his right. He pushed the button for *Wasp-Waisted*.

"Captain Guerin," he announced.

"Third floor, on the left." A woman's voice. The door clicked and he pushed it open.

Franck ignored the lift, preferring to test himself on the wide stairs that circled around the iron fretwork of its cage. The stairs were vitrified teak, with scarcely a mark to betray their age. He took them one at a time, keeping his breathing regular, passing no-one. At a slow, steady pace he felt no discomfort. Each landing had two doors, one to the right and one to the left: generously-sized apartments of another era. On the third floor the right hand door bore an advocate's name. The left was unmarked. He rang.

The door opened, framing the receptionist. A woman in her very early twenties. Almost-flat shoes, knee-length skirt, severe blouse, hair bound in a chignon, little or no make-up, no earrings. Very discreet for a firm founded on the trappings of the erotic. However, she was particularly pretty, and possessed the confident bearing that often bespoke a childhood in the sixteenth arrondissement.

"Good morning captain Guerin. Please come in."

She stepped aside to let Franck enter a spacious reception area. Parquet floor, white walls, a long and low red velvet sofa, and an open-fronted desk bearing a flat-screen PC, a telephone and little else. Off to one side sat a cabinet bearing an expresso machine and a bone-white set of small coffee cups and saucers. On the wall to his left hung a tall painting of a woman in a long, flowing, deep red evening gown which bared her spine as she turned away, leaving a cascade of long chestnut hair over one shoulder. To his right was its mirror image, except that his time the gown had gone, leaving a mini-skirt of red patterned lace floating over her buttocks and revealing the high stiletto shoes on which she expertly balanced her shifting weight.

"This way."

While Franck was distracted, the young woman had opened a door alongside the under-dressed painting. Franck turned at her command and stepped past her into the next room.

It must once have been the great salon, where the mistress of the house had received her robed or frock-coated guests, where over-stuffed sofas had offered respite during endless conversations, where heavily framed paintings had covered the walls and cut flowers had stood tall, then wilted, in china vases. A vast space once replete with wealth and comfort, now reduced to a barer state by the spartan aesthetics of a different age.

The mistress of the house, however, was still to hand.

"Maryam Sehati," she announced, moving out from behind a massive desk whose surface was irregularly hewn slate.

"Franck Guerin."

Having come round to the side of her desk she had stopped. It was up to Franck to close the distance between them and shake her hand. As he did so, she raised her own, sending more than a dozen bracelets sliding backwards from her upheld wrist, meshing together musically as they fell. Her grip was light, yielding. Just as he instinctively softened his hold in response, she slid away.

"Please. Be seated." She regained her chair, whose tall

leather back rose as high as her head and on whose armrests she slowly let fall her naked arms. Both bore a host of bracelets, all finely wrought, twisting in a variety of metals across her slightly olive skin.

Franck had the choice of two chairs on the opposite side of the desk. He took the one to the right, resisting the urge to push the other aside and position himself directly before her. He felt she would not appreciate him rearranging her furniture. This way he caught her slightly profiled. Noting her strong cheekbones, sharp chin, long neck, almond eyes and thick black hair, he assumed the angle was no accident. For a moment only the dark pupils of her eyes turned to him. Then she smiled and swivelled her chair so that they could look directly at each other.

"I've come …," he started.

"To talk about the murder of Laure Sarrault. First of all, may I offer you some coffee?"

"No thank you. How do you know I'm here about Sarrault?"

"People talk, captain Guerin. Luc du Bellay is one of my subscribers. He told me about your visit to him. He also asked me if I might be able to replace the copy of my magazine you carried away, if you happened not to return it. I think you should have some coffee."

"No, really, I'm fine."

She picked up her phone, touched a button.

"Claire, two coffees please."

A pause.

"Claire would like to know if you take milk or sugar?"

"No," said Franck.

"I should think not," she commented, before turning her attention back to the phone. "No," she said, and gently laid it down.

"Go ahead," she instructed. "I will answer your questions."

"You publish a magazine called *Wasp-Waisted*. I've seen one copy. It's high class pornography – perfect girls in expensive lingerie. The photo taken of Laure Sarrault and published in *Exposé* could easily have come from it."

"No, it could not."

Franck swung a slim briefcase onto his lap and flipped it open. He pulled out the copy of *Exposé* and tossed it onto the desktop. He then did the same thing with the copy of *Wasp-Waisted* he had borrowed from du Bellay's office and opened it at random.

A girl in red stockings and a suspender belt, one leg pulled up in front of her. Photographed from the side to catch the taught line of the suspender through the air from the belt to the stocking top. The photo ran up to her breasts, supported by silky scarlet, and cut off where the strap that held the cups stretched out to an unseen shoulder. Strained lines of delicate materiel whose snapping would leave uncovered flesh.

"Are you sure? Looks like much the same kind of thing do me," insisted Franck.

"Use your eyes, captain. Is that not part of your job? The photo of Sarrault is excellent, and I have nothing but praise for the gifts of whoever took it. However, it is in black and white. We publish in colour. I have no desire to live in a universe of shades of grey. Colour is the sign of life, of vitality, of passion, of desire. Flushed cheeks, a burgeoning nipple, vivid lips, painted nails – all pulsing with colour."

She spread her own nails, violently red, to make her point.

"I have nothing against black and white per se," she continued, "but I am no necrophiliac. Without colour, skin is marble, and marble is fit only for tombs. I do not find death erotic. Given that the erotic is my profession, if not my vocation, I do not publish in black and white. I fear for your investigation, captain. You have only started and you have already made two mistakes. First, this photo could not have come from *Wasp-Waisted*, as I have just explained. Secondly, my magazine is not high class pornography. It is high class erotica."

"I'm not here to debate semantics," Franck countered.

"No, but you are here to find the truth. The truth requires precision. *Wasp-Waisted* is not designed to give you an erection and make you come. That is pornography's job, and it is an easy one, particularly given the average male. *Wasp-Waisted* – if you're a man – is designed to make you think about what it is to desire. One talks to the penis, the other to the mind."

"OK," said Franck. "I apologise. I didn't mean to offend you."

His tone, however, suggested that he did not particularly care.

"I am not offended. I am disappointed, though. I had hoped to be dealing with someone a little more sophisticated."

The door opened and the receptionist came in carrying a steel tray from which she handed Franck an expresso cup on a saucer. She placed another on the desk near Maryam and left without saying a word.

Franck sipped his coffee. Even for him it was almost too hot, and almost too bitter. He frowned at the cup as he set it, half empty, on the desk.

"Too much character?" asked Maryam, who had drained hers slowly, without letting the cup leave her lip. When she set it down there was not a trace of lipstick on its pristine white rim.

"No more than I ought to have expected," he replied. "Let's come back to Sarraute later. Tell me about your magazine."

"I founded *Wasp-Waisted* four years ago. It's sold by subscription only. I started out with about a hundred subscribers. Now I have a little over a thousand. I publish four or five times a year with five shoots an issue. Girls under thirty. Lingerie. Imaginative photography. A little beauty and a frisson of sensuality for a world that badly needs it."

"Girls under thirty?" echoed Franck.

"Have you ever known a woman to be at her best undressed over thirty?" asked Maryam, archly.

Franck did not pursue the issue.

"How much does it cost? There's no price on the cover."

"A subscription? Five hundred euros a year."

"Not bad. It must make you a lot of money."

"Costs are higher than you might think. I print on high quality paper. The issues are stitched, not glued or stapled. I pay the girls well. I pay the photographers very well."

"And you have no advertisers. At least, not in that one." Franck indicated the issue he had taken from his briefcase.

"You didn't look hard enough. Or you did, and you're not much of a detective."

"Help me," suggested Franck.

Maryam smiled. She placed her elbows on the desk, causing the bracelets to cascade downwards once more, and rested her chin on her interlaced fingers.

"But you are a very calm detective. Not easily needled. I suppose you've seen much worse than me?"

"I don't know how bad you are yet."

"I hope not to disappoint you."

"The adverts?" Franck prompted.

Maryam extended an arm and drew the magazine towards her while leaving it the right way up for Franck. She slowly turned a few pages, smoothing the heavy paper down each time she did so. She stopped at one and let her finger hover over the image.

"Du Bellay. Bra, panties, suspender belt. Longford stockings, as you can see from the motif that forms the seam down the back of the legs."

She continued turning and chose another.

"Scherherazade. Halter babydoll. The impossibly high heels are Manolo."

"They pay you?"

Maryam nodded.

"And yet there's not a logo in sight," Franck commented. "No text either."

"It's a field for connoisseurs, captain. Those who don't recognise a piece make sure they find out who made it before another aficionado finds out they didn't know."

"And these brands are ready to pay to reach, what, a thousand readers?"

"For the thousand I give them, they're ready to pay a lot.

Haute couture doesn't just exist for dresses. A little lace and some fine stitching can fetch an awful lot of money."

"As can a few photos of young girls wearing nothing but a little lace and some fine stitching."

"You disapprove?"

"Normally, no. After all, what harm does it do?" Franck shrugged. "But now there's Laure Sarraute. A little lace and some fine stitching seems to have done her a lot of harm indeed."

"I doubt she was killed by her lingerie."

"But maybe because of it. Just how far are your aficionados ready to go for the perfect image?"

"That far? Very few indeed, I imagine. On the whole, art lovers do not go out of their way to destroy works of art."

"It has happened." The last slashing in the Louvre had taken place three years previously. A well dressed Italian in his early sixties, a deranged self-proclaimed Venetian aristocrat who set out to punish those who had robbed his city of its treasures. Napoleon's fault, as it so often was.

"I need your subscription list," Franck announced.

"I cannot give it to you. Not unless I am forced. This publication is founded on discretion. If only to protect my reputation, I will give you nothing without a court order."

"In which case, I will get one. But the time it takes may cause another girl's death. You can live with that?"

"As I don't believe it will – yes I can," replied Maryam.

Franck rose from his chair.

"Expect to hear from me soon," he said, as he gathered up the copies of *Exposé* and *Wasp-Waisted* and slid them into his briefcase. "Thanks for the coffee."

Maryam waited until he had almost reached the door.

"I'm not finished," she said. "You are missing something, captain. You shouldn't be so hasty."

Franck remained where he was. "So tell me."

Maryam left her seat and opened a black steel cabinet next to a wall. It was as tall as her, and would have been taller still had she slipped off her high heels. Inside Franck could see small piles of magazines. Back issues. She chose one off a stack that sat on the topmost shelf on the left hand side. As she returned to her desk she beckoned to Franck to do the same. He obeyed, settling back down on his original seat.

"This was my first issue. February 2003. Published on Saint Valentine's day."

She stroked the cover. The only words it bore were the magazine's title. No date. No issue number. A woman's back, caught in the tight embrace of a black bustier. Long black hair plunged vertically down her spine, bridging the gap between the end of the bustier and the horizontal line of a string cutting across her hips. It then continued its descent between her buttocks. The skin tone was rich and warm, blessed by the sun.

"Arresting cover, is it not?" asked Maryam, a conspiratorial smile on her face. "However, that's not what I wanted to show you. Look inside. The second girl." She slid the magazine over the cold slate of the desktop.

Franck turned the pages quickly, or as quickly as he could given their resilience. When he got to the second photo set he perched over it. The magazine's own weight and careful binding allowed it to lie open, almost completely flat.

A shawl of embroidered gauze, shimmering under angled light, was draped over a supine figure. It lay at an angle, running from her right shoulder to her left waist, following the curve of her breasts in between. Further down, a matching semi-transparent pair of narrow briefs melted into a green-blue marine-like haze between her legs. Above the shawl were shoulder-length blond hair and a young face both beautiful and severe, its cheekbones heightened dramatically by blusher and its eyes surrounded by deep-sea tints. Although it lacked the serene air of the *Exposé* cover, it was clearly Laure Sarraute's face.

The facing page showed Sarraute erect, bending her head so that her hair tumbled forward. A hanging curtain of gold, it stopped just short of her chest. Light blue straps looped over each shoulder. They tapered down to cups cut diagonally, facing each other, spilling her breasts together. The fabric that covered them contained waves of different hues of blue. A tanga of similar design clung to her hips, its surface ever so slightly raised by an unseen strip of public hair. She wore thigh-high boots moulded so closely to her legs it seemed that only peeling would ever get them off. They stopped dead a hands-breadth from her crotch without leaving the slightest pucker on her skin.

"Now, that's what a photo of Laure Sarraute taken for *Wasp-Waisted* would look like," commented Maryam.

"This was your first ever issue?"

Maryam nodded. "Tall oaks from little acorns grow. I had a print run of 150 copies. I signed up almost 100 subscribers. I subsequently sold a few dozen single copies. What's left I keep here. I've refused every request to sell one over the past two years. What's scarce is priceless, as I trust you know."

"You think this issue has something to do with Sarraute's murder?" Franck asked.

"Not at all," insisted Maryam. "However, you came here to discover a link between Laure and *Wasp-Waisted*. Well, there it is."

"I'd be more convinced that all this is innocuous if I had your subscriber list. Particularly the list of the hundred who received this." He lightly tapped the open magazine before him.

"As I said captain, I won't hand it over – not unless forced. And even then I will loudly protest."

Franck sat back in his seat, studying Maryam's face. He saw no hostility there.

"What do you suggest I do?" he asked.

"Force me, if you must," she offered.

Franck shrugged. If he had to play games, he would. "I'd rather not lose time with such formalities, but if I must, I will."

"Laure Sarraute is already dead," said Maryam. "There's no cause for haste on that score. And anyway, I'm in no rush to help you lose yourself in a dead end."

"Let me be the judge of that," insisted Franck. "You'll be hearing from me. May I take this?" He pointed to the copy of the first issue of *Wasp-Waisted.*

"On loan?" she asked.

Franck nodded.

"Of course," she assented. "Look after it, though. It's worth a lot."

"I promise I will."

"And study it well. Tell me when you've decided whether or not it's me on the cover."

Back on avenue Montaigne Franck paused to switch his mobile back on. A text message was awaiting him: "hotel bateliers rue vinaigriers 10th body discovered 08h00 one for you – Yves".

*

Franck emerged from the metro at Chateau d'Eau. As ever, it was hemmed with young black men touting for the neighbourhood's innumerable hair salons and wig vendors. Franck attracted no attention, his skin colour or his hair eliminating him as a prospect. He crossed the boulevard de Strasbourg, walked to the next intersection, took a left, and soon arrived at the diagonal sweep of the boulevard de Magenta. The rue de Vinaigriers awaited him on the other side. It ran from one neighbourhood to another: to the west, the blacks, the Indians, Turks and Arabs; to the east, the young professionals who had colonised the banks of the Saint Martin canal.

The Hotel des Bateliers sat right in the middle, offering its guests a taste of both worlds. It could also boast easy access to the Gare du Nord – to the once industrial stronghold of Lille, and through the tunnel to London – and the Gare de l'Est – to the flat plains that had long stood uneasily between France and Germany. Franck came up alongside it and stared up at the brick facade. A hotel for weekenders or professionals in transit whose modest budgets could cover a meal at one of the neighbourhood Indian restaurants or a few glasses at a canal-side wine bar.

A uniformed policeman stood outside the front door, scrutinising all who came and went. Franck showed his ID and was nodded through.

Inside he found himself in a narrow hall with a long reception counter running along one side. A block of pigeonholes was fixed behind the counter. Under half were empty, some had keys tethered to unwieldy iron tags bearing a room number, and others had passports slotted into them. At a glance, Franck estimated there were around twenty-five to thirty rooms. A perspex-covered sign screwed to the wall announced the going rates. At fifty to sixty euros a night, the hotel was charging modest rates, but not those of a fleapit. A far cry from the Lutetia nonetheless.

A couple in their fifties stood behind the counter, their faces both anxious and irritated.

Franck introduced himself. "Captain Guerin. You own this establishment?"

They both nodded, then the woman spoke up. "Janine Berroyer. This is my husband, Fernand. We've run this hotel for over twenty years. We've never had the slightest bit of trouble."

"Sometimes trouble chooses you. I doubt you had anything to do with it," offered Franck. Cold comfort, no doubt. "Where's the body?"

Madame Berroyer pointed to a narrow lift at the end of the hall. "Fifth floor. Room 504."

"One of you found it?"

"No, it was our cleaning girl, Yasmina. She knocked on the door shortly after starting her shift this morning – on weekdays, the guests tend to get up early. When she got no reply, she used her key. We heard her screaming and then she came running down the stairs. We called the police immediately."

"Is she here?" asked Franck.

"We let her go home. She was very upset."

"Fair enough. I'll need her details though, as she'll have to make a statement."

"Of course," said madame Berroyer. She lifted a sheet of paper from behind the counter and rapidly scribbled an address and a phone number. "She doesn't live far. That way she's never late."

Franck folded and pocketed the paper.

"When did the victim arrive?" he asked.

"Yesterday early afternoon. Paid for one night. In cash."

"Any special requests?"

"No, not really. Except that she wanted a room that overlooked the street, was high enough not to be noisy, and caught the sun."

"You have many rooms like that?" asked Franck.

"Anything from the fourth floor upwards," explained madame Berroyer. "The middle rooms on each floor have full floor-to-ceiling windows. The further up you go, the more light you get."

"What name did she give?"

"Tazi. Rachida Tazi," said madame Berroyer, adding, "*Maghrébine*. Young, early twenties. Rather too provocatively dressed to my taste."

"You think she was a prostitute?"

"If I had thought she was a prostitute, I would have told her we were fully booked," she insisted, indignant. "In actual fact she was quite polite. Came down in the middle of the afternoon and asked for an ice bucket. Didn't just call down and demand we send one up. Helped me fill it with ice too."

"She didn't have any luggage, though," pointed out her husband, emerging from his silence. "That made it pretty clear why she was here."

Franck saw his point, but said nothing.

"Had you ever seen her before?" he asked.

Both shook their heads.

"Can I ask you to think about everything that happened yesterday so that I can take a full statement later?" asked Franck. "I have to go up now."

He began to move off towards the lift.

"How long will this take?" madame Berroyer called out. "Our guests ... well, you can imagine."

Franck nodded. There were undoubtedly several similar hotels in the neighbourhood. There was nothing to stop their guests from fleeing the disturbance.

"We'll be as quick as we can. But room 504 will be off limits for some time."

"Well, at least she paid in advance," said the husband, resignedly. Business was probably already modest. It was about to get worse.

When he reached the lift, Franck noticed a door to a stairwell on his left. Rather than squeeze himself into a lift that could probably hold two at best, he took the stairs and spiralled slowly up to the fifth floor. It was a way of reminding his body to heal itself as quickly as possible.

The door to 504 was wide open. Electrical cords snaked into the room from two plug points in the corridor and harsh light spilled from it. A discussion in low voices could be heard from within. The forensic team was already there.

Franck stood in the doorway. There were two technicians, one bent over in a far corner, the other closely inspecting the surface of the surprisingly large floor-to-ceiling windows in the centre of the room. The latter glanced over at him.

"You're Guerin?"

"Yes."

"Apparently this one's for you. You can come in. We've taken photos and checked the floor. Best glove up, though."

The technician turned back to his work. Franck slipped on a pair of transparent plastic gloves but remained in the doorway.

The room was largely taken up by a double bed which sat with its head against the wall on Franck's left. Against the wall to his right were a dressing table with a hinged mirror and a flat wooden stool with an upholstered leather seat. There was about a metre of free space between it and the end of the bed. Another door ran off the room at that end. It was open, showing a tiled floor and a glimpse of white linen towels. The floor of the bedroom was heavily varnished parquet with uneven gaps between the boards. The walls were smooth plaster, white with a blue rinse. The place looked clean and well cared for.

The bed had a light blue cover and a generous selection of pillows and cushions. The victim lay amongst them, her head, shoulders, upper back and arms nestling within them. Her eyes lay half-shut, her face distant, even haughty. An imperious calm hung over her, like that of a despotic princess confident in the subjugating power of her beauty. An oriental princess, albeit hailing from the southern, rather than the eastern, shores of the Mediterranean.

Her arms were carelessly thrown above her head. Her hair was long and solidly, deeply black. It curled from her head over her right shoulder, down past her waist, fanning out alongside her buttocks. She was clad in a richly embroidered *guêpière*, a tangle of red and gold threads on a dark background. It gripped what little waist she had and clung to her ribs, forcing her breasts upwards to where it cut off, revealing two plump hemispheres. Above them her dun-coloured skin stretched across prominent bones from which emerged a long neck supporting her oval face. The contour of her eyes was precisely traced in kohl, her lips rouged, and her ears bore long silver pendants. Stockings suspended from the bottom of the *guêpière* covered long slim legs. Dark tapering panties stretched across the suspenders and tapered down to her crotch. They bore the same swirling scarlet and black motif.

"Which arm?" asked Franck.

"Left," replied one of the technicians, without looking up.

Franck moved to the bed and leant over the corpse. He thought he could see a faint puncture wound on the otherwise unblemished inside of the left arm.

"Champagne?" he asked.

This time the technician stood up and gazed, puzzled, at Franck. "How did you know that?"

Franck tapped the side of his nose. "Flair. That's what makes a detective. Where is it?"

"Ice bucket in the bath," said the technician, indicating the open door to the bathroom. "Half a bottle left. Henriet. You wouldn't think a hotel like this would stock such classy champagne."

"She probably brought it with her. How many glasses?"

"One so far. If there's another one, it's well hidden."

"Bagged for testing?"

"Of course. What should we be looking for?"

"Fast acting tranquilisers."

"Then the injection, when the subject can no longer defend herself?"

"That's the hypothesis," said Franck.

"So," said the other technician, coming to join his colleague. "It's Laure Sarraute all over again?"

"You were at the Lutetia?" asked Franck.

The man nodded, introducing himself, "Georges Sternberg."

"Looks like it, Georges" agreed Franck.

Which meant, he assumed, that the little the young woman on the bed was wearing was worth thousands of euros.

"Found her clothes?" he asked.

"In the chest of drawers."

Franck moved to a three-drawer chest in the corner between the dressing table and the window. In the top drawer he found, neatly folded, a pair of low-cut jeans, a zebra-print t-shirt, a high-cut leather jacket, a pair of sandals incrusted with fake gems, a flesh-coloured bra and matching panties. Alongside them was a small handbag, no more than a hand's breadth across, with a long looping handle.

"Can I?" he asked.

"Go ahead," he was told.

He picked up and unzipped the handbag, sorting through its contents with the tips of one gloved hand. A little cash, lipstick, mascara, a palm-sized mirror, two tampons, one condom, a set of keys, and a mobile phone, turned off. No ID, no bank cards, no social security card: nothing to confirm her identity. In a side pouch he found half a dozen brightly coloured cards advertising a night club called The Velvet Pussy, rue Froment in the ninth arrondissement. She wasn't carrying enough condoms for a prostitute, but her evocatively-named place of work suggested that she belonged to one of the less conventional professions.

Franck left the hotel half an hour later. He had given some instructions to the technicians, who listened patiently but distractedly. In particular, he had given his card to Sternberg, asking him to email him electronic copies of all the death scene photos once he got back from the field. He had also taken a statement from the owners, written on hotel stationary. He would type it up later and send it back to them to sign.

Once outside he tugged out his notebook, paged through it until he found the number he sought, and tapped it into his mobile phone. To his disappointment, Luc du Bellay was not available, or so his receptionist insisted. Franck told her that he would be sending a confidential email to du Bellay within the next few hours. He stressed how important it was that du Bellay read and respond to it as soon as possible. The receptionist assured him she would pass the message on.

Another thought occurred to him. Assuming that the victim was dressed in Du Bellay lingerie, just how far would the similarities go?

He searched through his notebook for another number and keyed it in. A female voice answered, which surprised him.

"This is captain Franck Guerin of the Brigade Criminelle," he announced. "I thought this was Jacques Beaufort's direct line."

"It is indeed," said the voice. "He's stepped out to yell at a photographer. Should I ask him to call you back?"

"No," said Franck. "Get him on the line."

"I'll see what I can do," said the woman, and disappeared.

Three minutes later Beaufort came on the line, his voice sprightly.

"Captain Guerin. I get the feeling you're about to tell me what I need to know."

"Have you received a photo?" asked Franck. "A North African girl, early twenties, some kind of corset, stockings and suspenders?"

"Who is she?" Beaufort fired back in return. "Is she dead? It's hard to tell. She could be sleeping."

"When did it arrive?"

"I'd guess about two this morning. That's when I got the text message, in any case. Same procedure as the last time. Envelope in the external mail slot. The print and a USB stick."

"Nobody saw anything?"

"Not as far as I know. There are not many people around at that time of night. We've got one security guard, but he seems to spend most of his time playing with his PlayStation. How about answering some of my questions, captain? It's this young woman's five minutes of fame. She wouldn't want to go through it anonymously. Or have wanted. I take it she is dead?"

"Don't you dare publish the photo Beaufort," Franck growled. "You don't have the right."

"The dead can't sue," countered Beaufort. "I'll take my chances. Give me a name, captain. Haven't I been cooperative? I gave you lot full access to my mobile phone records."

They had yielded nothing. The text message announcing the delivery of the Sarraute picture had come from a prepaid mobile phone that had been activated the day of her murder. Since then it had shown no sign of life – although Franck was confident he'd soon be told it had known a brief burst of activity early that morning. In any case, Beaufort had just forfeited whatever right he might have claimed to any reciprocity.

"I'm coming round there to tear that print from your hands."

"Do as you like. That'd make a nice photo – a police captain violently interfering with the freedom of the press. Anyhow, it's too late. We've already proofed the page. I just wasn't sure whether it was front cover material. Now I know. See you on the newsstands tomorrow morning."

Beaufort hung up.

Franck angrily pocketed his mobile. Beaufort had the rest of the afternoon to obtain Tazi's name. With *Exposé*'s resources and connections at his disposal, Franck had no doubt he would find it out.

But not from him.

Wednesday, 13th June

Two photos.

Dead centre, a newspaper kiosk, its tenant barricaded behind a mosaic of magazine covers and piles of newspapers, its wing-like doors swung open to the passing day, displaying their printed wares. Just inside one of the doors, a wire magazine holder, fully charged with fresh new issues. One is clipped to a vertical panel which reaches up from it, displaying its title and revealing itself to be *Exposé*. To the right, Franck Guerin, looking down at the pile of magazines. Dark brown trousers and shoes. A jacket of a similar shade over a light khaki shirt, worn without a tie. His lip is curled.

A windowless wall covered in stained whitewash, with a slab-like metallic door implanted dead-centre. Above it, on both sides, curved glass tubes attached to the wall, crude representations of buxom women cursed with multiple torsos but only one pair of legs. Stepping down from the entrance into the street, Franck Guerin, dressed as before. His eyes are scrunched, like a creature emerging from a tunnel into daylight.

*

Jacques Beaufort was as good as his word.

As dawn rose on the insomniac tenants of the capital's three hundred plus newspaper kiosks, bound stacks of the latest issue of *Exposé* were thrown at their feet, Rachida Tazi blazoned across the cover.

The photo showed exactly the same pose that Franck had seen on the bed at the Hotel des Bateliers. The image was bathed in the unhurried light of a declining afternoon. The embroidery on her *guêpière* glowed darkly, rendered molten by the black and white palette. Tazi's pupils seemed moist pools, glimpsed below lazily closed eyelids. Her long hair provided the deepest shade of night. The overall effect was of voluptuous indolence.

The title was: "A sleeping beauty no kiss can awake.

Sarraute's slayer strikes again."

Beaufort had once more provided a short text for the inside cover.

> Last week *Exposé* brought the world the last photo of Laure Sarraute. Today we publish another of her killer's fatal compositions. Rachida Tazi could not claim Sarraute's fame, but this photo proves that she was her sister in sensual beauty. Just as before, we have good reason to believe that the murderer was behind the lens that caught this image.
>
> When will this deadly connoisseur be brought to justice?

Franck found some slight solace in the text. So little was said of Tazi that it was clear *Exposé* had obtained nothing more than her name. Had they suspected she was a stripper, they would have been incapable of holding back the information.

Franck had called the number for The Velvet Pussy several times the previous evening. It had taken six attempts before someone finally answered, and several minutes before Franck succeeded in making himself understood by whoever was holding the phone to his ear in a cavern filled with pounding music. Persistence paid, and he finally got through to the night manager.

He was cagey when asked whether he employed a certain Rachida Tazi, but dropped his guard when Franck told him why she had not come in that evening. The news provoked an expression of almost genuine-sounding regret. The manager then insisted that Franck stay on the line while he brought a close friend of Tazi's in from the stage. A long wait ensued. Presumably her act was not one which could easily be interrupted.

Franck had spent the time reading the coroner's preliminary notes, which had been emailed to him minutes before. Tests had been run immediately to verify whether the corpse or evidence recovered from the crime scene bore traces of the same substances associated with Sarraute's death. The results were positive. Whatever else might have been done to Tazi, she had at the very least suffered the same treatment as Sarraute. Moreover, in all probability, nothing else had been done. Once again there was no sign of sexual contact.

There was also an email from Luc du Bellay. He had identified the lingerie from the digital photos Franck had sent him. It was one of his: a model called Salammbo, released two years previously and retailing in Europe at over 4000 euros a set. He offered to provide detailed sales data once Franck found out the exact size Tazi had been wearing. The message was short and to the point. Du Bellay had not taken the time to indicate his regret that his products had once more been appropriated as a murderer's tools.

Franck had almost forgotten that a phone lay cradled on his shoulder when a new voice came on the line – young, female, and impatient. The brusqueness vanished abruptly when Franck announced that Rachida Tazi had been found dead. He weathered a long disbelieving silence, followed by a squall of sobs, before he was able to ask who he was speaking to and get her to agree to see him the next day. He originally suggested an early meeting, but had to settle for the afternoon, since she would not clock off until four in the morning at the earliest. Close friend or not, clearly the show had to go on.

Tourist buses lined the boulevard de Clichy, the heart of the Pigalle neighbourhood. They turned its pavements into high-sided alleys, the over-sized windows of the coaches reflecting back those of the sex shops. Between the two, groups of tourists wandered slowly back and forwards. They guffawed and pointed, albeit more at each other than at the merchandise on show, which simply repeated itself from one shop front to the next.

Early afternoon was a lacklustre time for sales of DVDs, imported magazines and artificial genitalia. The entrances of the strip clubs that sat alongside the shops looked tawdry and abandoned in the daylight. All lacked their customary hawkers whose job, come dark, was to entice the gullible into over-priced drinks, shabby seats, poor lighting, and acres of exposed flesh. Pigalle by day was more a place of laughter than lust, almost childish in its crude vulgarity. Had there been no tourists, it would have been deserted.

Franck climbed the last of the steps from the depths of the metro. Where in the rest of Paris the tunnels sat just under the surface, here on the slopes of Montmartre the streets climbed while the underground remained obdurately on a horizontal plane. Getting in and out required tackling long flights of stairs or standing idly on escalators that slowly laboured their way up and down. Normally Franck belonged to the determined minority who preferred the stairs, although not to the select band of sprinters who always took them two at a time. This time, however, he drifted towards the escalators, not wishing to put his abdomen to the test. He was feeling tender today, and had already taken four painkillers in the course of the morning.

He was hungry, but knew this was no place to eat. Stale baguettes, kebabs of indeterminate origin or under-heated paninis were all that were immediately on offer. There was, of course, as in any corner of the city in which tour groups congregated, a MacDonalds to hand. This was an option he did not even consider.

To his left was a kiosk, hung with newspapers and magazines. A pile of *Exposé* was propped up before it. Franck felt sure it was out-selling the more graphic ware available all along the boulevard. Just as, he feared, Luc du Bellay was no doubt checking stocks of Salammbo and contemplating a new production run to bank them up. Two different enterprises were enjoying record sales thanks to Laure Sarraute and Rachida Tazi, or thanks to their fatal and unfortunate encounter with a talented photographer. He now had to discover what else they had in common. Tazi had brought him to Pigalle, whereas there was no connection between Sarraute and the sex industry. Undressing for fashion was somehow a whole different universe.

The Velvet Pussy was on a narrow street in the zone south

of the boulevard given over almost entirely to narrow bars where women dressed lightly and talked dirty to get men to squander their money on tepid champagne. The Pussy, to its credit, was one of the street's two honest-to-god strip clubs. Neon outlines of women bending over to touch their ankles flanked its door. They were unlit. Showtime was many hours away and the door was locked.

Franck found and pressed a buzzer. He waited three minutes before pressing again. The door was eventually tugged open from inside. An elderly man with an impassive North African face looked at him, saying nothing.

"Police," announced Franck, holding up his ID. "I've come to see Beatrice Moreau."

The man nodded and stepped back to let Franck through into a short corridor. He gave no directions. Franck walked past him. A few steps took him down and into a large semi-circular room with a bar at one side and a small stage at the other. The walls were lined with booths done up in cheap black velvet; the centre of the room held small circular tables ringed by cushioned chairs. Neon strips were on overhead. Franck assumed a different means of illumination took their place during business hours, as the neon revealed too cruelly the stains and bald patches on the fabric of the club's fittings.

A young woman sat in one of the booths, watching the entrance, waiting for him. She was smoking, and had been for some time, to judge by the ashtray before her. There was also a tall glass, empty, its rim smothered in red.

Her lips were thick and glossy, her eyes exaggerated by a rock-solid ring of black and her cheekbones highlighted with a similar lack of finesse. Franck wondered if he was looking at theatrical greasepaint. Perhaps she had simply got into the habit of making up for underlit bars and raking spotlights.

He walked towards her. She looked in her early twenties. She wore a red shirt with a gaping neck that allowed more than a glimpse of her bra. Its cups covered her breasts entirely, made from some synthetic material that shone under the lights. She did not look as if she could afford a Du Bellay. Nor was she likely to receive one as a gift from an admirer, given the circles in which she seemed to be moving.

She stood up. She wore a short skirt wrapped tightly across her hips. With the exception of her breasts, everything about her was slim and muscular. Beatrice Moreau appeared to be a stripper of the athletic persuasion.

"Franck Guerin." Franck extended her hand.

She shook it. "Beatrice Moreau"

"Please sit down," said Franck, sliding into the booth on the other side of the table, extracting his notebook and laying it down on the surface.

"You want a drink?" asked Moreau.

"I'll take a coffee, if it's possible."

"Farid," Moreau cried to the elderly man who had let Franck in. He was now standing behind the bar, watching them. "A coffee for the captain."

"You see *Exposé* today?" she asked.

Franck nodded.

"Is that a real photo? Was it really taken by the murderer?"

"Unfortunately, yes, it is a real photo," admitted Franck. "As for who took it, we're not yet at liberty to say."

"You mean you don't know," corrected Moreau.

Franck shrugged. "There are things I can't tell you, but I can't stop you working them out for yourself. What I really need, though, is to learn about Rachida. If I understood correctly yesterday, you and she lived together?"

"Sure, we lived together. Don't get too excited though. We lived together and we worked together – same club, same shifts, but different beds. Sometimes we danced together, though."

"Stripping?"

Moreau cast him a withering glance. "What else, in a place called the Velvet Pussy?"

"You said you worked the same shifts. What were they?"

"Fridays, Saturdays, three or four other nights a week."

"How long had both of you been doing this?"

"I've been here two years. Rachida, a little less."

"Tell me about her."

"She was twenty-two. She was pretty."

"She was more than pretty," Franck interrupted.

Moreau shrugged her shoulders. "Maybe. Her tits were small, but she had long arms and long legs. Long hair too. Black. Right down to her waist. If you go for the Arab type, yes, you could say she was beautiful."

She had sat up as she said this, moving her shoulders back and her chest forward. Her breasts were certainly bigger than Tazi's, but Franck was not about to compliment her on the fact.

"Where did she come from?"

"Tunisia. She was sent over when she was fourteen. Worked for her uncle in a couscous restaurant in the 93."

93 was the postcode for Seine-Saint-Denis, the region that sat to the north-east of Paris. Home to many first- and second-generation immigrants, its one and a half million inhabitants dreamed of the riches of their wealthy neighbour; few ever got close.

"Legal or illegal?"

"Never asked her."

"How was she paid here?"

Moreau said nothing.

"I'm not with the URSSAF. I don't care."

The URSSAF collected social security contributions from firms. Its inspectors did their best to clamp down on black market work and undeclared employment. Its Parisian team spent almost all their time raiding restaurants, bars and nightclubs: places rich in cash with staff who were none too concerned if they never received either a contract or a payslip. The DST, for its part, was rather fond of places whose management were taking a free ride and therefore easy to squeeze into giving up information. The dodgier the operation, the better the source, Catherine Vautrin was fond of saying. When they've got something to hide, they've got something to give. Little matter that steering inconvenient check-ups in other directions ensured that such places' staff remained at their employers' mercy and without cover when they fell ill or got old.

Franck found himself wondering whether he should not try a different approach this time, and call in the URSSAF when his own investigation was over. Although Beatrice Moreau would be unlikely to recognise it, he would be doing her a favour.

"Cash in hand," she admitted. "Two hundred euros a night. More on Fridays and Saturdays."

"You too?"

"I'm not illegal."

Franck did not pursue the point.

"So how did you two meet?"

"Here. She answered an ad for dancers. Wanted to get away from her family."

"You know why?"

"No, but I can imagine."

"Did they know she worked here?"

"No. She said they would kill her if they found out. Or send her home. Hard to say which would have been worse."

Given her looks, Franck imagined that Rachida might well have become one of the tawdry princesses of Pigalle. An easy enough job, her days free, an apartment with a girl her own age, dreams of better things, maybe even a Prince Charming. Better than Tunisia or the protective prison of her family. Except that Prince Charmings rarely frequented strip clubs. Whereas murderers sometimes did.

"Do they know she's dead?"

"Depends on whether they read *Exposé*."

"You haven't contacted them?"

"I don't know anything about them."

"You don't have an address for them?"

"No."

"If they don't come forward we'll have to search Rachida's things in your flat to find one. They have to be told."

"OK. Just don't touch my stuff."

"Is there anything there I shouldn't find?"

Beatrice shrugged.

"If there's cocaine, I can't ignore it. If there's just cannabis, I don't have the time to care."

"Promise?"

"Promise."

"There's a little shit in my room, but that's all."

"OK. How long had you two shared the same flat?"

"About as long as she's been working here. When she started she didn't seem to know anyone in Paris. She slept in a cheap hotel near here. We had some good laughs together, and my boyfriend had just disappeared, so I suggested she move in."

"You needed help with the rent?"

"Of course."

"A thousand euros a week doesn't cover everything?"

"I'm young. I'm here to have some fun. Fun costs money. No point spending it all on food and rent."

"You have no other income?"

Moreau sat back in her seat, her eyes flinty.

"What are you getting at?"

"You know full well, Beatrice. Some strippers just take their clothes off and stop there. Others go a little bit further. How much further depends on the money on offer."

"You asking me if I'm a whore?" Her tone was harsh but not indignant. Franck had not expected it to be.

"Actually, no. I don't particularly care about you. You have the good fortune to be alive. I'm not here to give you either trouble or advice. My real question is about Rachida. Was she involved in prostitution?"

Moreau shook her head.

"No, not Rachida."

"You're sure?"

"Of course I'm sure. I offered her some opportunities. She wouldn't."

"So you …" Franck let the question hang.

"Yes," replied Moreau bluntly. "Not often, but from time to time. Rachida could have done good trade. Four star hotels, that sort of thing. She had the looks, and the exotic bit. Her tits wouldn't have been a problem, not in that market."

"But she wasn't interested?"

"No. She said it was too risky. And didn't pay well enough. Which just proves she never tried, because there's good money to be had. She had other plans."

"Like?"

"Photo spreads. Then movies."

Was she moving into modelling and that was the link to Laure Sarraute?

"With or without her clothes?"

"Not just without her clothes. Hardcore. Getting paid to fuck with a guy before a camera."

"This is something she had done, or was going to do?"

"She had her first shoot two weeks ago. She managed to get Jean-Michel Rey interested. He's got connections. Knows people down on the Cote d'Azur."

The name meant nothing to Franck.

"The photos have been published?"

"I don't think so. Rachida would have shown me. We'd have had a party."

You celebrate what you can, thought Franck.

"Any other plans? A boyfriend?"

"No. She wasn't interested in the men around here. Not that you can blame her. She wanted something better."

"And where was she planning to find it, or him?"

"At the Beaux Arts."

Franck let his surprise show. L'Ecole Nationale Supérieure des Beaux Arts was the Left Bank's haven for the young with creative talent, a bohemian bent and, for most of its students, parents affluent enough to support studies that tended to be formless and never-ending. The Beaux Arts had been one of the focal points of the May 68 uprising. It remained tainted with nostalgia for that brief interlude, and was perhaps the last of the nation's institutions to be so. That said, 1968 was a long time ago. Franck doubted that many of its students had fraternised with workers from Renault's assembly lines, or any other proletarians, since then. In any case, they would have had a hard job doing so: Renault's massive operation on the outskirts of Paris had closed in 1992, making industrial workers a rarity within the capital. Was opening its arms to a young Tunisian stripper a contemporary manifestation of the Beaux Arts' revolutionary spirit?

"She was artistic?"

Moreau laughed.

"No. She knew how to peel off a stocking, but I never saw her paint or draw."

"So what's the connection?"

"Life classes. She modelled there some afternoons. Took off her clothes and stood still. Pays less than taking them off and shaking it about, but you meet a different kind of person. She went there some evenings too."

"How long had she been doing this?"

"Two, maybe three months."

"Was it working?"

"What do you mean?"

"Had she met someone?"

"Maybe. On Monday she was due to dance here, but said she couldn't. Said she had a special appointment."

"You saw her get dressed?"

"Yes. We left together. She walked me here just after lunch, then off she went."

"What was she wearing?" Franck asked.

"Tight jeans. Striped t-shirt cut high. That flat stomach of hers on show."

"What about underwear?"

Moreau raised her eyebrows. "Knickers. A bra. Why?"

"What kind?" Franck insisted.

"What kind? I don't know. Dim, probably. Something sensible in cotton."

"Nothing sexy, then? Not what she was wearing in the photo in *Exposé*?"

Moreau reflected before replying. "No. You're right. Those weren't hers. She didn't have the money for that kind of lingerie. Looks like my girl was moving upmarket after all."

"She didn't say who she was seeing? Where she was going? What she was going to do?"

"No. She was playful about it. Said she'd tell me later. No – that's not it – she said she'd show me later."

Show her what? A set of Du Bellay lingerie paid for by a new lover? An engagement ring offered by a wealthy and besotted student? He had to check her flat. He hoped the contents of her drawers and wardrobe knew more about her than her best, or only, friend.

"Can you take me to your flat?" he asked.

"No, I have things to do this afternoon."

"But this place doesn't open for hours," Franck objected.

"True. But, like I said, I have things to do."

Franck did not press the point.

"Can you give me keys?"

"Don't you have Rachida's?"

"They're filed away as evidence."

Moreau dipped into the handbag that lay beside her on the scuffed velvet seat. She dangled a ring with two keys before him.

"They're spares. Leave them in the flat when you're finished."

Franck took them.

"Thank you. Is there an address to go with them?"

"17 rue Ernest Roche. In the seventeenth."

"Porte de Clichy?" Franck's guess was an educated one. The magnetic poles of the seventeenth arrondissement were the place des Ternes to the south-west, a neighbourhood of imposing apartments and self-righteously respectable residents, and the porte de Clichy to the north-east, where both locals and buildings were somewhat less well-scrubbed.

"Of course."

As Franck pocketed the keys he warned Beatrice, "Be careful over the next few days. We know nothing about the man who did this. If it's not random, your connection to Rachida may put you in danger. If you see anything, phone the police. This is my number."

He laid his card on the table. Moreau picked it up and turned it between her fingers.

"I can look after myself."

"I bet that's what Rachida thought."

Franck shook her hand and left, showing himself out. Beatrice Moreau lit another cigarette.

Back on the street Franck's stomach reminded him that it was feeling neglected. He crossed the boulevard de Clichy, swapping the ninth for the eighteenth arrondissement. His destination was a café near the Abbesses metro station that had not lost the habit of making sandwiches to order. It was uphill all the way, for this was where Montmartre's slopes began in earnest. He set off slowly, embarrassed to find himself advancing little faster than the elderly on the street. Healing was a humbling process.

With few customers inside, he had his choice of tables but preferred to lean against the bar. He ordered a ham and cheese sandwich on half a baguette and a Perrier. The server whipped out a leg of ham, a block of gruyère and a steel butter dish from a cold store beneath the counter. He pared slices of cheese and butter with a wicked-looking carving knife. He used the same implement to halve and split a baguette snatched from a vertical wicker basket behind him. Without pausing he slathered the butter onto both halves of the bread, slapped down the ham and cheese, and slid the result across the counter to Franck. The Perrier followed in quick order. It took Franck only slightly more time to down it all. He placed a ten euro note on the counter. When his change came, on a small round plastic dish, he nudged it back and asked for a coffee in its place. His mobile phone chirped before it came.

A text message: "Have seen *Exposé*. Not one of mine. Maryam."

Franck was impressed. *Wasp-Waisted*'s editor was not quite as blasé as he had thought. Moreover, he now had her mobile number. He took the time to save it in his directory before tapping a reply: "But maybe one of your readers'?"

He had time to finish his coffee before Maryam reacted.
"Bring me a court order. I'm free tomorrow PM," it said.

Franck spent the rest of the afternoon, and a good chunk of the evening, in the one-bedroom flat that Tazi and Moreau had shared on the fifth floor of a crumbling brick building at 17 rue Ernest Roche. It did not take him long to work out that Moreau had colonised the salon, thereby gaining four or five square metres over Tazi, who was left the bedroom. He did so on the basis of the photos on display: in the salon Moreau was to be seen in the midst of an extended family, with several children perched on relatives' knees; in the bedroom there was only one photo, of a young Arab girl and an aged woman enveloped in a colourful shawl.

The photo, which he assumed to be of a grandmother left behind in Tunisia, sat on a flimsy table at the head of the bed. Alongside it was another framed image, this time a sketch of a naked young woman seen at an angle, her arms crossed across her breasts, one hand clutching each shoulder, her lower basin completely smooth. As the lack of pubic hair was consistent with the coroner's report, Franck took the drawing to be a gift from an anonymous admirer in one of the life classes at the Beaux Arts. He took both framed images and slipped them into evidence bags.

The bedroom contained a sagging wardrobe poorly assembled from woodchip panels and a chest of drawers that had probably first seen service in the 1950s. He went through both, his hands gloved, sifting clothes, checking inside shoes, and flicking through discarded magazines. He found a roll of banknotes, 2430 euros in all, hidden amongst her underwear, none of which seemed to be in the same league as Du Bellay. There was no correspondence, neither personal or administrative. More importantly, there was no sign of any passport. It was as if Tazi had deliberately discarded anything that might confirm her identity.

The room boasted not a single book, suggesting that her motives for frequenting the Beaux Arts were indeed far from scholarly. The posters on the walls featured pop singers ranging from Britney Spears to – to Franck's surprise – Celine Dion, Quebec's queen of the hysterically impassioned ballad. There was a small radio/CD player in one corner, the support for a precarious stack of CDs that evoked the same tastes, but there was no PC. With no computer and no diaries or notebooks, Franck quickly became pessimistic about finding any written trace of her rendezvous at the Hotel des Bateliers. As a last resort he drew the quilt and covers off Tazi's bed, but found nothing tucked beneath its mattress or in the dust beneath it.

He gave the salon – Moreau's room – a peremptory search without anything catching his eye and moved on to the kitchen, the only sizeable space the two girls held in common, the bathroom being nothing more than an ill-ventilated shower closet. He made himself some coffee in a stained cafetière as he went through the storage space. The search revealed nothing other than the girls' weakness for chocolate in all its forms, and a regrettable habit of leaving leftovers to die at the back of the fridge.

Franck took a place at the two-seater table that sat along one of the walls. He emptied the cafetière into a large cup and sipped his coffee, which proved insipid. The search had been fruitless. Unless someone came forward, there was no way to inform Tazi's family of her death. Franck found himself reduced to hoping that they read *Exposé*.

There was, perhaps, an alternative. There was good reason to assume that Rachida had chosen a new name when she struck out on her own. The only lead he had was Moreau's statement that Rachida had worked for an uncle when she first came to France – assuming she had not made that up too. There had to be hundreds of couscous restaurants in Seine-Saint-Denis, too many for him to visit carrying her photo. But the DST knew a lot about the immigrant communities in the Parisian suburbs. They might have a faster way.

The memory of his call to Pierre Halphen still smarted. If he tried his operational contacts again, he would no doubt run into the same brick wall. DST agents were nothing if not disciplined. He would have to go higher up.

Reluctantly, he pulled out his mobile phone and pulled up the first number in his directory. To his surprise, he got through straight away.

"Vautrin." It could have been a robot, for all the warmth the greeting contained.

"Catherine, this is Franck Guerin."

"My phone is away ahead of you, Franck. Tell me something I don't know."

"The case I'm working. I've got a new victim. An illegal immigrant. No ID, no passport, no social security. But she might have a family connection to a couscous restaurant in Seine-Saint-Denis. She may have worked there until two or three years ago."

"Might. May. No documents. No name. The only thing you seem to be sure of is that she's dead. You chasing a ghost, Franck?"

"You would know a thing or two about that," he countered. "All I'm looking for is some help – someone to float a photo and the name I've got for her through our networks in the 93."

"Is the nation in danger?"

Franck said nothing.

"I thought not. Stop wasting my time. And, unless you've got something to say to me about Corsica, stop calling this number."

"I'm on my own?"

"Not at all. Use your new colleagues. Ask the *flics* on the ground in Seine-Saint-Denis to give you a hand. I'm sure they have nothing better to do."

She hung up.

Franck tried his coffee again. Lukewarm dishwater.

His eyes drifted to a framed cork noticeboard that hung on the wall alongside him. A collection of business cards was haphazardly pinned to its surface. Most concerned carry-out places, some bore the names of bars and night clubs, not just in Pigalle, and the rest businesses such as hairdressers or plumbers. There was, however, one card that caught his eye: Jean-Michel Rey, photographer, 5 rue Victor Basch, Montrouge, with two phone numbers and an email address. Franck confiscated it

He nipped out just before nine, purchased a packet of decent coffee at a local all-night grocery store and trudged slowly back up the five flights of stairs. He emptied out the coffee jar he had found in the kitchen and sat it alongside the new packet in the middle of the table.

He hoped Moreau would appreciate the gesture, assuming she noticed anything when she returned in the early morning from a long night's stripping. He dropped the set of keys she had given him onto the table and walked out the apartment, gently closing the door behind him.

Thursday, 14th June

Two shots.

Early morning light playing with the surface of the Seine, glimpsed over the parapet of a bridge. Franck Guerin, striding purposefully, jacket swinging out behind him, one arm holding a worn leather briefcase, the other holding his watch up to his face. His regard is confident.

In the background, a featureless office block covered in huge rectangular panels of blue-tinted glass. Before it, scurrying extras hurrying about their business in dark suits or severe skirts, most clutching briefcases or computer cases, some with folded newspapers. In the foreground, Franck Guerin, his jacket and trousers crumpled by comparison with the others, his briefcase a shabby relic of another age. He gazes around, looking lost.

*

"That's it?" asked Franck, reaching out to the document wallet lying in the middle of Yves de Chaumont's otherwise unencumbered desk.

It was just after eight in the morning. He had come straight to Yves' office, having woken to a text message instructing him to do so.

"That is the best I can give you at this stage," Yves replied.

"It's not a court order?"

"Of course not. You have no probable cause. Laure Sarraute was photographed for dozens, if not hundreds, of publications, and far more recently than this *Wasp-Waisted* photo four years ago. If we're not going after the others, we can't go after *Wasp-Waisted*. Note that I deliberately avoid mentioning the fact that there is no link between Rachida Tazi and the magazine, which weakens the grounds for your request all the more."

"But there is clearly something in common between the death photos of Sarraute and Tazi and the fare that *Wasp-Waisted* serves up," insisted Franck. In the DST, they would have tunnelled in through the internet and quietly copied the list from Maryam's assistant's PC. They would have worried about demonstrating the relevance of the information after the fact. Playing by the rules might be good for one's conscience, but it could prove wearing on the nerves.

"Clearly?" mused Yves, casting a glance at Franck that suggested he was aware of his thoughts. "If you're saying that they belong to the same aesthetic universe, I'm inclined to agree. But that is a matter of artistic appreciation – dangerous territory for the law."

"So what's this then?" asked Franck, waving the stiff cardboard wallet in the air.

"As I said, the best I can do," said Yves. "I'm well aware it doesn't even come close to what Catherine Vautrin could have done, but I suspect it will suffice. In any case, it has the singular advantage of respecting not only the laws of the nation, but also those of chivalry."

Franck opened the wallet. Inside was an envelope cut from thick hand-made cream-coloured paper. It was addressed by hand to Maryam Sehati. On the unsealed flap at the back was stamped the de Chaumont family crest.

"May I?" asked Franck, before lifting the flap.

Yves acquiesced with a wave of his hand.

Franck extracted a sheet of the same creamy, textured paper, which had been folded in two. He unfolded it and read.

Paris, 14th June

Mademoiselle,

I have not had the pleasure of making your acquaintance. Based on what I have heard from my colleague, captain Guerin, the loss is considerable, and all mine. Perhaps one day I will be able to remedy this, but as an aging judge I serve the Republic from within its dusty corridors, whereas the captain does so on its streets.

You are aware, I believe, that two young women have

recently been slain in most peculiar circumstances. I speak of Laure Sarraute and of Rachida Tazi – one famous, the other unknown, but both stolen from us long before their time and, we must assume, against their will. Captain Guerin, of whose considerable gifts you cannot yet be aware, is convinced that possession of a list of subscribers of your magazine would help us bring the perpetrator to justice. My past experience inclines me to trust his instincts, but due process cannot compel you to obey his request.

May I respectfully solicit your favour in this matter, and ask that you provide the captain with the information he seeks?

Whatever your decision, I remain your faithful servant,

Yves de Chaumont
Juge d'instruction

"You think this will work?" asked Franck.

"Courtesy works wonders. You'll see."

Franck was far from sharing Yves' confidence, but he said nothing. He slipped the note back into the envelope, placed it on the folder, and tugged both to his side of the desk.

Yves watched him do so, saying nothing. He raised a quizzical eyebrow. Franck shrugged and slumped back in his seat.

"We don't know anything yet, do we?" asked Yves.

"Not really," admitted Franck. "Tazi and Sarraute don't seem to fit together."

"Similar age group. Stunning physiques," offered Yves.

"Four years' age difference. Different origins. Different metiers. Different social circles. Yet they both ran into the same man. It can't be a copycat – the MO is identical, we've never released details of the injections, and too little time had elapsed between the two killings for anything to get out. I'll bet he knew Tazi before Sarraute was killed, and planned both murders well in advance, particularly since his timing fits so neatly with *Exposé*'s printing schedule. In any case, he knew them well enough to buy the right size of lingerie for each of them."

"Unless the girls bought them," objected Yves.

"For Sarraute, that might have been a possibility. For Tazi, it seems far less likely. She didn't have the means."

"Aren't you underestimating the earning potential of her particular profession? In any case, she may have been given the means."

"I doubt it. Tazi arrived at the hotel wearing different underwear. She changed, or was changed, in the room. But the hotel's owners say she arrived with nothing more than the small handbag we found. She couldn't possibly have got what she was found wearing into it – not without crumpling it, and there was no sign of that. With Sarraute it's different. Her lingerie was smaller, and could have fitted into her bag. But if we're assuming the killer followed the same protocol both times, then what was true for Tazi ought to have been true for Sarraute."

"Tazi could have been sent in advance to purchase her lingerie and then passed it on to the killer, who brought it to the hotel."

"Try going to a Du Bellay boutique. It's pretty intimidating. Still, it's worth hoping for, because if Tazi did so, then one of the shop assistants may well remember her."

"Because of the colour of her skin?"

"Amongst other things. She was a stripper in Pigalle, grew up in the outer suburbs and lived in Tunisia until her teens. If the way she talked reflected her background, she'll certainly have stood out against the run of the mill Du Bellay customers."

"We have no idea how she talked," objected Yves.

"True, but it's unlikely she had either the accent or the vocabulary that goes with shopping in the Bon Marché."

"We're talking about someone who seems to have frequented the Ecole des Beaux Arts. It may have rubbed off."

"Yves, if you think you could have had a conversation about Rouen cathedral with Rachida Tazi, I think you're mistaken."

"Some would call that prejudice, Franck."

"I'll call it probability," insisted Franck.

"And this is why you're so interested in Du Bellay's sales records, since you believe the killer does his own shopping?"

Franck shifted in his seat. "Good question. I've got them, but in the absence of a suspect I don't know how aggressive we want to be with them."

"Du Bellay sent them through without the slightest hesitation? Maybe we should hold him up to mademoiselle Sehati as an example to follow."

"Yes he did. As good as his word. I've got credit card numbers for sales of Sarraute's size in Midnight Sun in all his French boutiques and about half his other outlets across the world. For Tazi's size in her lingerie I've got the details for France and a few other places. He's promised the rest as soon as he gets it."

"So he's cooperating."

"Very much so. He just wants us to warn him if we get in touch with the purchasers."

"What are the numbers?"

"Midnight Sun 85C bra – 17 sold in the two Paris outlets; 14 via credit card. 4 sold in Nice; 1 by card. As for neighbouring countries, I've got 4 out of 5 in Milan, 3 out of 3 in Geneva, and 12 out of 15 in London."

"That leaves 6 untraceable cash purchases in France," observed Yves. "What about the Tazi outfit?"

"Salammbo?"

"Salammbo," repeated Yves. "Flaubert would be pleased."

"Salammbo 80A – 8 out of 10 in Paris. None sold in Nice. 1 out of 1 in Geneva. 3 out of 5 in London."

"Not such a big seller," observed Yves.

"According to Luc du Bellay, it's a size issue. More of his clients are 85Cs than 80As."

"Makes sense. I don't suppose the same card number pops up on both lists?"

"Were it the case, I wouldn't be sitting here."

"What about the bank card we recovered from Sarraute's

bag?"

"Not on the lists," confirmed Franck.

"Given we're dealing with a careful planner, he's got to have been buying in cash. And in different outlets."

"It wouldn't take much effort to eliminate the traceable ones, though. 22 purchases in Paris. We could get the addresses and send a uniform round to see them."

"To do what?"

"Ask to see the lingerie. And if they don't have it, ask them why. And if the explanation's not convincing, ask where they were last Monday, or the previous Monday, depending on what's missing."

"What would you accept as a convincing explanation? Put on a few kilos? Ripped in a moment of passion? It would be a bit embarrassing both for the owners and whoever you sent. Best send a woman, that's for sure."

"In and of itself, it's probably a pointless exercise, but it might have a beneficial effect. If news of it got out it might scare him off. That could save the next one, if there is supposed to be a next one."

"Or just make him change brand," observed Yves. "To the best of my knowledge, Du Bellay is not the only upmarket purveyor of lingerie in the market. All this sounds like a dead end to me, Franck."

"It shows we're being thorough."

"It suggests we're desperate. You're also forgetting that we don't have the resources here that you were used to at the DST. Get the names for the credit card purchases and sit on them for the moment." Yves paused. "Are we desperate?"

"We're perplexed. But we're not desperate yet."

*

"Good morning, captain," said Claire, *Wasp-Waisted*'s receptionist, as she opened the door to Franck. "I can't quite recall you making an appointment."

"Don't worry, I didn't," said Franck. "I'd like to drop

something off for mademoiselle Sehati, and briefly talk to her if possible."

Claire smiled, "She's not here yet. Can you wait? She shouldn't be long, and she doesn't have any appointments before eleven thirty."

It was just before ten o'clock. After his early morning meeting Franck had called the Beaux Arts, fixing an appointment for the next day with its administrative staff to go over their employment records for life models. He had then left immediately, catching the metro at Louvre Rivoli and getting off at Franklin D. Roosevelt.

"Thank you," said Franck, as Claire gestured him in.

She led him to the red velvet sofa and invited him to sit.

"Would you like a coffee?" she asked, moving over to the cabinet that supported the expresso machine.

"Yes, I would."

Claire knelt down to extract a tray of different-coloured foil-wrapped doses for the machine.

"Any preferences?" she asked.

"Strong. Black. Hot."

"I'm more of a smooth girl myself," she observed, as she selected the colour that corresponded to Franck's description.

"Sugar?" she asked, as the machine filled a small white porcelain cup. "Don't forget – mademoiselle Sehati is not here. You might want to make the best of it."

"No thanks."

"Dark, powerful and bitter – how very masculine of you," she said as she passed him the cup, balanced on a tiny saucer. "Do you mind if I join you?"

"Not at all," said Franck, and watched her as she prepared a café for herself, humming slightly as she emptied two sachets of sugar into it.

"Not worried about your teeth then?" asked Franck.

"My father's a dentist. He'll look after me."

She sat sideways on the sofa beside Franck.

"Mademoiselle Sehati likes you, you know that?"

A frown of incredulity creased Franck's brow.

"I can't say it's the impression I got," he said.

For an instant he wondered if Claire had been told to say this, but it did not seem like her boss' style. If she had something to say, he felt sure she would delight in saying it herself. Maryam had proven herself sufficiently direct in the course of their last encounter. That, he was prepared to admit, was one of the few things he had liked about her. Along with her bracelets. And her eyes. He stopped himself there. Tallying up all the things liked about her was not the purpose of his visit.

"That's because you don't know her. You'll learn," said Claire. She winked at Franck, raised her cup to her lips and slowly drained its entire contents. "Now if you'll excuse me, I have to get back to my work."

She moved back to her desk across from the sofa and fixed her eyes on the flat screen of her PC. Franck watched her as she began to tap gently on her keyboard, waiting to see if she would come back to the subject she had just broached. She ignored him.

After a while he let his attention wander to the paintings hung in the reception area: the woman turning away from the spectator and dressed, more or less substantially depending on the canvas, in red. He began to mull over the skin colour, which was closer to that of Laure Sarraute than of Rachida Tazi. Then there was the red, which had figured prominently in the decoration of Tazi's lingerie. Rachida's hair, however, had been the deepest jade, whereas in the painting it was chestnut, which of course would not work for Sarraute, who was blonde.

Franck pulled himself up mentally. This way madness lay. Clues to the case were not to be found in every image of a half naked woman he might stumble across.

The main door to the office opened. Claire leapt to her feet.

"Good morning mademoiselle Sehati," she exclaimed, all smiles.

Maryam paused in the doorway in a short black skirt with a slightly longer semi-transparent darkly embroidered overlay that stopped well short of her knees. From there her legs ran bare down to a pair of dark ankle boots. She wore a white shirt liberally unbuttoned at the neck. Its cuffs had been folded back to leave room for the horde of bracelets that clung to her wrists. She was carrying a jacket that seemed to be knitted from thick strands of a wool-like material run through with silver and gold threads. She clutched a slim oblong purse in her other hand.

She vaguely nodded in Claire's direction, her eyes on Franck.

"Good morning Claire, I see we have an unscheduled visitor."

"Captain Guerin has been drinking our coffee and relaxing on our sofa," explained Clare. "He says he has a present for you."

Maryam arched one of her carefully plucked eyebrows.

"If the captain has brought me a present it's because he wants something. I don't think he's the type to offer up flowers or jewellery for the sheer delight of giving."

"Present is not a term I would have used," admitted Franck, rising to his feet. "I have a document for you, and I'd like to know your reaction to it. That's why I didn't just send it over."

"In which case," said Maryam, "you'd better come with me."

She opened the door to her office and ushered him through.

"Two coffees, Claire," she ordered, leaving the door open.

Franck waited until she had taken her place behind her desk before choosing one of the chairs across from her. He laid a large manila envelope marked Prefecture de Police on the cold slate desk where it lay uneasily on the irregular surface.

"That's your court order?" asked Maryam, indicating the envelope with her chin.

"Not exactly," said Franck. "It's a little more unusual than that."

"Well, well," said Maryam, reaching out, "Let's have a look."

She slid a hand inside the outer envelope and retrieved a smaller one bearing the de Chaumont crest. She held it for a moment with the thumbs and forefingers of her two hands, feeling the texture of the paper. She nodded appreciatively and then raised the flap, extracting the letter within.

While she read it, Claire slipped into and out of the room, pausing only to lay a coffee before each of them, carefully choosing an even stretch of the slate surface each time.

Maryam lay the single sheet down before her and looked up at Franck with sparkling eyes.

"You will introduce me to monsieur *le juge* one day, I trust?"

"At the earliest opportunity," Franck assured her.

"In which case I will confide my subscriber list to you and you will promise me to use it, if at all, with tact and discretion."

"You have my word."

"Don't give it lightly," warned Maryam, pointing to the letter. "When you do, you engage that of monsieur de Chaumont as well."

"You can both count on me," he insisted.

"Good," said Maryam, clapping her hands and leaning back. "In any case, given that *Wasp-Waisted* has no connection to the new girl ..."

"Rachida Tazi?" interrupted Franck.

"Yes. Given that, you must be coming to realise that I can't lead you to the killer?"

"Identifying how the killer chose his victims is one thing, understanding his tastes is another. Given his predilections, it wouldn't be surprising to find that he reads *Wasp-Waisted*."

"And what exactly are his, as you say, predilections?" enquired Maryam.

"Beautiful women in expensive lingerie. He seems to have the means to invest in Du Bellay outfits, which don't come cheap. The corset in which we found Tazi cost even more than what Sarraute was wearing, and Tazi certainly didn't have the wherewithal to pay for it."

Maryam held up a hand, commanding silence. She looked sternly at Franck with a mixture of disbelief and disappointment.

"The what?" she asked, stretching out the final word of her interrogation.

"The corset on Tazi. Costs over 4000 euros, the model is called ..."

Maryam silenced him once more, slicing her hand across his words.

"Salammbo. The eponymous Carthaginian princess from Flaubert's fantasy of eastern delight. Stitched with oriental motifs culled from carpets preserved in the Palace Museum in Rabat. Red and gold on black. I saw *Exposé*, captain. I know what it was. But I, unlike you, happen to know what it was not."

"Sorry?" asked Franck, unable to understand what she was objecting to.

"Rachida Tazi was wearing a *guêpière* with matching briefs, probably a thong. She was not wearing a corset. Du Bellay, for that matter, does not make corsets."

"I don't pretend to be a connoisseur," said Franck. "It looked like a corset to me. Anyhow, I don't think such fine distinctions will prove very important."

"Oh no?" challenged Maryam. "You think that a better grasp of the aesthetic criteria and erotic sensibility of my publication might help you decode your killer's motivation, but you don't think it's important to be able to distinguish a *guêpière* from a corset?"

Franck shrugged, willing to concede the point, and yet not entirely convinced. This only added fuel to Maryam's ire.

"What does lingerie mean to you, captain? What does it conjure up for you?"

Franck could do little other than shrug again.

"Oh no," she warned, "you're not going to get away with that. Laure Sarraute, what was she wearing?"

"White bra and panties. Du Bellay's Midnight Sun model," Franck recited. "85C," he added.

"A white bra you say. A push-up? A *corbeille*? A *balconnet*? A *bandeau*? Why not a sports bra while you're at it?" She threw up her hands, her bracelets clashing.

"You've lost me," admitted Franck.

"I would understand, captain, if you fell a little short of being a connoisseur. But I cannot accept your utter ignorance. Not only because it is an affront to a subject that I hold dear but also because, if your theories about this killer are correct, then your ignorance is going to stand between you and saving the next woman on the list."

There was a knock at the door and Claire stuck her head into the office.

"Sorry to interrupt, mademoiselle. I've got Janet Wolff on the phone from New York. She says she got up early specifically to call you."

"I'll take her," said Maryam, and then turned her disapproving glare back on Franck.

"What are you doing on Saturday night?" she demanded.

"Well ..." began Franck.

"Never mind. Whatever it is, cancel it. You're coming to dinner at my apartment. I will attempt to teach you something. Ask Claire for the address on your way out. Now go, so that I can calm myself and collect my thoughts. Janet Wolff, as you of course do not know, is one of the reigning queens of the lingerie world. She's also, much to her credit, one of the few who happens to be a woman."

As Franck quietly took his leave she murmured, loud enough for him to hear, "Can't even spot a joke. Some detective."

Claire beamed at Franck as she handed over a square card printed with the *Wasp-Waisted* logo on which she had carefully written an address in the seventh arrondissement. Beside it she noted nine o'clock.

"Told you," she whispered. "She likes you."

"It's not what you think," insisted Franck.

"Nonsense," she countered. "You think she's in the habit of inviting single men she scarcely knows over for dinner?"

"What makes you so sure I'm single?" enquired Franck.

"Apart from the way you dress?"

*

Franck hated La Défense. He hated everything about it: the concrete; the steel; the tinted glass; the vast, impersonal shopping centre; the pompous dimensions of its Grande Arche; the armoured shell of the CNIT; the labyrinth of roads and tunnels that meandered about beneath it; the hundred and fifty thousand who poured across its vast central esplanade at the beginning and the end of each working day; its brooding isolation at the edge of Paris, menacingly perched on the banks of the Seine. That a business district, summoned out of nothing by a combination of determined promoters and would-be visionary politicians, might possess as distinctive a character as the rest of the city was clearly too much to ask. Still, something could – and should – have been done to avoid the impression that a chunk of New York's, London's, or Shanghai's acres of office buildings had been hacked off and dumped on a site all too visible from the western half of Paris.

The café where Sylvie had told him to meet her was crafted from formica and perspex and filled with uncomfortable brightly-coloured moulded plastic seats. Assuming she had chosen it because there was nothing less objectionable in the immediate vicinity, he decided to keep his complaints to himself. He stood leaning against a counter-top that ran all the way around the inside of the place, looking out into the atrium of a recently completed behemoth of glass and steel already full to the brim with suits, skirts, mobile phones and blackberries, all rushing about in what he assumed to be the pursuit of greater profits. It was almost midday, but nobody seemed to be thinking about lunch.

When Sylvie approached, her pace, if anything, was faster than the others. She clicked into the café in heels, kissed Franck on each cheek, and slid a slim Louis Vuitton briefcase onto the counter, pushing aside his empty coffee cup.

"You want one?" he asked, pointing to the cup.

"Any good?"

"Weak. Lukewarm."

"I'll pass."

She opened the briefcase and extracted a single A4 sheet split into a number of rectangles containing a mixture of text and coloured diagrams.

"Everything I need to know about Du Bellay?" hazarded Franck.

"I hope so," replied Sylvie. "I'm not sure I could get much more. It's not a listed firm, so the information available from public sources is limited. I called in a few favours to draw this up." She tapped the sheet of paper.

"Thanks," said Franck.

"Don't mention it. Wait till I do, and then just give me whatever I'm asking for."

"If I can, I will," offered Franck.

"There's a lot hiding behind that 'if'," observed Sylvie. "Still, it doesn't matter. I don't expect you to be as ... how would I put it? ... as accommodating as me."

She glanced at her watch, a tiny bejewelled band around her left wrist.

"You have to go?" asked Franck.

"Yes. That's why I told you to meet me here. I'm supposed to be in a meeting room on the fourteenth floor of this building in four minutes."

"I'll walk you to the lift," said Franck, picking up the sheet of paper, folding it twice, and placing it in an inside pocket. He left two euros on the counter and followed Sylvie out the door. She walked fast, her heels resonating on a fake marble floor. He adopted her pace, hoping the twinges of discomfort he felt would not become anything worse.

"What's behind the figures?" he asked, as they traversed the atrium.

"Du Bellay is a family firm. Founded by Luc's grandfather. Manufacturers and importers of silks, lace and similar fine fabrics. Made a lot of money before the first World War. Made an astonishing amount during it – I didn't have the time to find out how, as I doubt our troops were that well dressed. Lost some ground in the thirties, almost went broke during the Occupation, picked itself up in the fifties, lost its way in the seventies, and dropped off the radar in 1994."

"Went broke?"

"Not at all. Liquidated all its assets – two remaining factories, stocks of fabric, distribution agreements, all that kind of stuff – but was never wound up. The only property they held on to was their headquarters – the building in the sixteenth arrondissement where you met Luc du Bellay, which belongs in its entirety to the firm, although today they only occupy one floor. After 1994 there was only a handful of staff, grouped around Luc's father, and a lot of money in the bank."

"What were they doing?"

"Ostensibly very little, just managing the firm's funds – modest by my standards, but respectable enough for a family concern. Du Bellay's father continued to offer himself a generous salary and probably spent a lot of time congratulating himself on getting out when he did."

"Why?"

"The textile industry doesn't really exist in France anymore. Not on an industrial scale, at any rate. The Du Bellay assets were sold when they were still worth something, which says something for the old man's foresight."

"So when Luc du Bellay took over, there was nothing but a well-stocked bank account?"

"No, not just that. He inherited two generations' worth of expertise in sourcing and exploiting quality fabric. He also inherited the Du Bellay brand, a hundred years old, unsullied by any recent experiments or failures, and ripe for recycling, since nothing had actually been branded with it for decades."

"So Luc went into lingerie?"

"With a family name that spoke of an intimate knowledge of silks, lace, and fine-spun cloth, it made perfectly good sense to move into a market where they featured so prominently. But Luc didn't just go into lingerie – he went into high-end lingerie, where quality is certainly important, but where image counts even more. The first two du Bellay generations were manufacturers and traders, the current one is all about marketing."

"So?" Franck was sure Sylvie was leading him towards something. He was also aware that they were now standing in front of the lift that was about to sweep her away to her meeting.

"Luc du Bellay had to spend a fortune to design and manufacture his product range from scratch. That was the fortune his father had so carefully managed and handed on to him. He spent a second fortune on marketing his products. That fortune came from a handful of banks who are waiting impatiently to be reimbursed."

"Which is proving difficult?"

"He's got good products. He asks high prices and gets away with it. But his sunk costs are huge and rumour has it he's nowhere near the volumes he'd require to start turning a profit."

The lift doors opened silently before them. There was no-one inside. Sylvie hopped into it and spun round to face Franck.

"Or at least, he wasn't. Not until ten days ago."

*

Getting to Montrouge from La Défense involved spending a lot of time in the metro. The distance and inconvenience made symbolic sense: La Défense was a triumphant temple to contemporary capitalism; Montrouge was a rusting relic from the days when a Communist-run Red Belt of suburban towns encircled Paris.

5 rue Victor Basch offered him four choices. Beijing-Paris Import-Export on the ground floor explained the two young Chinese men chain-smoking outside, doing their best to look like extras in a John Woo film with open-necked shirts, black leather jackets and stooped postures. Wystech one floor up explained the pile of empty cartons marked Dell in the skip by the side of the building. La Poste DRGP SCC explained the

two yellow cars parked in reserved slots on either side of the entrance. As for Rey Studios, it had to explain the woman with the enormous bust, gaping blouse and excessive make up who was waiting before the lift.

Franck caught up with her as the doors opened. A man in a charcoal suite leapt out, furiously stabbing a number into his mobile phone, a thin leather attaché case trapped under one arm. Had to be Wystech.

The woman clumped into the lift in her calf-high boots. She paused before the control panel and looked towards Franck, who had slid in beside her. Despite a sign insisting that the lift could hold four passengers, it seemed to have been designed to encourage perfect strangers to rub up against each other.

"Which floor?" the woman asked, painted nails hovering before numbered buttons.

"Fourth," said Franck.

She frowned slightly, pressed number four and then number three. Franck bit his lower lip. Some detective, right enough. With some three hundred thousand staff, La Poste did indeed have a place for everyone.

He reached the fourth floor alone and found himself in a neon-lit hall facing a single unmarked door with a wide mail slot cut low-down. That alone could explain the third floor's disapproval, for forcing a postal worker to bend his already over-strained back. Not to mention depriving him of the chance of a sly peep.

Franck rang the bell alongside the door. He heard an indistinct shout within. A few seconds passed before the door opened on a muscular man in his late twenties wearing a tight blue t-shirt and worn jeans. His hair had been shaved into a squared-off buzz cut. One of his ears was heavily pierced.

"Jean-Michel Rey?" Franck asked. He had not phoned ahead.

"No. There." The man jerked a thumb over his shoulder.

Franck walked around his monosyllabic greeter, passed an unmanned reception desk and continued down a short corridor. The doors leading off it were all open: a toilet; a coffee-making room equipped with a sink, two kettles, three cling-filmed tubes of plastic cups and a battered fridge unit that looked as if it had come from a hotel room; another toilet; a cloakroom ringed with metal pegs and a wooden bench.

Inside the latter a young woman was struggling into a pair of jeans, her attempts not helped by her refusal to relinquish the cigarette in her left hand. She wore a black thong. Her bra was hanging on a nearby peg, alongside a striped blue and white sweatshirt. Instinctively Franck paused, glancing at the bra. The girl looked up at him briefly, realised his eyes were not fixed on her swollen breasts, and went back to her task.

Franck continued to the end of the corridor. It opened onto what was once open-plan office space, as wide as the building itself. Every window was covered by shutters. The place was starkly lit by strip lights hung on struts that descended from a patchwork of stained polystyrene ceiling tiles.

Two cream coloured screens formed an angle in the centre of the vast space. They provided a backdrop to a makeshift stage where rugs covered industrial carpeting. A brown vinyl sofa, a glass coffee table and a standing lamp were grouped together. Behind one of the screens Franck could see clumps of furniture running back to the far wall. Each collection seemed to correspond to a theme: an office; a bedroom; a café; a workshop; and so on. Stranded amongst them were a collection of lighting rigs.

Closer to hand, to his left, was a long metal workbench on which three cameras were carefully laid. Alongside them, sandwiched between two servers, were a large flat screen and a keyboard. A cable ran from one of the servers to a fourth camera hung around the neck of a squat overweight man with an untidy beard. He was perched on a stool, bent eagerly towards the screen.

"Monsieur Rey?" Franck asked.

"Just call me Man," came the reply.

"That's a pity," said Franck, refusing to rise to the bait. "I was looking for a Jean-Michel."

The photographer lifted the wide strap that ran around his

neck and laid the camera on the bench. He swivelled on the stool, and stood to face Franck.

"It's a joke," he said, scornfully. "Man Ray, famous photographer. Photographed whores and flogged them as art. Pretty clever, for a nigger."

"Lived in Montparnasse from the twenties to the forties," Franck filled in. "Knew Breton, Ernst, Miro, Picasso, you name it. They didn't seem to worry about him being black."

"So what are you, some expert in art history, or a campaigner for S.O.S. Racisme?" Rey countered.

"Something like that. I'm captain Guerin from the Brigade Criminelle."

"Really?" Rey seemed unimpressed. "I know some of your colleagues. What can I do for you? If you've come for a show, you're a bit late – you've just missed Alex and Misha."

He switched his attention to the man who had let Franck in and was now lurking behind him.

"You two can go. Tomorrow three o'clock. After that, you get paid."

"Pay now!" demanded an Eastern European voice.

Franck turned his head. The girl had succeeded in getting into her jeans, but nothing else. She stood indignantly in the doorway, pushing her partner aside.

"Tomorrow. One more shoot. Then you get paid," insisted Rey. "And I wouldn't make too much of a fuss, or this nice policeman might ask to see your work permit."

She levelled a baleful glare on Franck, then turned and stormed away. The man followed her patiently. The door out to the landing slammed shut.

"Migrant labour, always a problem," sighed Rey. "Let's have a drink."

He led Franck into the room with the hotel fridge, which he tugged open, revealing a stock of bottled beer and a few cans of Orangina. Rey removed two bottles, one of which Franck declined, saying he would rather have a coffee. As he watched Rey ladle Nescafé into a plastic cup with a sugar-encrusted spoon, he questioned the wisdom of his choice. When the cup was handed to him, its sides buckling under the heat of the water Rey had just poured into it, there was no room for doubt. He laid it on a nearby table. Rey had already emptied half his beer.

"So why are you here?" he asked.

"Rachida Tazi," explained Franck. "Seen yesterday's *Exposé*?"

Rey nodded. "Recognised her right away. You think I killed her?"

"Did you?"

"I wouldn't have lasted long in this business if I was in the habit of killing my models," Rey pointed out.

"Well, if you didn't, do you know who did?"

"Whoever had just fucked her," Rey suggested. "Found in a hotel room dressed like a slut? Sounds like someone had their fun and wanted to make sure no-one else did. Or didn't have enough fun, wanted their money back, and things got out of hand."

"Very useful," said Franck. "Thanks for sharing those thoughts. Now, tell me about your dealings with Rachida Tazi."

"I met her at that club she strips at. I was in there one night with some men I know in the film business. She came over to us after her act. She was acting really interested, and did everything she could to get our attention. She had a short skirt with nothing underneath. When she sat down you could see her pussy. Just like Sharon Stone. Remember that film?"

Franck nodded. Stone had presided over the jury at the Cannes film festival, had acted for Scorsese in *Casino*, but she was doomed to remain the woman who crossed her legs in *Basic Instinct*.

"She wanted into the business badly. I think she would have sucked us all there and then. When Arabs go slutty, they go the whole way. Generations in the harems, it's probably coded in the genes. No wonder the mullahs keep them tied up in sacks."

He paused to finish his beer. Franck's coffee languished on the table.

"So we talk. Ask if she's ever done any video. She says no. Ask if she's done any photos. She says no. So I offer to take some pictures. If they're any good, my colleagues say they'll try her out. She agrees. Two weeks ago she comes here one afternoon. I take a set. Not bad. Not so keen on Arabs myself, and her tits were too small, but she was supple. Could bend herself into all sorts of positions. That's a gift. You can sell the same cunt twenty times if you've got twenty different angles."

"I imagine that's what you did right after – you sold it?" asked Franck.

"Not yet. I've had a busy schedule. A shoot a day, almost. Haven't shown them to anyone yet."

"Not even your friends in the film business?"

"No. She wasn't happy about that. Phoned me two, three days after the shoot. Wanted to know what was happening. I told her to calm down, wait for my call. She left me a couple of messages after that. Impatient bitch. Wouldn't be surprised if that's what got her killed."

"So no-one has seen these photos?" insisted Franck.

"Just me. Want to be the first?"

Rey took Franck back into his work area and steered him towards the bench. He took the stool before the workstation and left Franck standing behind him, watching over his shoulder.

Rey clicked away with his mouse, burrowing down through a series of directories on his server until he reached one entitled "Exotic". A double-click revealed maybe twenty sub-directories, each bearing a girl's name. There was only one Rachida.

"Here we go," said Rey.

The first image that took possession of the screen was bargain basement Ali Baba. Rachida was in full belly-dancer regalia: baggy trousers, bronze cups holding her breasts, a headdress with dangling coins, a black veil below her eyes, heavily rimmed with kohl, feet bare, dark polish on the nails of her toes and fingers. Behind her sheets had been hung and large pillows had been scattered around in a half-hearted attempt to suggest a Bedouin setting. To her right stood a bearded youth tricked out as an explorer, complete with coiled bullwhip in one hand.

Rey unfurled his photos as they had been taken, a crude stop-and-go narrative in which Rachida stripped under the menace first of the whip and then of an erect penis – which was soon in her mouth, between her breasts, and in her sex, before finally expiring over her buttocks. There were around a hundred shots, many but a slight variation on the previous one. From time to time Rey commented on his handiwork. He was right about the ease with which Rachida's limbs could be stretched, her back twisted, her neck bent back as her hair uncoiled down her spine. Having mimicked terror unconvincingly at the beginning of the shoot, her expression moved to one of feigned lust and ecstasy, a repertory presumably better known to her from her nights stripping.

One last photo had been taken after the end of the session. Naked and standing tall, Rachida menaced her partner, thrusting a handful of tissues towards his face as he recoiled. She had a broad mischievous smile, while his nose wrinkled in disgust and he caught her outstretched arm to hold it back. Not so keen on his own sperm, then.

"A good shoot," said Rey. "I'll sell it no bother, even though there's no anal."

"For any particular reason?" asked Franck.

"She wouldn't. Not this time. Wanted to keep something back for the future. Smart girl."

"Who's the buyer?"

"Any number of on-line porn sites," Rey explained. "Haven't decided yet."

"She authorised the sale?"

"Of course. Sign first, shoot later – that's one of the rules in this business."

"Can I have a copy of the authorisation form?"

"Sure. Want a copy of the shoot? Don't want you thinking I'm not cooperating."

Franck left with a bulging bright red plastic bag. Inside was a photocopy of Rachida's contract, disclaiming all rights on the pictures and acknowledging receipt of her fee. The address matched the flat she shared with Beatrice Moreau. There was also a copy of the equivalent document signed by her male partner from the shoot. His fee was half Rachida's. Then came a thick wad of sheets on which Rey had printed the photos. He had used plain paper, after Franck had assured him that he was not interested in the fine detail of the images.

Rey had shaken his head at this. "You wouldn't last long in my profession."

Friday, 15th June

Two photos.

One of the narrow streets of the Latin Quarter, lined with closely parked cars obscuring the windows of the art galleries behind them and the works they seek to reveal. Franck Guerin, sliding between two cars, heading across the road. Jeans, a grey t-shirt and a blue jacket sit oddly with the briefcase in his hand, like a university lecturer over-keen to show he remains close to the universe in which his students dwell.

The facade of a neighbourhood café, supporting a large chalk board announcing the day's specials. The entrance is to the left, preceded by a series of outside tables, each host to a motley pair of students, draining glasses and lighting cigarettes. To the right, striding into the frame, Franck Guerin, briefcase caught underneath one arm. By his side, partially obscuring him, is an elegant woman in a long silver-grey dress and raised heels. With a gauzy scarf around her neck, she seems better suited for an evening at the opera than a drink in the company of Guerin's worn jeans and tired jacket.

*

Franck shifted his weight, trying to get more comfortable on his office chair. He had spent over three hours hunched over his keyboard, having discovered a short email from Claire, Maryam's assistant, upon arriving that morning. Its title was "The Holy Grail" and it contained no text, only an attached file which proved to be the *Wasp-Waisted* subscriber database.

There were 1012 names with postal addresses, half of which also had phone numbers and email addresses. A date was appended to each line, marking the individual's debut as a subscriber, as was an issue number, which presumably referred to the point at which the current subscription would run out. Franck noted that some were marked "life".

He loaded the file into a spreadsheet and began playing with it.

The addresses spanned the globe. Japan was well represented, but America seemed the most frequent destination for *Wasp-Waisted*, with New York turning up time and again.

For the moment, Franck limited his focus to France. If his killer was from another country he would have to be taking an extended holiday in Paris and know his way around very well – from the catwalks of Sarraute to the strip clubs of Tazi. It seemed unlikely.

He had 162 French addresses, of which 112 were in the Paris region. Franck scanned the names, recognising a number of fashion designers even he had heard of. However, the only name that seemed connected with his investigations thus far was that of Luc du Bellay.

He printed off the 162 French names, set the list on the desk alongside his keyboard, and started checking them, one at a time, against police databases. This was the kind of thing that he was used to farming out to back-office teams in the DST. Throw enough resources at a problem and a solution will be found: that was the DST way. However, Franck was beginning to suspect that resolving problems and solving crimes were two quite distinct disciplines. In which case, what he was doing could prove a useful, if frustrating, exercise in humility.

It was nearly midday when he raised a weary pen and crossed out the last of the names. Apart from some financial delinquents and a host of driving convictions, *Wasp-Waisted*'s local subscriber base appeared relatively well-behaved.

Nonetheless, Franck was glad to have the list. Any name that came up now could be checked against it. The more information he had, the closer he ought to be. It was just a question of reaching critical mass. Or so he hoped.

*

Franck arrived at the entrance of L'Ecole Nationale Supérieure des Beaux Arts just after three in the afternoon, late enough for most of its students to have emerged from their disorderly bedsits and studios concealed in the nooks and crannies of the

Latin Quarter. They could be seen scattered across the main courtyard dressed in an infinite variety of styles but united by a shared passion – the nicotine furnished by the cigarettes omnipresent in their hands.

Franck had been told to cut diagonally across the courtyard and go through an arch marked "C". Once there a sign pointed him down a corridor marked "Administration".

He found himself walking past a series of small offices, none holding more than two people. Desktop PCs and printers took up much of the horizontal space, while the walls were shored up with antiquated filing cabinets. The only artwork to be seen had been done by young children, whose photos stood on small frames on desks or hung perilously around the edges of computer screens. All of the staff seemed to be female.

At the side of each open door was a blue enamel plaque with a number embossed in white. The plaques shone slightly. Somebody clearly looked after them.

Franck reached number 215 and introduced himself to madame Quignard, reminding her of their three fifteen appointment. She was in her early sixties, overweight, with tangled hair and thick-rimmed glasses. For a moment she looked formidable, but she smiled when she shook Franck's hand and offered him a seat.

"It's the first time I've had a policeman in my office," she explained.

"I hope I don't disappoint you," he replied, smiling himself. That said, unless his expectations were very much mistaken, she was going to disappoint him. Without a social security number, Rachida Tazi should figure nowhere on her records.

"If you keep smiling like that, I'll be more than happy," announced Quignard. "I don't get a lot of smiles in this office. The only reason anyone ever comes to see me is to complain. Never had anyone in to thank me for getting their pay right, or returning money we overpaid by mistake."

"You handle the pay for everyone?" Franck asked.

"Yes. Teachers, staff, part-timers, occasional workers. No-one gets a payslip without passing by me, or through this."

She indicated the PC on her desk.

"I'm looking for details on a young woman called Rachida Tazi. I'm told she did modelling for life classes."

Madame Quignard noted the name on a pad beside her keyboard.

"When? I've only got the past two years on line. We changed systems early 2005. Anything before then has been archived. It'll take a lot more time to find."

"That's not a problem. She's supposed to have started here three or four months ago."

Madame Quignard started typing and scrolling up and down on her screen.

"Got a Medhi Tazi, works on the maintenance staff, that's all."

"Do you know where he comes from?" demanded Franck. He was still inclined to think that Rachida had changed her name, but it would do no harm to check. Stumbling upon a relative would make things a lot easier.

"You mean, where he lives?"

"No, where does he come from. It's a North African name."

Madame Quignard frowned at Franck and raised a finger in warning. Perhaps she was formidable after all.

"We don't hold that kind of information. The Beaux Arts has nothing against immigrants, and neither should you."

Franck turned his smile on again to counter her nascent indignation.

"I don't. I just need to know if he's linked to Rachida Tazi. She was Tunisian."

"Was?"

"This week's *Exposé*. Front cover."

"No." Quignard looked at him, horrified. "Poor girl."

Shaking her head she picked up her phone and tapped a four digit number.

"Jules, how are you? I'm fine. Still making sure everyone gets their due. I've got a strange question for you. Mehdi Tazi. Where's he from? Originally, I mean. OK, thanks. No, no problem. Statistics. They're always asking us to count one way or another. You? Of course I have to count you too. What? Of course there's a special category if you come from Marseille! Thanks again."

Franck gave her an appreciative look.

"You're good at this. Ever thought of joining the police?"

Madame Quignard seemed pleased with the compliment. Either she had forgotten May 68, or her sympathies at the time had lain with de Gaulle. "I'll keep it in mind. Mehdi Tazi is Algerian."

No connection then.

"Are all models paid?" he asked.

"Would you take your clothes off for free?"

"Don't some people do it for Art's sake?" hazarded Franck.

"Standing or sitting in the same position for hours on end, shivering or dying for a pee, with a bunch of students staring at your private parts? You'd do that for free? That said, we don't pay them very much. Believe me, I wouldn't do it for twice what they get."

"Who hires them?"

"We hire them. All the contracts go through here. What you want to know is who picks them and decides how much work they do. That's the painting and drawing professors."

"Could they be bypassing you?"

"Not unless they're paying the models out of their own pocket."

"It's possible?"

"Unlikely." She nodded towards her screen. "Believe me, they're not that well paid either."

Franck pushed his chair back, ready to stand up.

"Can you try one last name?"

"Sure."

"Laure Sarraute."

"As in the model?"

"As in the model," Franck confirmed.

"So *Exposé* is right? It is the same killer?"

"That's the current hypothesis. The challenge is trying to find something that links them, other than the way they died."

Madame Quignard nodded. She began tapping, paused, tapped again, paused, and tried one last time.

"No. Nothing."

"Madame Quignard, thank you for your time and cooperation."

"It's been a pleasure."

They shook hands. Franck returned to the corridor, none the wiser.

He wandered back into the main courtyard. He stood in a corner for a while, watching the students. Most were caught up in animated conversations, with a lot of fast talking and jabbing of cigarettes into the air. New theories being hammered out? Tales of last night's happenings? Speculation about what the media were beginning to call the Du Bellay murders?

He did not bother listening to find out, but walked directly over to the quietest group he could see: two young men whose eyes rarely strayed from the cobbles at their feet and who muttered to each other in an undertone. Their faces swivelled up reluctantly when he arrived.

He did not show his ID, nor introduce himself.

"I'm looking for a professor who runs life classes," he stated.

"Which one?" asked one of them.

"Any one," he replied.

"Professor Subrini," said the other. "Or professor ..."

Franck cut him off. "One will do. Thank you."

He retraced his steps. Behind him the two students gratefully went back to staring at the ground.

Franck had to ask twice before he found professor Subrini's office. Its door was covered with notices: tutorial times; forthcoming exhibitions; scholarships; life class schedules.

He was about to knock when a timetable positioned in the centre of the door informed him that a tutorial was underway. It was the last of a series that had commenced at midday. The morning had been left blank, as had every previous day that week. He looked at his watch. Ten minutes to wait. He slipped to the side of the door and turned, leaning his back against the wall.

Franck closed his eyes and listened. He could hear occasional phrases from behind the door. Two female voices. Footsteps in the corridor came and went, slowing sometimes as they approached, but he never acknowledged them and was never challenged. Only someone who had the right to be there would be standing around with his eyes shut.

After eight minutes the door swung inwards. His eyelids lifted and he caught the back of a young student with short bristly hair, several earrings, a leather jacket, torn jeans, scuffed ankle books and a huge portfolio clutched with difficulty under her arm. She walked away briskly and never noticed him.

Professor Subrini, however, did. Standing in the doorway, she turned her head quizzically in his direction.

"Am I expecting you?" she asked.

"No," said Franck. He could not have said exactly what he had been expecting, but it certainly was not what he found before his eyes.

Professor Subrini wore a long dress of silky material whose light grey bordered on silver. From the base of her neck to the top of her heels, it clung to her frame, swelling over her breasts, pinching her waist, hugging her thighs and plunging perpendicularly towards her feet. A semi-transparent scarf, embroidered with streaks of velvet like shooting stars, was draped across her neck and shoulders. Her bare arms came to rest on her hips as she turned her head to one side and studied him.

"You teach in this?" Franck found himself asking, his mind switching back to the garb of the student that had just left the office.

"Rarely," came the reply. "I'm due at a vernissage this evening. An ex-student. An important show for her. She begged me to dress up, and I won't have time to nip home before I go there."

"I can understand why," said Franck.

"Why, you know where I live?"

"No," clarified Franck. "Why she begged you to dress up."

Her eyes were grey too. Her hair, for the moment largely auburn, had begun to follow their example. Her features were fine, a face that had always been slim, tapering down to a sharp chin. A scattering of lines ran from the side of her eyes. Her hair was shoulder length, hooped behind her ears, which were bare and unpierced.

"And you've been waiting outside my door all this time just to pay me a compliment?"

"If you have ten minutes, I'd like to ask you a few questions."

"So what are you? Art dealer, budding student, failed student, journalist, mysterious admirer?"

"I'm a policeman," Franck declared. "Franck Guerin. Captain. Brigade Criminelle. I'm investigating two murders."

The professor tipped her head a little more to the side and frowned at him.

"Can you show me some proof, just so that I can take you seriously?" she asked.

Franck brought out his ID and handed it to her. She took it and held it at shoulder height for some time.

"Terrible photo," she remarked, handing it back. She then extended a hand to shake his. "I'm Anne Subrini. I hope this has nothing to do with me."

"I'm sure it doesn't," Franck reassured her. "But you might be able to help me."

She gestured him inside and shut the door.

Subrini's office was large and filled with light from three tall windows facing south. Stuck in one corner was a hefty wooden desk that looked like it had outlived many previous occupants of the room. Its inlaid top was covered by a scattering of books, magazines and sheets of paper bearing a mixture of text and illustrations. A flat screen of generous dimensions had pride of place upon the desk, dominating a keyboard and mouse.

The wall through which they had come was given over to books, with shelves reaching two meters high to the ceiling. The walls to the right and to the left held a well-spaced collection of paintings of diverse styles. Two leather armchairs, worn by age, occupied the centre of the room, along with an oblong coffee table and a chaise longue draped with a bolt of purple silk. Anne Subrini sat herself down, dead centre, on this burst of imperial colour. Franck took one of the armchairs.

"You teach painting?" he asked.

"Drawing too," she corrected him. "Line and colour."

"It's just ..." He gestured around him. "No easel. No palette. No tubes of oil and stacks of brushes."

"This is an office, captain, not a studio. I talk about art here, but I don't make it here. At best, I hang it up."

"Your work?" Franck pointed towards one of the walls hung with pictures.

"Some of it."

Franck scanned the collection trying to guess which ones were hers. He pointed to a canvas showing the upper torso of a young woman seated behind a flat wooden surface on which her left forearm and right elbow rested. Her right hand was gathered into a fist that lay under her chin, supporting a head that tipped slightly forward, her pupils raised in their orbit to gaze at the spectator. Her blonde hair was brushed back from her forehead, but came cascading down around her shoulders and spilled over her breasts. Although naked, the subject of the portrait conveyed not the slightest vulnerability.

"Yours?"

"Well done," she replied. "How did you know?"

"I was told you organised life classes. It's the only nude here."

"So you're not a connoisseur, just a good guesser?"

"We call it detection."

"But you're not a detective, captain. Nor, unless I misread your ID, are you with the Brigade Criminelle. It's marked DST, is it not?"

"Yes," admitted Franck, impressed by her acumen, but

quick to brush the issue aside. "I'm on secondment ..."

"Doesn't that mean you're a spy?" she cut across him. "You don't look like a spy – which, I imagine, is what would qualify you to be one."

"Strictly speaking, at the DST there are no spies – only counter-spies," offered Franck. "And that's just a small part of what it does."

"Watching over the nation? Making sure we can sleep safely in our beds?"

Franck shrugged. "Basically, yes. We're just a division of the larger police force – there's nothing sinister about us."

"Don't worry captain," said Anne. "I'm not afraid of you."

She leant back in the chaise longue, an amused look on her face.

"So what can I do for you? You, and your two murders. It was two, wasn't it?"

"Do you read *Exposé*?" he asked.

Anne laughed, and drew herself up, lowering her eyebrows and watching him from under her eyelids, not unlike the portrait Franck had guessed was one of hers.

"Do I look like I read *Exposé*?"

"In that dress, actually, yes you do."

She chuckled again. "*Touché*. You caught me on a good day, captain. I don't normally look like this."

"Normally it's a paint-stained smock, tattered trousers and worn boots?" He could not imagine it.

"Something like that. Well, a little less nineteenth century bohemian," she conceded, "but just as practical. Anyway, to answer your question, no, I don't read *Exposé*. Should I?"

She leant forward, elbows on her knees, and cradled her chin in open palms, awaiting his reply. Franck had been waylaid by the exchange and was not quite sure how to proceed.

"Let me try another question," he said. "I'm trying to find out if someone can model in a life class here without featuring on the school's payroll."

"Of course," Anne replied. "If they don't ask to be paid, or get paid in kind."

"People do it for free?"

"Some, yes. We get a few exhibitionists every year, but we know how to weed them out. On the whole it's pensioners who do it for nothing. Gives them something to do. Gets them out and into the company of young people. The students, to their credit, are nice to them. Some see bodies on the verge of collapse as the greatest challenge for verisimilitude."

"You don't?" asked Franck, although her tone had rendered his question superfluous.

"I'm old-fashioned, captain. I think immortalising beauty is the greatest challenge. True, anyone can paint a pretty face, or taut young breasts, or athletic shoulders, or proud buttocks, or shapely thighs. But few can make them pulse with life, glow with warmth, express their sensual energy. Decay is surprisingly easy to capture. Its forms are multiple and banal. Beauty that is fierce and vital is much, much harder."

Franck sneaked a look up at her painting. She had not done so badly.

"So, retired people do it for free. What did you mean by those who get paid in kind?"

"The Beaux Arts runs evening classes. Art history on the whole, but also drawing, photography, some video. They're fairly expensive. We've got a prestigious name, after all. We also run our courses later than others – at eight or nine in the evening. We get the busy people who can't sneak off early to get to the Ecole du Louvre. Being busy people, they on the whole can afford our fees. However, not all can. And those who can't sometimes have something to trade. I believe our computer network is partially maintained by a budding photographer. The plants in the offices are watered and cared for by a chef in a restaurant round the corner who probably knows more about art history now than most of our students. Those who have no practical talents can always offer to do life modelling. It doesn't happen often, but it does happen sometimes."

"The last case?"

"I don't teach evening classes, so I can only tell you about cases that colleagues have decided to pass on to me. Three months ago, for instance, one of them told me about a girl who was prepared to model to pay for her courses. I used her for some of my life classes. Still do, in fact. She'll be here at six. Worth coming to see – extraordinary hair; proud and lithe; a real gazelle."

Franck tensed.

"What's her name?"

"Rachida Tazi."

Franck bit his lip. Not a wasted visit after all.

"You're going to have to find a substitute."

Anne sat back, spreading her arms along the top of the chaise. Her eyes never left Franck's. She held a breath for a long moment, and then let it out, very slowly.

"She's one of your two murder victims?" she asked, her voice low and quiet.

Franck nodded. "Her body was found last Tuesday. A photo of the corpse fell into the hands of *Exposé*, who put it on their front cover two days ago – that's why I asked whether you read it. You might have recognised the photo. There was a similar one of Laure Sarraute the week before."

Anne nodded slightly, her eyes not relinquishing their grip on Franck's.

"I had heard of Sarraute," she commented. "Why didn't anyone tell me about Rachida?"

It was the very question Franck was about to put. She might not have been an *Exposé* reader, but Tazi had been all over the media in the last forty-eight hours. The professor's link to the victim must have been known to her students, who were unlikely to be as disconnected from current events as she clearly was.

Moreover, there was something else in her tone. A hint that her connection with Rachida was not entirely impersonal.

"You were close?" asked Franck.

"Not really," explained Anne, although not dismissively. "Still, I've been back since this morning. I must have crossed paths which someone who knew ..."

"Back?" interrupted Franck.

"Yes. From Rome. I gave a lecture at the Villa Medicis last Saturday. I stayed over for much of this week. There is something magical about Rome I find difficult to resist. I got back this morning, by the night train. I went home, washed, changed, and came here for twelve."

"Since when you've been rather busy," Franck added, remembering the timetable on the door.

"True, and none of the students I've seen are in my life class. Still, a colleague could have popped in, or left a note." She stopped, momentarily pensive. "She's been dead, what, two days? Am I the only one here who remembers her?"

"I doubt that," offered Franck. "Anyone who saw her photo is unlikely to forget her."

Anne let this statement hang in the air, as if weighing it, and then shook her head ruefully. "We have never been so assailed by images, captain. We hold onto very few of them, otherwise we probably could not continue to function. This photo would have to be something rare indeed were it to grant Rachida a form of immortality."

"Wait till you've seen it."

"You are that sure?" Anne raised an eyebrow. "Can you describe it to me?"

"I think you'd be better looking at it yourself. I suspect I have neither your eye nor your vocabulary. It's your metier, after all."

"Humour me. When did you last see it?"

Franck shrugged. "It's stuck to the wall of my office. It's in my dossier. It's on newsstands all over the city. I see it all the time."

"No you don't," insisted Anne. "It may be there all the time, but you don't look at it, you don't really see it, all the time. The eye tires of what is ever present. It is attuned to change, to novelty, to predators emerging from the still grass. Yours more than most, I would suspect. But the first time you saw it, what did you see then?"

"Before I saw the photo, I had seen the corpse," Franck pointed out. "My judgement, if not my vision, was already clouded."

"All the more interesting then. When you saw the corpse, what did you see?"

"Our failure to protect a young woman. A meticulous killer's handiwork. His signature in the form of a piece of expensive lingerie."

Anne waited a few seconds, presumably in case Franck had anything to add, before observing, "You couldn't see Rachida at all. You could only see what she had become. A victim. A bit player in a tale that wasn't her own. But what about the photo?"

Franck was about to say that he had seen Jacques Beaufort's greed for a scoop, and all the money that was about to flow from a dead girl's image, but he didn't. For he had seen something else. Or rather, he had averted his eyes from something else.

"A young woman in full possession of her body, of her beauty, of her sensuality, prepared to offer herself up, lending her being to the spectator. It was too ..." Franck paused, realising that he was talking as if Tazi had been alive when the shutter had clicked, and finding it difficult to find his words while Anne observed him so intently. "Too ... not too painful to behold, but too intimate to behold."

He breathed out heavily and fell back in his seat.

"Or something like that," he added.

"Or something   like that," echoed Anne, smiling approvingly. "You underestimate yourself, captain. For something who has neither the eye nor the vocabulary, you offer a most intriguing description indeed. I must see this photo."

"It's still on the newsstands," said Franck. "Can I ask you some questions about Rachida?"

"Of course, but as I have been talking more or less nonstop for the past four hours, would you have any objection to asking them in a neighbouring café?"

"Not at all."

They settled down inside a café at the corner of rue Bonaparte and rue Jacob. Anne greeted the owner behind the bar, the waiter moving between tables, and a fair number of the students scattered around them. She ordered a mint tea and a Perrier for herself. Franck contented himself with a simple coffee.

Before their drinks arrived, a male student came across to their table.

"Professor," he said, bowing ever so slightly as he did so, "Have you heard? Rachida Tazi – our life model – she's been killed."

Anne raised an eyebrow to Franck before replying, "I was informed a few minutes ago, Pierre. I must say, I suspect I'm still in a mild form of shock. I'm afraid this means you'll never get to draw her again. I hope you were paying attention while you had the chance."

She gestured towards Franck.

"This is captain Guerin, from the police, who is investigating her death."

The student nodded to Franck before turning back to Anne. "The life class this evening at six. Is it cancelled? Wasn't she supposed to model this week?"

"Yes she was. And no, it isn't cancelled. We'll have a substitute. A quite different subject, but worth tackling. Don't be late."

She dismissed the student, picked up her tea and drained it. Franck followed her example.

"Go ahead," she invited. "Ask your questions, captain."

"How many times did Tazi do a life class for you?"

"Tonight would have been the sixth. So that makes five."

"Did you have much contact over that period?"

Anne shrugged. "Not an awful lot. She would arrive at my office ten minutes before the class. We would chat while we walked to the room together. She generally disappeared straight after."

"She didn't hang about with the students?"

"Not after the class. I believe she had to go to work."

"Do you know what her job was?"

Anne smiled. "Are you testing me, captain, or just being discreet? She was a stripper. Which was not that surprising, given her looks, her lack of education, and her illegal status."

"She was quite open about it?"

"To me, yes. I don't think any of the students knew, though."

"What evening classes did she sign up for?"

"Art history, I believe."

"Any idea why?"

"Other than an interest in the subject?" demanded Anne.

"It has been suggested to me that she saw the Beaux Arts as a way to meet, let's say, a better class of people. A better class of man, to be more specific. Maybe she planned on using her charms to climb into a different social milieu."

"Maybe so," conceded Anne. "Art history classes are a classic bourgeois pastime. If that was her plan, it wasn't a bad one. That said, I'm not sure Rachida was quite as clear and focussed as you suggest."

"Why do you say that?"

"If she was hoping to snare a rising young executive with a weakness for dusky beauty, she must have known that she'd have to get out of stripping pretty fast as soon as the opportunity presented itself."

"And?"

"Well, based on what she told me the last time I saw her, she was planning on moving into pornography. Not a smart move, if her big idea was to become a pampered housewife in the sixteenth arrondissement."

"You told her this?" Franck queried, still trying to fathom the nature of their relationship.

"Of course not. She wasn't my student. She wasn't mine to counsel." Anne stopped suddenly, frowned, and bit the edge of her thumb. "Is there some kind of pornography connection with her death? Was she killed because she backed out? Did she sense my disapproval and end up ..."

Franck held up a hand, shaking his head. "Don't get carried away. We might not know a lot about the whys and wherefores of this case, but I'm sure you have no reason to blame yourself for what happened. For what it's worth, she didn't back out. She went through with a shoot two weeks before she was killed. With a certain Jean-Michel Rey, who seems to be quite well known in the business. The photos have not yet been published."

Anne seemed perplex. "And you're sure this Rey had nothing to do with her death? I don't know anything about the pornography business and those who lurk within it, but I'd be surprised to learn they're all angels."

"It wouldn't make sense, at least not business sense. Milking Tazi over time would have been a lot more profitable than taking one set of pictures and then writing her off."

Anne raised her hands and then let them fall, as if in surrender. She sat back in her seat. "Enough theories from me, captain. It's your enquiry. Ask away."

"How many students take your life class?"

"Eighteen are registered for it. On average, I get about thirteen or fourteen each time. As the Beaux Arts goes, that's a pretty good turnout."

"How about the art history evening classes you think she took. How many people follow those?"

"I couldn't really tell you. I've never been involved in them. I believe they are relatively well frequented, though. Maybe forty people." She paused. "Shouldn't you be writing this down?"

Franck shook his head. "I've got a fairly good memory. Eighteen plus forty."

"Fifty eight suspects already, captain? If anyone who sat in the same room as Rachida is deemed suspect, you'd better add one on."

"You?"

"Yes, me". Anne shrugged, and then gestured casually at the young people gathered around the small circular tables inside the café. "You don't really think one of my students could have done this?"

"I'm looking for someone with a heightened aesthetic sense, who takes good photos, and who knew Rachida Tazi."

"And Laure Sarraute, if I've understood correctly," added Anne.

Franck nodded.

"The Beaux Arts does have a fair number of connections with the fashion world," admitted Anne. "You're right, it makes sense to look here. What do you want me to do?"

"Can I have a list of your life class students? If any have a particular interest in fashion, photography, or both, I'd be interested to know."

"OK."

"Who should I get in touch with to get a list of those registered for the art history evening classes?"

"I can do that for you too," said Anne. "Informal channels work faster than formal ones here. But I won't be able to tell you anything else about the evening students. I've never met them."

"Doesn't matter. Their addresses, and phone numbers if possible, will do."

Anne suddenly leant forward. "I have an idea. You think the photo of Rachida was taken by the same person who took the one *Exposé* published of Laure Sarraute?"

"Everything points in that direction, yes," affirmed Franck. "Same procedure followed for delivery of the print. Same use of black and white. Same inability to tell that the girl in the photo is dead. Same attention paid to both body and lingerie."

"They're like two fingerprints, then," suggested Anne. "Artistic fingerprints. I could study the shots for you and draw up a general description of the photographer's style. Would that be useful?"

"Yes it would. Particularly if you saw any traits that reminded you of a student's work. How quickly could you do this?"

"Do you have the original prints? I could work from copies

of *Exposé*, but the quality of the originals has to be better."

"I have both prints and digital files."

"Digital?" remarked Anne. "Not a traditionalist then."

"Is that significant?" asked Franck.

"In this day and age, not really. Still, it would have been easier to track a silver nitrate buff. There're not an awful lot of them left."

"When could you do this, professor?"

"Anne. Professor is for my students, captain."

"Fair enough. In which case you might want to call me Franck."

"I might indeed," she said, smiling. "As soon as you can get the prints or the digital files to me, I'll study them. You should come along when I do so. You might learn something."

"In which case I will. When would you be available?"

"How about this Sunday?" suggested Anne. "It's the one day of the week I can go to my office and get some work done without being interrupted by students. Still, I don't want to spoil your weekend, Franck."

"Don't worry about my weekends. Until I've found this killer, they'll all be spoilt."

"Come round Sunday morning then."

"Here – at the Beaux Arts?"

"Yes. The main entrance is always open. You'll have no trouble getting in."

"This is very generous of you," insisted Franck.

"Not really," replied Anne. "I owe you. You're about to do me a big favour."

A series of tall windows ran along one wall. They began at shoulder height and ran up to a high ceiling. Through them Franck could see a building on the other side of a courtyard. The windows of its topmost floor overlooked the classroom. He could see potted plants, a few heads, one complete with shoulders – a woman with her back to him.

Anne followed his gaze.

"They have other things to do than spy on you," she

reassured him.

"I suppose they've seen better specimens too," Franck added.

"Yes indeed. Still, you're not so bad. The proportions of your face are not quite right, but your nose, eyes, and eyebrows form an arresting group. I get the feeling you have muscular legs and shapely buttocks. The rest of you is so-so. For instance, either your back is not quite straight or you have developed a bad habit of hunching forward."

Franck assumed this was neither compliment nor criticism. She was playing him back to himself. That was what she was trained to do.

Still, he found himself strangely interested in her opinion.

"I have a slight curve in my spine," he offered, although he was not sure why.

"Maybe," she replied. "What is certain is that you do nothing to combat it."

He was about to tell her that she sounded just like his mother, but didn't. Nothing suggested to him that she had children. He assumed her to be four or five years older than himself. He did not think she would be pleased to be associated with the generation that had preceded them both.

"So where do I pose?" he asked.

Anne pointed towards the centre of the room, where a low platform had been raised above the parquet floor. In both of its rear corners were wooden bistro chairs.

Franck looked at his watch. Five minutes to go, if the class started on time.

"Do I wait for them to get here before I undress?"

Anne laughed and clapped her hands.

"This is not a strip club, Franck. There is a world of difference between a nude model and an undressed body. For centuries that distinction was the only thing that allowed life studies to be executed and hung where even the most innocent eyes could see them."

She nodded towards the far end of the room.

"That door there. It's a dressing room. Leave your clothes

there. You'll find something to cover you. Come out in that."

Franck crossed over to the door she had indicated. As he pulled it open he heard the first student enter the classroom behind him. He did not turn around.

Going above and beyond the call of duty had been a characteristic of his time in the force. Given the things he had volunteered to do in the course of his missions with the DST, this was fairly anodyne. He thought of himself as a private man, but not as a shy one. That said, he had no intention of writing this up in the case notes, even though it was just a question of furthering the investigation. Anne Subrini could clearly prove a useful contact, and was worth cultivating. Nothing more.

Franck smiled wryly and shook his head. So much for lucidity.

He undressed in the cramped surroundings, which were less dressing room than cupboard. The only light was provided by a bare bulb hung over his head. There were two pegs on the wall, but he preferred to fold his clothes up and lay them on a wooden desk that had been squeezed against the back wall. He extracted the magazine from his revolver and pushed it down inside one of his shoes. He slid the gun into the middle of the pile of his clothes. He laid his watch on top of it. He was now completely naked.

On one of the pegs hung what looked at first to be a shapeless dressing gown but turned out to be a voluminous beige woollen blanket. It scratched his skin as he wrapped it around himself. He waited for a few minutes, listening to chairs scraping and conversations mixing into each other on the other side of the door. Then things quietened down and a sole voice took over. Franck took a deep breath and pushed open the door.

He emerged from the changing room, feeling the wooden floor beneath his bare soles. Not quite knowing what to do next, he stopped where he was and scanned the room. He counted twelve students on the seats gathered in a semi-circle facing Anne, who stood on the platform in the middle of the room. She was talking in a firm voice that carried to every corner.

"Most of you are still not getting the depth. Look less at the body and more at the shadows. If you get that right, the body will emerge on its own. Today we're going to do four poses, fifteen minutes each. For the first two, I want you to sketch quickly, getting the model from head to toe. For the last two, pick a detail and work it finely. OK?"

Three students replied in kind. Amongst the others there was a scattering of nods.

"We have a new model today. His name is Franck. It's his first time. Be kind."

She beckoned him over.

Franck joined Anne. She reached out and lifted the blanket from his shoulders, letting it drop to the ground behind him. She took a half step backwards and looked at him, her head tilted. Briefly – very briefly – he saw her gaze fix on his abdomen, before continuing its inspection. She leant forward and with an outstretched finger pushed his chin slightly up. She then took his right arm and draped it across his waist, placing his hand flat along his left hip.

"Step back with your right foot," she instructed. "Keep your leg straight, otherwise you won't be able to hold the pose. That's right."

She stepped off the podium.

"Fifteen minutes."

Franck could see no clock in the classroom. This was going to be a long fifteen minutes.

He observed the students, his eyes shifting slowly from one to the next. He gave the seven young men most of his attention. Three of them shared a vaguely similar look: worn or torn jeans, tight t-shirts or coloured shirts, hair that reached down to the back of their necks, unshaven faces or goatee beards. The student who had approached their table in the café was amongst them. The rest were a motley crew, their dress more flamboyant, running from tweeds to black leather trousers and jacket, their hair either cropped to nothing or longer than that of the five young women. The latter offered him the spectacle of jeans, skirts, jeans with skirts, various shades of hair and hair extensions, baggy tops and skimpy t-shirts. He was faced with an indistinguishable mosaic of youth in its early twenties. The only thing they all had in common, apart from their drawing pads, was the fact that they were white.

The students sketched diligently, their hard-backed pads balanced on an arm of a chair or propped on a knee. Their eyes washed over him, but rarely met his. He was a form, not a person, and his outline counted more for them than his regard.

Little by little, Franck's capacity to concentrate on his audience left him. His muscles began to complain. Patches of his skin itched momentarily but intensely. His breathing seemed shallow and irregular. The fingers on his left hand, which hung by his side, began to curl up. He felt his right leg begin to shake. By the time Anne clapped her hands, his eyes no longer registered the students.

"New pose," said Anne as she walked towards him. Franck brought his legs back to the vertical, bent his head way forward, and stretched his arms behind him.

"Not so easy?" she asked.

"Whatever you pay, it's not enough," he replied.

"You're just not hungry enough, that's all," she countered, her hands gently pushing and pulling him into a second pose.

Franck emerged from the cupboard, dressed once more. He moved awkwardly, his limbs still suffering from their recent ordeal.

Anne sat waiting for him on one of the chairs abandoned by the students. She had a small circular mirror in her hand and was studying her face, her handbag open on her knees.

"You spot your killer?" she asked, without deflecting her eyes.

"Well, if he was there, he'll certainly spot me in a crowd when I come to tail him," observed Franck.

"Nonsense," adjudged Anne, snapping the mirror shut and depositing it in her bag. She swivelled her eyes towards Franck, who was awkwardly sitting himself down on a nearby chair. "The people in this room saw you naked. That means they are most unlikely to recognise you dressed. Clothes are a formidable means of transformation. When we are young, what we wear hints at or magnifies our graces. When we are old it transforms our figure and hides our disgraces."

"Which category do I fall into?" enquired Frank.

"You're a good example of the fact that flaws don't just come with age. I take it that the alarming collection of scars and stitches around your stomach and groin was acquired in the line of duty? Quite recently, too, by the looks of things."

Franck nodded. "A couple of bullets that were hard to get out."

"And hard to get over, I suspect," she added. "Well, they've certainly left you with an interesting calling card. Your killer, if he was in the room today, will remember you if you tear off your clothes in the course of the pursuit. That said, so long as you keep it all under wraps, he'll see just another badly-dressed far older man."

"Far older? There're only ten years between them and me," objected Franck. "Twelve, at the most."

"For the people who were in this room, ten years is an eternity. Ten years ago they were still caught in the grip of childhood. In ten years time you'll be battling a spreading waistline and slowing limbs. Time is moving at a different velocity for you and for them."

Franck, bent over in his seat to massage his calf muscles, glanced sideways at Anne.

"I take it you weren't impressed by the show then."

Anne smiled broadly, stood up, and swept towards him, her dress alternately clinging to and releasing her legs as she did so. "*Carpe diem*. That's the only conclusion worth taking from what I just said. Let the future worry about itself. What you need right now is a walk."

"And a drink," added Franck.

"I know where we can get both."

She deposited a thick cardboard invitation into one of Franck's hands.

"The vernissage you're due at tonight?"

She nodded. "It's only ten minutes' walk from here. I think you'll make it."

"Yes, but I'm not invited, and I'm scarcely dressed for it, if what you're wearing is the general standard," Franck objected.

"As my guest, you'd get in even if you were a tramp I'd just picked off the street. Anyhow, they'll find you quite 'authentic' – which I believe is all the rage at the moment – particularly once they find out you're with the police. And if you let them see your gun they'll be in seventh heaven. Come on."

She moved towards the door. Franck levered himself out of his seat and followed.

Furthering the investigation. Nothing more.

"So what's the exhibition about?" asked Franck as they got within twenty metres of the gallery.

"It's a new show from Juliette Sollers. I don't have many protégés, but she is one. She left us five years ago and has made quite a name for herself. She's signed with a gallery in New York which – as I trust you know – is where everything happens these days. Paris, by comparison, is a tranquil backwater, a simple curiosity. However Juliette remains strangely loyal to her roots, and still insists from time to time on opening shows here."

"What does she do?" asked Franck.

"What does she do?" echoed Anne. "She's an artist. She looks closely at things and tries to reproduce what she sees. Or what she has learned to see."

"No, what I meant was, am I about to see paintings, photos, sculptures, videos, or something indescribable?"

"She's a painter. As for whether what she does is describable, you come and tell me in fifteen minutes' time."

With that Anne thrust her invitation into the hands of a young, sturdy, besuited black man standing outside the gallery entrance. She gestured towards Franck to indicate that he was with her and swept through the open door. By the time Franck followed, Anne was already caught up in a hug with a young woman wearing an extravagant ballroom dress of red organza. Given the way that all around them had stood back to admire and applaud the encounter, Franck assumed this was the artist herself.

He slipped off to his right, towards a table laden with bottles and equipped with a white-jacketed barman. He drained a tall glass of orange juice before accepting another and wandering off to cast an eye over the paintings.

There were fourteen in all, all portraits of naked mothers carrying young babies. In two cases a naked male, presumably the father, could be seen observing from one edge of the painting. It appeared that Anne's protégé was quite a traditionalist, given the verisimilitude of the portraits, and the painstaking care she had taken to reproduce skin tones and, through some artistic sleight of hand, texture.

Franck was finishing his second orange juice before one canvas when Anne appeared at his shoulder.

"Describable?" she enquired.

"Madonna and Child?" suggested Franck.

"Very good," said Anne, closing one hand around his left arm and leaning in close to him. "And as with a fair number of Madonnas, things are not quite as serene as convention or tradition would have us believe. Mary feared the Christ child's destiny. What do these mothers fear?"

"Hard to say," admitted Franck. "They all seem quite absorbed in gazing upon their offspring."

"They're not gazing, Franck," insisted Anne. "They're studying. And what they're studying is their child's skin. Who can blame them? Look at it. Look how she has caught the smooth, unsullied, moist and yielding nature of a baby's skin. It's one of the miracles of the very young – they are wrapped in a perfect material that we cannot resist, that we are driven compulsively to touch and stroke. All the more so because we know it won't last – life is waiting around the corner to scar, burn, dehydrate, crack, and blemish. These women are acutely aware of that. They just have to look at their own skin. Look how Juliette has caught how fatigue bruises, how the sun desiccates, how surgery scars, how pollution discolours, and all the other ways these mothers' skins have suffered. Little wonder that mixed in with their spellbound admiration there's a little drop of jealousy. Not to mention, at least in the paintings with the father as observer, a nascent sense of embarrassment, an unexpressed fear that what before was so embraceable – for how else was the child made? – now no longer deserves to be desired. That is what Juliette sees. Which, for one so young, is quite remarkable. I'm very proud of her."

Franck released his lower lip from between his teeth, where it had sought refuge during Anne's commentary. "I didn't see that at all," he admitted.

"Of course you didn't. You haven't sat through my courses for years on end. But you're no fool, Franck. You'll learn. Come on."

Using the hand that – as Franck was acutely aware – had never relinquished its grasp upon his arm, she tugged him into the centre of the gallery.

"Now this, Juliette, is a man who knows the difference between the quick and the dead," she proclaimed.

He left some forty minutes later, having done his best to listen politely to the inane questions which had been thrown at him once Anne had revealed his profession to all and sundry. On five separate occasions he had declined to display his service revolver, making little effort to hide the fact that he found the request at best misplaced and at worst in poor taste. He had thanked Anne for the experience and reminded her he would be back next Sunday to look over the photos. It had been an unexpected and no doubt profitable afternoon and evening, but it was time to go. He was beginning to feel like a curiosity which, if nothing else, was incompatible with the dignity of his calling.

Back on the pavement he bid goodnight to the doorman and nodded to a young woman waiting outside in a short coat from which emerged long, slender legs. She was staring at her mobile phone, perhaps willing it to ring. He began to walk away.

"Am I that hard to remember, captain?" came her voice from behind him.

He turned slowly. She had put her phone back in her pocket and cocked her head to one side.

"You're the girl with the tattoo," he said.

Sonia Delemazure clapped her hands with delight. "So I did make an impression! But wasn't I supposed to hear from you?"

It was true. Rachida Tazi's murder had waylaid Franck's investigations into Laure Sarraute's boyfriends.

"You will," he promised. "Is that what you're doing with your phone – pleading with it to make me call?"

"Don't flatter yourself," she said, albeit with good humour. "I was wondering what had happened to my date."

"Believe me, he'll come," said Franck. "You're not the kind of girl men stand up."

"You don't know his reputation. Neither the most punctual nor the most faithful of men."

At that, a taxi pulled up outside the gallery.

Franck pointed inside where a figure could be seen handing money to the driver.

"Prince Charming has arrived," he announced. "Enjoy the vernissage."

He turned on his heels but curiosity made him glance back a minute later.

Luc du Bellay had his arm around Sonia Delemazure's waist and was propelling her through the door.

<u>Saturday, 16th June</u>

Two photos.

The Eiffel Tower in the distance, softly lit in the evening sky. Franck Guerin, walking quickly from right to left in black trousers, polished shoes, a white shirt, and a black jacket. His eyes focus straight ahead.

A balcony built from carefully shaped sandstone blocks and equipped with a waist high parapet. Franck Guerin, in an open-necked white shirt, holds a glass of champagne to his lips, his hand ready to tip it back. The detail is not perfect, and it is impossible to read the expression on his face.

*

"Captain Franck Guerin," he announced. "As promised."

"Good morning captain," said Sonia Delemazure. "You know this is no time to call a girl?"

"It's eleven forty," Franck pointed out. He had been up since seven and had reached his office just after eight, walking through largely deserted streets as Paris enjoyed the first lazy morning of the weekend. "Some people would already be thinking of lunch."

"Well, just so you know the next time, eleven forty is no time to call a girl."

"In which case I apologise. Would you like me to call back at a more convenient time?" he offered.

"Ever the gentleman. You should give a few lessons to Fred. He's always waking me up, but he goes ballistic if anyone ever does it to him. Now's fine. Just as long as you've got nothing against talking to a naked woman."

"I'll keep my eyes averted," assured Franck. "How did you enjoy the vernissage?"

"A bit cruel, if you ask me. Those women did not look good. Let's hope having a child is sufficient compensation."

"I believe it is," offered Franck.

"Because you have a child?"

"I know a few women who do. There might be a very high divorce rate amongst the police, but there's a high birth rate too. Dangerous professions encourage people to secure the gene pool early on. Anyhow, it seems you didn't much appreciate your evening."

"I didn't say that. I said the exhibition made me shiver. But vernissages are always good fun – the arty people meet the fashion people meet the media people meet the money people."

"And Luc du Bellay? Where does he fit – fashion or money?"

"Both, I suspect. He must be worth a mint. Next time take a look at his shoes. Even his socks are a dead give-away."

"I don't spend a lot of time looking at people's socks."

"It's a miracle you ever catch anyone, captain. Where do yours come from?"

"My socks?"

"Yes."

"I have no idea."

"OK. How many holes do they have?"

Franck mused a little. "A few. Not enough to threaten the integrity of the sock."

"Never sleep with a man with holes in his socks. That's one of the things they teach you when you've just arrived in the big city. No man with holes in his socks has ever bought a girl a diamond necklace."

"Isn't it something you find out too late?"

"Hey, once the shoe is off, you can still say 'No'."

"Let's hope Du Bellay doesn't disappoint you."

"He didn't. I've even got one here, as a souvenir. He left early this morning. He says he's got a lot on at the moment."

"Whatever it is, let's hope he can do it sockless."

"I'd be willing to bet he's got an entire change of clothing in his office. Don't you, captain? I believe it's standard practice for men on the prowl."

"In my case, where I'm going to wake up tends to be fairly predictable. I also watch where I put my socks. They're old friends."

"Just so long as – what was it you said – their integrity hasn't been compromised?"

"Exactly." Franck paused. "Can I get to the point?"

"Sure."

"Can you give me Laure Sarraute's old boyfriends?"

"Off the top of my head, I could give you most of the names. But if you want phone numbers, that's going to be trickier."

"I have her address book. If I have the names I should be able to find the numbers."

"OK, let's think." She went silent. "What counts?"

"Sorry?"

"What counts as a boyfriend?"

"Anyone who bore the title."

"Yeah, well, there's not exactly an official ceremony."

"How about anyone you would have recognised as her boyfriend?"

"Right. So not just the guys she slept with, for instance?"

Franck exhaled noisily. "OK. Let's do two lists. The boyfriends, as you saw it, and the additional men she slept with. No, let's do three – boyfriends; casual sexual contact; regular sexual contact, but still not a boyfriend."

"The difference between casual and regular being ...?"

"Twice."

"So that's why you're a gentleman, captain. You're living in another century. Let me sit down with a pad. Can I send you an email with the results?"

"Sure. When?"

"I've got a studio shoot at five today. I'll do it before then."

"That will do fine. Thanks for your help Sonia."

"It's all in a good ... hang on, there's someone at the door."

Franck listened distractedly as Sonia dropped her mobile, presumably to put on some clothing, went quiet, distantly opened the door to her apartment, greeted a delivery man, went silent again for a while, and then came back.

"I think I've got something better than the sock now," she said excitedly.

"What?"

"I'm looking at a large purple box. Want to open it with me?"

"If you like," said Franck.

Sonia laid down her phone once more, created a lot of rustling noise, and cried out in a mixture of surprise and delight.

"Guess what it is?" she challenged, having repossessed her phone.

"Roses?" suggested Franck.

"A Midnight Sun ensemble. 85B. Just right. Shows he knows how to measure with his hands. A real professional, that Luc du Bellay."

"A real professional," echoed Franck.

*

"I wouldn't call this a smoking gun," said Yves, glasses perched on his nose as he looked down at the one page analysis of Du Bellay's finances.

Franck had knocked on his office door – Saturday being the one day the judge did not have madame Alba to protect him from distracting visitors – just before one in the afternoon, in a failed attempt to interest him in lunch. Yves had politely turned him down, announcing his intention to finish the dossier before him and then escape back to his family. True to form, he nonetheless asked Franck to give him a rapid briefing on the Sarraute case. Franck, equally true to form, had come prepared. He gave a brief account of his last visit to the *Wasp-Waisted* offices, his interviews with Rey and Subrini, his accidental acquaintance with the private life of Sonia Delemazure, and the results of Sylvie's incursion into industrial espionage.

"Remarkable information, though," continued Yves. "We should arrest people like Sylvie Thomas more often."

"As a tribe, I don't think investment bankers would react well to being arrested," observed Franck. "Sylvie's quite a unique case."

Yves looked up at him over the top of his glasses, which he wore only to read. "If my memory serves me well, you were the arresting officer. That's why Sylvie's a unique case. Had one of your arrogant and impenetrable colleagues from the DST gone in your place, I doubt she'd be helping us in this way. Quite what she sees in you, though, escapes me. Look at your shoes, for instance. A little polish would not go amiss. Not to mention the fact that I can see a hole in your sock from here."

Franck looked down at his right foot, which was resting on his left knee. Yves was right.

"You should have a talk with Sonia Delemazure. You have things in common."

"So what about this Sonia?" asked Yves. "You think she's in danger? Was this a portentous gift?"

"Normally she shouldn't be. Although her connection with du Bellay seems to be recent I suspect it is already well known in her entourage. She's not the shy and retiring type. I'd even be willing to bet I'm not the only person who'll hear of this morning's present and who it came from. If she turns up dead in it du Bellay's got to know we'd be at his door in an instant."

"In which case maybe we should accept that he is the unwitting beneficiary of someone else's acts?" suggested Yves.

"Unless ...," began Franck.

"Unless he is the killer," interrupted Yves, confident he knew where Franck was going, "and therefore deranged in some way we don't understand, and feels invulnerable, and may even have done this to play with us." He paused, before adding, "Something like that?"

"Something like that," admitted Franck.

"Well let's find out more about him," concluded Yves. "You say he's known as a bit of a playboy. Find out whether there are any dark corners to his reputation."

Franck thought of the easiest way to do so, and then shook his head.

Yves smiled. "I suspect the spectre of Catherine Vautrin has just flitted through your mind."

"It is the kind of thing the DST makes it its business to know."

"She's been asking about you," said Yves casually, as if it had slipped his mind.

"Catherine?"

Yves nodded. "Your commanding officer. I ran into her yesterday."

"How on earth do you run into Catherine Vautrin? She's not the kind of person you bump into a cocktail party."

Yves chuckled. "I think Catherine would be a challenge for even the most talented of hostesses. No, if I bumped into her, we can safely assume it was because she wanted to bump into me."

"What did she want?"

"To know how you are doing."

"She's got my number," Franck pointed out.

"But she's unlikely to use it," countered Yves. "You are *persona non grata*, after all."

"What did you tell her?"

"Never you mind," said Yves, his eyes crinkled with amusement. "However, she did tell me something you should know."

"Which is?"

"The enquiry into the Corsican incident. It's fast approaching. There are some who believe you'll make an excellent scapegoat for what went wrong."

"Including Catherine?"

"Who knows? She's not the kind of person who shares her opinions. And even if she did, what reason would we have to believe her? That said, she's not forgotten about you, Franck. So don't give up on her."

"You weren't there the last time I talked to her. Or the previous time, for that matter. It wasn't particularly encouraging. In any case, I've given up asking for favours from the DST."

"It's not a great loss. The secret files of the DST are not all they are made out to be. Particularly if you have to be able to bring a case in a court of law some day. Anyhow, nothing is worth a piece of information you gleaned yourself."

"Any suggestions how? Sonia Delemazure?"

"If she had any doubts about du Bellay, I imagine – or I can only hope – she wouldn't be seeing him. No, try your friend at *Exposé*."

"My what?"

"That nice monsieur Beaufort. If there's anything amiss, he'll surely know."

*

Franck got out the metro at Ecole Militaire and started walking towards the fifteenth arrondissement, crossing the top of the Champ de Mars. He ignored the Eiffel Tower to his right, still mulling over his impressions from the meeting he had just left at the *Exposé* offices.

Beaufort had been keen to help, and had invited Franck over that afternoon, insisting that he would take the time out from his assessment of his photographers' haul from Friday night's whirl of galas, parties, and misbehaviour. Not once did he ask Franck's reasons for taking such an interest in Luc du Bellay's social life. That said, he could not possibly have missed the implications, and was no doubt even now earmarking illustrations for the article that would accompany any forthcoming arrest.

Beaufort had confirmed that du Bellay was a regular feature at fashion shows and a standard fixture of the nightlife that fed off them. His firm was known for sponsoring events at a number of clubs whose doors remained closed to those who were not in the know. It was therefore scarcely surprising that he had crossed paths with Laure Sarraute and that he had been able to attract the attention of someone like Sonia Delemazure.

He moved in other spheres too, playing on his family name to push himself forward as one whose opinion was to be sought on business matters. A few months before he had been at the Elysée, invited along with a number of other young entrepreneurs to talk about reinforcing France's place in the luxury goods market. Beaufort had fewer images to offer of this aspect of du Bellay's life – there was not much call for paparazzi around business conferences.

The third pillar underpinning du Bellay's social existence was firmly rooted in the sixteenth arrondissement. He was a member of the Racing Club de France, and was a regular Sunday visitor to its tennis courts in the bois de Boulogne, not to mention the nearby clubhouse. When the *haute bourgeoisie* of the capital gathered itself together, he was generally to be seen in impeccable evening dress with an attractive young woman in flowing robes on his arm.

Of scandal, however, Beaufort had offered not a whiff. Aside from the frequency with which he changed girlfriends, supposing anyone took exception to that, du Bellay respected the codes of the circles in which he moved.

Franck had left *Exposé* with hundreds of images on a memory stick and a potentially embarrassing debt to its photo editor. The afternoon spent together had not brought them any closer. Franck had found Beaufort too light-hearted, too content with himself, as if he knew something that Franck did not.

When he arrived at Maryam Sehati's apartment building Franck endeavoured to thrust this uneasy feeling aside. He would not allow Beaufort to cloud his mind for the rest of the evening.

He tapped the code Maryam's assistant had given him and gained access to the marble-floored entrance of a building on avenue Charles Floquet. One street away from a direct view over the Champ de Mars, the avenue played host to a number of overseas embassies, and no doubt housed its fair share of their families. It was not an address for those of limited means.

At the end of the hall was an interphone panel with buttons for each inhabitant. Franck pushed the one marked Sehati and waited for a response.

He had to ring five times, waiting a little longer between each attempt, before he obtained a reply.

"Captain, good evening," said Maryam. "If I'm not mistaken you are on time."

Franck glanced at his watch. "I think I was when I first rang. Now I'm a few minutes late."

"Well go away and come back when you're thirty minutes late," came the reply, and the interphone went dead.

He did as he was told. He wandered over to the Champ de Mars, following its gravel paths aimlessly and dodging the occasional nocturnal jogger. He gazed alternatively at Napoleon's alma mater at one end, the classical façade of the Ecole Militaire, still home to the army's theorists, and at Gustave Eiffel's curiosity at the other, a structure for which he had the same instinctive fondness as the rest of the city's inhabitants.

He strolled past a number of tourists, mostly Japanese, dismantling portable tripods and gently storing lens of multiple dimensions in silver-sided, boxy cases. They had been there to catch the Tower's shimmering lights, ten minutes of scintillation provided every hour, on the hour, once evening fell. A few diehards remained, waiting for the next show at ten o'clock.

Franck retraced his steps and tapped on Maryam's interphone at exactly nine thirty. She replied immediately.

"Such precision, captain. You should have been an accountant."

"I lack the necessary respect for large sums of money," he said.

"How little we have in common. Third floor."

She buzzed him through. The stairs were hidden behind an unmarked door next to the lift. He walked slowly up three flights, content not to feel a single twinge. He emerged onto a wide landing that boasted four doors, two to his right and two to his left. One was slightly ajar. He moved over to it and pushed it slowly open.

"Mademoiselle Sehati?" he called softly.

"Captain Guerin," replied an unseen voice. "Do come in and shut the door. You can leave your gun on the small table to your left."

He was on the edge of a large salon, big enough to count five double sided floor-to-ceiling windows, two of which were open, providing a glimpse of the stone balustrade of a balcony. The floor was of meticulously polished herring-bone parquet, hidden at two spots by sizeable richly-coloured oriental carpets. One, to his right, played host to a four-seater canapé facing two armchairs over a low coffee table. The other, to his left, supported a dining table that could have sat eight but tonight was set for two. On the wall to his right hung five large framed black and white photos of desert landscapes. To his left were three paintings, all female nudes. An opening at the edge of the wall led off into a corridor.

At the end of it, advancing towards him, was Maryam Sehati, barefoot and dressed in black trousers and what seemed to be a dark blue man's shirt. Sitting loosely on her torso, its sleeves were rolled up to her elbows and its neck generously unbuttoned.

"Beside you," she said, as she entered the salon, pointing to a waist-high table that sat like a patient dog to Franck's left. Its mosaic surface bore a vase of orchids and a set of keys.

Franck reached inside his jacket, pulled out his revolver, ejected the magazine, and set both down on the table.

"That's better," said Maryam as she came up to him, kissing him lightly on each cheek. "As you can imagine, I feel nervous around guns."

"I wouldn't have thought you'd had much exposure to them."

"My parents carried me out of Iran in 82. I was five. I still remember the rifles of the bearded men in long robes. Probably because they were pointed at us. That's why I fight my battles with other weapons."

She took one of Franck's hands in her own and led him to the seating area to the right.

"Welcome to my home, and thank you for coming."

She released him at the canapé, into which he sank, and remained standing over him. Her gesture had surprised him. It seemed to Franck that he could still feel the soft imprint of her hand in his palm.

"I take it you do drink?" she asked.

"As a general rule, not when I'm carrying a gun. But now you've relieved me of that burden, I'll happily join you."

"Good," she said, clapping her hands and wandering briefly out of the room into what Franck took to be the kitchen. She returned with a chilled bottle of champagne and two long, thin glasses.

"Will this do?" she asked, holding the label up for inspection.

"Henriet?" said Franck. It made sense that Maryam would prefer one of Reims' most select producers. "Very well."

He stood up and reached out for the bottle. Maryam tossed it to him and he caught it tightly with both hands. He twisted off the foil cover, loosened the wire around the cork, flattened it in his hand, slipped it into a back pocket, and then used his thumb to ease the bottle open. Maryam was waiting with the glasses and had one immediately in position to catch the first drop. She handed the first glass to Franck, who then filled the one remaining in her hand.

They raised their glasses.

"To finding your killer," she proposed.

"Let justice be done," added Franck, gently touching his glass against Maryam's, his eyes on hers.

She slowly sipped at her champagne, holding his gaze as she did so. Franck followed her example, and drained half his glass. She smiled, lowered herself to the canapé, sat sideways, and motioned him down beside her.

"Now that you've accepted my invitation, can I call you Franck?"

"Of course."

"In which case there'll be no more of that mademoiselle Sehati nonsense. That's all very well for Claire, but I think you can just call me Maryam."

"Fair enough," agreed Franck. "I'm sorry I arrived empty-handed. I've had a busy day."

"Actually, that's no excuse," Maryam pointed out. "Everyone in Paris has busy days. However, I'm no great admirer of bouquets of flowers, I can't say I'd spontaneously trust your taste in wine or chocolates, and I don't think you have the means to turn up with a little something from Cartier, so you're forgiven."

She pulled both her legs up underneath her and leant back into the canapé's embrace.

"So how's the investigation going?" she asked.

"Slowly," admitted Franck. He had a decision to make about how much to share with Maryam, given he had no objective reason to trust her. Then again, Claire had said that she liked him. He also happened to be sitting in her apartment, close enough to smell her perfume. And she had taken his hand like an old friend. Or a new lover. Or maybe just a new plaything.

"I have to find a link between Rachida Tazi and Laure Sarrault," he offered. "For the moment I've got one launching a career in pornography and the other poised to sign with Ephémère."

"Sarraute was to be an Ephémère girl?" exclaimed Maryam. "I hadn't heard."

"So it seems."

"That would have been a huge leap for her – a long term, exclusive contract with international exposure. Are you looking at the jealous rival angle?"

Franck shrugged. "Would the same person feel jealous of Rachida Tazi for allowing a certain Jean-Michel Rey to photograph an erect penis lodged in every orifice she had to offer?"

"It would probably depend whose penis it was," observed Maryam. "But you're right. Although porn and fashion are beginning to mix, it remains very much a marginal phenomenon. I don't know anyone who has a finger in both pies." She sipped her champagne. "So all you've got is the lingerie – the common link is the killer's indisputably excellent taste."

"You say that almost with admiration."

"You disapprove?"

"Of course I disapprove," said Franck. "He's killed two young women."

"True," conceded Maryam. "But try to look beyond that. Look at what he has done with them. Look at the pictures he's given us."

"If he'd sent them to you rather than *Exposé*, would you have published them?"

"No, I've already told you. We don't do black and white."

"If they'd been in colour?"

Maryam waited for a while before replying. "They would have been hard to resist." She looked up at Franck. "Now you definitely disapprove, don't you?"

"I don't judge you, Maryam. But your reaction does worry me. If it's widespread – and I suspect it is – it means that unconsciously a significant number of people might feel some kind of empathy with this killer. And it's a short step from empathy to complicity."

"Whereas you, like Justice, are blind, and therefore immune to the aesthetic side of this crime?"

"I hope so," declared Franck, not realising that he had just handed Maryam her cue.

"Except, in this case," she said, leaning over and jabbing Franck in the chest with a pointed finger, "being blind is going to stand in your way. Until you can look upon lingerie the way he does, you're never going to understand this guy. Luckily for you, you have access to an undisputed expert in the field. Are you ready for your lesson?"

"Let me put this down," said Franck, placing his champagne glass on the low table, where Maryam's stood already. "Should I have brought a notebook?"

"That from a man who never takes notes? Relax, Franck, this won't hurt."

Maryam slid from her end of the canapé and knelt on the rug before him. Her fingers raced down the front of her shirt, unbuttoning it until, with a shrug, she let it fall on the floor behind her. All the time her eyes rested on Franck's. Having instinctively hunched forward towards her when she moved to the floor, he had then frozen in place.

"It is very gallant of you to gaze so steadily at my face," she remarked. "But if you are to learn anything, you will have to look a little lower."

Franck did as he was bid. Maryam's breasts were held in black diagonally-cut lace cups, out of which their upper halves proudly rose. Her perfume was stronger now, unless it was just the heightening of his senses. Or the quickening of his pulse.

"This is a *corbeille*. This is the basket –" With her index fingers she traced the edge of each cup, starting from the point where they joined the straps looped over her shoulders and ending where they met each other. "– and this is the fruit." She gently prodded each breast, her skin sinking then rebounding as she released the pressure. "It pushes the breasts up, and draws the eyes down." Her right index finger slowly slid from the centre of her collarbone down into the diminishing gap between her breasts. "It provides the décolleté required by an aggressively open shirt or plunging v-cut dress."

Franck nodded, unsure what else to say or do.

"And who made this admirable piece?" Maryam asked.

With a little difficulty, Franck found his voice. "Du Bellay?" he suggested.

"Very good. How do you know?"

"A guess," he admitted. "A pretty safe one, given the circumstances."

"Du Bellay uses very expensive French lace. His cups and panels are both remarkably supple and strong. The breasts nestle within them and are caressed into shape. This is highly unusual – most bras force the breasts into one form or another. The touch of a Du Bellay is said to be gentler than even the most considerate lover." She passed a hand, palm upwards, lightly under both breasts. The slightest of rustles could be heard in the silence of the apartment. "Du Bellay's lace is woven not just to order, but to shape, which means the threads can be as dense or as sparse as required. This allows a whole host of subtle effects, teasing and directing the eye. For instance, my breasts are not as big as you currently believe them to be. Much of that is engineering – the structure pushing them into the centre of your gaze – but some of it is patterning. The observer's eyes do what the Du Bellay wants – a trick made easier by the fact that it generally coincides with what the observer wants to see and to believe. As for my nipples – " She arched backwards ever so slightly. "– you cannot see them, for the pattern clusters around them, but you cannot mistake their exact position. The lace thickens at this point so that whatever their current state, you will believe them erect and impatient."

She reached out, caught Franck's right hand by the wrist, and cupped it around her left breast. Franck's fingers were rigid, straining away from the fabric. She held his hand until they relaxed, melting into place.

"As you touch you feel a fragile surface, the narrowest of barriers between you and me, so sheer that the heat of your palm and that of my body pass through it unchallenged. It is said there is no need to remove a Du Bellay when making love. It becomes the flesh it enhances."

With that Maryam rose gracefully. Franck's palm remained as it was, immobile, bereft, as she buttoned up her shirt.

"Stay there," she commanded, and stalked from the room.

Franck did as he was told, recovering the mastery of his hand and pushing himself back into the canapé. Inappropriate interaction with parties of interest in an investigation. There were rules against it – in the DST rulebook, in any case. He had never checked to see if the Brigade Criminelle applied the same constraints. Then again, the definition of inappropriate was always open to interpretation. Intimacy in the pursuit of information was an arm the DST had been known to deploy. Or maybe it was just an excuse that agents offered up when caught.

Ten minutes or so went past. Franck got up, wondering whether there was a problem. He had taken a few uncertain paces when Maryam returned. She had abandoned the shirt for a tight black t-shirt whose scooped neck offered a generous view of the curved tops of her breasts.

"Back there," she commanded, pointing to the sofa.

Franck sat back down as Maryam once more kneeled before him.

"Well?" she asked.

Franck said nothing for a few seconds, and then offered, "Smaller?"

"Not exactly," Maryam corrected. "Rounder. You are looking at two perfect half-spheres, and you are no longer looking at the gap between them."

She expertly lifted the t-shirt over her head in one smooth movement, shaking out her hair as it came free.

"This is a *balconnet*. It holds the breasts up and only nudges them together. It creates a perfect equilibrium – one side resembles the other; what is above is equal to what is below." Her hands glided from right to left and from top to bottom, hovering over her breasts, to illustrate the point. "It provides a more stately décolleté, while recalling the budding and gravity-defying breasts of a teenager. Both prim and perverse, you might say. Particularly this model."

The bra she was now swivelling lightly under Franck's nose, as she slowly twisted at the waist, was once more black. This time, however, it was a solid black. Its half cups and plain straps threw off a glossy sheen.

"This is a Longford. It possesses the flesh. The fabric is a smooth as silk – see how clearly my nipples are outlined – but taut and elastic. Wearing a Longford is like having two strong proprietary hands gripping you. It keeps you on edge, but ensures an impeccable profile. If a Du Bellay is a lure to seduce, a Longford is an arm to dominate. Touch me." She once more took Franck's right hand and drew the palm alongside her left breast. This time he put up no resistance. "See – nothing moves. A Longford produces a marble-breasted Amazon."

Franck retrieved his hand and nodded.

"Remember this – a *balconnet* nudges the breasts into shape, whereas a *corbeille* pushes them. You may also come across a third category, which the Americans have taught us to call a push-up, which squeezes them. Maybe you should be taking notes after all?"

"Nudges, pushes, squeezes," Franck recited dutifully. "I'll remember."

"Now, if you will excuse me, I will change for dinner. You may mull over what you have learned."

With that she left the room.

For a while, Franck just stayed where he was on the canapé, absorbing what had just happened. He found Maryam impossible to read. With most women, what she had just done could be construed as an invitation to follow her to her bedroom, which he imagined vast, luxurious and enticingly close to where he sat. She, however, had seemed quite serious in her determination to impart to him a basic understanding of different forms of lingerie. Which was not to say she had not taken great pleasure in surprising and destabilising him. He suspected she was fully capable of helping him and playing with him at the same time. He was the detective, after all. It was up to him to work out her true intent.

And what it meant for the case. There was, after all, a difference between what he had just experienced and what had gone on in the two fatal hotel rooms. When Maryam had placed his hand against her breast its heat could be sensed, as could the distant shudder of her heart. Had the killer done the same he would have encountered icy silence, having leached the life from his lingerie-clad beauties.

Franck poured himself some more champagne and got up, wandering over to the open windows and out onto the balcony. The street was quiet, as befitted a neighbourhood known for its diplomatic discretion. A large black car was emerging from an underground garage to his left. Across from it, leaning against a lamppost, stood a tall figure in a bulky jacket with a shapeless bob on his head. His jacket was open, letting Franck glimpse what looked like the end of a long camera lens. He seemed to be watching the car complete its manoeuvre into the street. Its windows were tinted: the paparazzi's curse. He wondered whether this was one of Beaufort's envoys, frustrated in his mission to capture an illicit couple.

That aside, there was nothing to see. Not even a dog being walked. This was a neighbourhood that kept its evenings indoors.

"I cannot believe you find more to admire out there than in here," came Maryam's voice.

Franck returned to the salon. Maryam stood alongside the table on the opposite side of the room from the canapé. She had a circular tray poised on one hand from which she was transferring a series of small white bowls to the tabletop. When she had finished she looked up at him.

"Be seated," she commanded.

She had bound up her hair in a chignon and changed into a simple black cocktail dress revealing her knees, her collarbone and the long sweep of her arms. Her legs sported seamed stockings and a pair of insubstantial stilettos showcased her feet. Each wrist bore a collection of thin, slightly twisted, bracelets. They jostled each other gently, sliding backwards as she raised one arm to beckon Franck towards her.

She indicated his spot as he neared the table and slid around to place herself on the opposite side.

"This is where you say something flattering about my dress," she indicated.

"It's very classy," offered Franck. "Goes with the neighbourhood."

"Indeed it does. And, like the neighbourhood, it appears positively demure but has its secrets. It is, of course, an original."

"Of course," echoed Franck. "An original what?"

"Chanel, 1958. This dress is older than me. There's a little boutique in the Palais Royal that sells vintage models like this."

"It's aged well."

"How very true. Which can't be said for many dresses. Or for those who wear them."

"You're a long way from having to worry about that."

"At last!" cried Maryam, triumphantly. "A compliment! I was beginning to wonder whether you found me strangely hideous. I was about to suggest a good optician."

She reached over to a bottle of wine that stood already open, its cork beside it, on one side of the table. She filled half a delicately-stemmed glass for Franck before serving herself.

Franck lifted his glass.

"To a young woman in an old dress," he said.

"May the reverse never come to pass," she replied.

Franck took a sip of his wine and then stopped. He held the glass before his eyes.

"This is an excellent wine," he observed, turning the glass by the stem and watching its contents slowly rise and fall.

"Not all the finer things are wasted on you, then," commented Maryam. "Côte Rôtie, 95."

"From your cellar?" asked Franck.

Maryam laughed. "From my traiteur. Who has the time – or the faith in the future – to build up a cellar these days?"

"You should meet Yves de Chaumont," said Franck. "He'd change your mind."

"Ah, monsieur *le juge*, my courteous correspondent – yes, I should, and I'm counting on you, Franck, to organise that."

"I'll do what I can," said Franck. "But he's a busy man."

"And a particularly wise one," she commented. "Or so it seems to me. A worthy choice of mentor."

"I'm not sure I'd call him that."

"Too proud to do so?" challenged Maryam. "If wily Odysseus thought that his own son should have one – more to the point, if there is someone upon whom even I would confer such a title – someone whose judgement I have never known to be wrong, and whom I trust and admire without reserve – why shouldn't you?"

"It's not that," insisted Franck. "I've only been working for Yves for two weeks. I've worked with him on a number of occasions before, but this is the first time I've actually been under his command. That said, you're probably right – there is a lot I could learn from him."

"Of that I have no doubt. He, for one, would surely already have expressed delight, wonder and curiosity about all this." She swept her hands over the multitude of ceramic bowls that sat to one side of their plates. "Having first, of course, spontaneously paid homage to my beauty and my choice of wine."

"So I score one out of three?"

"I count on you being a quick learner. We'll see how much better you do next time."

"I promise to try harder."

"I will hold you to that," she insisted, her voice serious although her eyes were not. "But first, let me give you a first taste of my homeland. Every dish on this table represents a little piece of Persia."

"Memories of your childhood?" asked Franck.

"Memories of my traiteur's childhood," she corrected. "My mother always had a weakness for French cuisine."

And so they ate, with Maryam explaining the dishes as she served Franck a portion from each bowl.

She quizzed him on his past. Franck offered up the basic facts: his studious youth, his military service with the Chasseurs Alpins, the sense of vocation that took him into the police against everyone's expectations, a vague description of his time at the Direction de la Surveillance du Territoire, and an even vaguer account of his temporary transfer to the Brigade Criminelle. She did not push for detail, letting him decide what she should or should not know.

When her turn came, she chose the opposite approach, flooding Franck with a anecdotally-rich account of her family's flight from Iran, their arrival in Paris, her father's business dealings, her two brother's dutiful careers and even more dutiful marriages, her own chaotic studies and career, all leading up to her decision to publish *Wasp-Waisted*, and its current success.

"Not that it's making any money," she clarified. "But it is making its mark, and in time that will be worth a fortune."

They had both finished eating. Or rather, she had finished

ferrying food to Franck's plate and, on occasion, directly into his mouth. She had scarcely touched the rare portions she occasionally placed before herself.

"Ready for the final lesson?" she suddenly asked, pushing back her seat and getting to her feet.

"I didn't realise there was to be another one," admitted Franck, as he watched Maryam circle the table towards him.

"I'll need your help this time," she murmured, and extended her arms, bracelets gently clashing. Franck raised his hands to meet hers and let her draw him from his seat. Her playful smile, with which he was now familiar, was back on her face.

She turned her back to him, her delicate neck exposed beneath her bound-up hair.

"Unzip me," she said.

With clumsy fingers, Franck did as he was told, locating the top of the zip in the heavy fabric of her dress and drawing it downwards, slowly but steadily.

"Thank you," said Maryam, "I can see you've done this before."

She turned back to him, pushing the dress off her shoulders as she did so. It hovered precariously for a moment until she shrugged, sending it down her arms, over her hips, and to the floor. Delicately she stepped out of it and stalked to the centre of the room, one hand leading Franck behind her.

Her torso was clad in a fine semi-transparent weave of dark thread that swelled over her breasts, followed the contour of her ribs, and hugged her waist tightly. Thin straps raced over her shoulders and fed into a darker framework that traced a path down her sides, under her breasts, and across her stomach. Silver threads followed this frame with tightly undulating curves, before bursting out into delicate foliage that ran from her left hip to her right breast. Scallop-edged straps descended from the bottom of the garment, stretched taught under a pair of similarly decorated panties, to grip the top of her stockings.

Maryam turned slowly on her toes, her arms held away from her body.

"This is a *guêpière*," she announced. "A busy little piece, that has to support the bust, flatten the stomach, tighten the waist, and hold the stockings." She used her fingertip to trace each element as she described its role. "Unlike the corset, which works by brute force, dominating the body it moulds, a *guêpière* must be both light and strong. It's like a ballerina's partner, the strength behind the grace. Always behind, though. Never before."

She stepped right up against Franck and leant into him, her arms circling behind his back, her head tucked alongside his neck.

"You feel that?" she whispered into his ear. "That's me. If I were wearing a corset, what you would feel would be the corset."

She leant back, moving her hands up and linking her fingers behind his neck, arching her spine and looking into his eyes.

"It all has to mean something, Franck," she said. "That's why you have to learn to decode these things. Rachida Tazi was not wearing a corset. She was not bound and left to die. She was wearing something designed to flatter and seduce. She was looking her best. Her last appearance was to be one that nobody could ever forget."

She let her fingers slip past each other, stood up straight, and folded her arms under her breasts, studying Franck from beneath quizzical eyelashes.

He did not respond, his eyes lost in the lingerie she wore and his thoughts in a distant hotel room.

Maryam leant towards him once more, her cheek brushing his and her lips close to his ear.

"Time for dessert, I think," she whispered.

Sunday, 17th June

One photo.

The arched entrance to the Ecole Nationale Supérieure des Beaux Arts, its wooden doors pulled back, offering a glimpse of the cobbled inner courtyard. A solitary figure emerging from it, in dark blue trousers and a similarly coloured shirt, with no jacket. Franck Guerin carries his faithful leather briefcase, holding it slightly behind him, as if it contained state secrets he was sworn to protect.

*

Anne Subrini had a small, chunky glass in her hand when she opened her office door. She was the first living soul Franck had seen since he had walked through the open gates of the Beaux Arts. Anne had been right about Sundays creating an oasis of tranquillity within its walls.

She wore a blue and white striped top, dark blue trousers cut off just above her ankles and a pair of sandals. Her hair was bunched behind her head, held in place by two delicate skewers of wood. She leant against the door frame, smiling at Franck.

"I hope you weren't expecting me to be all dressed up?" she said.

Franck shook his head. In a sense he had: their last encounter had left him with an indelible image of Anne in her silver-grey dress.

"Just as well you didn't," he said. "I can't say I made much of an effort myself."

Anne laughed, gazing at Franck like a mother with a wayward child.

"No-one could mistake you for a honey-tongued flatterer, Franck," she observed.

Franck smiled and shrugged his shoulders. However, he knew better than to correct his words. She was teasing him. Without malice.

"Come in and join me in some sparkling water."

Franck stepped into the office. Anne gestured towards the pair of leather armchairs that sat before the windows. As Franck sat she filled a new glass from a bottle of San Pellegrino on her desk and brought it over to him.

"Thanks," said Franck, laying the glass on the floor beside his armchair and hoisting his briefcase onto his knees.

"Drink it," instructed Anne, pointing to the abandoned glass. "Hydration keeps the skin young. Even losing battles have to be fought."

Franck retrieved his glass, drained its contents, and held it up for Anne to inspect.

"Good boy," she said, sitting in the other armchair. "How's your weekend going?"

"Yesterday was busy, but I'm hoping things will calm down today. How about yours?"

"Quite the reverse – it's been quiet, but I think it's about to get quite hectic. One thing I have done, though, is get you the lists you wanted."

She returned to her desk to retrieve a beige cardboard folder and laid it on the coffee table beside the armchairs.

"Names and contact details of the students in my life class," she explained. "The same for the art history evening class Rachida took – or at least, registered for. I've talked to the professor who taught it, and he says that her attendance was patchy. After the first few classes she rarely came at all."

"Thanks," said Franck, drawing the folder towards him with an outstretched finger. He opened it to study the two sheets of paper inside: 18 names on one, 36 on the other. The address given for Tazi corresponded to her flat in the seventeenth arrondissement. Those of the other participants in the evening class were scattered all over Paris, plus a few from the suburbs. None of the names were familiar to him.

"Thank me if they turn out to be useful," said Anne. "Now, I believe you have something to show me."

Franck pulled out two large envelopes, extracted the prints of Sarraute and Tazi received by *Exposé*, and handed them over. Anne laid them down side by side on the low table in front of her.

"These, we are assuming, are the killer's shots. Printed on high quality photographic paper from digital images. Three thousand DPI. No sign of flash ..."

"Shhh," said Anne, quietly but insistently. "I'm looking."

Franck lapsed into silence and waited. Anne hung over the two photos for nearly ten minutes, occasionally sipping from the glass in her hand. Franck watched her, her brow tilted forward, her eyes making slow sweeps within each image and then rapid jumps between the two. The open neck of her striped top hung forward, offering distracting glimpses of her collarbone and an edge of white lace. At one point she stretched out her hands and swapped the two photos over, only to resume her silent inspection.

Finally she sat back in her seat, finished off her glass of water, and let her gaze drift up to meet Franck's.

"Definitely the same photographer," she announced. "And a singularly talented one, too. I reckon he had a lot of time at his disposal. Both pictures were taken with the available light, so he probably ran through a whole series of apertures, discarding every shot but these. The images are steady – given the exposure time necessary with natural light he must have been using a tripod."

"Do you think the subjects were dead when the pictures were taken?"

"Hard to say. If they had been breathing normally, I think we would have seen it. Since the breasts echo and exaggerate the expansion and contraction of the lungs, there might have been a blur around the edge of the cups. A slight blur, but a blur all the same. That said, if their breathing was very shallow – in deep sleep, for instance – it would probably leave no trace." Anne paused. "Can I ask how they were killed?"

"You can," said Franck. "But I can't tell you."

"No external damage, clearly," commented Anne.

Franck nodded. "Clearly. That's as much as I can say."

"However it was done, it looks like a very gentle death. There is not a hint of suffering in these photos. Quite the opposite, in fact. I would say the photographer was trying to suggest a form of omnipotent ease."

"Omnipotent?"

"These are very sensual images. Both women are a flawless example of a particular physical type. Sarraute is the busty beauty, a fertile wonder crafted by Mother Nature herself. Tazi is the lithe Amazon, whose bone structure and taut skin, rather than curves, are the source of her attraction. That's probably why she's wearing a *guêpière*, a far more overt statement of femininity than Sarraute's bra. It softens her androgynous side. But neither piece of lingerie looks like an imposition. Each woman seems completely at ease, as if the lingerie were a second skin. And yet it clearly is nothing of the sort. This is the most expensive, the most artfully contrived lingerie money can buy. They couldn't be more underdressed, nor more artfully clothed. That's where the overwhelming sense of power comes from. Here you have two women apparently slumbering, two Sleeping Beauties dressed to entice and snare. It is the helplessness, the seeming passivity, that renders them irresistible – you cannot help but look; you cannot help but desire. The onlooker – traditionally the one with all the power, with the divine right to look where he chooses – is transformed, deprived of his capacity to choose. When he looks at these, his reaction may be one of admiration, reverence or lust, but it cannot be indifference. So what we have here, paradoxically, are photos of tyrants at the height of their powers."

"That's a strange way to describe a pair of murder victims," objected Franck.

"The murder is not in the photo," insisted Anne. "The murder is the context you supply when you tell me who it is and how she was found."

Anne paused, directing her gaze once more at the images. When she looked up it was to add, "Ironically, having said that, the murder may be what made these images possible. It provided the abandonment of slumber without sleep's unpredictable inconveniences – the sudden moves, the unfortunate or absurd rearrangements of the limbs. Insofar as these images were staged – and they are clearly the fruit of artifice and not of natural hazard – then murder, or at least very powerful sedation, may have been a precondition of success."

"So I'm dealing with an artist?" said Franck.

"I'm afraid so. A worshipper of beauty whose devotion knows no limit."

"Which suggests the Beaux Arts is a good place to look."

The solemnity of Anne's face was broken by a rueful smile.

"Not one of my students could have taken these photos. Not one. And if any other student of this institution was capable of doing so, I'd have heard about it, believe me."

"The evening classes?"

"Amateurs, idlers and dilettantes, I fear."

"So what do I do? Sweep the garrets of the Latin Quarter for some unrecognised genius?"

"I would be very much surprised if someone this good has gone unnoticed," said Anne, rubbing her fingers in small circles at the side of her eyes, as if to drive away sudden fatigue. "Look to those who have published or exhibited, not those who are languishing unknown."

"If I was a killer in the habit of taking photos of my victims, I might be given to discretion or tempted to keep my talents to myself," objected Franck.

"This one sends his work to *Exposé*. How shy and retiring is that?"

Anne scooped up the two photos, slid them back into their envelopes, and tendered them to Franck.

"I take it I don't get to keep them?" she enquired.

Franck shook his head, sliding them back into his briefcase, along with the folder she had given him. "I'm afraid not. Can I ask you to look at some other images?"

"Suspected handiwork of your killer?"

"I wouldn't say that. Just other things that have come up in the course of the investigation. I'd like to have your initial reaction – whether you think they're connected at all with what you've just seen."

Anne shrugged. "Go ahead."

Franck retrieved a thick folder from the briefcase, unhooked the elastic strings that kept it shut, and passed it over to her. She extracted a wad of sheets, each bearing a poor reproduction of a colour shot. She flicked quickly through them, her brow creased, stopping around half-way.

"This is pornography," she commented. "Pure and simple. Actually, not pure at all, let's just say simple – too much light, too little shadow, not a shred of creativity. I can see it's Rachida Tazi. That said, it's not the same girl as your killer's photo. Not even close."

"What do you mean?" asked Franck.

Anne chose a sheet at random and held it up to him. "This could be anyone Franck. Anyone with four limbs, breasts and a vagina."

"Nothing about the photography that links it to the *Exposé* shot?"

"Quite the opposite. Whoever did this could not have taken the *Exposé* shot," insisted Anne, thrusting the pile back at Franck.

Franck took it and hid it from sight. "You ready for one more?"

"Depends," said Anne. "Does it get worse?"

"No, this is definitely a step up from Jean-Michel Rey."

He extracted the copy of *Wasp-Waisted* he had borrowed from the Du Bellay offices and handed it to her. She gave the cover an appraising glance, raised her eyebrows, and settled back into her armchair.

"*Wasp-Waisted*," she read aloud. "What can you tell me about this?"

"It's a high-end publication dedicated to lingerie shots. Published in colour four or five times a year. Only available by subscription. Seems to be something of an industry bible."

"The upmarket segment of the industry," commented Anne, leafing through the pages. "I doubt much of this stuff features in your average neighbourhood lingerie store."

"That's what interests me," admitted Franck. "I have two victims artistically killed in expensive lingerie. I have a publication dedicated to attractive young women artistically draped in expensive lingerie. Makes you wonder ..."

"You think whoever did the one reads the other?" suggested Anne.

"Or works for, or publishes, or whatever," continued Franck. "What I really need to know is whether you think there's any similarity between the images."

"You mean the same photographer?"

"Not necessarily. Just the same sensibility. That'd be a start."

"At first glance, I can see why you're asking the question," admitted Anne, having paged to the end of the magazine. "I'd like to take a longer look at this. You have any more?"

Franck nodded. He retrieved the February 2003 copy Maryam had given him.

"This was the first issue of the magazine," he passed it to Anne. "It features Laure Sarraute. Page 8 and following."

Anne slowly turned the pages until she reached the images of Sarraute.

"A younger Laure," she mused. "Not quite the beauty she was to become. Not quite, but what promise ..." She tailed off. "How did you get these?"

"One from a subscriber, the other from the publisher."

"Suspects?" asked Anne.

"I wouldn't say that."

"What would you say?"

Franck did not have to cast about for a phrase. It lay where he had left it the previous evening. "Parties of interest in the investigation."

Anne slid the second copy of *Wasp-Waisted* on top of the first and set them down on the coffee table. Her gaze hovered over them, her eyes lost in thought.

Then they suddenly snapped up and fixed on Franck's.

"Am I at risk?" she asked.

"Sorry?" said Franck, not understanding the question, and surprised by the edge of anxiety in her voice. Her Olympian calm and confidence was perhaps not as all-encompassing as he had begun to assume.

"Does anyone know I'm analysing the photos? It's just I'd rather not end up in *Exposé* myself, trussed and dead on an anonymous bed. It's a publication I've never liked."

"You've got nothing to fear," insisted Franck. "Nobody knows you exist."

"I'd prefer it if you keep it that way," insisted Anne.

"Don't worry. You're my secret weapon."

*

Franck drained his coffee and slid the plastic goblet into the stack he had been building up all afternoon.

On reaching his office – the only living presence in the corridor on this Sunday afternoon – he had found an email from Sonia Delemazure, sent the previous day. It contained her list of Sarraute's male friends: four official boyfriends, three men she had frequently slept with without according them any particular title, and nine one-offs, although Sonia had appended a note insisting that there could have been others that Laure had not confessed to her. She had provided phone numbers for all the boyfriends and one of the regular partners; for the others she could only furnish names and a description of their profession, which generally had nothing to do with the fashion industry.

Franck recognised none of the names. None of them subscribed to *Wasp-Waisted*. None were students in Anne Subrini's life class. Feeding them into the standard databases revealed two potential incidents of possession (both one-offs) and one of disorderly contact (one of the boyfriends). None of them had registered for the evening class Tazi had briefly attended.

He laid the boyfriends aside. He turned to the life class students, dutifully checking them out despite what Anne had said about them lacking the necessary photographic gifts. He checked for criminal records, coming up blank, and added them to his case database alongside the *Wasp-Waisted* subscribers. Data was never worthless – one of the DST's mantras. A bell would ring if any mention of them ever came up again.

Franck turned to his last list, the art history evening class, and started running their names. He came up with no criminal pasts. None were *Wasp-Waisted* subscribers either.

He then started calling their numbers, but managed to talk to only twelve of them, a sunny Sunday afternoon not being the best time to catch people on the phone. The exchanges rarely lasted more than five minutes, enough to explain who he was and why he was phoning, and ask for their recollections of Tazi. A few had no memory of her. Others talked of a slim North African girl who seemed way out of her depth, and whose attendance quickly became infrequent. None could recall her striking up any particular attachment with another member of the class.

He checked off those he had talked to, which left 25 still to go. He laid down his telephone, only then realising how numb his right ear felt, and switched his attention back to his computer. He retrieved the USB stick Jacques Beaufort had given him the previous day and started looking through the collection of photos of Luc du Bellay taken from the *Exposé* archives

He was well past the hundred mark – arched forward, his fists balled against his mouth, his gaze on the screen – before he realised how much his back hurt, not to mention the complaints from his eyes. Telling himself that he was more than half-way through the task helped him to ignore the signs of discomfort. In any case, if it persisted he had an ample supply of painkillers to hand.

Franck scanned each image, looking at every face, attempting to bludgeon his brain into spotting something significant about the women du Bellay frequented. Thus far all he could say was that du Bellay liked his women young and pretty, although he was not averse to sharing laughs or polite smiles with elderly matrons, provided they were sprinkled with gems or wore extravagant gowns.

Twice a tremor of excitement ran through him when he spotted Laure Sarraute in the same frame as du Bellay, but they were never in close proximity, and the shots came from fashion events they both had good reason to attend.

A fair number of the photos Beaufort had provided came from Du Bellay shows, allowing Franck to test his eye on different sets of lingerie, trying to sift the *corbeilles* from the *balconnets*. He felt little confidence in his ability to do so, but was pretty sure he had spotted the Midnight Sun collection when featured alongside a waving du Bellay on a catwalk.

He glanced at his watch, sighed, and called up the next photo.

Yet another lingerie show, with du Bellay holding court in the foreground, surrounded by a knot of dark-clad men and women, while three models pivoted in undergarments on a raised stage behind him. Franck dutifully scanned the group of admirers, drew nothing from it, and moved on to the next image. The exact same shot, only with a closer focus, beaming in on du Bellay, cutting out much of the crowd, and including only one of the models in the background. He moved on once more, only to find himself a few seconds later in the same event, the photographer having zoomed in exclusively on du Bellay's animated face and raised hand. Franck's index finger automatically moved to click the next photo into view but instinct froze it in place. Something familiar was missing.

He displaced his mouse to the controls at the bottom of his screen in order to move backwards rather than forwards.

That was what was missing: Rachida Tazi in a dark blue and green ensemble, poised on her lean, strong legs on the stage behind du Bellay.

He sat up straight in his seat and spooled back to the first of the images from this particular event. This time he advanced more slowly and caught a first glimpse of Tazi, albeit from behind, a few photos in. He continued, winding through another twelve images without seeing anything new until he spotted another familiar face: Sonia Delemazure, one hand accepting a glass from du Bellay while the other shot off in the opposite direction, out of the frame.

Franck hopped to the next photo, only to find a close-up of Delemazure. He noticed she was wearing a strapless top, although the slightly blurred shot failed to catch the exact contours of her shoulders. Franck clicked again and was rewarded with a wider angle. Du Bellay featured once more on the left, dispensing what was probably champagne. Sonia stood dead centre, a link in a chain of moving glasses. To the right, hand outstretched to receive the second glass Sonia bore, stood Laure Sarraute.

Franck clicked the right side of his mouse, calling up a block of information about the photo. If nothing else, at least Jacques Beaufort had introduced him to the concept of metadata. He skipped line after line of useless facts and numbers until he found the date on which the photo had been taken.

Six months ago. Sarraute, Tazi, du Bellay, Delemazure: same time, same place.

He needed to know more. He reached for his telephone.

*

"Try the tropical juice cocktail," insisted Sonia. "It's freshly squeezed and the mix is terrific."

Franck had been planning on asking for a coffee in the hope it would wash away the taste of those he had thrown back all afternoon, but he was not about to spurn Sonia's advice. He nodded to the waiter who hovered attentively beside the two of them.

"Same for me," said Sonia. The young man in an impeccable white shirt, short black jacket and matching bow tie nodded, folded his silver tray under his arm, and turned on his heels.

"I so love the Raphael," confided Sonia. "So stuffy, yet so chic."

"I'll take your word for it," said Franck.

A modestly sized luxury hotel adrift on an otherwise

anonymous stretch of avenue Kleber, Franck knew the Raphael as a haunt for diplomats attending meetings in a conference centre just across the road operated by the Ministère des Affaires Etrangères. He had participated in a couple of delicate operations in and around its walls, but he was not about to explain to Sonia that he could, if required, take her on a guided tour of its service corridors.

They were sitting in a corner of its lobby bar in armchairs so low and so deep that Franck refused to do more than perch on the edge of his. Sonia had collapsed into hers, as if exhausted by her day, so that Franck's eyes had to graze across her extended legs and bare thighs before meeting her face.

"Thank you for seeing me so quickly," he said. "Particularly since it's a Sunday. I'll try not to make a habit of muscling into your day of rest."

"Day of rest?" Sonia snorted. "Four hours ago I was caked with make-up and stalking across the flagstones of La Défense in thigh-high boots."

"What on earth were you doing at La Défense? It's a ghost town on a Sunday."

"Which makes it the perfect day for photo shoots with all those glass facades glistening behind you," explained Sonia. "Anyhow, when you called we'd just finished. It was either meet you or go drinking with a bunch of bitchy assistants, make-up girls and young women of my scandalous profession."

"They sound more fun than me."

"Sure, but you're more exotic. So, what's happened? You got him?"

"I've got something for you to look at. Here."

Franck handed over the print he had made from Beaufort's collection of images. Having failed to find a printer at the Brigade Criminelle capable of producing a decent quality reproduction, he had been reduced to using a coin-operated printing booth in the metro. As a result the print was smaller than he would have liked, but at least it was sharp and clear.

Sonia curled forward from her recumbent position to

retrieve the photo.

"That's Luc," she said. "And me. And Laure."

"December last year," said Franck. "What was the occasion?"

"Luc was showing his collections for some charity. Breast cancer, I think. There was a big party afterwards. Laure was invited. She dragged me along. There were a lot of business types – severe suits, straight from the office – whereas we were all dressed to party. Not a bad night, though – good champagne and decent music. Luc's events are always very well done. He's known for that."

"Ever seen this girl before?" asked Franck, pointing to the stage behind Luc du Bellay.

Sonia peered once more at the photo and shook her head.

"No. Quite a looker, though. See how she carries herself? She's got tiny tits, yet she's pulling off a lingerie show – quite a feat."

"You're sure you don't recognise her?" insisted Franck.

Sonia made a show of looking once again.

"I'm sure," she announced.

"It's Rachida Tazi," said Franck. "She was on the cover of *Exposé* last week."

"The second victim?"

"The second victim," repeated Franck. "So in this photo I have the first victim, the second victim, and the man who made the lingerie they both died in."

"And me," added Sonia.

"Exactly," said Franck. "I'm not sure it's a good time to be getting close to Luc du Bellay."

"You're joking!" she protested, sitting backwards and frowning at Franck. "You can't possibly think he's the killer! Have you ever met Luc du Bellay?"

"Have you ever met a killer?" countered Franck. "They come in all shapes and sizes. This one dresses his victims in the finest lingerie money can buy. What kind of present has du Bellay been giving you recently?"

"He gave me one of his company's products. If he made

upscale perfume, I expect he'd have given me some of it. Come on! He wouldn't be that stupid! A killer who drapes his victims in what his own firm is famous for? You disappoint me, captain."

"I'm just asking you to be careful," insisted Franck.

"It's not in my nature. I take it you don't want me to tell Luc about all this – you and your crazy suspicions?"

"I'd rather you didn't. When will you next see him?"

"Tonight. We're having dinner here. I believe he's even booked a room. We've both got a soft spot for the Raphael."

"What are you wearing?" asked Franck.

"You can see what I'm wearing," said Sonia, with a puzzled tone, pointing towards her silky blouse and short skirt.

"No. Not that," insisted Franck. "Underneath."

Sonia paused, glancing unconsciously at herself.

"What do you expect – it's our first date since he sent it to me." she said. "It would be ungrateful not to. And I look great in it."

Franck lapsed into silence, considering his options. Their tropical cocktails arrived. Sonia drained hers in the time it took Franck to make up his mind.

"I'll make you a deal," he said. "Don't drink any champagne, that's all I ask."

"Why?" she asked.

"Never mind why. Can you promise me that?"

"Why should I?" she demanded, petulantly.

"To keep an old man happy."

"That would be you?"

"That would be me," he confirmed.

She sighed and shook her head, mixing scorn with what might have been a hint of affection.

"OK," she said. "I promise."

"Good," said Franck. "One other thing."

"What about 'that's all I ask'?" she objected.

"This doesn't involve any sacrifice. Just something we agree on."

"What?"

p.191

"If for any reason you're frightened, or something seems wrong, open one of the windows of your room."

"Isn't that a bit cloak and dagger? Wouldn't I be better picking up a phone and calling the front desk?" said Sonia, irritation once more infusing her voice.

"You wouldn't use the phone unless you were really convinced something was wrong. By that stage, believe me, you wouldn't be able to get anywhere near it."

"So what will happen if I open a window?"

"Nothing. Keep that in mind – nothing will happen, so there's no reason not to do it. If the slightest thing is said or happens that makes you uneasy, don't hesitate – just wander over to one and open it. It's a warm evening, it won't seem strange."

"What's the point, if nothing will happen?"

"If you open a window, I'll make sure I'm close enough to know if you need help."

Sonia's eyes softened.

"You'll be standing out there, watching over me?" she asked.

"Sitting, with any luck," corrected Franck.

"You'll lose a night's sleep for nothing."

"Let's hope so, for your sake."

*

It happened at quarter to three in the morning.

Franck was bundled into an office doorway in the rue de la Perouse, diagonally across from the Raphael. He had gone home to change, choosing old jeans, a dark knitted jumper, and a long thick and tattered coat which had done sterling service on a number of previous occasions. He had eaten quickly, warned the neighbourhood police station what he was up to, and called the hotel's general manager.

The latter, who recalled an occasion on which Franck had extracted a terrified girl from the hands of two Korean diplomats without provoking an international incident or, more importantly, a disturbance within the hotel, had good reason to trust him. Without asking for any explanation, he listened to Franck's request, gave him the number of the room reserved for du Bellay and explained where it lay on the fifth floor. He asked whether any of the night staff should be warned of a potential intervention. Franck told him that it would not be necessary. As he hung up, he wistfully thought of the in-room surveillance the DST could have put into place in a matter of minutes. He thrust the thought aside.

When he returned to the neighbourhood at nine thirty he gave the hotel a wide berth, in case du Bellay had not yet arrived for his dinner reservation with Sonia. Franck sat down inside a bus shelter on the other side of avenue Kleber and stayed there for the next two hours, not once taking his eyes from the Raphael's main entrance.

There was no sign of du Bellay. This time, at least, he had proved punctual.

At eleven thirty he crossed the road, continued down one side of the hotel, and chose the doorway offering the best view of room 504. He took two large plastic water bottles from the deep pockets of his coat, one full and one empty, and squatted down to wait.

Lights went on in the room about ten minutes later. Nobody got around to shutting the room's heavy curtains, leaving only a screen of fine gauze drawn across the windows. From time to time shadows flitted across it.

A little over an hour later all the lights went out.

Franck continued his vigil, changing position every fifteen minutes or so as his back or limbs complained. His abdomen joined in from time to time, whenever he let himself slump forward. Having left his painkillers in his flat, given their potential soporific effects, Franck just put up with it. He took regular sips of water, and was once obliged to use the empty bottle.

He was waiting for one of two things – either an opened window or a sudden return of illumination within the room. Du Bellay could not take photos in the dark. Thus far the killer had always worked with daylight but this time he would have to turn to artificial means, and Franck felt confident some sign of them would leach from the window.

At a quarter to three something quite different came to pass.

He heard the footsteps first. Nobody had walked by for nearly two hours, and the traffic on nearby avenue Kleber was too intermittent to hide any sound that the night offered up.

A figure came round the side of the hotel and cut diagonally across to where Franck was lying. He tensed himself, ready to spring to his feet.

The footsteps came closer. A man's shoes, walking briskly. A dark-clad figure wearing a shirt and jacket, whose hands were outstretched to support something round and flat.

Franck rolled onto his knees, and then drew himself upright. One hand hovered close to the pocket where his revolver lay.

"I've brought you some hot chocolate," announced Luc du Bellay. "I thought it might cheer you up."

Franck floundered for a few seconds before finding a reply.

"You're quite the gentleman," he said.

"I try," admitted du Bellay. "But crouching on stone slabs in the dark to watch over a damsel in distress beats me in the chivalry stakes every time."

Franck was reaching out for the cup of hot chocolate when he froze, his gaze fixed over du Bellay's right shoulder. A light had come on in room 504. A few seconds later one of its windows swung open.

"Shit!" he muttered, as he thrust du Bellay aside, sending the chocolate flying.

He had only sprinted a few paces, though, before his eyes pulled him up.

The gauze covering of the window was tugged aside and a figure stood there, visible from the knees upwards. Sonia gazed down at Franck with not a stitch of clothing. She raised a hand to her lips, blew him a kiss, waved, and then turned and disappeared.

"Quite a girl," said du Bellay, picking himself up off the ground. "Very much alive and kicking, as you can see."

Two photos.

A polished BMW parked in the street before a stately building of hewn stone whose windows are almost too high off the ground to feature in the frame. Franck Guerin, in khaki chinos, a rust-coloured shirt and a light jacket, crosses the street into front of the BMW, one hand securely underneath his briefcase. His face is drawn, and visibly unshaven.

Tinted glass doors, violently orange as they catch the sun, tugged open by a tall young woman with blonde hair and a skirt so short that it scarcely seems to go beyond the edge of her buttocks. Striding in the opposite direction, away from the doors, is Franck Guerin, the holster containing his service revolver clearly visible by his side. The young woman's head is turned backwards over her shoulder, her eyes fixed on Guerin's hip.

*

"Caught some sleep?" asked Luc du Bellay, striding into the reception area.

He looked crisp and sharp. Since the Raphael was just around the corner from his office, and it was now midday, this did not count as an exploit.

Franck had gone home, slept badly for a few hours, and brooded over Sonia Delemazure's behaviour ever since. On balance, he was inclined to believe she was just young, insouciant, and wholly unconvinced by his suspicions. That said, indeed for those very reasons, he ought to be a little more wary with her in the future. Which would not be easy – her headlong charm was difficult to resist.

Du Bellay shook his hand, scanned Franck's face, and commented, "Not as much as me, I'm willing to bet."

As he guided Franck into his office he spoke over his shoulder to his receptionist, "Can we have some coffee for the captain? Large, black and very strong should do the trick."

He deposited Franck in one of the seats beside the windows that overlooked the place des Etats-Unis. He chose the next one along for himself. They were to talk side by side, rather than looking across at each other. Du Bellay was positioning himself as an ally, not an opponent.

"Although you haven't arrested me – for which I'm most grateful, I do assure you – I can't help feeling you've got me down as one of your suspects," said du Bellay.

"How are sales?" asked Franck, bluntly.

"Sales are excellent. Advance orders have overtaken the extra production I organised. I'm currently looking at ways of catching up without sacrificing quality. Suddenly everyone's interested in Du Bellay, even in the most surprising of quarters. Business could not be better. You want to slap the handcuffs on now?"

"You must agree, it doesn't look good," said Franck.

"To someone trained to look at things the way you do, no I suppose it doesn't. However, I assure you, the 'follow the money' rule doesn't apply in this case. Take my fingerprints. Take my DNA. Take whatever it takes to make you believe me."

"For the moment an explanation will do."

Franck pulled out the photo he had shown Sonia the previous day in the Raphael and laid it on the table.

"To your left, Laure Sarraute, victim number one. Right behind you, Rachida Tazi, victim number two."

Du Bellay picked up the photo and studied the girl on the stage modelling his lingerie.

"You're right," he said. "That is the other *Exposé* girl. But this means nothing. I'd already told you that Sarraute and I sometimes moved in the same circles."

"But you didn't tell me that Rachida Tazi worked for you."

"She didn't."

"What's she doing in one of your fashion shows, wearing your product line?"

"Working for someone else who was working for me," said du Bellay, getting to his feet.

He walked over to his desk, taking the photo with him.

"This looks like a show we did at the end of last year," he said, sitting down behind his laptop.

"December," offered Franck.

"Yes, the fifth of December," confirmed du Bellay, reading off his screen. "Six runway models. All provided by an agency called Elegance, via a certain Frédéric Bonneau. Would you like his phone number?"

"I already have it. So you're saying you'd never seen Rachida Tazi before this show, nor afterwards?"

"Not in any real sense of the term, no. Elegance will have sent me a bunch of profiles and photos before the show. So I must have okayed her, but I don't think I'd ever met her."

"And after?"

"I have no recollection of ever seeing her again. Elegance did a show for me in February this year. Let me check."

He busied himself with his mouse and keyboard for a few minutes. Franck got up and wandered over to his desk in order to look over his shoulder.

"No, they didn't send her in February. In any case, her name's not on the invoice. I might have asked for different dimensions – it depends on what I'm showing. Having said that, I see here they sent Julie Morand, and I'd guess she has much the same figure."

"So you never used her again in a show. What about privately?"

"Definitely not."

"You'd swear to that? You go through a lot of women. You're sure she wasn't somewhere amongst them?"

"My reputation is somewhat exaggerated, captain," protested du Bellay. "I'd be more inclined to say that a lot of women have gone through me."

"But not this one?"

"No. Not this one."

Franck left du Bellay at his desk and wandered into the middle of the room. Du Bellay watched him, waiting.

"Are you serious about the DNA and the fingerprints?"

asked Franck.

"Absolutely."

"I'll make an appointment for you. I'll be in touch."

"You have my number. Any time."

"I'll see myself out."

Franck moved towards the door, pausing before he opened it. He turned back. Du Bellay was still at his desk, looking at Franck over the top of his screen.

"If anything happens to Sonia Delemazure ...," he began.

"Were I the killer, would I be that stupid?" asked du Bellay.

Franck kept his reply to himself.

Were he the killer, he might see it as a worthy challenge.

*

It took Franck about an hour to walk to Elegance's offices in the rue des Haudriettes on the fringes of the Marais. They were on the ground floor of a building set back from the street, behind a gravel-filled, carefully raked, courtyard. A cluster of smokers were out front, blowing into the air and holding their cigarettes as far from themselves as possible – a clutch of models, make-up and management, judging by their variegated appearances.

To complete the collection, a mountain bike skidded up behind Franck as he arrived and a tall youth leapt off it, camera and lens case slung across his back. He whipped out a packet of cigarettes and joined the others in search of a light.

Franck walked around them, pushed open the double orange-tinted glass doors and walked up to a zinc-topped reception counter. A girl perched on a tall stool behind it smiled eagerly at him.

"I need to see Frédéric Bonneau," announced Franck.

The girl leant forward and asked in a half whisper, "You have an appointment?"

Franck shook his head, pulled out his ID, and laid it on the counter, "No, but I have this."

"Wow," said the girl, picking up his ID. "Is this real?"

"There's a number on it you can call," said Franck. "If you have any doubts."

She laid it back on the counter, pushed it towards him, and held up her hands.

"Hey, you're the man with the gun. I believe you."

She clicked on the screen that sat just beneath the counter ledge and flicked the microphone of her headset down before her lips.

"Fred? It's Andrea at reception. They've come for you." She winked at Franck. "The police. There's a big strong man here aching to get you in cuffs."

Frédéric Bonneau declared himself delighted to see Franck once more, and ushered him into his office. He made sure he was comfortably seated in the leather canapé that squatted in one corner of the room, called for coffee, ostentatiously cut off his mobile phone, and sat himself diagonally across from his visitor.

"You've caught him?" he asked. "I'm worried sick. It'll soon be Wednesday – and that means a new *Exposé*. I'm dreading seeing another one after Laure and that poor Arab girl."

"No I haven't," said Franck. "But let's talk about that poor Arab girl."

He drew out the photo from the Du Bellay show and tossed it to Bonneau.

Bonneau studied it, tenderly. "Laure and Sonia. What a pair. That poor Luc du Bellay probably didn't know what hit him."

"He survived," said Franck. "Look at the girl on the stage behind him. She didn't."

Bonneau's smile gave way to a frown. He shifted in his seat, peering at the photo.

"When was this taken?" he asked.

"Last December. A charity show given by Du Bellay."

"We did that show," said Bonneau. "I did that show."

"So I heard."

"That's her, isn't it?" asked Bonneau, looking up at Franck.

"That's the second *Exposé* girl?"

"That's right. You supplied her for the evening."

"Shit. Shit. Shit," intoned Bonneau, softly. "Now that I see her, I remember her. The stripper. What was her name?"

"You tell me."

He moved to his desk, taking the photo with him, picked up a telephone, and pressed a single key.

"Marianne? Fred. I'm going to test your memory. Cast your mind back to the end of last year. We did a show for Luc du Bellay, tried out a few new girls. There was an Arab girl, lithe, boyish, long black hair. We only used her that once. Remember her name? Yes, that was it."

He abandoned the receiver and came back to the canapé.

"Rachida Tazi. Shit. She'd never crossed my mind again from that day to this. Even when I saw her photo in *Exposé* – and you know why? I didn't remember her being that beautiful."

"So what's the story?" demanded Franck. "You never used her again?"

"That's right. For private shows like that we sometimes use new girls. See how they look on a catwalk. See how they behave under pressure, with the lights and the attention and all the panic backstage. This Rachida, she had walked into the agency a few days before. Didn't have a book, didn't have a CV, didn't have a hope. But I was standing there and she caught my eye, so we had a chat, I had one of the photographers take a few pictures, and I had her measured up. When du Bellay phoned, I thought, why not? There was place for a profile like hers, so I did it. A bit of a rush. There was no time to sign anything."

"So what went wrong?"

"On the night? Nothing. She looked good. She was completely at ease. Surprisingly so, even. I said to myself – not the first time this girl's been on a stage. How right I was! It all came out two days later, when I called her in and handed over her to Marianne – Marianne does the administrative stuff. First we find out she's got no insurance number, and wants to be paid cash. Then it comes out that she's stripping in Pigalle. And that's where we parted company. She got paid, of course, although God knows how Marianne covered it up. We're not thieves, even when we're dealing with the dishonest."

"What was the problem – that she was illegal, or that she was a stripper?"

"Both. If I'd known either, I'd never have used her."

"That she didn't have a work permit, I can understand. But what's the problem with a stripper?"

Bonneau shook his head. He sat down, clasped his hands, and attempted to explain.

"Of course it shouldn't matter. If the girl's got the look, she's got the look. But ask any marketing executive if he's happy with an ex-stripper in his catalogue, or pushing his perfume, or onstage in his brand's show, and he'll look at you, say nothing, and walk across the street to the next agency. There's a line you can't cross. You can walk naked down a catwalk wearing nothing but designer heels, but you can't shake your tits in a strip club in Pigalle. I didn't draw that line, but it's my business to know it exists."

"So you never saw, or heard from, Tazi again?"

"No."

"Do you know if she struck up any friendships with any of your models, or any of your staff?"

"It's one big happy family here, captain," said Bonneau. "We work together, we party together. I would have seen her."

"So this." Franck reached out to retrieve the photo from Bonneau. "Laure Sarraute, Sonia Delemazure, Rachida Tazi, all standing next to each other – this is just a coincidence?"

Bonneau opened his palms and peered at Franck over them.

"You don't believe in coincidences?"

"They make me uneasy."

Back out on the street, Franck's mobile phone started ringing. He held it to his ear.

"Guerin," he announced.

"Is that how you were taught to answer the phone?" asked a

calm voice.

"Madame Alba," said Franck. "This is a pleasure. I take it Yves wants to see me?"

"He's always happy to see you captain, but that's not why I'm calling. There's been an incident, and Yves reckons it belongs to you."

"What's happened?"

"You've had some contact with a certain Jean-Michel Rey?"

"Yes. What's he done?"

"It's more a question of what's been done to him."

*

Some things were the same as the last time Franck had come to Montrouge. The Chinese were still in their leather jackets, still smoking, still saying nothing. The post office vehicles were still resplendently yellow. However, the backwater atmosphere, the lack of buzz that came from being on the wrong side of the ring road that served to separate Paris from its suburbs, had momentarily disappeared.

Two marked police cars were illegally parked before the building. An unmarked van, which Franck knew to be a mobile lab for crime scene technicians, was perched on the pavement across the street. Inside the entrance half a dozen people milled about, clutching plastic goblets of coffee and smoking. They were not waiting for the lift. Or if they were, it was to see what might come out.

Franck slipped through them and pressed the lift button. He felt everyone watching him, wondering who he was. He did not look round. When the lift arrived, no-one got in alongside him.

On the fourth floor he surprised a bored-looking uniformed policewoman lighting up a cigarette. Before she could challenge him he slipped his ID from his pocket and held it up. She nodded, and gave her attention back to her lighter and the tip of her cigarette.

"They chase you out?" he asked.

The policewoman looked back up at him. "Nothing worse than technicians when they get their hand on a scene. Can't go anywhere. Can't touch anything. Best not even breathe."

The unmarked door to Rey's studio was open. A bustle of activity, but no voices, could be heard from the other end of the corridor. Franck's ears picked out the sound of a camera. Jean-Michel Rey was finally the star of his own photo shoot.

"Franck Guerin," said Franck, extending his hand to shake the policewoman's.

"I know who you are, captain. They told me you'd be over. Although why the DST is interested in this I can't imagine."

"As a general rule, when the DST is involved, it's best not even trying to imagine," observed Franck. "But I'm here for the Brigade Criminelle."

She nodded. "They're holding you at arm's length until that mess in Corsica gets cleared up. In the meantime you get to slum it with the rest of us."

Franck was surprised. It was the first time anyone in uniform had come right out and mentioned the Corsican incident to him. It suggested that the rumours about what had happened were becoming a flood.

Franck's hand was still held in front of him, waiting to be shaken. He let it drop.

"I don't see this as slumming," he said. "The DST is part of the police, not some alien race."

"Yeah, right. They just don't play by the same rules, that's all. If you didn't already know that captain, you're about to find out."

"What makes you so sure?" enquired Franck, keeping his voice even and calm.

"I'm a union representative. UNSA Police. We hear things."

"Thanks for the concern," offered Franck. "But I have confidence in my superiors." He said this with as much conviction as he could muster. Doubts still remained from his last two chats with Catherine, even though Yves seemed inclined to believe that his old boss was still on his side.

He offered his hand once more. This time she looked at it,

snorted, then shook it while observing, "More fool you". Maybe she knew more about Catherine Vautrin than he did.

It was time to change the subject.

"You been here long?" he asked, nodding at the door behind her.

"Maybe three hours. Interviewed the guy who found him. Talked to some of the other workers in the building."

"Who found him?"

"Guy worked downstairs. Wystech. Said he was due to do some work on his computers. Said Rey had a maintenance agreement. Came up here at half nine this morning, found the door closed but unlocked. Came in, found Rey, phoned us. There isn't much left of the computers to maintain anyway. You want his name?"

Franck nodded. She brought out a notebook and flipped backwards through it.

"Paul Bannel."

She waited for Franck to bring out something and note it down. He did not.

"What about the others? They see anything?" he asked.

"No. Nobody gets in here before eight at the earliest. Even the post office people. It's some kind of headquarters operation – no envelopes to be sorted, no bags to be made up, no reason to get in at the crack of dawn."

"What's your take?" asked Franck, taking an ostensible interest in her opinion. At times it paid to placate the gods. Even the most minor and insignificant of deities.

The policewoman took a drag on her cigarette, blew out the smoke, all the time toying with the notebook in her other hand.

"It could have happened any time yesterday. Nobody's here from Wystech or La Poste on Sundays. I've spoken to a couple of the Chinese, and they say they're here seven days a week, but nobody can remember anything out of the ordinary yesterday. In any case, they were all gone by six. So let's say the killer comes in the early evening. The door wasn't forced, so Rey either knew him or had arranged a meeting with him. They go through to the main area. They talk, enough time for the murderer to get the shutters down on the windows so that no-one sees anything from the outside. He overpowers Rey and kills him – the forensic team says by injection. He smashes the place up. He walks out. Doesn't bother to lock the door."

"The shutters are always down," Franck informed her. "Naked people here all day long. Stops the neighbours complaining. Or gaping."

"You've been here before?"

"Yes," replied Franck. "That's why I'm here again. Thanks for your help."

He walked down the rest of the corridor.

The policewoman had exaggerated. Whoever had killed Rey had not smashed the place up. With one exception, things were much as they had been on Franck's last visit. The exception was the workbench: the wide flat screen was still there, but the two servers that had flanked it were now on the floor. They were in pieces – pieces that had been disassembled rather than smashed. The drawers from the workbench, their contents tipped out, lay haphazardly around them.

Franck wandered over and looked at the scattered components. He was searching for a screwdriver, but could not see one.

"Not interested in the body, captain?"

The question came from behind him. He turned and recognised the face. It was the technician who had been at the Hotel des Bateliers and the Lutetia – Georges something, Franck recalled.

Franck joined the technician, shaking his hand and kneeling down beside him before the slightly raised stage in the centre of the room. On it stood two tired leather armchairs, their skin dull and warped. In one sat Rey, his head back, his arms hanging stiffly down each side of the chair, one leg hooked behind the other. His position looked most uncomfortable, but his face was placid, his eyes lightly shut.

"Our boy had to roll up a sleeve this time," said the technician, pointing to Rey's left arm. His shirt cuff had been unbuttoned and the sleeve forced up above his elbow.

"Injection mark?" asked Franck.

"One fresh one. Several others, too. It seems Rey wasn't averse to the needle."

"Where's the champagne?" asked Franck, looking around.

"There isn't any. Smell the tumbler on the floor."

Franck did as he was told. A chunky-bottomed glass with a film of tea-coloured liquid at the bottom. He did not touch it, just hung his nose over it.

"Whisky," he said. "Rey didn't have any whisky."

Franck went back into the corridor, pulling on plastic gloves as he went.

In the room off the corridor that played host to Rey's hotel fridge he found a bottle of Johnny Walker Black Label. It was missing maybe five centimetres.

He went back into the studio area.

"There's a whisky bottle back there. Bag it and print it."

"Not that we'll find anything," predicted the technician.

"Probably not," admitted Franck. "Our killer might have changed his tipple of choice, but I doubt he's become sufficiently careless to carry it with his bare hands."

"So why whisky this time?"

Franck nodded towards Rey's corpse. "Not the champagne type. Anyone looked at the computer equipment over there?"

"No", said the technician. "It's important?"

"Could be. Once you've checked for prints, spread it out neatly and get someone up from Wystech to look at it. Two floors down. Ask for someone called Paul Bannel, he seems to have looked after Rey's gear."

"OK," said the technician. "What's he supposed to look for?"

"To see what's missing."

By eight in the evening, the technicians had all they wanted. Paul Bannel from Wystech had been summoned and had delivered his verdict on the servers: both hard disks had been spirited away, but nothing else was missing.

Franck was helping the technicians load their gear back into their van when he decided there were two last things he wanted to check. He pulled out his phone and dialled Luc du Bellay's mobile number. It barely had time to ring before it was answered.

"Good evening captain," said du Bellay. "I'm in the middle of a meeting, so please excuse me if I seem curt. What can I do for you?"

"Can you account for your movements early yesterday evening?"

Du Bellay paused. "Account in what sense?"

"Provide proof of where you were and what you were doing."

"Yes, I think I can. From when to when?"

"Let's say from five until you arrived at the Raphael, which must have been around nine."

"I was in a meeting."

"On a Sunday?" said Franck, instantly sceptical. "What kind of a meeting?"

"A business meeting. It does happen, you know," said du Bellay, almost apologetically. "In fact, I was with some of the people who are currently sitting around a conference table with me."

"OK. I may need their names. Sorry to disturb you."

"Always a pleasure, captain. Have a good evening."

"That's most unlikely," said Franck, and rang off.

One more call. He dialled Jacques Beaufort.

"Have you received a photo?" he demanded, knowing that the timing would be right for the next issue.

"No. Should I have?"

Franck did not bother replying, and simply hung up.

Tuesday, 19th June

Three photos.

The facade of Le Nemours, with its tall stone pillars, brass-framed windows and host of external tables, all but one of which has been taken over by customers, watched over by the vigilant eye of a long-aproned waiter. Franck Guerin entering the frame from the right in tired chinos, reddish shirt and a creased jacket, his briefcase close to hand. All the customers ignore him.

The facade of Le Nemours, unchanged. A young woman in tight, low-cut jeans, open sandals, a bright pink top hanging off her left shoulder, her hair cut to the nape of her neck, standing back from the door as a smiling waiter opens it for her. Four of the customers sitting outside, all male, cast surreptitious glances in her direction.

A bookshop, its window populated by severe looking tomes, its only concession to frivolity a wire rack of paperbacks just to the right of its main entrance. Franck Guerin stands before it, one arm clutching his briefcase, the other reaching up to scratch his nose as he looks around him, as if for something he has lost.

*

"I'm curious to know whether you got one of these" said Yves.

He held aloft an oblong envelope made of stiff black cardboard. In the top right hand corner, where the stamp should have been, was the *Wasp-Waisted* logo. "Yves de Chaumont *juge d'instruction*" had been written dead centre in a calligrapher's hand, in flowing gold ink.

"Delivered by courier this morning," said Franck, pulling his own out from the file he had brought with him to Yves' office.

"I've been waiting for you to come to open it," said Yves. "What is it?"

"Go ahead," insisted Franck. "It's quite safe."

Yves retrieved a paper knife from a desk drawer, carefully slit open the envelope and held it at an angle to let its contents slide onto his desk: a rectangle of similar material, of slightly smaller dimensions. The same logo was to be found in the top right hand corner, followed by a printed text, again in gold.

Mademoiselle Maryam Sehati invites you to join her on the 6th of July at La Maison Blanche, avenue Montaigne, at 21h00.
As connoisseurs will know, two auspicious events will take place on this date: the publication of the 20th issue of *Wasp-Waisted*, and mademoiselle Sehati's thirtieth birthday.
Dress will be formal and the inelegant will be turned away.
No partners, please.
R.S.V.P.

It was signed by Maryam herself, in the same hand that had inscribed the recipient's name on the envelope.

"Will you go?" asked Franck.

"As no other opportunity has yet presented itself to meet the intriguing mademoiselle Sehati, I fear I have to," said Yves. "How about you?"

"Given that our killer might be in the room, I can scarcely say no."

"Dress will be formal, and the inelegant will be turned away," read Yves. "If you're going after the killer, you're professionally obliged to make an effort, sartorially speaking."

"I'll try."

"That would make a nice change," commented Yves, casting an eye over Franck.

Franck now had two largely sleepless nights to his credit. He had convinced the crime scene technicians to work on the samples from Rey's studio through most of Monday night, and had felt honour-bound to stay with them. He had then got up early this morning to be with the coroner when he dissected the corpse, in order to get his impressions first hand. In his haste he had simply slipped on the same clothes he had stripped off before collapsing on his bed a few hours before. To say that he looked crumpled would have been a kindness.

Yves, however, did not pursue the subject. He slid the invitation back into its envelope and pushed it to one side of his desk.

"To business," he announced. "Jean-Michel Rey – we're sure it was the same killer?"

"No sign of a struggle. Flunitrazepam found in the whiskey and in his blood. Traces of potassium chloride at the injection point."

"Against which I could cite – no champagne, no lingerie, no attractive young woman, no photo sent to *Exposé*," enumerated Yves.

"It may have been a different kind of target, but it was exactly the same means of execution. We've never released details of the way he kills. This can't be a copycat. It's him."

"So what's the link with the others? Where's the aesthetic side to this one? If we're sticking to the hypothesis that our killer sees himself as some kind of an artist, where's his signature on this one?"

"There's a clear link to Rachida Tazi. Rey took a set of photos of her a few days before the killer did the same."

"Not the kind of photos our killer is in the habit of taking," observed Yves.

"Anne Subrini would agree with you on that. I've shown her the images and she is adamant that they have no artistic value and nothing in common with the *Exposé* photos. But if that's true, why steal Rey's hard disk, which contained every image from the shoot? Why take such an interest in his rival's work?"

"I'm not sure our killer would see Rey as a rival. An intruder, perhaps, but not a rival. Anyhow, we don't know what else was on those hard disks. Didn't he keep backups somewhere? Isn't that what you're supposed to do?"

"He did. He had two servers. Each of them backed up onto the other. The guy from Wystech had set it up. Worked automatically twice a day. It just so happens that the hard disks from both servers are gone."

"Not very far-sighted, this man from Wystech," Yves commented.

"Or Rey was too cheap to pay for anything else. Which would seem in character to me."

"Just how shady was this Rey?" asked Yves.

"More than enough. We know he was a drug user – there was a shooting kit hidden in the studio and a lot of scars on his inner arm. And there's worse – we found half a box of 9mm parabellum shells in a drawer beside where his computer gear had been. A drawer that had been pulled out, thrown to the floor, and raked through."

"9mm shells," mused Yves. "Yet another PA50 on the loose."

Over three hundred thousand 1950 automatic pistols – or PA50s – had been manufactured for the French army over a period of fifty years. Still in active service, it was also the arm most frequently found in illegal circulation.

"Think the killer found it?" asked Yves.

"If it was in the drawer, he'd have to have been blind not to."

"Something else to worry about then," observed Yves. "That said, firearms don't seem to be his style. Too messy."

"Let's hope it stays that way."

"You think the servers were attacked to steal Rey's photos – presumably those of Rachida Tazi – from the hard disks," said Yves. "But they hadn't been published. How did he know they existed? Who knew about the shoot?"

"Beatrice Moreau, half the staff of The Velvet Pussy, the guy in the photos with Rachida, and an unknown number of people in Rey's circle. That's a lot of possibilities. And then there's Tazi herself. She could have told the killer. We don't know what they said to each other in the Hotel des Bateliers. Maybe that's part of the reason she was killed."

"That's unlikely," insisted Yves. "Tazi was there to be killed, whatever she said or heard once she got into room ...

what was it?"

"504," supplied Franck. "OK, so he didn't kill her for that, but she might have told him all the same. They were clearly close. She trusted him right up to the minute he passed her a glass of champagne. He could have been her confidant. He could have known her past, her dreams, her projects, everything."

"In which case maybe it's not the shoot," said Yves.

"Why not?"

"Because if he knew everything, he knew about the shoot before it happened. But he killed Tazi – and Rey for that matter – after it had taken place."

"Whatever the reason, the photos, aside from their commercial value, have nothing of interest in them," said Franck. "I've analysed the full set Rey gave me. Even though the print quality is poor, it's clear there's nothing incriminating. There's nobody in the background. All you see are Tazi and her partner."

"That's another thing that seems odd," interjected Yves. "Like you say, we already have the photos. If making them disappear was the point of the murder, then our killer has failed in his endeavours. Up until now he's not looked like someone who makes mistakes."

"You think it may have been something else?" asked Franck. "Something else on the servers? Photos or files, or whatever?"

"Maybe something we don't have a copy of," continued Yves. "Something whose very existence we have to guess. So tell me Franck, what else could have been on those servers?"

"Something else connected with Tazi?"

"Or something connected with Laure Sarraute."

*

"No hard feelings?" asked Sonia Delemazure, as she kissed Franck lightly on both cheeks.

"I should have known you liked playing with fire," he

replied.

Sonia sat across from him at the same table at the back of Le Nemours where they had first talked.

"Look. No burns." She wiggled her fingers in the air. "I don't think you'll be seeing me on the front cover of *Exposé* tomorrow. Anyhow, Luc says he's patched things up with you."

Franck shrugged. "Du Bellay has provided an explanation for Rachida Tazi's presence at his show. Turns out she was working for your agency."

Sonia twisted her lips into a pout. "Well I never met her."

"I have a photo of you standing a few metres from her," Franck pointed out.

"Doesn't count. I'm an easy-going girl – I'll stand next to anyone. Hey, all you have to do is call me and I jump."

This part, at least, was true. Franck had called her the moment he stepped out of Yves' office and she had agreed to meet him that very afternoon.

"For which I'm very grateful," insisted Franck. "As for Luc du Bellay, even though his story about Tazi checks out that doesn't mean you shouldn't be careful."

"He had his chance. He didn't take it. At least, not to do what you thought he might."

"Of course he didn't," objected Franck. "He knew I was there."

"No he didn't," insisted Sonia. "Not until afterwards, anyway. As soon as I told him, he got up out of bed and brought you that hot chocolate. Wasn't that sweet?"

"Hot chocolate with a hint of mockery – sweet and sour, if you ask me. But it doesn't matter." Franck was not there to rehash the embarrassment of Sunday night at the Raphael. "I need to ask you some more questions about Laure."

"Sure," said Sonia, sitting up straight in her seat. "Can I order something first, or are we boycotting courtesy completely simply because Luc is so attached to it?"

Franck raised a hand to call over a waiter.

"Mademoiselle would like ..." he said.

"Freshly squeezed lemon and a Perrier," she requested.

"And another coffee for me," added Franck.

Sonia pointed towards the two empty cups already on the table. Franck had got there half an hour before her and had used coffee to while away the time.

"You might be calmer if you drank less of that," she suggested.

"If it was good enough to kill Balzac, it's good enough for me." He reached down into his briefcase. "Take a look at this." It was one of the paper printouts from the Rey session with Tazi.

"Well, well," said Sonia. "You brought me here to show me dirty pictures? Isn't there a law against that?"

"Actually, it's one of the less explicit ones. And no, there isn't a law against it – not with someone your age. You recognise the girl?"

"Of course. It's the one that caused all the trouble for Luc."

"You don't think that's a bit unfair?" chastised Franck. "I doubt very much that Rachida Tazi set out to cause trouble for anyone. It's whoever caused her so much trouble that she ended up dead and on the cover of *Exposé* that interests me."

"So, why the photo?" asked Sonia.

"Rachida did a porn shoot a few days before she died. The man who took these pictures is himself now dead."

"Dead as in dead, or dead as in murdered?"

"Dead as in murdered. It hasn't got out in the media yet, but everything suggests he was the latest victim of our killer. If at all possible, I'd rather you kept this to yourself for the moment."

"Hey, you can trust me," insisted Sonia, hand on heart.

"Like I trusted you at the Raphael," commented Franck archly.

"You're slow at forgiving, aren't you?"

"The police don't forgive. Juries might, and the penitentiary system almost always does in the end, but it's not our style. Neither is forgetting, come to that."

"You have my word of honour," insisted Sonia. "I'll tell no-one, at least not until it's all over the news."

"Not even during pillow talk?"

"I tend just to fall asleep. The Raphael was an exception."

"OK," said Franck, tapping his forefinger on the photo. "Let's come back to this. What I need to know is whether Laure Sarraute ever did anything similar."

Sonia stared at him, incredulous. "You're kidding, right?"

At that the waiter arrived, sat down their drinks, added another flimsy receipt to those Franck had already accumulated, and wandered off.

Franck waited until he was a few paces away. "I'm perfectly serious," he insisted.

"Of course she didn't." Sonia slowed her voice down, as if speaking to someone mentally challenged. "She signed with Elegance. She was a successful haute couture model. She was about to become the face of Ephémère. You think that all that would have been possible if she'd done porn? Have you learned nothing about our profession?"

"I know all that," said Franck, patiently. "But what about the beginning? What about when she'd just arrived in Paris, when she was still no-one and had nothing?"

"I didn't know her then. We met at the agency – remember? I think you should start taking notes after all."

"Yes, but did you never talk about those early days? Are you sure she mentioned nothing like this?"

"Believe me, if she'd done it, she'd never have talked about it. She'd have done everything in her power to cover the traces – anything and everything. But even then, it would have got out. These things always do. You think the Ephémère people don't run background checks? I'd reckon there's nothing about her they don't know. And if they'd caught a whiff of porn, they'd never have signed her."

Sonia was indignant. Her hands gripped the edge of the table between them, and she stared down at Franck as if daring him to contradict her.

"And in any case," she added. "Laure wouldn't have done it. Not her. Not even if she was starving to death. She wouldn't have taken her clothes off for money. For Art, sure. For money, no way."

"For Art?" echoed Franck.

"Sure. She was a life model for a while – way back in the beginning, like you said, before Elegance. But that's OK. Nobody cares about that. Particularly when it's for the Beaux Arts."

Franck frowned, not quite sure he should believe what he had just heard. He had, after all, checked Laure Sarraute's name with the payroll woman – madame Guignard – at the Beaux Arts. He looked down at his coffee and began to turn the cup on its saucer, very slowly, with one finger. Sonia took this as a cue to pour some Perrier into her squeezed lemon and start stirring it.

Franck stopped playing with his coffee, drained it, and set it down. Something had come back to him – something about a change in the payroll system a few years ago, and how older records were no longer on-line.

"You're sure about this?"

"Of course I'm sure. She told me herself. She was even quite proud of it. But, like I said, it doesn't matter."

"Oh yes it does," he insisted. He pushed back his seat, digging into his pocket for some money.

"That's it?" asked Sonia. "You're done with me? I've not even finished my drink."

Franck slapped down a twenty euro note.

"Take your time. Mull over what you else you might have forgotten to tell me about Laure Sarraute's life before Elegance."

Sonia let Franck take a few paces before she called out. "Want to know what I'm doing later on this afternoon?"

"Not particularly," he called over his shoulder, and made his way out of the door.

Sonia kept her eyes on him as he walked outside. He advanced a few paces and then pulled a mobile phone from his jacket. He tapped in a number and held it to his ear. Not once did he look back at her.

His call was not answered for some time, and he was waiting for voicemail to kick in when he finally heard Anne Subrini's voice.

"Captain," she said. "This is a pleasant surprise. Do hang on a minute."

Franck could hear a muffled exchange on the other end of the line, involving what sounded like another woman. Then movement, and a door opening and closing.

"Sorry about that," continued Anne. "One of my students."

"I didn't mean to disturb you," said Franck. "I can phone back at a more convenient time."

"Not at all," Anne assured him. "It's one of those tutorials that never seem to come to an end. A student who clings like a barnacle and always has an extra question. Anyhow, you've given me an excuse to step outside, so I'm already in your debt."

"Not for much longer," said Franck. "I have something to ask you. I could go through the administrative people in the school, but I suspect you can do this faster and better."

"What is it you want?"

"I have reason to believe that Laure Sarraute – the first *Exposé* victim ..."

"I remember," said Anne.

"It seems she was a life model in the Beaux Arts some time back, probably 2002 or 2003."

"You want me to check?"

"Yes. And if it's true, is there any way you could find out which students attended the classes she posed for?"

"Probably. There might be a confidentiality issue, though. Do you have some kind of a warrant?"

"Not yet. That's why I'm asking you. Could you do it?"

"I expect so. When do you need this information?"

"As quickly as possible," declared Franck. "Sorry about that."

"It's all in a good cause," conceded Anne, with good humour. "Come around tomorrow afternoon. I'll gather together what I can for then."

"I really appreciate this."

"It's nothing. And anyway, I'm glad you called. I have something for you."

"The two copies of *Wasp-Waisted*?" said Franck. "There's no hurry. I don't need them right now."

"Something else. A surprise. You'll see. Till tomorrow then?"

"Till tomorrow," agreed Franck.

Anne rang off.

Franck pocketed his phone. He looked around the paved square where he stood, unsure whether to head back to his office.

Something caught his eye. Behind one of the pillars that ringed the base of the Comédie Française: a zoom lens; it was pointing at him.

He forced his regard up into the sky, keeping his head moving as if he had seen nothing. He cast around for something in which he might credibly seem interested. His eyes fell on a bookshop on the other side of the road and he headed towards it, walking briskly across a gap in the traffic. Once there he stopped and pretended to be studying its window display.

After a few minutes he slowly turned around, allowing his gaze to sweep across the entire facade of the Comédie Française before carrying on to rest on the tables set up outside Le Nemours. The lens was still there: same pillar; the second from the end at the left. Although he had moved maybe thirty metres and significantly changed the angle between him and the building, the lens was still pointing at him. Whoever was behind it was there for him.

He waited for the traffic between him and place Colette to calm down and then cut across the road, seemingly heading back to Le Nemours. But as soon as he stepped off the road surface and was back on paving stones he pivoted and started moving towards the Comédie Française.

The lens was no longer visible. He sped up, breaking into a run, dashing around the bystanders who froze suddenly in his path. He reached the line of pillars and penetrated the shade behind them. Apart from two tourists puzzling over a much-folded map of the city, there was no-one there. Franck sprinted to the end of the building, ignoring the pain in his abdomen, and turned the corner. He was now looking up the row of columns that marked the principal facade, the one that looked out over the avenue de l'Opéra, the one that had been blocked by crowds when he was leaving the theatre twelve days before with Sylvie Thomas.

There were a handful of people strolling or loitering before him. But only one running – with a camera slung over his back. Franck picked up speed, his teeth set as his body protested, but his prey had turned the corner at the far end of the building before he had closed half the distance.

Franck hurtled on, shot round the corner, only to see the photographer grab a mountain bike from against the wall of the Comédie Française, leap upon it, and start moving forward.

"Stop!" cried Franck, as much a gasp of pain as anything else, sprinting as fast as he could. He had a couple of seconds before the bike built up speed and outpaced him. They were not enough. The bike shot forward towards one of the side entrances to the Palais Royal before turning rapidly to the left into the rue de Montpensier.

Franck gave chase, counting on the fact that Montpensier was a one way street and that the bike was going the wrong way. He turned the corner. The bike was speeding away. There was no traffic coming to slow it down.

Franck stopped, knowing he was beaten, each gasping breath causing his stomach muscles to clench in agony.

His stalker had bested him. There wasn't even a registration plate to note and call in. As his fingers rifled his pockets for painkillers, he concentrated on the diminishing silhouette before him.

Particularly the shapeless bob on its head.

Wednesday, 20th June

One photo.

A bistrot proudly rooted at the corner of a street with several outside tables seating hungry customers hung over their meals like vultures. Franck Guerin stands off to the left, leaning forward to kiss a woman on the cheek. Whereas his dress is casual, hers is sober, tightly-drawn and intimidatingly professional. Her left hand reaches out, touching Franck's right sleeve with apparent affection.

*

It was just after five thirty in the morning when Catherine Vautrin left her apartment building in avenue du Colonel Bonnet, the only living being on a street whose otherwise impeccably respectable inhabitants were still contentedly asleep in their beds. A tired raincoat drawn around her allowed occasional glimpses of gray trousers and flat black shoes. Her destination was a nearby taxi rank where a handful of cabs were always to be found in the predawn, awaiting their first fares of the day.

Catherine tapped on the side window of the first of two parked taxis, drawing the driver's attention from the newspaper deployed over his steering wheel. She received a nod in return. The driver folded up his paper and released the central locking mechanism on the car, allowing Catherine to open the back door that faced the pavement. She slid inside, offered a tired good morning, and gave the address of the DST offices. The driver nodded, tossed his newspaper onto the seat beside him, and started the engine.

Just as he was about to pull out a figure stole up alongside the driver's side rear door and tugged it open. By the time he had slid into the back of the car Catherine's revolver was firmly clutched in her right hand and pointed directly at his chest.

"Good morning Catherine," said Franck, not particularly

surprised to find his heart in close proximity to a handgun whose safety mechanism had, he was sure, been disengaged.

"You're lucky I'm still half asleep," she observed. "Do that to me mid-morning and you're a dead man."

She had not lowered her weapon. Franck slowly extended his right arm and offered her his palm, on which sat two packets of Gitanes.

"I thought about bringing some croissants, but reckoned you'd rather have these," he said.

Catherine swung her handbag up onto the seat between them. It was already unzipped. She briefly pointed to it with the tip of her revolver. Franck widened the opening with his left hand and tossed the two packets into it, spotting at least three others as he did so.

"That buys you two minutes," said Catherine. "We'll soon be on our way." That was for the taxi driver, who sat frozen in his seat, his eyes held by the sight of gun in his rear view mirror.

"You won't take my calls," explained Franck. "I tried several times yesterday evening."

"Maybe I was busy."

"Maybe I don't count."

"Maybe."

"Anyhow, this was the only way I knew to get a hold of you," said Franck. "Even if it does mean getting up before the sun."

"Sunlight is overrated," observed Catherine. "Darkness is our element."

"Speak for yourself."

"I always do."

"Do you have a tail on me?" demanded Franck.

Catherine's head jerked back slightly. This was a movement she had rarely been seen to perform. He had surprised her.

"Do we have a tail on you?" she echoed, at last lowering her revolver and thumbing the safety back on. "Why on earth would we do that?"

"Any number of reasons," offered Franck. "Like the need to

keep tabs on an agent under suspicion."

Catherine snorted as she slipped her gun into a shoulder holster under her raincoat.

"Delusions of grandeur," she said, more to herself than to him. She then swivelled her gaze back to him. "You have, of course, no reason to believe me, but I haven't put a tail on you. And I don't think anyone else would have without asking me first."

Franck looked into her dark eyes. He was inclined to believe her.

"I didn't think so," he said. "But I had to check. Just being thorough. You taught me that."

"Wonder who it is," she mused. He had succeeded in intriguing her. "Think it's the Corsicans? If it is, then we should have you under observation."

"No," he said. "I'm washed up. I'm of no interest to them. It's got to be the case I'm working."

"Your model killer?"

"He's extended his range a little since last we talked."

"True," she conceded. "A stripper and a pornographer, if I'm not mistaken."

Franck raised a quizzical eyebrow. Catherine allowed herself a brief smile.

"Of course I'm taking an interest," she said. "Since you're still in theory one of the staff, if you screw this up the DST is going to lose face. So I keep an eye on how well you're defending our honour."

"Would it shock you to know that's not my primary motivation?"

"I'm used to being disappointed, so no, not really."

"Well, I think I've used up my two packets' worth of time," said Franck. "I'll let you go."

"Good."

Franck opened the door and stepped outside. He was about to close it when Catherine called out to him.

"Franck. You really think the killer's on your tail?"

"Looks like it."

"Officially, I can't do anything for you. Unofficially, if you want backup, I can get it."

Franck suppressed a smile. He had never really believed the DST might be tailing him. If they had been, he would never have spotted them. He had come for something else, and Catherine had just given it to him.

He appeared to think for a moment, considering her offer.

"No. I should do this myself," he said. "It's all part of the learning experience."

"Just make sure it doesn't become part of the dying experience."

With that she motioned for him to shut the door and told the driver he could pull out.

Franck moved to the pavement and watched the taxi drive away.

It was time for some coffee. If the killer was indeed a few steps behind him, he had better be on his toes.

*

"Just be wary of anyone carrying a camera," insisted Franck, aware of how ridiculous he must sound.

Sylvie Thomas looked at him mockingly and gestured around them.

"This is Paris," she pointed out. "One of the most visited cities in the world. The streets are awash with tourists determined to immortalise everything they see in pixels."

She had phoned him in his office that morning, suggesting that they meet for lunch. Franck turned her down, explaining that he could not take the time out from the investigation. Sylvie pointed out that the cover of that morning's *Exposé* did not appear to feature a corpse, since it was given over the beaming face of the recently elected President Sarkozy. Faced with her insistence, Franck explained that he now had three corpses on his hands. When she began to question his arithmetic, he briefly explained about the murder of Jean-Michel Rey, which had still not attracted much attention from the media.

True to form, at least as far as his relations with Sylvie were concerned, he lost the argument. She promised that she would not take up more than an hour of his time – no starter, no dessert – and would tear herself away from La Défense to come into the centre of the city to make things more convenient for him. This came as some surprise, since experience had taught Franck that Sylvie valued her time very highly. Browbeaten, he suggested they meet at half twelve at a bistro on the quai de Bourbon on the neighbouring Ile Saint Louis.

Sylvie was pulling up in a taxi when Franck arrived on foot, having walked a little over five minutes from his office.

As it turned out, Sylvie did not seem to have anything urgent to tell him. As they ate – perch fillet with a mushroom sauce for her; blood sausage and fried potatoes for him – Franck ended up giving her an account of the recent events of the case. He had just finished recounting his fruitless pursuit around the Comédie Française as the waiter brought two coffees.

"I know," conceded Franck. "Just keep it in mind. He may have seen you with me. I think he's been on my trail for some time. He was certainly in the street when I went to Maryam Sehati's apartment for dinner."

"Aha, the entrancing mademoiselle Sehati," interrupted Sylvie. "You're very coy about what happened that night."

She dipped her head, angling her eyes up at him.

"If she roused the seducer within you, I'd like to know how she did it. I never got close."

Franck ignored her and continued with his train of thought. "And I have the feeling he was outside Elegance the last time I was there. It may be that he followed me to Jean-Michel Rey, realised we were getting close to him, and intervened to kill Rey and destroy whatever was on his servers."

Sylvie played with her coffee spoon, biting back a smile.

"You've got to admit, it is ironic," she said. "Franck Guerin, the man trained to track the bad guys down, can't spot one tailing him. No wonder the DST is asking itself questions about you."

Franck looked at her askance, twisting a paper sachet of sugar between his fingers. It broke open in the process, showering the tabletop with white grains. He tossed it aside. "You don't see what you're not expecting to see. That's the only reason why it's possible to tail anyone, even for us. If he hadn't had a camera, I'd never have spotted him. Which means he's not that good. He should have known I'd be hypersensitive to cameras – it's his fault, after all."

"So why did he bring it?"

"Because that's what he does. He takes photos – Sarraute, Tazi, no doubt Rey, and now me. Anne's got to be right. It's one big, sick artistic project."

Sylvie cocked her head. "Anne?"

Franck waved a dismissive hand. "A colleague. I've been discussing the case with her."

"First time you've ever mentioned her. I thought you were handling this case on your own"

"Right now, it looks like I need all the help I can get," said Franck.

"So how useful has my help been? What's happening with Luc du Bellay?"

"Unless he was the mystery man on the bike, I've got nothing on du Bellay. He may be making a mint out of these deaths, but he seems to have an alibi for Rey, and his links with Sarraute and Tazi seem pretty tenuous."

"You're saying it's not his fault the killer adores his lingerie?"

"Something like that," conceded Franck. "After all, he's not the one flocking into the Bon Marché to snap up the models featured in *Exposé*."

"So if you're not planning on arresting Luc du Bellay, he remains respectable," concluded Sylvie. "He's a man you can do business with."

Franck frowned at her. "You're planning on doing business with him?"

"In a way. I thought I might buy something from him."

Franck shook his head, disappointed but not entirely surprised. Sylvie's profession was a savagely pragmatic and cynical one. It was only to be expected that it would spill over into other aspects of her life.

"You too? Can't wait to dress yourself up like Laure Sarraute?"

Sylvie leant teasingly across the table until her nose was hovering close to his.

"Come on Franck. No girl could resist such stunning lingerie."

"Captain, this is Georges Sternberg," said the voice. Franck was on foot, walking alongside Notre Dame, heading back to his office and his files.

"Sternberg?" repeated Franck, failing to recognise the name.

"I'm the crime scene technician from Rey's studio, and the Bateliers and the Lutetia."

"Of course. Sorry. I should have ..."

"Doesn't matter," interrupted Sternberg. "You're a busy man. And judging by what I'm looking at, you're about to get busier."

"Where are you?"

"The Meurice. Fourth floor. Room 403."

"I'm on my way."

*

The Meurice was a relatively discreet member of the capital's collection of grand hotels. It had stood on the rue de Rivoli since the first half of the nineteenth century. Expanded and remodelled several times since then, it maintained a running battle with the Ritz, the Plaza Athenée, the Crillon, the Bristol, and the Georges V for the custom of visiting heads of state, ministerial and diplomatic delegations, chief executive officers, and troublesome celebrities. Luxury and discretion were its two guiding principles, and its reputation was its most cherished asset. Its management policed its good name with fanatical devotion: they had even succeeded in recasting the dubious honour of having housed the German high command during the Occupation into the glory of having moved von Choltitz to refuse Hitler's order to raze the city in the face of the Allied advance.

Today's challenge was more mundane: dissimulating from their guests the presence within their walls of a crime scene.

When Franck arrived before the main entrance a liveried groom swept one of the doors open for him. He nodded his thanks and stepped through it into a vast reception area through which wandered a scattering of well-dressed guests. All was calm. There was not a uniform to be seen, aside from those borne by the hotel's staff.

Franck had the choice between the wide reception desk, with two eager young women sporting identical tightly knotted chignons, or the concierge's box to his left. Based on his knowledge of the codes of such establishments, he unhesitatingly chose the concierge.

His approach was monitored impassively by the short, stout man who stood proudly within the box. He had three keys embroidered on the epaulette of his jacket, witnesses to his long service.

"Good afternoon sir," he greeted Franck.

"Good afternoon," said Franck, retrieving his ID from his jacket and laying it flat on the counter between them.

"I think you'll be wanting the fourth floor, captain," said the concierge in a low voice. "May I tell the management you're here?"

"Of course," said Franck, matching his soft tone. "Where's the crime scene van?"

"We put it in the delivery bay round the back. Took them up in the service lift."

"Fair enough," said Franck. "Should I do the same?"

"Not at all, captain," said the concierge, lifting a section of the counter beside him and stepping out to join Franck. "Allow me."

The concierge escorted Franck to the main lift. He slowed his pace as they approached so as to allow the doors to close on a Japanese couple who were slightly before them. They waited a short while together in silence before they found themselves alone in an ascending cabin.

"Another one for *Exposé*," commented the concierge. "At least he's come back to a quality establishment after that fleapit in the tenth."

Franck cast a disbelieving glance at him. "You were worried he was dropping his standards?"

"A murder's not a problem, so long as it's compatible with the standing of the establishment," the concierge pointed out. "Today management's running around desperate, trying to keep this quiet. In six months time it'll be a tale to tell the guests. Part of the legend."

The doors opened and a uniformed policeman swivelled his head towards them from where he stood propped against the wall a short distance down a corridor perpendicular to the lift.

"This corridor's yours," said the concierge as Franck stepped out. "All the guests are out, and we'll try to keep it that way as long as we can."

"Thanks," said Franck.

The concierge nodded as the lift doors closed on him.

Franck showed his ID and the policeman silently indicated a room some distance down the corridor behind him. Franck knocked at 403, received no reply, and slowly opened the door.

It was a substantial room, facing south with three large windows overlooking the Jardin des Tuileries on the other side of the rue de Rivoli. The entrance was in one corner, opening onto a seating area containing a patterned chaise longue, two upholstered armchairs and a scattering of small tables. A sleeping area then followed, dominated by an oversized bed at the foot of which stood a dark velvet canapé. Then came a dressing area with an elegant commode topped by a vast oval mirror. The wall against which it sat contained two doors, both open, one for the toilet, the other for the bathroom.

Georges Sternberg was kneeling in the centre of the sitting area. He was working on a bottle of champagne nestled in an ice bucket on a low table. He looked up at Franck, and then at his watch.

"You're fast," he commented.

"Not fast enough, though," said Franck. "You always get there first."

Georges reached out and picked up a transparent zip-locked bag from the carpet near him. "Here's the glass. Just the one, as ever."

"Anything different this time?" asked Franck.

"This, for a start." Sternberg ran his hands through the thick pile of the carpet that covered the floor of the room. "First time we've had anything other than parquet."

"So?"

"So," said Sternberg, getting to his feet and pointing to a spot near the bed. "Slight indentations. Three of them. Tripod marks."

"Can I go over?" asked Franck.

"Shoes off. These on." Sternberg tossed a pair of elasticated plastic foot coverings to Franck. "You need gloves?"

"Got my own," said Franck, sliding off his shoes and pushing them back out into the corridor. He encased his feet and hands in plastic, shut the door behind him, and then moved slowly through the room, averting his eyes from the bed for the moment.

"Where are the marks?" he asked.

"At the foot of the bed. Right hand side as you face the wall. About fifty centimetres from the edge of the canapé."

Franck spotted them. He delicately positioned his feet slightly behind them and then raised his eyes, previewing the shot that he assumed would soon come into his hands.

His first sight of the corpse produced a slight jolt of recognition. For several minutes he stood in silence, chasing down the face, hunting for the name. Then it came to him.

"They're going to need a new Bond girl," he observed

He had last seen Marie Goubert resplendent in folds of gold

cloth, proclaiming her passion and scorn in *Le Cid*. She was much calmer now, her eyes shut amidst her celebrated chiselled features. She lay on her left side, an outstretched arm serving as a pillow, her right hand nestled between it and her cheek. Her chestnut hair was tousled, a few strands toying with her eyelashes, the rest spread luxuriantly over her shoulder, throwing her fine neck into shadow. Her breasts were hidden in half-cups of a velvety texture, alternately suffused with rich dark colours or worn away to semi-transparency. They glowed and beckoned from within the cavern formed by the crook of her elbow. Her taut waist emerged from this enticing gloom, preceding slightly twisted hips around which stretched the narrowest of briefs in the same mosaic of richly-coloured and almost absent fabric. The panties burrowed down between her legs and beneath her right thigh, which slid across her left to allow both her knees to sink into the covering of the bed. Her delicate feet were bare, the toes on each of them describing a perfect arc.

The overall effect was of deceptive slumber, the vigilant rest of the goddess Diana, ready to spring to her feet and draw her bow at the slightest rustle.

Franck changed position, crouching along the side of the bed. There was a torch on the floor there, no doubt left by Sternberg or his colleague, who was working quietly in the bathroom. Franck switched it on and trained it on her extended left arm. The mark, albeit tiny, was there. The goddess of the Comédie Française had slept through the approach of a needle that had spelled her death.

He extinguished the torch and got to his feet.

"The scene's yours," he said to Sternberg. "I'm going to see the management."

He left the room and sat down in the corridor to put his shoes back on. While he was there he pulled out his mobile phone. Although the timing was wrong – *Exposé* had come out that morning, and he could not believe that its photo editor would have preferred Sarkozy's grinning features to this – he nonetheless called Jacques Beaufort.

"Have you received a photo?" he demanded.

"Who is it this time?" asked Beaufort.

So something was different. They were not dealing with a Rachida Tazi this time around: if a photo had been received by *Exposé*, Beaufort would certainly have recognised the victim.

"Check your mail slots. Check the entire building. Make sure there's not an envelope somewhere."

"You weren't so anxious the last time I told you I didn't have one," Beaufort observed. "Then again, who would want a photo of that ugly bastard Rey? This one's different, isn't it? Our boy's back on track."

"Have you changed security? Have you put something in place that might have scared him off?" demanded Franck.

"You're kidding. Scare off our best photographer – not to mention one who works for free? What about you lot? Have you got an unmarked car sitting outside our building every night with a couple of snoring detectives?"

"We don't have the resources," said Franck. "Just check. I'll call you back later."

He ended the call and started off down the corridor, only to stop and turn back.

He popped his head into room 403.

"Georges, can you do something for me?"

Sternberg had moved on from the champagne bottle. He was now combing through the upholstery in the seating area.

"Sure, captain."

"Take a photo of the body from where the tripod marks are."

Sternberg glanced over at the bed.

"OK. How high?"

"How what?"

"How high do you want me to hold the camera? Level with the bed? Level with the corpse? Head height? Ceiling height?"

"Whatever gives the prettiest picture," said Franck.

"You serious?"

"Perfectly."

*

It was ten o'clock in the evening by the time he had finished collating his notes. An hour previously hunger had slowed him down, tugging at his concentration. Now he felt nothing other than thirst for some decent coffee. He contemplated the papers on his desk with frustration and no little fatigue. It was Laure Sarraute all over again.

Marie Goubert had arrived just after midday the previous day. She had booked the room herself two days earlier, having called the director of the Meurice. As the latter was an assiduous presence at the Comédie Française and a vocal admirer of Goubert, they had met on several occasions. Each time the director had assured her that his hotel – which, after all, was no more than ten minutes walk from the theatre – was at her disposal were she to require the services of its restaurants, spa, or most luxurious rooms. When she enquired whether he could lend her a quiet, light and airy room in which she could shut herself away for an afternoon before taking to the stage once more as Chimène in *Le Cid*, he was delighted to oblige.

When the day came the director had hurried to the front desk to greet her, offered to invite her to lunch in the main restaurant, which she declined, and shown her to room 403, assuring her that no-one would disturb her in the course of the afternoon. An hour later she had called down for champagne, and the director had personally signed the chit for the sommelier, determined that no bill be presented for any element of her stay.

At six in the evening, the stage manager at the Comédie Française began calling Marie Goubert's mobile, never getting beyond her voicemail. At six thirty, having interrogated the rest of the cast of *Le Cid*, he sent his assistant round to her apartment in the eighteenth arrondissement. Just after seven he called her understudy into his office and told her to start getting ready. At eight o'clock he stood on the stage just before curtain up and announced that Marie Goubert would be replaced in this evening's performance by Pauline Le Goff and sensed disappointment seep through the auditorium. Le Goff, however, gave a creditable performance and received the congratulations of her peers when the curtain fell. Through the rest of the evening and into the early hours of the night, messages continued to pile up on Goubert's voicemail. Most were solicitous, some complicit and a few simply curious. Nobody thought to phone the Meurice, because nobody knew she was there.

When the director arrived the next morning he spent some time, as was his habit, chatting with guests in the lobby as they emerged from the breakfast room. Upon enquiring whether a cosmopolitan Canadian couple, whom he had urged to seize the opportunity to go and see *Le Cid* during their stay in Paris, had enjoyed their evening, he learned of Goubert's mysterious absence. As a result he was the first to enter room 403 that morning and learn that the French stage had just lost its reigning princess.

The coroner's initial estimate placed the time of death between three and four in the afternoon. The champagne glass tested positive for flunitrazepam. The pinprick on the inner vein of Goubert's arm showed traces of potassium chloride. There had been no sexual contact. A detailed report would follow within twenty-four hours.

Marie Goubert's clothes were neatly folded on the commode in the dressing area of the room. She had abandoned a plain white bra and briefs for the lingerie in which she was found. Her handbag contained the keys to her apartment, her mobile phone, a Christian Dior purse with a little over a hundred euros in cash and three bank cards, a small make-up bag, an oval palm-sized mirror, two unopened letters, both utility bills, her pass for the Comédie Française, her national ID card, two untouched muesli bars and an article cut from *Variety* which recounted, in English, the successful conclusion to the recent search for the female star of the next Bond blockbuster.

Front desk staff could cite no suspicious comings or goings

during the afternoon or evening. A ministerial delegation from Qatar had checked in the course of the afternoon, generating substantial traffic both in the lobby and in the lifts. Franck had quizzed staff about any guests or visitors carrying prominent photographic equipment, but had drawn a blank. He had recovered tapes from the very discreet cameras that scanned the main entrance area and the secondary entrance on the rue de Castiglione, but there were none for the corridors of the fourth floor, or for the staff entrance and delivery bay on the rue du Mont Thabor. He would look through all the available recordings, but he was not optimistic.

Against his better judgement, Franck headed down the corridor to the coffee machine, searching in his pockets for some centimes. His mobile phone rang.

"Guerin," he answered.

"You forgot to call me back," said Jacques Beaufort.

"You find anything?"

"No. You going to tell me anything?"

"You haven't found out by now?" asked Franck.

"Come on, who is it?"

"Your network's slipping up, Jacques. I would have thought you'd have someone on the payroll in every grand hotel in Paris."

"We do. But clearly one of them's not doing his job. At least, not today. Which hotel?"

"This is Wednesday," Franck pointed out. "You've just put the new issue on the newsstands. You've got a whole week to find out."

"Which also means it doesn't matter if you tell me," insisted Beaufort. "I'll find out over the next few days for sure."

Franck thought it over. It could count as payoff for the Luc du Bellay photos.

"OK," he said. "Marie Goubert has been killed."

"The actress?"

"Yes."

"Where? How?"

"First, tell me what you know about her."

"What do you want to know?"

"Anything that might help. Did she have any connections to the fashion world?"

"Not directly. Christian Lacroix does a lot of costumes for the Comédie Française, so she must have met people. But beyond that, I've never heard of her on a catwalk. Though she must have had offers – everyone said she was one of the great beauties of her generation."

"Was being the operative word," mused Franck. "So where did the Bond thing come from?"

"Out of the blue, as far as I know. She's made a few trips to Hollywood over the past year, but I don't think anyone expected anything quite so big. Or quite so vulgar, depending on who you talk to."

"There was criticism?"

"This is France. Since when did success meet universal applause? Envy inspired its usual eloquence – a pupil of our finest tragic tradition stooping to play the whore of an agent of American imperialism, that sort of thing."

"British imperialism," corrected Franck. "Anglo-Saxon, if you want something more generic."

"Whatever. In any case, it was a far cry from Corneille and Racine. Too far for some. But I doubt your killer's to be found amongst such critics. He wasn't too fussy to kill a stripper, so I don't think a future starlet posed a particular problem."

"OK. None of this is particularly useful, though," said Franck.

"Try this," said Beaufort. "Your friend Luc du Bellay. Take a look at the collection of photos I gave you, she must be in there. He dated her maybe eighteen months ago. Lucky bastard."

"Thank you," said Franck. Luc du Bellay, once again. He decided to offer something in return. "It happened in the Meurice."

"How?" demanded Beaufort.

Franck had already hung up.

Beaufort immediately called back – twice – but he refused

to answer.

He was heading back down the corridor to his office, a stained plastic cup of coffee in his hand, when he recalled something else.

Although hesitant to call so late, he turned once more to his mobile phone, and called Anne Subrini.

"Good evening Anne, it's Franck."

"Didn't you stand me up today?" she asked, although with amusement rather than anger in her tone. "After I ran myself ragged compiling lists for you?"

"I'm sorry, Anne. There was an emergency – I'm still dealing with it."

"You're forgiven." She did not ask what had come up – a deliberate lack of curiosity that said much for her tact. "You can come and see me anytime, Franck, I'm almost always here. What about tomorrow?"

"I doubt I'll be free. What about Friday – sometime in the morning?" asked Franck.

"That's fine. Now get back to doing whatever it is you're supposed to be doing."

She rang off, leaving him feeling like a student whose term paper was long overdue. Which, with four bodies stacked against him, it certainly was.

Thursday, 21st June

Two photos.

Franck Guerin, seen from the waist upwards, his face angry, his lips tightly shut. Across from him, an attractive woman of a similar age in a cream blouse and a tightly-fitting jacket squared off across her shoulders. Her eyes are determined, and her lips move in speech. One arm outstretched, she plants an accusing finger on Guerin's chest.

Franck Guerin, his head turning, slightly blurred, his eyes narrowing. He is leaning forward, his body building momentum for a sudden move.

*

"I need to see him right now," insisted Franck.

It was after ten in the morning. Franck had been delayed by his search for a shop that could provide a large-scale colour print of the shot Georges Sternberg, the crime scene technician, had taken for him.

Luc du Bellay's receptionist was losing her amiable veneer. She had already explained three times that her boss was hosting a very important meeting and could not be disturbed. Franck had tried pulling out his mobile and calling directly, but du Bellay's phone was cut off.

"I'm going through that door," warned Franck, pointing to the entrance to du Bellay's office.

"You want to see me lose my job?"

Her phone rang. She picked it up.

"Certainly," she said. "Right away."

She hung up and got off her seat. Her tone had changed. Her professional smile was back.

"He's finished? I can go in?" asked Franck.

"He's just asked me to bring in some champagne."

"In the middle of the morning? Is that how he does business?"

"Sometimes," said the young woman.

"Let me get it," suggested Franck. "Where's it kept?"

She directed him to a storage room hidden behind a door in a corner of the reception area. Inside was a full-sized fridge filled with bottles of water, fruit juice, and a case of Pommery champagne. Piled on top was a series of cardboard cartons, each containing six glasses.

"How many?" he asked over his shoulder.

"Four," she said.

He found a carton that contained champagne flutes, unpacked them, set them on a tray, and added a bottle of chilled champagne. He carried it all back to the reception counter.

"Can I take it in?" he asked.

"Why not?" she said. Before he could move off, she added, "Hang on." She stalked over to the storage area, slowed by her heels, and retrieved another glass. "Might as well have one for yourself," she said, adding it to his tray.

"I'm not really in the mood," said Franck.

"Just wait," she insisted. "Moods are contagious."

She opened the door to the office and ushered him through. Franck advanced, the tray held before him, and then stopped to announce his presence.

Luc du Bellay was sitting behind his desk, whose surface was covered in neat piles of paper. Three additional chairs had been pulled around it. Two bore elderly, dark-suited men who looked quizzically over the tops of their spectacles at Franck. The last, its back to him, was occupied by a woman in a short skirt, patterned stockings, a cream blouse, and a boxy black jacket, her hair carefully piled on top of her head.

"Captain!" cried du Bellay. "Always one for the dramatic entrance!"

He stood up, clearing a space on his desk for the tray.

"You've arrived just in time to meet the new owners of Du Bellay," he said, beckoning Franck forward.

Franck took two paces and then stopped.

The woman who sat across from du Bellay had just turned around.

"Good morning Franck," said Sylvie Thomas.

"What are you doing here?" asked Franck.

"Like monsieur du Bellay just said, my colleagues and I have just bought his firm," explained Sylvie. "For a consortium of investors, of course."

Franck stared at her. She smiled back.

He switched his attention to du Bellay. "Can I give you this?" he asked, indicating the tray with his chin.

"Of course," said du Bellay. He moved round the desk and relieved Franck of the champagne.

"I think we should talk," said Franck, his attention focused once more on Sylvie. "Outside."

Sylvie mimed remorse, biting her lower lip and dipping her shoulders like a child chastised by its parents. "Are you going to arrest me again?"

"Outside," repeated Franck.

He strode through the Du Bellay reception area, across the lobby of the building, and outside onto the pavement facing the trees of the place des Etats-Unis. Sylvie followed behind at a more moderate pace.

"What is going on?" he asked her.

"I've just bought a financially embarrassed family firm with huge brand potential," she stated. "Well, I didn't buy it personally, but I arranged for it to be bought. As far as I'm aware, when last I enquired, that's not a crime."

"You should have told me. You're dealing with a suspect in a murder investigation."

"Ah no," insisted Sylvie, pointing a determined finger at Franck's chest. "He's not a suspect. You told me yourself. And, in any case, even if he was, it wouldn't be against the law to sign a contract with him."

"Since when was your bank interested in small-time family lingerie businesses?"

"Since you asked me to look into Du Bellay's finances. That showed us their weakness. You also tipped me off about the sudden boom in their sales. That showed us their potential.

You've only got yourself to blame. Don't forget – you came to me."

"What about the victims? That's what your so-called 'potential' is founded on. Sounds pretty distasteful to me."

"Money has no smell, Franck. Ask Vespasian. If it makes you feel any better, it's unlikely we'll hold on to Du Bellay. We'll flip it in nine to twelve months, before this whole *Exposé* effect begins to fade."

"Unless the killer happens still to be out there, notching them up, keeping the tills ringing and profits high."

"You'll catch him. I have every confidence in you."

"Tell that to Marie Goubert," muttered Franck, turning away from Sylvie in disgust, as much at himself as at her. He liked Sylvie too much – despite the fact that she served a quite different cause from his own. Seeing her was always a refreshing change from his normal routine, offering distracting glimpses of a world he would never wish to inhabit but was curious to observe. But he should have known she could not be trusted.

"What?" demanded Sylvie, but Franck did not hear her.

He had caught a flash of light in a bush in the park opposite them: sun catching glass. There was a figure behind it, hunched down to conceal as much of his bulk as possible.

Franck surged forward, leaving Sylvie marooned behind him. He crossed the road and leaped the low barrier that ringed the park, an involuntary cry breaking from his lips as he did so.

The figure had moved too, pushing one of the park gates and sprinting down the road that ran along its south side. Franck struck a parallel course, skirting trees and ploughing across flowerbeds as he attempted to keep pace. His brow was instantly damp with sweat and his midriff pleaded with him to stop, but this time he would not let the pain slow him down.

His prey was moving quickly, a long-nosed camera dangling on a strap at his side, jiggling wildly as he ran. Franck looked ahead. He could see a mountain bike propped up against the fence that marked the park boundary where it met the avenue de Iéna. Time to even up the match. He tugged out his revolver and aimed it as best he could without breaking his stride. He fired. Once. Twice. Three times.

The bike toppled over just as the photographer was a few metres short of it. He stopped dead, and suddenly changed direction to head down avenue de Iéna. As he did so the strap of his camera detached itself from his shoulder and started sliding down his arm. He paused instinctively, his left arm swinging across his body to seize the strap and stop the camera lens from touching the ground. Just as he secured it, Franck cannoned into him from behind and both men fell.

Franck rolled over him and got to his knees. He still had his revolver in his hand, having thumbed the safety mechanism back on before the collision. He brought it up, disengaged the safety and locked both hands into firing position, his face a grimace of pain. The photographer was not paying him any attention. He was reaching out for the lens that was now rolling away from the body of his camera.

"Shit," he muttered. He looked up, pulled the bob from his head, and threw it at Franck. "You broke my fucking camera!" he yelled.

Franck lowered his gun, his thumb once more neutralising it. He was panting through clenched teeth while he pushed his left hand firmly into his stomach, as if to calm it.

"Who are you, and why are you following me?" he asked.

The photographer dug into his pocket and tugged out a mobile phone. He flipped it open, tapped a few keys, and handed it to Franck.

"Ask him," he said.

"First of all, you put these on," said Franck, drawing a set of cuffs from the back of his belt. The photographer dutifully extended both hands and Franck clipped each wrist in turn. He then extracted the mobile phone from his captive's grasp.

"Who is this?" demanded Franck.

"Sounds like my favourite captain," said Jacques Beaufort. "And as you're calling me with Didier Fabre's phone, I reckon this means you've caught him out."

"He works for you?"

"He works for me," confirmed Luc. "And he's very good at what he does. You should be flattered. Last assignment he did was some freelancing in Afghanistan. Before that Lebanon. Only the best for you."

"How long has he been stalking me?" demanded Franck.

"More or less since you first came to see me. Just goes to show the amount we're prepared to invest in this story. You see – it's not just about free front page covers. The day you bring the killer in, I'll have a photo essay retracing your entire enquiry. You'll be a big star."

"Sure," said Franck. "The detective who took two weeks to spot his tail. Real star material."

"Hey, don't feel bad about it," said Beaufort. "He's used to dodging snipers and avoiding bombs. You should be quite pleased with yourself for catching him."

"He shot my bike and broke my fucking camera!" shouted Fabre.

"What's he saying?" asked Beaufort.

"Somebody broke his toys," explained Franck.

"Tell him I'll buy him some new ones."

Franck held the phone at a slight distance as he addressed Fabre, who was fingering the cuffs uneasily. "Your boss says he'll replace everything. No expense spared."

He turned his attention back to the phone. "You call him off right now."

"You can't make me do that, captain," objected Beaufort. "There's no law against following a police officer. So long as he doesn't obstruct your enquiry, there's nothing you can do against us."

"That's what you think," said Franck, closing the phone.

"Uncomfortable?" he asked Fabre, nodding towards the cuffs.

"You could say that," confirmed the photographer.

Franck found his keys and unlocked Fabre's left hand. While the photographer flexed it, Franck suddenly took a step towards one of the cars parked alongside them on avenue de Iéna. He raised the empty cuff, tugging Fabre behind him, and snapped it shut over the handle of the car.

"Hey!" protested Fabre. "What're you doing?"

"Buying myself some peace and quiet," said Franck, getting to his feet. "If the driver comes along, tell him to phone the local commissariat. They'll know what to do. Meantime I'll keep this."

He waved Fabre's mobile phone in the air and walked back towards the place des Etats-Unis, leaving the photographer's cries behind him. He advanced slowly, doing his best to regulate his breathing and calm his abdomen. He tossed the phone into the first rubbish bin he passed.

When Franck got back to the Du Bellay building, Sylvie and her two colleagues had gone.

"You mind telling me what that was all about with Sylvie Thomas?" asked Luc du Bellay, who had welcomed Franck back into his office.

Du Bellay was still toying with a glass of champagne. Franck asked for some coffee to wash down two painkillers he had retrieved from one of his pockets.

"I think I found you your buyer," explained Franck. "I know Sylvie Thomas. I had asked her to check into your finances. I think that's what sparked her interest in buying your firm."

"Does that mean I have to pay you a finder's fee?"

"Provided you pay your capital gains taxes, let's say it's all part of the service," suggested Franck.

Du Bellay put down his glass.

"You know, part of me doesn't feel that grateful. I wasn't really planning on selling the firm. But the banks had me by the throat. I'd borrowed heavily to build up the brand. I've spent a lot of time renegotiating loans over the past year, month after month."

"What about the sudden leap in sales?" asked Franck.

"What about the exceptional production costs to keep pace and take advantage of it?" countered du Bellay. "The fundamentals were looking better and better, but my cash flow was all screwed up. A classic error. Your friend Sylvie

Thomas, however, seems to have access to as much cash as she wants."

"So what happens to you?"

"Oh, I stay on," said du Bellay. "General manager. With a small equity stake to make sure I still give my all. Just as well – investment bankers might know a lot about money, but they don't have a clue about manufacturing and marketing lingerie."

"So to the outside world nothing will have changed?"

"In the short term. With time, the connoisseurs will notice. My mission was to make the best lingerie in the world. That, of course, is what got me so deeply into the red."

"From now on it'll be to make the most profitable lingerie in the world?"

"Something like that," conceded du Bellay. "Still, can I hope this means you no longer suspect me of killing my clients to keep sales up?"

"That depends," said Franck. "Where were you on Tuesday afternoon?"

"At La Défense. In a meeting room in Sylvie Thomas' offices. There were at lot of us, including three lawyers."

"Not the best witnesses," observed Franck, "But they'll do."

"So, what happened on Tuesday?" asked du Bellay. "I've been stuck in negotiations for days. I've no idea what else is happening in the world."

"This."

Franck had retrieved the briefcase he had abandoned in the reception area upon arriving that morning. Inside was an A4 colour print of the photo he had asked Georges Sternberg to take in the Meurice. He slid it from its protective envelope and laid it on the table.

"I believe you knew her," he said.

Du Bellay did not reply. He reached out towards the photo, but did not touch it, his fingers hovering over Marie Goubert's face. After a moment he withdrew them, folding his hands into his lap.

"Marie," he softly pronounced her name.

Franck watched him intently. Neither Sarraute nor Tazi had

elicited such a response.

"We were together for a while," explained du Bellay. "Two years ago. She was incredible. Every day she astounded me. I couldn't keep up. I was fun, but she was ..." He left the phrase hanging, a mute witness to the gulf he had not been able to bridge.

"I'm sorry for your loss," said Franck. He had assumed Goubert had been just another conquest for du Bellay. Now it looked as if he had been the conquered one, left prone in the dust.

"The same killer?" asked du Bellay.

"Looks like it," said Franck. "Providing you can confirm that she's wearing Du Bellay."

Du Bellay returned to the photo, picking it up this time.

"Yes," he said. "She's wearing a Tisserand – *balconnet* bra and tanga."

He turned the photo towards Franck and pointed to the fabric covering Goubert's breasts. He had slipped back in his professional world. "The Tisserand is the most expensive model we've ever produced. The foundation is silk muslin, almost totally transparent, onto which we weave velvet, which is then painted. We apply six different colours, all by hand. We use a workshop in Lyon that's been perfecting this technique since the nineteenth century. It's painstaking work. To get the mix of muslin and velvet just right so that when we cut it the colours and the transparency sit correctly on the body – covering what should be covered, and revealing what should be revealed – we have to weave different patterns for every size."

Du Bellay brought the photo back to himself and mused over it for a few seconds.

"It's our chef d'œuvre," he concluded. "She looks magnificent in it."

"In which case, it's our killer," concluded Franck. "I'll need your sales records again. I'll get confirmation of Marie Goubert's size through to you. Unless, of course, ..." he hesitated.

Du Bellay turned to face him. "Judging from this, she

hadn't changed over the past two years. So yes, I already know it. As for the sales records, well those for the previous models didn't seem to help you that much ..."

"True," admitted Franck. "But if this model is so expensive, maybe we're dealing with smaller volumes?"

"Smaller than you could possibly imagine," said du Bellay. "The Tisserand is not on the market. It's scheduled for release in six weeks' time. There have been no sales."

Friday, 22nd June

One photo.

Franck Guerin, walking forcefully past a pair of shoppers, both women in their early thirties dressed with expensive flair. He wears black trousers, a light blue shirt, and a blue jacket. His faithful briefcase is absent. His hands are bunched into fists, his eyes straight ahead, his brow furrowed, as if he were heading towards a fight.

*

"He's back on track," said Franck, concluding his briefing on Marie Goubert, early on Friday morning.

The full crime scene and coroner reports had come through, but were short on revelations: flunitrazepam in the champagne glass and nestling alongside potassium chloride in her blood; a whole host of fingerprints, none of which matched those retrieved from the previous sites; no marks of violence and no sexual contact. An all too familiar signature.

"With one exception," objected Yves, pointing towards the Sternberg shot. "No photo."

"There has to be a photo," insisted Franck. "There were tripod marks right beside the bed."

"So where is it?"

"It happened late on Tuesday afternoon. *Exposé* went to press a few hours later. Maybe he missed the deadline," Franck suggested. "Maybe he'll now wait until next week."

"Up until now he's always timed the murder to allow himself to deliver the photo within a matter of hours and has never come close to missing the deadline. Your friend Beaufort always got the photo before we got the corpse. It's as if the killer is losing control of his planning. Anyhow, I don't see him delivering it now. He'll assume we're waiting for him."

"Are we?" asked Franck.

"Unfortunately, even though it's pointless, we're now obliged to do so. I put a team onto *Exposé* yesterday. They'll watch the building twenty-four hours a day until it goes to press next Wednesday. The accountants won't be happy, and with good reason. Just this once, it would have been nice to have been able to mobilise the DST. I'd feel better squandering their surveillance budget rather than ours."

"All he has to do is post it from a mailbox anywhere in the country," agreed Franck. "Given the timing, there's no need for him to approach *Exposé* in person."

"Maybe you should go over there and brief their mail room staff about suspicious packages," said Yves.

"I will."

"Will Beaufort cooperate?"

"I imagine so."

"Despite what you did to his photographer? What was his name?"

"Didier Fabre."

"You really had to leave him cuffed to that car?" asked Yves.

"I'm sure it gave him a lot of time to reflect on what it means to interfere with an active investigation."

"He was scarcely interfering. If he had been, I suspect we wouldn't have taken two weeks to spot him. I can understand why you were upset, Franck, but the press have rights too. And it's our job to uphold them."

Franck shrugged. "He's probably sitting outside as we speak, watching that window with a new telephoto lens."

"Mustn't disappoint him then," said Yves, getting up from his desk and wandering over to his office window, looking out over the boulevard du Palais.

"See him?" asked Franck.

"Mountain bike, shapeless hat, big camera? No, no sign of him. Maybe he's getting better at concealing himself."

Yves turned his gaze back to Franck.

"I take it our killer's not lost his touch in that department. Nothing on the Meurice observation tapes?"

"Nothing that strikes me. People flow in and out of these grand hotels all day long, carrying all sorts of stuff."

"I wouldn't have thought that the clients of the Meurice carried their own luggage to their rooms," Yves pointed out.

"They don't. But you should see the size and quantity of the shopping bags. All our man has to hide is a collapsible tripod, a camera, and a syringe or two."

"True," Yves conceded. "It's not as if he's sneaking the bodies out afterwards."

"You know what surprises me?" asked Franck.

Yves moved back behind his desk. "What?"

"That's the third time he's set the same trap – hotel, lingerie, champagne – and the victims keep falling into it. Sarraute couldn't have known better, and it probably never occurred to Tazi that what had happened to Laure Sarraute could happen to her, but Marie Goubert must have heard about the previous two killings. And yet she seems to have walked into it without a care."

"Hotel and lingerie," corrected Yves. "They couldn't know about the champagne – we've never talked about it and it's never been in the media. As for the lingerie, we don't know when it's being put on."

"Forensics say there's no trace of superficial bruising from awkward dressing. Anne Subrini read the death photos as saying that the victims had dressed themselves."

"With all due respect for professor Subrini's gifts," objected Yves, "I don't think that's something you can tell from a photo. As for the one other common feature – the hotel – don't forget that our killer is not luring unsuspecting women into hotel rooms. They're booking them and inviting him in."

"It all goes back to that," said Franck. "He knows them. They know him. They trust him."

"Trust or affection?" asked Yves. "If the victims are dressing themselves, what are they expecting if not a tryst?"

"No sexual contact," Franck reminded him. "Forensics are formal."

"That it didn't happen doesn't mean it wasn't expected."

"We've already eliminated one serial seducer in the person of Luc du Bellay. Do I have to find another?"

"Luc du Bellay – the man who dressed them but never touched them," mused Yves. "What are we doing about this latest model? The one that isn't yet available, and yet turns up on the fourth floor of the Meurice? Doesn't that make him look rather suspicious all over again?"

"Except that he's got an alibi for Goubert. And for Rey, for that matter."

"An alibi that just happens to be our friend Sylvie Thomas. She ran rings round you on this one, Franck."

"She ran rings round me the last time too," observed Franck, recalling the arrest that had first brought him into contact with Sylvie.

"And yet now, as then, we can only stand by and applaud. We really should be thinking about recruiting her."

"We can't afford her. Believe me – I've seen the figures. Even you'd be jealous if you knew how much she earned."

"I doubt that," stated Yves, with calm conviction.

Franck smiled, sure that this was the indubitable truth.

"We're best using her on a voluntary basis," he suggested.

"Given the way she used us, I'm not sure who's volunteering who. Still, no harm done. Which is more than we can say about this mysterious Tisserand ensemble. It's the nearest thing to a smoking gun we've found thus far – whoever took it has to have a connection with, or know something about, Du Bellay's production setup."

"It turns out the first production run was completed three weeks ago," explained Franck. "The stocks are supposed to be sitting in a warehouse in Lyon. I've asked du Bellay to go down there and check them himself. I've told him not to alert any of the personnel. If one is missing, in the right size, then we know our killer had access to the warehouse. If none are missing, then something strange is going on with his suppliers and workshops."

"When will we know?"

"He drove down to Lyon last night. I had forensics release the lingerie taken from Goubert's body so that he could take it with him. That way he can check to see if it's a copy, although he seems very sceptical that such a thing is possible. I'm expecting to hear from him sometime today."

"Exemplary cooperation once again," observed Yves. "Our once favourite suspect is proving a valuable ally."

Franck sighed. "Add to that the fact that my mysterious stalker turns out to have everything to do with the case, but nothing to do with the killer, and it means we currently have precisely zero suspects. Four corpses, and we're still nowhere near."

Yves tutted, shook his head, and raised a finger. Franck sat back in his seat, sure he was about to be given a lesson.

"Not at all," insisted Yves. "We have three victims that fit a pattern – with a minor variation, as far as the photos are concerned – but we've still got a clear pattern. We've got a fourth one who does not. So we set him aside."

"We don't care about Jean-Michel Rey?" asked Franck, unwilling to admit that he was somebody about whom it was hard to care.

"Of course we do. We'll get back to him. In the meantime, let's stop trying to find a person who has links to Sarrault, Tazi, and now Goubert. Let's try identifying a characteristic that all three of them had in common."

"Sarrault and Tazi were life models at the Beaux Arts. For the moment that's all we've got, but I'll check with Anne Subrini for Goubert."

"Sarrault and Tazi were there years apart. Think about the present – each victim's present. What was going on?"

"Sarrault was modelling, Tazi was stripping, Goubert was acting," recited Franck. "They were all using their bodies in their line of work. Unfortunately, there's a whole host of professions for women for which that's true."

"Sarrault had signed with Ephémère, and was about to go from being a couture model to being a publicity icon. Tazi was moving into pornography. Her body, and its most intimate parts, were about to be visible not only in a seedy club in Pigalle but all across the internet. Rey, it's worth noting, was her accomplice in this, if not the actual instigator. Goubert ..."

"Was to be the next Bond girl," said Franck. "She was the darling of the Comédie Française and its, what, two or three hundred thousand spectators a year? Thanks to Hollywood ..."

"Not to mention Pinewood," interjected Yves.

"OK, thanks to the movie business," continued Franck. "She was about to be seen by millions and probably launch an international career as a film star."

"You see," said Yves. "They were all at watersheds. And somebody didn't want them to cross them."

*

Anne Subrini opened her office door.

"Come in, Franck. As you can see, my students have left me in peace for a moment."

She was expecting him. He had called her when he emerged from his meeting with Yves, checking that she was free to see him. Franck had walked to the Beaux Arts from Ile de la Cité, mulling over the fact that only a week had passed since his first visit. A week, and two corpses.

He stepped through the door, which she closed behind him. She led him towards the chaise longue and armchairs near the windows of her office. She wore a light yellow dress that flirted with her knees. Identically coloured ballet pumps held her feet.

"You're dressing up again," observed Franck, conscious of a fleeting hope that she had done so for him.

"I'm having lunch with Juliette and the woman who owns the gallery she's showing in. Juliette Sollers. You remember? We went to her vernissage."

Franck nodded. "I remember. Anxious Madonnas envious of their children."

"Good for you. Well, as ever, I dressed up for Juliette."

"It suits you," said Franck. Perched on the chaise longue, the simple cut and natural radiance of the dress endowed Anne with an almost bucolic charm and innocence. A far cry from the worldly sophistication in which he had first beheld her.

She smiled and shook her head. "It's a trick, Franck. This dress is far younger than me, both literally – obviously – and symbolically. It showcases what is ageing well" – she swung her slender and slightly tanned legs up in front of her and held up the delicate arms that emerged from its short sleeves – "and hides or distracts from the rest." She touched her throat, around which a gauzy scarf of a slightly darker yellow was casually thrown. "My neck is obscured, my bust is primly hidden, and the voluminous skirt works wonders with my thighs. Still, your compliment is most welcome. Artifice merits applause, if not always admiration."

"You are a harsh critic," observed Franck.

"That's my job. However, I can assure you, I'm just as hard with everyone else. For instance, you look terrible. Your skin is dry, your hair a tangled mess, and your eyes more bloodshot than pupil. What's more, you've made no attempt to hide it."

"I'll take your word for it. I've not spent much time in front of a mirror recently."

"Only recently?" chided Anne. "I suspect you've no time for mirrors, full stop. You don't believe in what you see."

"Whereas?"

"Whereas I only believe in what I see. You pursue naked truth; I prefer artful beauty."

"I believe in that," remarked Franck, pointing to one corner of the low table that separated him from Anne. An Italian cafetière and two substantial cups sat on a square tray.

"To business, then," said Anne. "Since you warned me of your arrival, I made us some coffee. I assume you prefer yours scalding hot, excessively strong and unapologetically bitter. Coffee in its ur-state, stripped to its essence. I hope you're not disappointed."

She leant over and poured the dark liquid, filling one cup for Franck and a half cup for herself. Franck sipped and nodded his appreciation.

"Have you got anywhere with Laure Sarraute and the life classes?" he asked.

"Yes I have," said Anne. "Laure had regular work as a life

model, once a week, give or take the odd absence, for a six month period in 2003. She was paid for it, and there don't seem to have been any reciprocal arrangements, unlike with Rachida Tazi. I assume she needed the money. That said, she couldn't have lived off what we were giving her, so she must have had other employment at the same time. Presumably she gave up the life classes when her modelling career began to take off." Two folders lay on the table, one beige, the other light yellow, not unlike her dress. She motioned with her chin towards the former. "In there are the dates of all the classes she posed for."

"Great," said Franck. "Any luck with the students?"

"That was trickier," said Anne. "But I've done what I can. Given how long she was here, any number of students could have sat in on a class for which she was modelling. That said, two teachers used her regularly for their painting and drawing classes. I've noted the names of the students enrolled in those classes."

"Are any of those students still here?" asked Franck.

Anne shook her head. "I don't think so, given this took place four years ago. That said, students have been known to cling on in dark corners for astonishing periods of time. What I am certain of, is that none of the students in my class with Rachida Tazi are on the list."

"Thanks anyway," said Franck. "I'll give the list a thorough check back at my office, and run the names through the computer."

"Discreetly," requested Anne.

"Discreetly," confirmed Franck. "I'm a man of my word."

"That I do not doubt."

"Anyhow, it may be that the Beaux Arts connection is a false trail," announced Franck.

"Why do you say that?" asked Anne.

"It depends what you can tell me about this," said Franck. He lifted his briefcase onto the table, extracted an oversized envelope from it, and allowed Sternberg's photo to slide out. With the tip of one finger he swivelled it around to face Anne.

She swung her legs up onto the chaise longue and leant

forward over the table.

"Marie Goubert," she said, unhesitatingly. "Our Sarah Bernhardt, our Rachel, our Champmeslé, and a divine beauty to boot. She's ...?"

"Yes," confirmed Franck. "Unless I'm much mistaken, she's our killer's number four."

"No," said Anne, somewhat distracted, as if she had not heard Franck.

"I'm afraid so," insisted Franck. "Her body was found two days ago."

"No," repeated Anne. "This photograph – it is inconceivable that it was taken by the same person as those of Sarraute and Tazi. The lighting is harsh. The framing is wrong. The body is flat and lifeless. Most of her face is hidden. There is also the fact that it is in colour. Given our killer seems to use digital equipment, that may not be a significant difference, but this is poorly tamed colour – the shades of velvet look electric. Technically, it's a weak shot, but that's the least of its problems. It has no soul."

"That's not surprising," said Franck, although such criticism had never occurred to him. "This was taken by a crime scene technician."

"Ah. In which case, a little soul would be asking a lot. Why not bring the original?"

"I don't have the original," admitted Franck. "I don't even know if there is an original. *Exposé* has received nothing. That's the one big discrepancy."

"So why are you convinced it's the same killer?"

"Because everything else is the same. She's dressed in Du Bellay lingerie. She was killed in a hotel room by someone she knew. And there is other corroborating evidence I can't tell you about."

"Poor Marie," said Anne.

"You knew her?" asked Franck.

"Of course. I've been going to the Comédie Française for as long as I can remember. I've watched Marie bloom on stage, like others before her. Only they eventually faded, or worse. It seems she's not going to have to face that."

"That's not what I meant. Do you know of any connection to the Beaux Arts – was she a life model, or student, or linked to a student or a member of staff?"

"Not that I know of. We have many former students at the Comédie Française, but all backstage – visual design, costumes, scenery, that sort of thing. I don't think any have ever trodden the boards."

"Could you check?" asked Franck.

"Of course."

Franck drew her attention back to the photograph.

"Forget the shot," he said. "Look at the scene. Is there anything here that might explain why we haven't received a photo? Is the pose wrong? Is the setting wrong? Is there something that would have made it impossible to take a shot he would have been happy with?"

Anne studied the photo for many minutes, her attention clearly focused on the figure of Marie Goubert.

"No. There's nothing wrong. The pose is more modest than the two previous victims. The folded limbs, both arms and legs, signal a desire to conceal. And yet what she is wearing is probably more revealing than what was found on Sarraute and Tazi. There is a lot of almost transparent fabric, like mist blown across her skin, mist suffused by patches of colour. If the light was more kind and the contrast more pronounced, you would have the impression that her body had been painted. Tazi was tricked out, admitting that there was something meretricious in her beauty. Sarraute was sculpted, staked out on a pedestal for the world to admire the sheer geometry of desire in her curves. There is something more sensuous, smouldering, in Goubert's pose. That might explain why so much is hidden. To see more might be unbearable – like staring at the sun."

Anne stopped, took a deep breath, and withdrew her regard from the photo. "I'm sorry," she said. "I'm talking about what the photo failed to capture, what could – or should – have been there. And here was me saying I only believe in what I see."

"Don't apologise," insisted Franck. "What you've said is very important."

"It is?" she asked, with more than a note of scepticism.

"It means there is a photo. We just don't have it yet."

"Can I ask something, even if it sounds strange?"

"Sure."

"If there is a photo, will you let me see it?"

"If there is a photo, all you'll have to do is buy *Exposé*."

"I'd rather see the original," she insisted.

"I'll see what I can do," said Franck. "And you're right."

"About what?"

"The request does sound a little strange."

Anne shrugged. "I see a portrait. You see a crime scene."

Voiced by anyone else, such a remark would have irritated Franck. A crime was a crime. Verbal niceties and fine distinctions were too often the arms of apologists who failed to see that every misdeed shook the foundations of the civilisation they took for granted.

But he knew that Anne's observation was sincere. Her calling determined the way she saw the world. As did his. And although their vocations were markedly different, he respected hers and the conviction with which she exercised it.

"Unfortunately, the one thing I don't see is the criminal," he admitted, unable to keep a hint of defeat from creeping into his voice.

"Not yet," countered Anne. "A little patience, Franck. A little determination."

"Is that what you tell your students?"

She laughed, folding her feet back underneath her again, suddenly carefree.

"Sometimes."

He picked up the beige folder with the life class information concerning Laure Sarraute.

"Thanks again for this," he said. "And if you find any mention or trace of Marie Goubert here, at any time over the past years, let me know."

He put the Sternberg photo back in its envelope, lay it on

p.257

top of the folder, and opened his briefcase to slide both in. It was time to go. No matter how much he admired Anne or enjoyed her company, he had too much work to do. Now that he had more information to process, the sooner he did so, the faster he would know where it might lead him.

Just as he was about to get to his feet, Anne leant towards him with an outstretched hand and gently grasped one of his arms.

"I have something else for you," she said.

She released him and laid her hand on the other, yellow, folder.

"This. It's a present."

"A present?" repeated Franck. "Why?"

"Never ask 'why'," she said, firmly. "Just say 'thank you'. Moreover, as a rule, you should do so before you open a present. It reduces the risk of any hint of disappointment sneaking into your tone."

"OK," said Franck. "Thank you." He grasped one corner of the folder. "May I?"

"Be my guest."

When opened the folder revealed a square of thick, heavily-grained paper on which a male nude had been sketched. Caught while turning, ribs, a twisted waist, a scarred pelvis and smoothly contoured buttocks were its most prominent features. The head was seen from behind, a mass of tousled hair emerging behind the peak of the right shoulder. The one visible arm was held down along the torso and bent at the elbow so as to allow the hand to clutch at the air alongside the head.

The scars looked all too familiar.

"Is this me?" asked Franck.

"Sketched very roughly during your life class," said Anne. "But yes, it's you. Like a knotted branch or trunk, grown resilient through time. Since you don't pay much attention to mirrors, keep it as a reminder of what you can't see."

"I will," said Franck. "I'm touched."

He leant across the table and kissed Anne on one cheek. She very lightly stroked his hair as he drew back. For the first time,

Franck allowed himself to believe that something might come of their encounter.

"Will you sign it?" he asked.

Anne snorted. "Of course not. It took me maybe three minutes. I don't sign my paintings, at least not visibly, so I can scarcely sign this."

"Please," urged Franck. "I won't tell anybody."

Anne shook her head, but chose to indulge him. She slipped off the chaise longue, went to her desk, and came back with a thick soft-leaded pencil. She flipped the sketch over and signed the back.

"Isn't it common practice to sign the front?" he asked.

"Like you say, it's a practice that is common, and the one the market prefers. It is not, however, mine."

"Fair enough," said Franck. He carefully closed the yellow folder and slid it alongside the other in his briefcase.

"I'll let you get back to your students," he said, this time getting to his feet.

Anne rose with him, but headed back to her desk rather than to the door.

"Don't forget these," she said, holding up the two copies of *Wasp-Waisted* he had left with her.

She brought them to him. "Remarkable publication," she commented. "Now there's one of our students who developed a very specific eye."

"What?"

Anne opened one of the copies to the back page, and pointed to Maryam's name at the top of the publishing details.

"Mademoiselle Sehati. You'll find her in the beige folder."

*

"Captain, this is Luc du Bellay."

"Are you at the warehouse?" asked Franck into his telephone, once more in his office. It was mid afternoon and he had begun to get impatient waiting for news from Lyon.

"Yes. I've checked the Tisserand stocks. I opened every

single box."

"And?" prompted Franck.

"All present and accounted for."

"Shit," said Franck. "That makes things a lot more complicated. Could somebody in the production line have run off an extra ensemble without you ever knowing about it?"

"I doubt it. The Tisserand uses very expensive custom-made fabric. I'd be very surprised if our supplier wove any more than the absolute minimum. According to our records, five units – either the bra or the tanga – didn't meet quality control after assembly, but normally they'll have been destroyed. I received the ensemble from the Meurice yesterday, and I can assure you it wasn't a sub-standard piece."

"Or a copy?"

"Of course not. I told you before – I'd defy anyone to copy the Tisserand. You would need the original material, and to get that you would need our supplier in Lyon. This may be a perfidious world, but he's been dealing with my family over three generations. I'd stake my business on his honesty."

"Strictly speaking, it's no longer yours to stake," observed Franck.

"Thank you for that little reminder, captain."

"Sorry," apologised Franck. He had nothing to gain by alienating du Bellay. "So nothing's missing, and we're not dealing with a copy – what's left?"

"I think I may have misled you when I said all were present and accounted for," said du Bellay.

"Doesn't sound ambiguous to me," observed Franck.

"All are accounted for, that's all."

"I'm not following you."

"324 units came out of the initial production run. That's 162 pairs of bras and tangas. Five units were lost to quality control."

"Why not 320 or 330?" asked Franck.

"We don't have an obsession with round numbers. The production run was determined by anticipated sales by unit size, based on the performance of similar ensembles. Once the calculation was done, our target was 324."

"OK," said Franck. "I'll stop the stupid questions."

"In all, 58 bras and 72 tangas were Marie Goubert's size."

"OK."

"Of those, there are 56 bras and 70 tangas in the warehouse."

"I thought you said all were accounted for?" asked Franck, suddenly lost.

"The two missing ensembles are accounted for. They're clearly marked in the stock register."

"Marked as what?"

"Promotion samples."

"Which are?"

"Ensembles that we send off ahead of release date to privileged partners. Who, as a general rule, request specific sizes. In all, sixteen units were shipped as promotion samples, but the six other pairs had different size combinations."

"So who got the two that interest us?" demanded Franck.

"A certain Saudi princess who will remain anonymous."

"And?"

"*Wasp-Waisted*. They're to feature it in their twentieth issue."

Once he had hung up, Franck set feverishly to work. He took out the beige folder Anne Subrini had given him and glanced at the traces left by Laure Sarraute's brief career as a life model at the Beaux Arts. For each session there was a date and a code for the class which had been present. Listed separately were the students enrolled in each class that year, between fifteen and twenty, each identified by name and a seven digit figure that Franck assumed to be some kind of matriculation number. He found her half-way down the list for class PD2: Sehati, Maryam, 1003504.

He thought back to the evening they had spent together, trying to recall exactly what she had said to him about her education. As far as he could remember, she had been vague and dismissive, implying that she had flitted between many options before finding her feet. For once, he wished he had taken notes. It had been a very distracting evening. Visually, he could recall everything – the way she had sipped her champagne, the three ensembles, the skin they had hidden or revealed, the way Maryam had moved towards him, how she had drawn his hands to her – but the very precision of these images seemed to have pushed the words they had exchanged to some murky place at the back of his memory.

The way she had sipped her champagne.

He turned to the shelves behind him, snatched the case files, and spread them out on his desk. The crime scene report from the Meurice was at the top of the pile. He ran his eyes down the detailed description of the room and all its contents until he found the paragraph devoted to the seating area with the ice bucket, the single glass, and the open bottle of Henriet champagne.

He left the file lying open and dug through the others until he found the equivalent report from the Hotel des Bateliers: an ice bucket in the bathroom and a half-empty bottle of Henriet.

He soon had the third report aligned alongside the other two. The Lutetia: an ice bucket on a small table in the corner of the room, cork and wire casing laid beside it, one open bottle of Henriet champagne.

He did not have a file for the fourth occurrence, just a recollection: a bottle tossed towards him; the chill, straight from the fridge, as he caught it with his two hands; Maryam hovering before him with two glasses as he freed the cork; the casual assurance with which she asked his approval of her choice; his appreciative nod on reading the Henriet label.

Hotels; lingerie; champagne. The only element of the killer's modus operandi that hadn't leaked to the media just happened to point straight to Maryam.

*

By the time Franck got there, early on Friday evening, avenue Montaigne was winding down. Those affluent enough to shop there were now heading elsewhere, carrying stiff, oversized paper bags which proudly bore the blazons of their preferred brands: Chanel, Louis Vuitton, Gucci, Ephémère, Armani, Christian Dior, Prada, Fendi, not to mention others that were completely unknown to him.

Franck strode hurriedly past the scattered women laden with their purchases. He thought back to the surveillance video from the Meurice: the luggage stopped at the front desk; the shopping bags carried on, almost always hung from a woman's arm.

At number 51 the sturdy doors that led to the entrance hall were once again propped open. He headed inside to the glass partition that guarded the access to the lift and stairs, only to find three young men in suits clustered around the intercom. A loud buzz resonated and one of them pushed on the inner door. Once they were through, the last of them held it open, beckoning to Franck.

"Thanks," he said and left them the lift, heading straight for the stairs, pain or no pain. When he reached the third floor he could hear the ageing lift continue its stately progress above him. He knocked on *Wasp-Waisted*'s door.

It was opened by Claire, Maryam's assistant, in a sober charcoal skirt, dark stockings and a light grey blouse.

"Captain Guerin," she said. "Not only do you not have an appointment, but I didn't even buzz you up. Just because you had dinner with Maryam doesn't mean it's open house."

Despite her chiding tone, she pulled the door wide open and beckoned him through.

"Can I see her?" he asked.

"I'll see," said Claire. She pointed to the red velvet sofa and waited until Franck had sat himself upon it. "Don't move from there."

She moved over to the door that led into Maryam's office, gently opened it, and slipped through.

Franck did as he was told, albeit with difficulty. He sat on the sofa, ignoring the contents of the room and the paintings on the wall, his head churning with all that Maryam had to explain.

Claire slid back into the reception area.

"She's on the phone," she said. "But as soon as she's finished, she's yours."

Franck nodded curtly. Claire remained where she was.

"Can I offer you some coffee?" she suggested.

"No thanks," said Franck. "I'm fine."

Claire raised a sceptical eyebrow.

"You're refusing coffee, but you're fine? Now that's an unlikely combination."

"Really," insisted Franck. "I'm fine."

Clearly unconvinced, Claire nonetheless returned to her desk and transferred her attention to her screen. She typed and clicked for a few minutes before looking across at Franck once more.

"You are coming?" she asked.

"Sorry?"

"To Maryam's party. You haven't replied. Yves de Chaumont sent us a delightful note, but you're still on my pending list."

"If there's a party, I'll be there," said Franck.

"That's very magnanimous of you captain," observed Maryam from the doorway to her office. "Although the 'if' is a bit puzzling."

"I'll explain," said Franck, getting to his feet.

Maryam stepped aside from the entrance to her office. "Be my guest".

As Franck brushed past her, she said to Claire, "Two coffees, please."

"I've already tried to tempt the captain," said Claire. "He says he's fine."

"Nonsense," said Maryam. "Two coffees. He's looking a little drained."

Franck had already taken a seat on one side of her slate desk. Maryam paced round to the other, her bracelets softly jangling.

"I've heard about Marie Goubert," she said. "But nobody

has said anything about a photo. Was it like the others? What was she wearing?"

"Where were you last Tuesday afternoon?" asked Franck, abruptly.

"Where was I?" Maryam seemed surprised, although not offended, by the question. "Here. Then at the Maison Blanche, taste-testing. Then at the Petit Palais, just to clear my head. Then back here. Then drinks with some friends at the bar of the Plaza Athenée." She paused. "I think that's right."

"Claire was here?"

"Yes. I took her to the Maison Blanche, and then sent her back here."

"So you were at the Petit Palais alone?"

Sitting near the foot of the Champs Elysées, housing the art collection of the Ville de Paris, recently reopened after an extensive refurbishment, the Petit Palais was a short walk from avenue Montaigne. It was also twenty minutes by foot, at most, from the Meurice.

"Not exactly," said Maryam. "Studious tourists, idle students, bored staff – you're rarely alone in a museum in Paris, particularly one that happens to be free."

"How long were you there?"

"I have no idea. An hour? Two? Claire left just after I got back here, so that must have been around seven. So, yes, maybe two hours, maybe a little longer."

Franck's elbows were planted on the top of her desk, his hands clenched together, one knuckle against his lower lip.

"Why?" he asked.

"Why what?"

"Why did you spend so long at the Petit Palais?"

Maryam sat back in her chair, opened the fingers of one hand, and began counting them off with the other. "Maillol's *La vague*, Clesinger's *Bacchante*, Devallières' *Madame Blanchard*, Alaphilippe's *Femme au singe* – you tell me, captain, how much time are you supposed to spend looking at such things?"

"While you say you were doing so, someone was killing

Marie Goubert", stated Franck.

A frown knotted Maryam's brow, and she narrowed her eyes.

"All of a sudden, I'm a suspect?" she protested. "Last I recall, I was helping you in this investigation, Franck. Helping in a way few others would."

She stopped. Franck continued to fix her with eyes of stone. He would not allow her to conjure up the memory of the previous Saturday's complicity.

"This is patently ridiculous," she continued. "I knew Marie Goubert."

"That, unfortunately, doesn't make it ridiculous," insisted Franck. "Marie Goubert knew and trusted whoever killed her. So, tell me, how did you know her?"

"I've known Marie for years. She's not a close friend, but we regularly cross each other's path at dinner parties. She is – was – an exceptionally beautiful woman, as well as an extraordinarily talented one. I asked her to pose for *Wasp-Waisted* shortly after I launched it. She declined the offer – she didn't refuse, she simply said she wasn't ready. I always felt she was less conscious of her beauty than we were. Her touchstones were texts, performances, and the passion they unleashed. To be frozen, mute, caught for eternity in a single image was foreign to her. But, with time, she mellowed – she got used to having her photo taken, even her portrait painted. Two months ago, I asked her again for *Wasp-Waisted* and she finally accepted. She knew my policy. She knew I wouldn't – couldn't – make the offer again."

"Because?" interrupted Franck.

"We are – were – the same age. This summer she would have turned thirty."

"Your arbitrary cut-off point," said Franck, adding, almost involuntarily, "Your watershed."

Maryam glanced at him with curiosity. "If you like, yes, my watershed. Is it arbitrary? Perhaps, but it's no less worthy for that. I've worked hard to create a very particular universe within *Wasp-Waisted*, where beauty and sensuality not only reign but are omnipresent. As you can't have failed to notice, the real world – the place in which you live and work, Franck – is not like that. *Wasp-Waisted* is an artificial construct, maintained by constant effort, critical vigilance, and a few unyielding principles. The under thirty rule is one of them."

"It makes no sense," insisted Franck. "Nothing dictates that a woman of thirty-one must be less attractive than one who is twenty-nine."

"It makes no sense?" she echoed. "Of course it makes sense – it calls sense into being. Nothing worthwhile was ever created without constraint: the twelve feet of the alexandrine; the frame that isolates the portrait; the three acts of the classical drama; the code of manners that separates a civilised dinner from a savage feast. *Wasp-Waisted* presents a world without age – in my Arcadia, neither death nor decay have gained a foothold; to ensure this, its boundaries are defined by the thirtieth year."

"So Goubert had agreed to take her last chance?" prompted Franck.

"Yes. I saw her a few weeks ago to discuss what she would wear. I talked to her about something new Du Bellay is about to bring out – the Tisserand. It's an extraordinary ensemble – evanescent, rich, incredibly difficult to make – and just right for Marie. I persuaded Luc du Bellay to send me an advance sample. We were supposed to shoot Marie in it in a matter of days."

"Where is it?" asked Franck.

"Where is what?"

"The sample."

"You want to see it?" asked Maryam. She lifted the phone on her desk. "Claire, can you get me the Tisserand sample we got from Du Bellay?" She hung up. "You won't get the full effect. You have to see it worn, and it's not my size."

"I have seen it worn," said Franck.

Maryam looked puzzled. "In which case you must have been spending a lot of time with Luc du Bellay recently. The next time you see him, ask him from me how he's going to maintain the same standards with a bunch of new investors breathing down his neck."

Claire opened the door from the reception area.

"I don't understand," she said. "The Tisserand is missing."

Maryam tossed her hands in the air to the clashing accompaniment of her bracelets. "Well find it Claire!" she shouted. "How far can it have gone?"

"Just from here to the Meurice," said Franck.

Both Maryam and Claire froze, their eyes on him.

"That's what Marie Goubert was wearing," continued Franck. "Your sample."

"Claire," snapped Maryam. "Out!"

Claire disappeared. Maryam slowly ran the tips of her fingers over the ridges on her slate desk. Franck said nothing, waiting for her to speak.

"I don't know what is going on," she said. "But I did not kill Marie Goubert."

"You've no alibi. You had the perfect pretext to lure her into a meeting. You had the only sample of the lingerie in which she was found – aside from those stockpiled in a warehouse in Lyon or in the hands of some princess in Saudi Arabia. You tell me – how does it look to you?"

Maryam placed her hands flat down on the desk and leant across them, closing the distance between them.

"This makes no sense. Why would I do such a thing? I admired Marie Goubert."

"Like you admired Laure Sarraute? Just how well did you know Laure?"

"As you know, she posed for *Wasp-Waisted* – just the once. Since then we bumped into each other from time to time, but nothing more than that."

"What about before?"

"Before what?"

"Before she posed for *Wasp-Waisted*. What about when she was stripping off for life classes at the Beaux Arts and you were sitting there, brush or pencil in hand?"

Maryam pulled back, her face uncertain.

"What's your point? Yes, I knew Laure before she succeeded as a model. So what? We weren't close."

"My point is that you never told me. I had two victims on my hands, both of whom had ties to the Beaux Arts, and you hid from me the fact that you had been there."

"No I didn't," stated Maryam, quite calmly. "I don't recall you asking me about the Beaux Arts, and I don't remember ever denying that I'd gone there. I only lasted a year anyway."

"So what about Rachida Tazi?" demanded Franck, forcefully. "Any half-forgotten connection to her? And Jean-Michel Rey, while we're at it? If I ask du Bellay to check their stock records for promotional samples, will I find a Midnight Sun and a Salammbo ensemble in Sarraute's and Tazi's sizes sent to you?"

Maryam remained unperturbed. "Midnight Sun, quite possible. Salammbo, I doubt it. I'd have asked for a larger sized bust."

"You're playing with fire," warned Franck.

"I'm not playing," she stated flatly. "You've seen me play, Franck. You should know the difference."

There was a timid knock at the door.

Maryam cast an arch look at Franck. "May I?"

Franck waved his assent.

"Yes?" she said.

Claire opened the door. She had a large, flat express delivery package under her arm.

"I'm sorry to disturb, mademoiselle," she said. "But this just arrived. It's marked very urgent".

Maryam raised a hand and held it horizontally, keeping her eyes on Franck. Claire crossed the office and gently deposited the package onto Maryam's palm. She left without another word.

Maryam tipped her hand and let the package fall onto her desk. She then pushed it aside.

"Shall we continue?" she asked.

Franck had followed the package with his eyes, taking in its length and breadth.

"I think you should open that," he said.

"I think we should get back to our discussion," she countered.

"No, really," insisted Franck. "Open the package. Please."

Maryam sighed and retrieved the pre-printed cardboard envelope, one of the standard sizes sold by La Poste for guaranteed next-day delivery. She used one of her sizeable fingernails to catch and pull the serrated-edged strip that unsealed it. She then turned it upright and shook it lightly. A USB stick fell onto the slate surface of her desk. Franck's hand shot out and grabbed the package from Maryam. He laid it on the desk while he retrieved a pair of transparent plastic gloves from his jacket pocket. He then picked up the package once more and, holding it with the fingertips of one hand, sent the other gingerly inside to extract the rest of its contents.

A large photographic print slid out.

Marie Goubert: just as Franck had seen her; just as Georges Sternberg had failed to capture her; just as Anne Subrini had imagined the perfect photo.

The print was in colour, as required by *Wasp-Waisted*'s publication policy.

"You might not be the killer," observed Franck. "But he's definitely thinking of you."

Maryam rose from her seat and came around to Franck's side of the desk. She placed one hand on his shoulder and leant over the photo.

"He might have abandoned black and white, but he's not lost his touch," she observed.

They both remained as they were for some time, lost in contemplation of the image. Maryam was the first to break the silence.

"You believe I sent this to myself?" she asked.

Franck reached for the cardboard envelope. It had been sent from the city's central post office, rue du Louvre: the busiest post office in the capital, open twenty-four hours. A counter clerk had stamped the package and noted the time of deposit: nine twenty-three the previous morning.

"Have you got a decent alibi for yesterday morning?" he asked.

"I'm afraid so, captain," she said. "I was at our printers from eight thirty until around eleven, discussing production standards for our twentieth issue. I was with two delightful and highly competent men all that time, and I'm sure they'll confirm it."

"Where was this?"

"Issy les Moulineaux," said Maryam, naming a suburban town on the southern fringe of Paris.

"I'll need their names and numbers," stated Franck.

"Of course," said Maryam. She patted him consolingly on the head, her bracelets softly chiming. "Back to square one."

She then pointed to the USB stick, asking, "What's that for?"

"If he's true to form, that's the digital file of the print," explained Franck.

Maryam pointed to Franck's gloves, "Have you got another pair of those?"

Franck reached into his jacket and retrieved a spare set of gloves. Maryam took them, raised her arms to send her bracelets tumbling towards her elbows, and pulled them on. She grasped the USB stick with two fingers, circled her desk, and inserted it into the laptop that lay brooding on a far corner. She clicked the built-in mouse twice.

"You're right," she confirmed. "Exactly the same image."

"OK," said Franck. "Can I have that back?"

"Of course," said Maryam. She clicked a few more times, then extracted the stick and laid it on Franck's side of the desk. "Now what?"

"I'm taking the envelope and its contents", said Franck, gathering them together. "What about the names and contact details for yesterday?"

"Ask Claire on your way out. She'll give you the details of everyone we work with at our printers."

Franck stood up, still gloved, holding the express package with both hands.

"At least he won't have the satisfaction of seeing his handiwork published this time," he said.

"That's rather a rash assumption," said Maryam.

Franck tapped the express package with a fingertip. "Not so long as I hold onto this."

"I'll say it again, that's rather a rash assumption," said Maryam, holding his gaze.

Franck pointed to her laptop. "Have you just taken a copy of the picture file?"

Maryam laid a finger vertically on her lips and held her silence.

"You can't do that!" hissed Franck. "If you do, you're playing his game."

"*Exposé* could do it," she pointed out. "I don't see why I cannot. Now, whether I should, or should not, that's a quite different issue. In any case, I don't go to press for another ten days. Catch him before then, and the question becomes academic."

One photo.

In the background, off to the right, the multi-coloured beads of the metro entrance in place Colette. Scattered across the frame, haphazard figures of wandering tourists or Parisians, idling towards unknown destinations. Slightly to the left, but striding into centre frame, Franck Guerin, in jeans and a dark grey sweatshirt, his leather briefcase in one hand. His eyes are hooded, half-reproving, while at the same time a smile is fighting its way across his lips.

*

Marie Goubert had no connection with the Beaux Arts, neither as a student nor as a life model. Anne Subrini had left Franck a message to this effect and Goubert's colleagues at the Comédie Française had confirmed it in the course of a long series of interviews that stretched across Saturday and much of Sunday. Two of her fellow actors had told of being present at dinner parties where Marie and Maryam Sehati had spoken to each other with warmth and affection. All professed deep shock at Marie's death and declared themselves perplexed by the circumstances in which it had happened. None could tell of any connection with Laure Sarraute and none had ever heard of Rachida Tazi, aside from her apparition in *Exposé*.

Goubert's pact with Hollywood was decried by a minority of her colleagues as positively Faustien, but most saw it as a smart way to supplement the relatively modest stipends that accompanied the prestige of working for the troupe that Molière had once overseen. The hope had been widespread that Goubert's prolonged absence during filming would prove temporary.

Her liaison with Luc du Bellay was recalled by some as an error of taste or judgement, by others as an illustration of her curiosity, and by her closest acquaintances as an affair as passionate as it had been short-lived. Only with the latter did

Franck broach the subject of Goubert's sex life. He heard nothing out of the ordinary. Indeed, for one whose beauty was so universally saluted, she was said to have been remarkably chaste, although some suggested that this was in part because so few men had dared to approach her.

Franck stepped out of the actor's entrance to the Comédie Française late Sunday afternoon, hungry and thirsty, having been there since mid-morning, wandering its labyrinthine corridors, posing his questions and dodging the hubbub of that day's matinee performance. He cast a longing glance across place Colette towards Le Nemours and contemplated nipping in for a sandwich.

A figure seated at one of the outside tables raised a hand and waved to him, inviting him over. Having at first hesitated, Franck headed towards him. As he did so the man lifted a short-barrelled camera and caught Franck's progress in a series of shots.

Franck sat himself down on a wicker chair alongside the one that held Didier Fabre, who put down his camera and offered his hand. Franck shook it.

"You're not making much of an attempt to hide yourself today," he observed.

"You've already chased me around those pillars once," explained Didier. "I didn't fancy going through that again."

"To be frank, me neither," admitted Franck. "You might have noticed – I'm not at my fittest at the moment."

"Something to do with all those pills you keeping popping?"

"Don't get excited – they're all on prescription," insisted Franck. "What's this?" he continued, pointing to a dark blue open-faced helmet that sat under the table.

"Goes with that," said Didier, pointing to the metro entrance off to the side of the square. Propped against the web of glass and baubles that surrounded it was a very clean looking scooter.

"You're illegally parked," Franck informed him. "New camera too?" he asked, pointing to the piece of equipment on the table.

"Yes," said Didier picking it up and offering it to Franck, who waved it away. "It's a very expensive model, but we've not had enough time to get to know each other yet. I don't know to what extent I can really rely on it."

"I don't imagine following me around is really putting it to the test," observed Franck.

"Not really. Still, I got one nice shot on avenue Montaigne yesterday. You didn't look too happy, neither going in nor coming out."

"Don't expect me to look happy until this case is solved," said Franck, attracting the attention of the waiter and asking for a ham and cheese sandwich, a glass of water and a double coffee. "You can quote me on that."

"Words," said Didier dismissively. "Not my department."

"So how much longer are you going to be trailing me?" asked Franck.

"Till Beaufort says to stop."

"How is the boss?"

"Not so happy. He's still waiting for the photo of Marie Goubert. Says the surveillance you lot have put in place is keeping the killer away, depriving him of another top-selling issue."

"As if we could scare this killer away," murmured Franck.

"Losing faith?" asked Didier, studying him closely.

"No," declared Franck. "But only a fool underestimates his opponent. And this one is very good."

"Can I quote you on that?"

"Words," Franck reminded him. "Not your department."

The waiter arrived with a third of a baguette generously provisioned with thin-sliced ham and thickly-sliced comté. He placed a large coffee, a glass of water, and a fluttering receipt alongside it. Franck emptied the water, did the same with the coffee, and grabbed the sandwich as he got to his feet.

"I'll put it on expenses," Didier assured him as he walked away.

Franck sat down at his desk, the inevitable coffee in one hand, the other reaching out to turn on his PC. He had to go back through the list of students from the life classes for which Sarraute had posed in 2003, since the last time he had stopped dead at Maryam's name. It was time to crunch the data the DST way: slowly and methodically.

He dug out the beige folder Anne Subrini had given him, extracted the two class lists and scanned them. Only one other name looked familiar to him, although it took him a few moments to remember why. It was on the list for class PD2, just slightly below Sehati, Maryam, 1003504: Sollers, Juliette, 1007402. He began to wonder whether there was anyone in this case to whom Maryam was not connected, and then reminded himself that this time around he had promised himself to be thorough.

He went back to the beginning of the two lists and began dutifully throwing the other students' names at the national crime databases. When that produced nothing of interest, he ran them against his own, which contained the names from the *Wasp-Waisted* subscription list, the Du Bellay sales records for Midnight Sun and Salammbo, Laure Sarraute's male acquaintances, and those who had participated in Tazi's life class and evening class at the Beaux Arts. Still nothing.

Only then did he allow himself to do the same with Juliette Sollers. The result was quite different: not only was she was a *Wasp-Waisted* subscriber, she had also bought an 85C Midnight Sun ensemble in New York in January, from a store called Barneys. Franck tried to recall her physical appearance, wondering whether she really was the same size as Laure Sarraute, but the only image he could conjure up from her vernissage was that of Anne Subrini in her elegant silver-grey dress.

Sollers lived abroad, of course, as confirmed by the location of her Du Bellay purchase. That said, if she had come to Paris ahead of the opening of her new show on the Left Bank, she might well have been in the city when Sarraute and Tazi were killed. As for Rey and Goubert, their deaths had occurred respectively two and four days after the vernissage he had attended – and Franck knew Sollers was still around, as she was the reason behind the yellow dress Anne was wearing when last he saw her.

He reached for his mobile phone, and then paused. Anne had been extraordinarily cooperative up until now, but how would she react to her protégé being treated, even briefly, as a suspect? Would it cause her to look askance at him, and suddenly come to see nothing beyond his profession?

Ashamed of his hesitation – whatever else might happen, the investigation had to come first – Franck pulled up Anne's number and called her. He got her voice mail.

"Anne, this is Franck Guerin," he said. "I've got a question for you that might seem strange, but I have to ask it. Do you happen to know – or could you guess – what size bra Juliette Sollers would take? Phone me back any time, on my mobile. I'll explain."

Maybe the internet could help. If Sollers was seen as a rising star in artistic circles, there was probably a photo of her out there somewhere. Franck knew he did not have Luc du Bellay's eye, but he reckoned he could by now identify a pair of breasts that were not too distant from those of Sarraute.

Just as he was calling up his browser, a small envelope flashed at him from the bottom corner of his screen. He had email. Succumbing to the tug of curiosity, he opened his mailbox to find a message entitled "Look familiar?" sent from Sonia Delemazure's email account.

He clicked on it, finding no text, but a substantial file attachment. He clicked again, and his screen filled with a photo.

Sonia lay on her back on a smooth purple silk sheet, her arms cast out on either side of her, her blond hair gathered behind her head on a plump pillow. The shot framed her from the hips upwards, which was enough to allow Franck to recognise the white lingerie she wore. His heart started to race.

Sonia's eyes were closed, and her celebrated shoulders relaxed, as if slumber had just stolen over her.

"No, no, no," Franck whispered vehemently, grabbing his phone and calling Sonia's mobile number. It rang six times and then, just as he expected her voice mail to kick in, was answered.

"Thought that would grab your attention," she said.

When Franck recognised Sonia's voice, a wave of anger shook him.

"This is not a game Sonia!" he yelled. "People are dying!"

"Hey, watch your blood pressure, captain," she replied, apparently unconcerned by his outburst. "I just wanted to know if you liked it."

"What's to like?" he thundered. "A morbid parody of the death of a woman you called your friend?"

A short silence followed.

"Ah," she said. "It's the Midnight Sun, isn't it? That's all you saw. Luc would be pleased. Look again, captain."

Franck did as he was told, frowning up at the screen, his heart decelerating. This time he noticed that the white strap of her bra encountered something when it ran up to her left shoulder. He used the zoom feature on his photo browser to get a closer look: the paws of some kind of mythological beast, its jaws open above them, the body behind curved to raised hindquarters throwing out long and supple legs. It was traced in black in a single continuous line and its interior was split into geometric cells, like those of a stained glass window, each coloured differently from its neighbour. He guessed it was no more than five centimetres long, poised between the edge of her shoulder and her collarbone. As tattoos went, it was relatively discreet.

He breathed out, long and slow, before bringing his phone back to his mouth.

"So you did it," he said.

"Last Tuesday – just after I saw you," explained Sonia. "It's still healing. Stings like hell, though. But I'm very pleased with it. I trust you spotted the Celtic motif?"

"Can't say I did," admitted Franck. "But I'm not at my best."

"You've not been at your best for some time," observed Sonia.

"I hate to say it, but you're not helping. Between this and the Raphael, you've not been particularly kind to my nerves."

"You should be thanking me," she offered, flippantly. "When your heart goes overtime, at least you know you're alive. But you didn't answer my question – do you like it?"

"Am I allowed to say I preferred your shoulders as Nature made them?"

"Only because it's you," she conceded. "Although I have to tell you that you find yourself in the same camp as Fred Bonneau. Still, that could explain a lot – like why you're in your mid-thirties and you're not married. Got something you want to share with me, captain?"

"Actually, yes," said Franck. "A question that's been niggling me. You remember that vernissage where I met you coming out?"

"The wrinkly women with the cute babies?"

"Yes, that one. Did you meet the artist?"

"Sure. Can't go to a thing like that and not shake the hand of the evening's celebrity. What was her name again?"

"Juliette Sollers."

"So what's the question?"

"Do you think she's an 85C?"

"Wow," exhaled Sonia. "Now there's question! Maybe you're not Fred's type after all. I don't have her phone number, if that's what you're going to ask for next."

"No, her breast size will do."

"The 85 I can't comment on, but yes, I'd say she had above average breasts, so she may well be a C cup. Want to explain now?"

"No," said Franck. "But thanks anyway. That makes up for nearly giving me a heart attack."

"Try lying back and relaxing," suggested Sonia. "Always does a world of good."

"I'll keep it in mind. I'll let you get back to plotting your next spot of mischief. Have a good evening."

"Thanks. You too."

She hung up.

Franck dismissed the photo from his screen and slumped back in his seat.

Maybe he was getting carried away with Juliette Sollers.

Maybe it was time to go home.

Monday, 25th June

One photo.

The regular, honey-coloured stone blocks that make up avenue Montaigne, dozing in the late afternoon sun. Resplendent against this backdrop, Maryam Sehati in an all-white dress fringed with an interlocking mosaic in gold thread, its unsullied brilliance underscoring the tone of her skin. White heels cling to her feet by virtue of a spiralling band that runs most of the way up each calf. A white canvas tote bag hangs from one shoulder, identical in colour to the slim leather purse she holds up in one hand. The other tugs a pair of sizeable sunglasses down her nose, allowing her to look over the top of them directly at the lens. The eyes speak of amusement at the uninvited, but surely not unwarranted, attention.

*

Franck slid the drawer out as far as it would go, sent his hands underneath to free the locking mechanism, pulled it completely free and carried it to the bed.

He knelt down before it and contemplated Marie Goubert's collection of lingerie. The drawer's contents appeared haphazard, although everything was neatly folded. Working methodically, he removed item after item with his gloved hands, and searched for some indication of the brands she favoured. Thanks to his apprenticeship at Maryam's hands he was even able to perform some basic classification, noting the types of bras and briefs, and correctly identifying four separate *guêpières* for what they were. When he had finished, he was left with a pile of what he took to be everyday underwear and an extensive collection of more delicate or elaborate items. He had identified five Du Bellay ensembles, which could well date from her time with Luc, given what Frank had seen of his open-handedness towards Sonia Delemazure.

When he reached the bottom he came across a slim cardboard box whose lid was embossed with the words

Giardino Segreto. On opening it he was confronted with several layers of diaphanous paper, which he teased aside to be confronted with a carefully folded garment of scarlet lace. He picked it up and smoothed it out on the bed cover. It seemed to be a pair of miniscule briefs overlaid with a skirt of lace a hand's-breadth in length. He eased his hand underneath it and raised it from the bed. It weighed nothing at all, and slid from his open palm as soon as he tilted it ever so slightly.

Franck pulled out his mobile and called Maryam. Having been greeted by her voicemail, he hung up and tried the *Wasp-Waisted* office number. Claire answered.

"Good afternoon Claire," he said. "This is captain Guerin."

"Good afternoon captain," she replied.

"I hope you took this morning off, given you had to work Saturday," said Franck.

He had arranged for a friendly locksmith to check the security of the *Wasp-Waisted* offices on Saturday morning, and Maryam had ordered Claire to be present. The results were what Franck had feared: the locks on the office door and on the inner glass door in the downstairs lobby looked impressive, but could be picked in under a minute by someone who knew what he was doing. Access to *Wasp-Waisted*'s stock of lingerie samples was open to any gifted amateur.

"If you think such a thing is possible, you've never worked for mademoiselle Sehati," observed Claire.

"I don't think I'd be up to it."

"I hope you haven't had any problems getting through to the men from the printers?" she enquired.

"No, no," he assured her. "I spoke to both of them on Saturday. Looks like your boss is in the clear."

"I'll be sure to let her know when she gets back. I must say, it's a relief. I'm not sure I'm quite ready to take over running *Wasp-Waisted* just yet."

"Let me test you on that," said Franck. "Does *Giardino Segreto* mean anything to you?"

"Of course," she said. "Milan's much-lamented *Giardino Segreto*, or Secret Garden. They made ultra-delicate lingerie, all of it hand-woven in the region. It is said there are women who have never actually dared put on their *Giardino Segreto* ensembles for fear of destroying them."

"Why much-lamented?"

"They went out of business two years ago. Partly due to Luc du Bellay, since he stole a large chunk of their market."

"Deservedly so?"

"If you want my opinion, yes," declared Claire. "If you can't put your lingerie on, or have it taken off, then I really don't see the point."

"OK," said Franck. "Thanks for the expert opinion."

"Any time captain," said Claire, and rung off.

Franck folded the fragile confection of lace and returned it to its box. Clearly Marie Goubert was no stranger to the world of fine lingerie. She and Maryam would have had a ready topic of conversation on the occasions when they met.

Franck replaced everything in the drawer, and returned the latter to its slot. He cast a final look around her bedroom, hoping that his eye would snag on something, and then left it.

Marie Goubert's apartment was generously proportioned by Parisian standards, particularly for someone who lived alone. Franck had already checked almost all the other rooms, starting just before ten that morning: the second bedroom, presumably intended for friends and guests; the kitchen, tightly gathered around a row of appliances; the surprisingly large bathroom that accommodated a tub, a separate shower unit, and a mirrored dressing table. Ostensibly he was looking for a something – a letter, a scribbled note, anything – linked to her decision to reserve a room at the Meurice. In reality, he was blindly searching for a trace of the web that had to link her to Sarraute, Tazi and Rey.

Thus far he had found nothing, aside from a password-protected laptop that sat on an elegant bureau in the bedroom. He had packed it away in its case, which lay propped against the tapering legs of the bureau, and would take it to the computer fraud unit, who would soon give him access to her email records and other files.

He now stood at the entrance to the salon, which overlooked the building on the opposite side of the street, providing a vista of Parisian rooftops: the singular advantage of living on the slopes of Montmartre. Clustered in the centre of the room were two canapés set at ninety degrees to each other and flanking a low table which bore a scattering of magazines. Diagonally opposite them was a large TV set. To the right was an oval dining table that could seat six. The wall to the left was completely hidden by built-in shelving, occupied by neat rows of books, stacks of CDs and DVDs, and a number of framed photos. On the wall behind him hung three paintings, identical in size, framed in the same fashion, all brightly coloured abstracts.

He checked the magazines on the coffee table, and then moved onto the shelves, reading the spines of the books and shuffling the CDs and DVDs like packs of cards. He looked at each photo in turn, recognising a few faces of those he had questioned the previous day at the Comédie Française. There were only two of Goubert herself. One was a rehearsal shot in which she appeared in regal splendour, no doubt incarnating one of Racine's formidable heroines, in a multi-layered robe that swept out behind her. The photo was signed by Christian Lacroix. The other showed her as herself, draped in what looked like a linen dressing gown. She stood with bare feet on scuffed or stained parquet and was smiling broadly, her chestnut hair gathered on her head and secured with what at first Franck took to be chopsticks, but which he then identified as slim paintbrushes. A canvas as tall as her, supported by a barely visible easel, stood on either side of her. One showed a woman seen from behind in a long, flowing open-backed red dress, her hair tossed over one shoulder. In the other the pose was the same, but the gown had disappeared to be replaced by a band of red patterned lace around her buttocks.

Franck pried the photo from the frame and turned it over. Nothing was noted on the back. Hastily he slid it into the inside pocket of his jacket. Before leaving the apartment he headed back into the main bedroom, but came out without the laptop.

He would return for that later.

He pulled out his phone and redialled the last number he had called.

"Maryam's still not there?" he asked Claire.

"She'll be out all afternoon."

"I'm coming over."

"You just can't keep away, can you captain?"

*

"Where have you been?"

It was Didier Fabre, sitting on his scooter squeezed between two cars a short distance down from 51 avenue Montaigne.

"If you don't know that, you're losing your touch," remarked Franck, as he strode by.

"She's not here." Fabre offered this information to Franck's back. "Your Iranian princess left well over an hour ago."

"I know," said Franck, without turning round.

"Got her photo, though," continued Fabre. "Looking good."

"That's scarcely a surprise", muttered Franck, going through the ever-open entrance door to number 51.

Claire buzzed him up and was waiting for him when he reached the top of the stairs to the third floor.

"More questions about *Giardino Segreto*?" she asked, standing aside to let him in. "We have a few samples stashed away. I could show you them."

Franck handed her the compact cardboard box he had taken from Goubert's bedroom. "I've brought one of my own."

Claire took it from him, laid it on her desk, carefully lifted the cover, sifted through the crepe paper, and extracted the contents. She held up the wisp of red lace, a thumb and index finger at each extremity, and turned it before her admiring gaze.

"Exquisite," she said. "Where on earth did you get this?"

"From a dead woman," said Franck, brutally. "Look familiar?"

Before she could reply he pointed to one of the two life-sized portraits that hung on the walls. The one without the dress with the plunging back. The one in which Marie Goubert was wearing only a pair of stilettos and the garment Claire held in her hands.

Claire drew in her breath. "You're right. I never thought to ask mademoiselle Sehati what it was."

"Nor who it was," added Franck. He held up the photo of Goubert standing beside the two unframed canvases.

"That's ..."

Franck provided the answer. "Victim number three, or four, depending on how you count them. How did Maryam get these paintings?"

"I have no idea," said Claire. "They were here when I started working for her."

"When was that?"

"Two years ago."

"She never talked about them?"

"Never," confirmed Claire.

Franck walked up to the nearest painting, the one with the red dress, and studied it closely. There could be no doubt that it was the painting in the photograph. It bore no trace of the artist's name.

"Could she have painted this?" he asked.

"Mademoiselle Sehati?"

"Yes, Maryam," said Franck, impatiently.

"She doesn't paint," said Claire, who had sidled up alongside Franck. "At least, not any more. I know she studied at the Beaux Arts, but not for very long."

"She must have had some talent," insisted Franck. "Otherwise she would never have got in."

He leant forward and grasped the right hand side and the bottom of the frame.

"Could you help me?" he asked.

Claire did the same on the opposite side and together they lifted the painting, detached it from the wall, and stepped back.

"Slide it down," said Franck.

Claire followed his lead, resting the frame on the floor.

Switching hands, Franck used his left one to hold the picture vertical and stepped round to scan the rear of the canvas. He crouched down. There was a signature in one of the bottom corners. A signature he recognised.

"Anne Subrini," he half-read, half-whispered, his heart sinking. What else had she not told him?

"Well, that makes sense," announced Claire.

Franck glanced sharply at her. "Why?"

"She's mademoiselle – Maryam's – muse," she paused. "No, that's not right. Her mentor. That's what she says."

"Who says?"

"Maryam." Claire was quite unconcerned. Judging by her tone, she was reciting a banal fact, something everybody already knew. "I don't think she paints much anymore, but I'm sure she did. After all, she was Maryam's teacher at the Beaux Arts."

"You've met her?"

"Of course. She comes by from time to time, and whenever she does they shut themselves away for hours. Maryam says she owes her everything – without Anne, *Wasp-Waisted* would never have got off the ground."

"What does she mean?"

"I'll show you," said Claire.

She disappeared through the door into Maryam's office. While she was absent Franck propped the painting up against the wall from which he had unhooked it.

Claire came back with an issue of *Wasp-Waisted* in her hands. He recognised the cover from the bustier and the long black hair. It was the first issue, February 2003: the one with Laure Sarraute. One of the two he had shown to Anne in her office in the Beaux Arts. One of the two she had pored over lovingly.

"Anne Subrini took every shot in this issue," explained Claire. "She set the tone. She defined the aesthetic."

"That was the only issue she was ever involved with?"

"As a photographer, yes, I believe so. Until now, of course."

"Of course?"

"She agreed to shoot a number of sessions for the twentieth issue. She was supposed to do Marie Goubert. And Maryam insisted that she be the one to catch her own final appearance."

Claire pointed to the cover of the February 2003 issue.

"You must have worked it out," she said. "That's her. Apparently it was Anne Subrini who insisted Maryam use herself as a model for the first issue. It was also her idea that Maryam make a return appearance."

"Before it's too late," commented Franck. "Before she hits the watershed."

"That's right," said Claire. "Thirtieth birthday – twentieth issue."

"When is this supposed to happen?" asked Franck.

"What?"

"The photo shoot. With Maryam."

"As we speak," said Claire. "That's why Maryam's out all afternoon."

Franck grabbed Claire, who recoiled with surprise and squirmed in his unforgiving grip.

"Where?" he demanded, his voice low and urgent.

"The Crillon," said Claire, faintly.

Franck released her and was gone, sprinting down the stairs.

Minutes later he shot out of the entrance to number 51, one hand clenching his stomach and his teeth gritted. He glanced to his left, where Didier Fabre was swinging his camera up at him.

"Start the engine," shouted Franck, running towards him. The photographer faltered, abandoned his shot, and had stowed the camera in a pouch hung by his side by the time Franck had circled behind him.

Didier grabbed his helmet from where it hung on a handlebar, slid his head inside it, turned a key, walked the scooter backwards onto the road, shifted forward in the seat to allow Franck to clamber on behind him, and engaged the gears.

"Where to?" he asked.

"The Crillon," shouted Franck. "Fast!"

Didier cut across to the other side of the road, heading

towards the Champs Elysées. The light was red at the junction, forcing them to wait while a stream of cars hurtled across before them. As soon as it turned green, Didier shot forward, causing a couple of shoppers who had blithely stepped out in front of him to scream and leap back to the safety of the pavement. He turned to the right and hurtled down the lower section of the Champs Elysées, competing with the taxis for the use of the bus lane. The lights were with them when they reached the place de la Concorde. Didier headed straight for the obelisk at its centre, braking suddenly and veering to his left as he circled behind it. Five lanes of cross-traffic now separated them from the eighteenth century facade of the Crillon. Didier sat there, gunning his motor, waiting for a path to clear. As soon as it did he surged forward and pulled up just short of the wide pavement in front of the hotel's red-carpeted entrance.

Franck slid off behind him.

"Stay here!" he shouted to Didier as he ran towards the entrance, watched with excitement by bystanders and with apprehension by the hotel's liveried staff.

He hurtled through the revolving door and hastened to the concierge's lodge.

"Good afternoon sir," greeted the head concierge, calm and collected. Constructed under Louis XV, the hotel had played host down the centuries to queens, kings, presidents and emperors, rendering its staff impressively imperturbable. "In a bit of a hurry?"

Franck slapped his ID onto the desktop between them.

"You have a room booked in the name of Sehati." His speech was breathless but urgent. "I need the number and a key card."

The concierge eyed the ID. "Like hotel security to give you a hand, captain?"

"Shouldn't be necessary. If I can do this quietly, I will," said Franck, recovering his ID.

The concierge turned to his computer. "Like to spell that for me?" he requested. Franck duly complied, spelling out

Maryam's surname.

"302. One of the presidential suites," said the concierge. He slid a hand inside his jacket and produced a white plastic card. "Opens every door in the place. I'd like it back when you've finished."

"Thanks," said Franck, and headed for the stairs.

He ran into a quartet of Russians as he reached the third floor: hard-set men with women half their age. They bustled noisily into room 305, just down and across from the room that interested him. Franck waited until they had shut their door.

He drew his revolver with his right hand, flipped the safety off, held it high, and dipped the key card into the locking mechanism, in and out. As it clicked he turned the handle, pushed the door open with his hip, and stepped sideways into the room, gun straight out in front of him.

The room overlooked the place de la Concorde. All its floor-to-ceiling windows had been opened, providing a constant background hum of tyres on cobbles. The substantial room was divided by its furnishings into two halves: first, a seating and entertaining area equipped with three canapés set in an open square; beyond it, a sleeping area with a massive four poster bed. Two doors were set into the far wall, both shut.

An ice bucket sat on a cloth-covered pedestal alongside one of the canapés, an open bottle of champagne leaning drunkenly inside it. On the elaborately inlaid surface of a low table crouching nearby sat two tall glasses. Beside them sat a small, unzipped, soft leather pouch. On another of the canapés lay a slim handbag, a monogrammed canvas tote bag, a carefully draped white dress, and a pair of white high-heels with permanently coiled leggings sprouting from them. Alongside them teetered two substantial, but apparently empty, branded shopping bags.

A tripod was set up at the foot of the bed, jutting no more than twenty centimetres above the level of the mattress. A heavy-bodied camera was screwed to the top of it. It gazed across at the only other figure in the room.

Maryam lay on her stomach at a slight diagonal across the

bed. Her arms were folded beneath a thick pillow that supported her head, which rested on her left cheek, her face tilted slightly forward. Her long black hair had been gathered together and draped in a lazy curve across her back, shifting to the left and then to the right. It spilled onto the bed at the point where her hips began. There it met the thick band of a suspender belt, woven in a dark mesh and sprinkled with what appeared to be tiny gemstones, that extended down to the base of her spine. From there two straight-edged straps cut into the swell of her buttocks before stretching forward to seize the dark tops of her stockings with serpentine heads and tiny, menacing teeth.

She wore nothing else.

For about thirty seconds Franck did not move, his eyes sweeping around the room, his ears listening intently for any sound. Using his left hand he very slowly closed the door behind him, holding the handle down so that it did not click shut. He then advanced carefully across the room, skirting the bed and coming up alongside the first of the two doors that lay beyond it.

With a twist and a sudden push the door flew open. It led to the toilet. Registering that it was empty, Franck stepped back immediately and swivelled to face the other door. This had to be the bathroom, which could be substantially larger, offering more space to hide and more lines of fire. He had not forgotten that a handgun had gone missing from Jean-Michel Rey's studio.

Franck breathed deeply three times to slow his heart and steady his hand, although it did nothing for the ache in his abdomen. He then grasped the handle with his left hand, turned it quickly, and pushed the door inwards. He could see a massive jacuzzi and an enclosed shower stall, both empty. He entered the bathroom, sliding along the wall, and then reached out to tug the door closed. To his left he could now see a long marble counter bearing two raised washbasins and a knee-high commode piled with thick white towels. His killer was nowhere to be seen.

Franck opened the bathroom door and returned to the main room. He laid his revolver on the bed cover and leant across to check Maryam's neck for a pulse.

"Don't touch her," came a voice to his right. He turned his head to see Anne Subrini standing in one of the open windows, holding a PA50 automatic pistol in both hands.

"Before you try to retrieve your gun, know that I am a very poor shot, so I may well miss you and hit her," she informed him. "I've only had this a week, and I've only tested it a couple of times."

Franck decided not to move. Anne walked into the room to the foot of the bed.

"Now that I'm closer I'm fairly confident I won't miss, so I suggest you slide very slowly back off the bed and put your hands on top of your head."

Franck did as he was told. Anne put one knee on the bedcover, bent forwards, and grabbed his revolver. At no point did the barrel of her gun waver.

"You've got a very steady hand," remarked Franck.

"You can't control the brush if you can't control your hand," she told him. "I'm going to step backwards. Once I'm sufficiently far from the bed, I want you to walk round it and go to the canapé facing the window. You think you can do that, slowly and steadily?"

Franck nodded.

"Do not bump into the tripod, if at all possible. It has taken me a long time to get the right angle."

Anne backed up and Franck followed her instructions, sitting on the canapé that backed onto the entrance to the room and was flanked by the two others. He sat at one end, the table bearing the champagne glasses blocking his access to the other. As Maryam's discarded clothing occupied the canapé to his right, Anne sat at the far end of the one to his left, allowing her to watch him and the bed simultaneously.

"By good fortune, I was on the balcony when you made your spectacular progress around the obelisk," she explained. "I realised you had to be coming for me."

"Is she dead?" asked Franck, pointing towards Maryam's body.

"Not yet."

"What are you waiting for?"

"For the clouds to move," Anne motioned with her head towards the windows behind her, without disturbing her revolver's stubborn scrutiny of Franck. "I need a little more light spilling into the room."

"She has to be alive for you to take a photo?"

"Of course," said Anne, as calm as if she were guiding a student out of ignorance. "I led you somewhat astray the last time we talked about this – the risk of movement while she is sedated is very small. But in any case there's a non-technical reason why that tiny risk has to be taken. I'm here to capture her vital spark, the beauty that has bloomed within her and is now at its peak. Were she dead, she'd already be on the path to decay at the moment the shutter closed."

"But you're happy enough to send her on that path once you've got your photo?"

"She'd set foot on it soon enough – she'll be thirty in a matter of days. You know that, captain, you've been invited to her party."

"And Goubert?"

"Her age aside, Marie was a few months short of being irredeemably tainted by vulgarity – a unique tragedienne, a peerless beauty, sacrificing herself to keep the Hollywood money mills turning. At least Maryam could not help ageing, but Marie chose to fall."

She was serious. Deadly serious. Insanely serious. Whatever Franck had seen, whatever he had felt, when chatting to her in her office at the Beaux Arts was gone. That Anne Subrini had been tossed aside and a strange new creature had emerged to take its place.

"Spare me the rest," said Franck.

"And spoil your understanding? No, Franck, you have to learn. Rachida and Laure were like Marie – careless with the gifts they had been given. That Laure offered her impeccable frame to other creators was understandable; that she felt free to surrender it to commerce, to become just another face endlessly reproduced to sell bottles of perfume was presumptuous. It was to forget that gifts remain the property of the gods who lent them. As for Rachida, she was a wild creature who lived in a half-savage world, but abandoning her intimacy to the pornographers was to espouse the cause of those who would destroy the realm of beauty."

"So you punished them all."

"It may seem that way, but no. I saved them all. I captured their essence in photos that will be admired for as long as we continue to hold beauty a special form of truth. At the same time I ensured the immortality of those images by saving their subjects from their own errors of judgement and the ravages of time. The only person who was punished was Jean-Michel Rey, for leading Rachida astray and for hoarding images of her that might have destroyed my efforts."

"What on earth makes you think you have the right to make such judgements? Who appointed you high priestess of this murderous cult?"

"In all simplicity and modesty," said Anne, her voice far calmer than Franck's, "I appointed myself, although I cannot agree with your notion of some kind of sacrificial rite. For a start, you must have noticed than no blood was ever spilt. I have slain as mercifully as I can, for the very killing I do is an act of mercy. It has fallen to me because nobody else took up the mantle. I have watched this world – my world, your world Franck – pay lip-service to beauty while delighting in debasing it. I decided to stand up and be counted."

"After Maryam, what then?"

"I think my time has come to an end. I managed to conceal everything up until now. This time it will, I fear, prove impossible."

"I agree," said Franck. "In which case my advice would be to cut your losses and let Maryam live."

"Except that, from my point of view, that wouldn't count as cutting my losses," objected Anne, rising to her feet. "If you'll excuse me a minute. I think the clouds have finally shifted."

She sidled across the room to the camera, her arm still extended and directed at Franck.

"Don't move from the canapé," she warned him. "Don't underestimate my peripheral vision."

She glanced through the camera's viewfinder and then bent her knees to retrieve the bulbous end of a cable that hung from it to the floor.

She turned her head towards Franck. "Try the champagne, if you like."

"Henriet," said Franck. "It was Maryam's favourite too."

"That's one of the many things she learned from me," said Anne. "Use my glass. Maryam's is the one that's almost empty. There are probably still traces of sedatives in hers. I don't imagine they'd appeal to you."

"If you insist," muttered Franck. He extended a hand towards the small table where the two glasses had been abandoned.

Anne cast a lingering gaze over Maryam's unconscious body and squeezed the bulb. She then glanced at the small screen on the rear of her camera.

"I think that's it," she declared. "Just one more to make sure."

She squeezed the bulb again, and then let it drop to the floor.

Franck had not taken one of the glasses. He had snatched up the leather pouch that lay beside them and scooped out its contents. It contained two empty syringes, their needles still capped, and a thumb-sized glass bottle of transparent liquid. He grabbed it, set his thumb alongside its rubber stopper, just as if it were a champagne cork, and pushed it off.

"Stop!" cried Anne as he reversed it and let its contents spill onto the floor. She abandoned the camera and rushed towards him.

"I hope that wasn't your only bottle of potassium chloride," said Franck.

He was rewarded with a sharp blow as Anne smashed the

butt of her revolver into his right temple.

When Franck regained consciousness his head was arched over the back of the canapé and blood had begun to coagulate where the skin had been torn from his forehead. He tried to right his head but was immediately hit by a wave of nausea and had to let it fall back. The attempt awoke a thudding pain behind his eyes.

After a while he tried again, far more slowly, and managed to move himself to a crouching position on top of the canapé. Gingerly he extended his right hand towards the pedestal with the champagne. He plunged his fingers into the bucket and retrieved a handful of ice which he held against his temple. Little by little the cubes slipped from his grasp, but by the time they had all escaped he felt a little more in control.

He very slowly got to his feet and stumbled across the room to the bed. Maryam's position had not changed, and neither the tripod nor the camera had been moved. He sat himself gently on the bed and touched the side of her neck. A vein throbbed under his touch. Franck withdrew his hand, closed his eyes, and blew the air from his lungs in a quiet sigh of gratitude and relief. He then touched her hair and gently slid the back of his hand across her cheek.

He had been right. Anne had been unable to bring herself to deface Maryam's body with a gunshot wound.

Franck picked up the receiver on the phone that sat on the night table on one side of the bed.

"This is room 302. I need an ambulance right away," he said, then hung up.

He got to his feet, still feeling dizzy. Judging it likely that he had been out for no more than ten or fifteen minutes, he had to check whether Anne had left the hotel. He could not count on her showing the same reticence with the PA50 – or his gun, for that matter – as regarded other, less gracious, targets.

He crossed the room towards the door but was stopped by his own peripheral vision – not to be underestimated either – as he tugged it open. On one of the canapés, on top of Maryam's carefully folded clothes, lay his service revolver. He crossed over to it, snatched it up, and checked the magazine. It was fully loaded.

Troubled by this, Franck nonetheless slipped off the safety and walked out into the corridor barrel first.

There was nobody in sight, but by the time he reached the stairs a groom came into sight, running up the steps towards him. He froze at the sight of Franck's gun.

"Room 302," instructed Franck, jerking his thumb over his shoulder. "Go!"

The groom surged forward and passed him by.

Franck continued down the stairs, lowering his revolver to his side as he did so. When he reached the main lobby he stopped and surveyed every corner, spotting no trace of Anne.

Didier Fabre, however, stood conspicuously just inside the main entrance, unsuccessfully trying to talk his way past one of the porters.

Franck walked, somewhat unsteadily, over to him. He flashed his ID at the porter.

"He's with me," he said, grabbing Didier's arm to make his point, and to give himself some support.

"Very good sir," uttered the porter, and stepped away from them.

"You ever follow me to the Beaux Arts?" he asked Didier.

"Twice," admitted the photographer.

"You ever see me there with a teacher a little older than me – tall, attractive?"

"Once," said Didier. "You mean the one that came out the lift maybe seven or eight minutes ago?"

Franck dug his fingers into Didier's arm. "Where did she go?"

Didier nodded towards the far end of the lobby. "I think she went into the bar."

"What's she playing at?" muttered Franck, releasing Didier and heading through the lobby.

After a few paces the head concierge got into step alongside him.

"Are you alright captain?" he asked. "Your head doesn't look too good."

"I'm fine," said Franck. "Just make sure the medical team goes straight to 302."

"Very good sir," said the concierge, allowing Franck to forge ahead without him.

The bar of the Crillon was all dark wood, marbled glass and plush red velvet. A single barman stood watch over its reserves of bottles and decanters, while a waiter busied himself with six businessmen in one corner.

Anne was the only other client, as distant as possible from the men in suits. An untouched flute of champagne stood on a low table beside the low-slung armchair in which she sat, facing the entrance.

She nodded to Franck, raised her glass to him, took a sip, and replaced it on the table.

Franck swung his revolver up from his side and aimed it at her.

"You're under arrest," he stated.

There was a sudden commotion at the other end of the bar. He shot a glance at the horrified group of businessmen.

"Stay where you are. You'll come to no harm," he ordered.

"I was hoping you'd find me here," said Anne, sitting very straight, one leg folded modestly across the other. Franck only now noticed that she was wearing a knee-length black cocktail dress and low-cut shoes with kitten heels.

She sent one of her hands down the side of her chair and came out with the PA50, which she propped on the armrest.

"Put the gun down," instructed Franck. "You're going nowhere."

"I was aware of that, Franck," she replied, with good-humoured forbearance.

She then pulled the trigger.

Franck fired twice in quick succession, catching her in the chest and shoulder. Anne crumpled forward. Her own shot had gone high, tearing into the ceiling above him.

She was dead by the time he knelt beside her.

"Good shot," said Didier, crouching in the doorway, one forefinger moving busily over his camera. He may have been talking to himself.

Wednesday, 27th June

It made the cover of *Exposé*.

The raised glass, ever so slightly tilted. The half-smile and the amused eyes. The clear and simple silhouette of the dress, sharply outlined by the encounter between the unadorned black cloth and the softer tone of her skin. The twisted skein of grey silk around her neck. The demurely crossed legs, shaped and smoothed by sheer stockings, one foot playfully dangling above the floor.

Framed by the expensive and immaculate furnishings of the bar of the Crillon, Anne Subrini had the triumphant ease that was once the birthright of high nobility, secure from others' judgements.

Didier Fabre had lived up to his reputation: in the halcyon calm before the first gunshot, he had taken a perfect picture.

Unthinkingly, he had rendered Anne the service she claimed to provide to others.

Friday, 29th June

Franck was walking down the rue Dumont d'Urville, heading towards the Du Bellay offices. Inside his trusty briefcase lay the copy of *Wasp-Waisted* he had borrowed on his first visit. True to his word, he was taking it back. Beside it lay another envelope which had been delivered to his apartment the previous day. It was the official notification of the opening of an enquiry into the Corsican incident, warning Franck that he should make himself available as a key witness, and confirming that his suspension from the DST would be maintained for the duration of the inquest.

Already sombre since the death of Anne Subrini, Franck's mood had darkened all the more at the thought of the months ahead. He was about to discover what it was like to be the suspect: to have his every move, his every word, his every decision scrutinised by those whose interest in him was icily professional. Moreover, the urgency that characterised the past few weeks would be completely absent from the proceedings that were about to start. He would be lucky to see a decision before the end of the year.

"Good morning captain!" came a familiar voice from behind.

Franck stopped and turned. Sonia Delemazure was bearing down upon him, resplendent in light blue sandals, worn jeans cut off below her knees, and a wide-necked blue and white striped cotton top, inevitably tugged down to expose her left shoulder.

She pulled herself up and leant forward, kissing him directly on the lips, taking him by surprise.

"You did it!" she proclaimed. "I, of course, knew you would."

"Thanks for your confidence," replied Franck. "But I'm not sure congratulations are in order."

"You caught the killer!" insisted Sonia.

"I shot the killer. It's not quite the same thing."

"Well, for a man they say was trigger-shy the last time, you certainly proved them wrong."

"What?" demanded Franck, frowning at her.

A blue Longchamp bag hung by Sonia's side. She reached into it and brought out a folded newspaper. It was that morning's copy of *Libération*.

"Pages 4 and 5," she announced. "Something they're calling the Corsican incident. There's even a picture of you, but you're not looking your best. Still, you're on a stretcher and you didn't have a make-up girl to hand, so no excuses are necessary."

Franck sighed. The clouds were indeed gathering.

"You can keep it," said Sonia, handing him the paper. "I'm going to see Luc. Thought I'd pop in and annoy him a little. Keep him on his toes. You had the same idea?"

"Not exactly," said Franck. He opened his briefcase, slipped the paper inside and extracted the copy of *Wasp-Waisted*.

"Can you give this to him?"

Sonia took the magazine from Franck.

"You don't want to keep it as a souvenir?" she asked.

"I don't think I'm in any danger of forgetting anything about this case. Anyhow, I promised I'd give it back."

"In which case, I will be your trusty messenger. You're not coming then?"

Franck shook his head.

"On you go. Annoy him for me."

Sonia stalked off with a wave.

Franck watched her go, wondering at how carefree she seemed, and whether he would ever know such a state.

His mobile started ringing.

"Guerin," he announced, having retrieved it from the inside pocket of his jacket.

"Good morning, captain," said madame Alba. "Monsieur *le juge* was wondering if you could call upon him sometime today. He has something to keep you busy."

"I'll be there as soon as I can," said Franck.

A little honest-to-god police work. Why not?

vernissage

Literally: the act of applying varnish, once done to paintings at the last minute before they were exhibited in order to heighten their impact. By extension, the term is used to refer to a private show of works of art in advance of the opening to the general public.

Vespasian

Roman Emperor (69-79), credited with the maxim "pecunia non olet" (money has no smell) in defence of a tax he introduced on the sale of urine collected in Rome's public toilets (the urine was used by tanners in treating leather). When public urinals were first introduced in Paris in the 1830s they were known as "vespasiennes".

Rachel	Elisabeth Rachel Felix, known simply as Rachel, was the most famous classical actress of the first half of the 19th century.
Racing Club de France	Created near the end of the 19th century, the Racing Club de France, comfortably installed in the Bois de Boulogne, has long been the preserve of the capital's wealthy sportsmen.
Robespierre	An emblematic figure of the French Revolution, leader of the Jacobins, praised for his ideals and incorruptibility by his admirers and condemned by his opponents for his willingness to use terror and bloodshed to advance his vision of the revolutionary cause. Guillotined in 1794.
SOS Racisme	An organisation created to fight racial discrimination which had much success amongst French youth during the 1980s when the National Front was muscling into the political scene.
Saint-Just	Ally of Robespierre and an unapologetic supporter of political violence during the French Revolution. Known as "the archangel of the Terror", he was guillotined alongside Robespierre in 1794.
Salammbo (strictly, Salammbô)	Title of a novel by Flaubert published in 1862 and set in Carthage. Intended to be a painstaking reconstruction of a distant historical era, it takes its title from the name of its heroine, daughter of a Carthaginian general, priestess and legendary beauty.

PMU (Pari Mutuel Urbain)	A state-supervised monopoly that manages bets on horse races.
Paris vaut bien une messe	Literally: "Paris is well worth a mass". Attributed to Henri IV, who was crowned king in the midst of the sixteenth-century Wars of Religion. Henri, originally king of Navarre (a tiny kingdom on the then border of France and Spain), was the champion of the Protestant cause but converted to Catholicism in 1593 as a means of reconciling the warring parties and clearing his path to the crown (which required, amongst other things, being able to live and reign in Paris, which was a stronghold of Catholicism and had been the scene of an infamous massacre of Protestants in 1572). Paris proved fatal to the king: in 1610 he was assassinated in the rue de la Ferronnerie by a fanatical Catholic (François Ravaillac).
La Poste	The French post office, one of the nation's most important employers (with 300 000 staff) and one of the pillars of the Republic (an isolated village knows that its existence is threatened the day the state school and the local post office close their doors). The distinguishing colour of La Poste – to be found on post boxes, delivery vans, and all its publicity – is a cheerful yellow.

flic	Widely-used slang for "cop". In the first half of the twentieth century, *flic* had largely negative connotations. However, as often happens with such terms, with the passage of time it has been adopted by those it is used to designate.
juge d'instruction	A *juge d'instruction* is a magistrate whose job is to carry out preliminary investigations of crimes and misdeeds and judge whether they are ripe for prosecution. Once charged with an inquiry, a *juge* has complete autonomy to proceed as he wishes and is almost impossible to stop (only the nation's highest court – the *cour de Cassation* – can wrestle an affair from the hands of a *juge*, which makes it very difficult to do so discreetly). A *juge* neither prosecutes cases nor decides their outcome – his sole mission is to determine whether they merit to be tried before a court of law. The *juges* handle very complex or sensitive cases deemed more suitable to elucidation by a powerful, independent and highly experienced judicial expert than by the normal police and bureaucratic process. It is said that the *juges d'instruction* are the sole actors capable of keeping the nation's elite in check, as it is well-nigh impossible to pull their strings.
maghrébine	The Maghreb is a name used for the countries of the north-west of Africa (Morocco, Tunisia and Algeria) which were once part of France's colonial sphere. A *maghrébine* is a woman who comes from this region.

DST (Direction de la Surveillance du Territoire)	Part of the nation's police structure, the DST is a secretive organisation in charge of counter-espionage, counter-terrorism and protecting the French economy. It is not to be confused with its sister organisation, the DGSE (Direction Générale de la Sécurité Extérieure), which carries out operations outside national borders. The DGSE is part of the Ministry of Defence, whereas the DST is attached to the Ministry of the Interior. In 2008 (the events of this book take place in 2007) the DST was merged with another intelligence service and changed its name.
La Défense	A massive business district to the west of Paris. Born out of nothing in the late 1950s, it now boasts a host of ever-changing skyscrapers built above a massive concrete plateau. Many French and overseas firms are headquartered here. Its most notable structure is the Grande Arche de la Défense, built for the two hundredth anniversary of the Revolution, which is visible from the Arc de Triomphe at the top of the Champs Elysées.
défilé	Literally, a parade (often military, like the massed tanks and troops that roll down the Champs Elysees every year on the 14th of July). Used without qualification, the term generally designates a fashion show.

Brigade Criminelle	Also known as "la Crim", the Brigade Criminelle investigates the city's murders and most serious crimes. Its offices are to be found at 36 quai des Orfèvres on the Ile de la Cité, an address well known to readers of Georges Simenon.
Champmeslé	Marie Desmares, known as la Champmeslé, an actress from the 17th century, who was the first to play many of Racine's great tragic heroines.
Le Cid	The most famous play by the seventeenth-century playwright Pierre Corneille. First performed in 1636, it tells of two star-crossed lovers, Rodrigue, the unproved warrior son of an ageing pillar of the Spanish aristocracy, and Chimène, the beautiful and principled daughter of a rival family. Rodrigue slays Chimène's father in a dual after he has insulted his own father's honour, creating a potent cocktail of love and hate in Chimène's heart whose resolution requires a Moorish invasion and some royal trickery. Hugely controversial in its time for neglecting the manners and principles then reigning on the stage, it has been a mainstay of the Comédie Française's repertoire ever since.
Comédie Française	The guardian of the nation's dramatic heritage, the Comédie Française is a state-subsidised theatre company whose origins date back to a royal decree issued in 1680.

Glossary

Many of the French words used in this tale have been adopted into English. Those which have not, but which were deemed useful in reminding the reader that the action takes place in Paris and not, say, London or New York, are presented in italics.

Although delving into a dictionary (or just typing an unknown term into Google) is always worth doing (as countless surprises await the curious), it is rarely practical if sitting in a plane, bus or train, or idling at the beach. This short glossary is intended to help those who dislike stumbling over unknown words or terms.

arrondissement   For administrative purposes Paris is divided into twenty arrondissements, each with its own local government. Their size and population varies widely (from 18 000 to 230 000 inhabitants). In the course of the city's history each arrondissement has evolved a distinct social character.

Balzac   Honoré de Balzac (1799-1850), an incredibly industrious and prolific novelist. Legend has it that he drank himself to death (although in his case, his tipple of choice was coffee, drunk in vast quantities to fuel marathon sessions of writing and proof correction). His cafetière is on proud display in the Maison de Balzac in the sixteenth arrondissement.

bouquinistes   The *bouquinistes* sell second-hand books on the banks of the Seine at the level of the Ile de la Cité. Their wares are stocked and displayed in large wooden and iron trunks that are mounted on the stone parapets that line the river.